HEARTLESS

BOOK FOUR: AGE OF CONQUEST

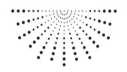

TAMARA LEIGH

TAMARA LEIGH

THE WULFRITHS. IT ALL BEGAN WITH A WOMAN.

A battle. A crown. The conqueror. The conquered. Medieval England—forever changed by the Battle of Hastings. And the rise of the formidable Wulfriths.

A HEARTLESS NORMAN

Chevalier Maël D'Argent lost more than his striking looks when he aided the Duke of Normandy in taking the English throne from King Harold. As much by his own actions at the Battle of Hastings as those of the enemy, he lost his sire and his honor in breaking faith with his family. Believing himself unworthy of forgiveness, his ruined face the least due him, Maël now serves a ruthless man bent on subduing Saxons resistant to Norman rule. But when his mission to safeguard King William's dignity leads to the rescue of a curiously familiar Saxon woman who causes the empty place inside him to strain its seams, he discovers he may not be as heartless as the one he serves—nor resistant to the wiles of one he ought to count an enemy.

A FALSE ABBESS

In the guise of Abbess Mary Sarah, the illegitimate Mercia has served the Saxon resistance for years in anticipation of learning who sired her. At last ordered to cast off the habit and veil, Mercia is told that revelation of her parentage hinges on acceptance of another role that could see her sacrificed by the noble family who refuses to acknowledge her. When she resists and is abducted by Saxon allies, her savior proves the scarred Norman warrior who spared her following the great battle. Once more, something sorrowfully empty in Sir Maël makes her long to fill his emptiness with what little she possesses, even if his captivity renders it impossible for him to forgive one as deceptive as she. Even if she never discovers who she is…

From the coronation of William the Conqueror at Westminster, to the amassing of the Danish fleet intent on dethroning England's Norman king, Sir Maël and Mercia's tale unfolds in the fourth book in the AGE OF CONQUEST series revealing the origins of the Wulfriths of the bestselling AGE OF FAITH series. Watch for RECKLESS: Book Five releasing Autumn 2020.

For new releases and special promotions, subscribe to Tamara Leigh's mailing list: www.tamaraleigh.com

PROLOGUE

Westminster Abbey, England
December 25, 1066

*W*illiam seethed. And well he should. Even a bad king, which he could prove, ought not suffer so inauspicious a coronation.

As if carved of stone where he faced an anxious audience of Normans and Saxons about whose feet smoke had begun to drift, he remained unmoving, only his eyes stirring when he caught sight of one of two D'Argents who had accompanied a dozen of his personal guard outside the chapel.

Chevalier Maël, returning by way of a side door, inclined his head, assuring his liege and what remained of his guard there was no need to halt the ceremony that was to see the Duke of Normandy crowned King of England. Rather, no need yet.

The service had proceeded smoothly and according to long-established tradition—William prostrated before the altar, anthems sung in praise of the one who would be king, and oaths sworn to govern his subjects justly and defend the Church. It was the next part that shattered the solemnity, causing the congregation to tense in anticipation of fleeing hallowed ground.

After the English archbishop asked if the people would accept William as their king, and the Norman bishop of Coutances translated his words into French, hundreds of Saxon and Norman nobles had shouted their approval.

Though William would be a fool to believe the enthusiasm of his fellow Normans was matched by Saxons who had lost their country when their king fell at the great battle, some of the latter were well with being a beaten people since there could be great gain in turning against their own. As for those who believed England's throne lost to a thief, they but feigned acceptance of the conqueror in the hope of protecting themselves and preserving what remained of their possessions.

Unfortunately, the Saxon shouts elevated by the Normans' had caused soldiers stationed outside to suspect an assassination attempt against William. For that, they set fire to nearby buildings. Or so said those confronted by the duke's personal guard.

Maël did not believe it, nor had his cousin, Theriot.

If the soldiers truly feared William was in danger, sound reason and loyalty would have bade them hasten inside to defend him. Had Maël to wager, it would be that the duke's mercenary soldiers seen emerging from homes and shops with bulging sacks had used the din inside the abbey as an excuse to return to burning and pillaging. And the temptation for William's own liegemen to enrich themselves had been too great for many to abstain.

When the man soon crowned king learned his forces, rather than rebellious Saxons, had caused the disturbance, he would have much to say about the near ruination of his coronation. But it would be naught compared to his wrath were it necessary to halt the ceremony.

Having alerted William it was safe to proceed, Maël was

eager to return to Theriot to aid in ensuring those out of control were reined in before Saxons fleeing ruined homes and businesses were moved from fear to anger. If that happened, rioting would ensue. And slaughter.

He had no love for the people of this land, and less so after losing his sire to them, but further bloodshed of city folk not given to warring would benefit none.

As the bishop once more translated the archbishop's words, Maël started back toward the side door. And paused when he caught movement on the dim balcony above that provided an unobstructed view of William before the altar—and a path for arrows and blades.

Through narrowed eyes, he sought the source but found none. Might it have been a bird searching for a way out? A rodent scurrying across the rail?

The rising shouts of those in the streets beyond the chapel and the sharpening scent of smoke causing the congregation to turn more restless, Maël hesitated. He was needed outside, but more here lest the coronation was interrupted not by the actions of greedy men but an assassin in truth.

Bypassing the side door, he nodded at one of the king's guard whose presence there ensured the congregation remained seated. Hoping the man had not allowed someone to gain the balcony unseen, he stepped onto tightly-turning stairs. As they were constructed without regard to defense, providing little space in which to wield a sword, Maël drew the family dagger he continued to wear only so none question its absence from a warrior no longer worthy of the esteemed weapon.

It was wrong it should fit his hand so well, and the price paid for the momentary comfort was recall of his sire awarding it to his only son. Rather, *legitimate* son.

Thrusting aside that memory of the day his accomplishment was honored by the man who had commanded if Maël could not be the worthiest of the family D'Argent, he be *among* the worthiest, he climbed the stairs cautiously so he might hear and not be heard above the holy words intoned.

However, he was expected by the two who stood at the center of the balcony in the light of a single torch flickering at their backs.

Ladies, as told by veiled hair, embroidered skirts beneath mantles fastened with brooches, and noble bearing. *Saxon* ladies, as evidenced by their presence in a city recently surrendered to Normans. But the same as the young of these conquered people, a handful of whom were responsible for the corpse made of Maël's sire, they could prove far from harmless.

Tossing out another memory, seeing no others here and that the hands clasped before the women were empty, he strode forward.

Their faces were mostly in shadow, but as he neared he discerned the one on the right was elderly, a hunch to her shoulders and the pale braids visible on either side of her veil thin and grey. The taller one was young, the lower loops of the braids brushing her shoulders thick and darkly gleaming.

From her sharply drawn breath, he knew the moment her eyes made sense of the side of his face come out of shadow. It was the same reaction of most women who looked upon a visage so ruined its contrast with the mostly unspoiled side shocked.

The king's physician had assured Maël that, given time, the livid and swollen flesh would heal sufficiently so the monster made of him at Hastings would once more look the man, but it was assurance he had not sought. Worse should have been done him, and not merely the loss of a limb as suffered by a cousin. Rather, loss of life the same as his sire and, possibly, another cousin whose body had not been recovered from that godforsaken meadow.

Maël halted a stride from the women. "What do you here?" he demanded with just enough volume to be heard above the men of God and the congregation's restlessness that boded they would make for the doors if what transpired outside was not soon resolved.

"What do *we* here, Chevalier?" the old woman said in a voice still melodious despite a crackle, and well enough accented it was obvious she knew his language well. "We mark this momentous day in the history of *our* country by bearing witness to what goes inside *our* abbey."

Unlike the Saxons below, she was openly disaffected, a prerogative of the elderly who often believed they had little to lose—and unlike her companion who set a hand on her arm to calm her and for it was jabbed with an elbow.

As the young woman jumped back, Maël shifted his regard to that one's face, and immediately the glitter in her eyes extinguished.

Since her proud bearing did not falter, he was certain she had not lowered her lids out of fear nor deference. She hid something. Unfortunately, it was impossible to look nearer on one whose features were mostly obscured the same as the older woman's. However, of note was hair peaked on her brow and a generous mouth.

She might be pretty, she might not, but unlike before the great battle, it mattered not to one whose face would no longer give him the pick of women worth courting.

Returning to the old woman, he said, "Who are you?"

She snorted. "You are not quick of wit, are you, Norman? As should be obvious, we are Saxons."

"Your names," he growled.

She set her head to the side. "For what would you know? So you might persecute us the same as your countrymen and mercenaries who continue to set fires and pillage though this city surrendered to Le Bâtard?"

The young woman gasped, stepped in front of the older one, and raised her gaze. The glitter there of such height and breadth it bespoke large eyes, she said, "Forgive my grandmother. So dear and great the number of those lost to her at Hastings, it is difficult to see any good come of the rule of your people."

Though her Norman-French accent was somewhat aslant, her speech was beautifully precise as of one given to much thought ere letting words off her tongue.

When he did not respond, she raised her chin higher. "Have mercy, Chevalier. Of an honorable age, my grandmother is of no danger to you nor your duke."

"Her *king*," he corrected.

"Her king—*our* king," she acceded. And stumbled forward.

Certain a blow had landed to her back, Maël bit, "Cease, old woman, else your granddaughter's pleading will be for naught."

So quickly that lady came out from behind the other that were Maël incapable of swiftly assessing a threat, impulse would have caused him to wield his dagger against her. The old one was empty-handed, but were it not impossible for her to escape following a struggle that would alert the guards, likely she would have drawn whatever blade was fixed to her girdle.

Stepping so near his dagger's point grazed her mantle, she spat, "Nithing! Thief! Murderer!"

As Maël wavered between delivering her to the king's guard and honoring the younger one's request by escorting them from the chapel, the decision was snatched from him by a rise in the commotion outside the abbey. Immediately, it was answered by the congregation. As if having held its breath, they expelled exclamations and cries. Then came the pound of boots and scrape of slippers.

Maël crossed to the railing. Though William remained flanked by the archbishop and bishop, monks, and personal guard, all was becoming chaos. Even before the doors were flung open to permit the panicked to flee, it was obvious the smoke's penetration of the chapel had intensified. Still the duke did not stir. Naught but the certainty of death would prevent him from departing Westminster absent crown, ring, sword, scepter, and rod.

As more smoke entered by way of the congregation's exit, Maël swung around. He had sensed no movement from the women, but he was surprised they were where he had left them —until he realized they had no cause to join the exodus. They had not slipped past William's guard and ascended the stairs that delivered Maël here. Somewhere on the balcony was a concealed door that could have seen an arrow put through William were these two of murderous intent.

Thrusting his dagger in its scabbard, he returned to them. "Show me the passage, and you may depart the way you came. Refuse me, and the guard will detain you and themselves learn its location."

As hoped, the young one yielded. "We are without choice," she said and pivoted and strode past the torch.

Maël gripped the older woman's arm through her mantle. "Make haste."

"You dare!" she snarled as if not only were he the enemy but beneath her. Though she was mistaken to assume he was not as noble as she, he let it pass and allowed her to pull free.

Less hunched than before, she followed her companion.

The passage in the far corner was accessed by an empty sconce. Turned to the right, the wooden panel whispered inward to reveal descending stairs.

The young woman entered and reached behind. When her hand was slapped aside, she entreated, "We must not delay."

The old woman turned back. Torchlight now upon her face, Maël's cast in shadow, she said, "I pray it was one of mine who spoiled your comeliness, *Norman*." She coughed, surely from the smoke. "A pity he did not also gut you."

Since he was mostly in accord, her attempt to offend was wasted. "Go, *Saxon*."

She grunted, swung around, and stepped into the passage.

As Maël closed the women into darkness, he assured himself if the elderly one continued to refuse aid and tumbled down the steps, it would be her fault alone.

After engaging the sconce's lever that locked it in place so no longer could it be opened from the inside, he descended the narrow stairs and found the last of the congregation shoving past William's guard amid smoke as eager to enter as they were to exit.

As he moved toward doors soon to be closed to allow the officiating clergy to complete the coronation, he looked behind.

No longer did William appear cut from stone, his color high and chest rising and falling rapidly. Doubtless, the reward to be distributed to the men who had greatly aided in seating him on England's throne would be denied those responsible for making a mockery of his ascendancy that could prove impossible to remove from memory.

Though Maël believed his own reward was secure, he would decline and return to Normandy. Or so he planned, unaware his efforts in the riotous hours ahead would see many of those who started the fires and looting drop to their knees before a wrathful William. And Maël elevated not to the lordship he refused after Theriot accepted lands for his brother, but to something of greater benefit to England's new king.

A position fit for one who had betrayed his family by not keeping his word and forgetting where his loyalties lay.

A position requiring he ensure no murderous Saxon, Norman, or otherwise thwart his liege's plan to bring England fully under the conqueror's control.

A position that could render him bereft of family and friends, though already that was earned.

But God help him did he become as heartless as the king he served.

HIS FACE. Beneath dark hair streaked with silver that did not belong on a man less than two and three score aged, she had thought it so handsome as to be nearly beautiful—until long strides carried him fully into torchlight to which she and her grandmother had turned their backs upon realizing there was no time to retreat.

For a moment, Mercia had thought herself afforded a glimpse of evil disguised as a thing of beauty to seduce women otherwise destined for heaven, but his mask had not slipped— was no mask at all, merely a ruined face.

Considering how fresh the scar scoring the left side of his brow and grossly ridging the right down past his eye and across his cheek to his ear, she guessed it dealt two months past during the clash now known as the Battle of Hastings though it had been fought upon the meadow of Senlac.

Might one of her grandmother's fallen sons have been the warrior who disfigured a Norman unworthy of such a face? Might it have been Mercia's own sire? Unlikely and never to be known, not even when the old woman made good her promise to answer a question that was not to be asked of her again.

"There!" that one said, voice coarse and brittle less from age than the smoke of precious things devoured by fire. She pointed at the inn on the opposite side of the street where the rendezvous had been set in the event her men drew the attention of Normans. And so they had, forced to depart the stables where earlier they had aided the women in dismounting.

"Praise the Lord," Mercia gasped.

The escape from Westminster had been frightening. Amid smoke and great heat, screaming, shouting, cursing, even laughter, they had run street to street, turning back here, turning aside there. And once they were forced to crawl to escape the notice of Normans whose stuffed sacks had begun moving their victims from fear to anger, as evidenced by Saxons making weapons of whatever they brought to hand.

"Halt!" her grandmother commanded.

"For what?" Mercia exclaimed. "The inn is ahead." And as far as she could see, the only people about were few and Saxon. As evidenced by the many her grandmother and she had passed and those who fled ahead of them, the foolishly curious were drawn to the commotion surrounding the abbey, the wisely fearful quick to distance themselves.

"Here!" The old woman turned into an alley between buildings.

Mercia followed and was unprepared when her grandmother swung around and backhanded her.

She cried out, stumbled sideways into the building, and slid down wooden slats onto her knees.

"You dare!"

Quelling the impulse to raise an arm to shield her lest the attack had only begun, berating herself for not expecting it ahead of forgiveness for what instinct had demanded she do to keep them safe, Mercia pressed a palm against lips bleeding onto her tongue.

She had known her grandmother's ire was not all for the chevalier, having been subjected to it when jabbed with an elbow, struck in the back, and her hand slapped away. But as there was no further show of aggression during their flight, she had believed that the worst of it.

So was this the end or just the beginning? If the latter, she would suffer without protest.

The hem of the old woman's soiled, embroidered skirt sweeping the dirt, she stepped near. "Never are you to name me *grandmother,* neither in private nor public, and yet you did so before our enemy."

Mercia's thoughts returned to the Norman as done often throughout their flight, but this time they cast further back—rather, deeper—and she acknowledged how greatly he had disturbed beyond fear of the enemy. What was it about him that tugged at her? On such short and near disastrous acquaintance, it was impossible to know, but something sorrowfully empty in him had made her long to fill that emptiness with what little she possessed that he did not.

Foolish! she silently rebuked. *Were your grandmother to reveal that never has she been kin to you, here much proof. You must cease being fanciful, Mercia.*

"Have you naught to say?" demanded the old woman.

"I spoke as I did to calm the Norman's impatience and rouse his sympathy in the hope he would let us go," Mercia rasped. "And so he did."

"What if that barbarian had instead dragged us before others and I was recognized, hmm? All I have done to keep you safe would be for naught were it known you are of my son's blood."

Which son? wondered the one named for the place of her birth.

"And then for you to speak to that knave of my great loss and beseech his mercy!" She spat on the ground, snatched up her granddaughter's chin. "Show me."

Lowering her bloodied hand, curling fingers into the slick warmth, Mercia watched the aged eyes move over her mouth.

"Regrettable." It was said with what sounded sincerity. "But deserved for speaking of me as if I am helpless and senseless—worse, acknowledging Le Bâtard as king."

"Gran—" She nearly named her that again as if the title of kinship were more familiar than that by which ever she addressed her. The old woman's teeth beginning to bare, Mercia said, "Forgive me, Countess. I could think of no other way to deliver us, but we are here now and soon shall be safe in Exeter."

Her grandmother's gaze wavered, then she released Mercia. "Safe for how long? Le Bâtard will set his army at that city's walls as well…will not be content until all of England bends the knee."

"We shall beat him and his kind back across the sea," Mercia said. "That is as you told, and that Harold's son will take back the throne."

As if the old woman needed to hear that, her shoulders and back straightened. "Aye, Harold's son will sit the throne, and higher it will be raised upon the bones of the usurper. Ere I breathe my last, I shall see it done."

Would she? Mercia wondered and startled when her grandmother extended a hand. Though no frail thing, it was not for a lady of years to bear the weight of one of many fewer years. However, lest she offend, Mercia placed one hand in her grandmother's, pressed her other bloodied hand to the ground, and pushed upright.

"Mercia," the old woman bemoaned as she looked closer on the damage. "Your lip is cut and begins to swell. I..." She swallowed.

"'Twas deserved," Mercia sought to console her though her heart was not in it. She had been disrespectful as never before, but she was certain the humbling of one of two Saxons had moved the chevalier to allow them to depart unmolested.

Raised and educated in letters and numbers at a convent that aspired to shape her into a woman fearful of displeasing the Lord, next tutored in the ways of the nobility whilst tending the lady of a great house that would have become greater had King Harold been victorious at Hastings, Mercia had begun learning the art of reading women and men and flattering and being flattered.

Having sensed the chevalier on the balcony was not given to the behavior of fellow Normans who threatened to ruin Le Bâtard's coronation, she had trampled pride nearly to the point of scraping and bowing. And for it, this. But she would not have her grandmother know how strong her resentment. Blessedly, it would ease, the countess's loss of loved ones so great she must be excused for grief-induced rage. It was her due as it was not

Mercia's whose own loss remained uncertain and could never be that of a loved one.

Blinking away tears, her grandmother said, "Aye, deserved, but I am glad for the disrespect shown me."

"I do not understand."

"Though I know you are of fine demeanor and sharp intelligence, I was not aware you could be so wily."

"Wily?"

"A kind word for deceitful," her grandmother misinterpreted the question, and as Mercia struggled against revealing how much it offended, continued, "Of good benefit to our cause." She arched pale eyebrows. "You will not accompany me to Exeter."

Mercia caught her breath. "My punishment is to be parted from you?"

"Not punishment. Reward. A pity I took you from the convent ere your profession was made, but you were raised well enough to play the part so none will discover your true purpose."

Mercia frowned. "What part and what purpose?"

"I am sending you to Wulfenshire."

"For what?"

"'Tis where you are needed, and since God has made a place for you there, it is His will."

Heart pounding, Mercia clamped her teeth lest she spill words that would see her dealt another blow.

"Mercia," her grandmother murmured as if to herself. "Though few know what you are to me, that name could prove your undoing in the midst of our enemies. You must take another, and methinks a biblical one best serves where you go."

Somewhere upon Wulfenshire, far northeast of the city of Exeter where her grandmother would journey without her.

"Have you a name to mind, Mercia?"

"I must think on it."

"Best one similar to your own so you not forget to answer to it."

Fearful of the pressure in her chest evidencing screams circled there, Mercia lowered stinging eyes.

An aged hand settled on her arm. "Look at me, Granddaughter."

Never named that, neither in private nor public, Mercia flew her gaze to rheumy eyes darkened by vengeful sorrow and resolve.

"Other than the danger which names present in the face of our enemies, they are no longer of great import. Who you are inside is all you must be." She stepped nearer. Skirts brushing Mercia's, she cupped the younger woman's jaw. "Never forget— ever embrace—you are Saxon. Strong of mind, body, and spirit. True to the blood, the bone, the marrow."

Mercia shivered over words with which her grandmother had rallied thousands of noble and common Saxons since the flower of England were slain upon that meadow, many of whom were now dead as well.

Thus, it mattered not the exact role she would play. It was enough to know that just as she had been no mere companion to the lady she served less than a year, no mere companion would she be upon Wulfenshire. This, however, would be dangerous. Like it or nay, Mercia of Mercia's aid in overthrowing the usurper would make of her an enemy to Normans.

A rebel.

CHAPTER ONE

Northern England
Late Winter, 1070

*W*illiam smiled. Non, *smirked.* He was not happy—
could not be under these circumstances—but he
was pleased. And in the way of one satisfied with himself, it
appeared.

If not that he and his guard had become separated from the
great host struggling across vast, snow-swept mountains to
reach Cheshire that was once more astir with rebellion, those
among William's warriors who had recently threatened to
desert would surely make sport of the conqueror, suggesting the
satisfaction he exuded was due to the reason he entered the cave
alone.

They would snigger, though only amongst themselves lest
they incur greater wrath than already gained in speaking out
against the march in frigid weather and the loss of horses that
saw many accustomed to riding now trudging alongside foot
soldiers.

Before all, the king had named the first deserters cowards

and idle weaklings and those who had yet to desert sniveling boys, then delivered a threat of his own should they turn back—no matter the service given thus far, their greatest chance of survival would be to keep going until they reached France with woefully limp purses.

Though that quieted most, William had further punished the disaffected, few of whom were his own Normans, by pushing his army harder and commanding them to follow his example. And so they had until the snowstorm.

As the captain of the king's guard, Maël had urged William to wait out the weather. Instead, the king quickened the pace and the six chevaliers tasked with protecting him remained at his side—all the more imperative when the army fell so far behind they became as unheard as they were unseen, rendering William and his guard vulnerable to any of the resistance who had survived extermination these past months.

Not until the storm began to abate had William halted. The hood draping his head coated in crusted snow, he had turned sharply in the saddle and looked between the warriors who shivered as much as he.

"You live!" he had snarled as if in response to an accusation of recklessness, then settled his gaze on Maël.

Having learned the king's anger, whether it burned within or without, was as dangerous as unbridled drink—and deadly when the two made allies of themselves—Maël had stayed in the cold place inside himself and stared back.

With a grunt of disgust, William had looked back the way they had come. Had he expected his army to emerge from swirling snow that had begun to drift, he was disappointed.

Certain those left behind had taken shelter and it would be hours before they appeared, Maël had suggested they make camp and rest the horses.

For answer, the king had thrust the frozen hood off his head and urged his mount onward. As if to more greatly shame his army for lacking endurance, they had ridden another hour and might have continued on if not for the needs of the body.

Maël had advised against the craggy, sparsely wooded area the king set his sights on, there being enough cover to conceal a dozen vengeful Saxons, but William ignored him, then scorned him when he sought to confirm the state of the cave his liege intended to enter.

Now, having been ordered to keep watch at a distance while the others under his command scouted the area and relieved themselves, Maël eased his weapon-ready stance as the king neared.

Just as ten minutes earlier he had likened William's boots fouling the pristine snow to the heinous solution to the northern rebellion, Maël did so again. Just as done often since accepting the position of captain of the guard vacated by the warrior deemed responsible for the spectacle made of the coronation, once more he questioned why still he served this man. Just as never the answer kept him waiting, neither did it now.

Because you sought to drown anger and hurt in drink, thinking of yourself and your feelings ahead of those it was your honor and duty to fight alongside and protect as they would have protected you. Non, you are not as monstrously heartless as William, but worthier of keeping company with the conqueror than the family D'Argent who, if they knew how greatly you broke faith, would have every right to do worse than strip you of that dagger. And your mother...

As Maël had done often in the three and a half years since Lady Chanson was widowed, he pushed that fine woman from his thoughts—and easier it was now she had wed again despite his objection to the one who replaced his sire.

Satisfaction more evident, the king halted. But something else was visible in the lines of his face and stiff of his bearing— anger that had been less easily roused since the beginning of the year when success after success in ending the rebellion lightened his mood. However, this was not anger like that provoked by those who had threatened to desert. If Maël read him right, and he was fairly adept at such, this anger was directed inward.

"All is well, Your Majesty?"

Beyond satisfaction and anger was glimpsed the relief of one rarely given to that emotion for how accomplished and fierce a warrior he was. "I live, do I not, Sir Maël?"

It sounded sarcasm, as if he sought to school the unlearned in his prowess, evidence of which was provided by his emergence from the cave unscathed. But though the king could be petty, there was something more to this mood, and Maël guessed relief played a greater role than its brief sighting revealed.

Knowing William would tell it in his own time, Maël said, "Forgive me. Whether mountain or plain, these northern lands are treacherous, and I would be answerable to God did I not do all in my power to protect you from the hidden things as well as the visible."

No lie. He had little liking for the conqueror before the harrying and none now that thousands of non-combatant Saxons, including women and children, paid for the resistance's exploits, but he had given his oath in the sight of God to protect William with his life and would not fail him—providing duty to his king did not require him to fail his family again as he had at Hastings.

First, in between, and in the end, you are a D'Argent, his father and uncle had said. Unworthy though he was, he would not neglect that again.

"Steadfast and cool as ever," the king commended his captain of the guard.

"As I strive to be, Your Majesty."

William nodded a head which, whitened by snow before he

entered the cave, was now darkly damp. "So you do, though sometimes your king thwarts you, eh?"

"I trust you know what is best—"

"You do not!"

Though mostly William presented as calm and self-assured, Maël had witnessed enough royal aggression—on occasion directed at him—to maintain a passive expression.

The king breathed deep. "Treacherous lands, these. More, treacherous Saxons. I should have heeded you, Chevalier."

"Your Majesty?"

He jerked his head toward the cave. "The Goliath thinks himself David."

Raised alongside cousins whose father was God-fearing, unlike his own sire who had trained them into men of the sword, Maël was familiar with biblical tales, especially those of great warriors. Though among those tales was that of the future King David who slew the giant, Goliath, he could make no sense of William. Had the long, cold ride skewed the king's mind?

As if his liege knew his thoughts, he snorted. "I speak of the red-haired and bearded Goliath."

Now sense made of him—and yet not. "Surely the leader of the Rebels of the Pale is not in the cave."

"He was, and quite the exchange we had."

Before or after William slew Vitalis to emerge from that place where he, like King Saul, encountered the rebel he hunted? More, how was it possible the clash between mighty warriors had not sounded across the cold air?

"He is dead?"

William shrugged his turned down mouth as he was wont to do in belaboring a lack of concern. "Non, I left him as I found him."

Then he had been perilously outnumbered.

Thrusting back his mantle, Maël gripped his sword hilt. The answer to what awaited him and his men of greater import than the answer to why Vitalis and his followers had not slain the most hated Norman, he asked, "How many?"

"They are gone."

Maël glanced at the cave that had swallowed and expelled the king alone.

"They departed by way of what the knave told are numerous tunnels," William said.

Even so, they could not be so long gone it was impossible to overtake them, nor of great number to have eschewed the opportunity to slay or capture their greatest enemy. "How many?" Maël asked again to determine which of his men to take and which to leave behind to guard William.

The king gripped Maël's shoulder so hard, the links of his armor were felt through the woolen undertunic that was his last defense against Northern England's cruel winter. "Leave it be, Chevalier. As told, they are gone." He grunted, released his captain of the guard. "Vitalis but sought to take a piece of me. And that he did."

Maël lowered his gaze down William but saw no crimson upon his mantle, the over tunic visible between its lapels, nor his boots.

"Not flesh," William said. "Cloth."

"I do not understand, Your Majesty."

William drew forth the back of his mantle, the lower portion of which his wife had embroidered with black thread boasting a single strand of gold. Proudly worked among the stitched flourishes at regular intervals were the letters *W* for William and *R* for Rex.

"As told," the king growled, "the Goliath thinks himself David."

Maël stared at proof the Saxon had stolen upon the King of England the same as David had done the King of Israel who also sought privacy in which to relieve himself, both rebels cutting away a sizable piece of cloth as proof they had spared their enemy's life.

Great was William's humiliation, and for that he directed anger at himself. Great was the blessing of escaping death, and for that relief. But what of satisfaction?

"Oui, shamed," the king said, and Maël was struck by the irony that, in setting an example his army could not match, he had been more shamed than ever they could be.

William flung the ruined mantle behind. As if to mock him, it cast a swaying shadow that magnified the jagged gap center of its hem. "But never humbled," he growled.

Never, Maël silently agreed. "And yet something pleases Your Majesty," he said. "You have plans to repay Vitalis's offense?"

William eyed the distant snow-covered peaks beginning to reappear now the storm had passed. "Would that I did, but foul weather, the rebels' greater knowledge of these godforsaken mountains and valleys, and my army's inability to keep pace stand in the way of justice. For now."

He returned his regard to Maël and smiled. Rather, smirked. Again. "Hence, pleasure found elsewhere. On one side, Vitalis's fear of slaying the anointed one, whether by guile or open combat, serves as recognition of my right to the throne. On the other side, that I have so worthy an opponent."

Unlike Edgar the Aetheling and his advisors, the former having fled to Scotland to once more gain King Malcolm's protection, the latter renewing their submissions to William weeks past when the king marched his army far north of York. It was then the first deserters had made their dissension felt, especially those who left not because of weather that threatened to take fingers and toes but in protest against laying waste to the region.

Though the indiscriminate destruction of homes, food stores, and animals was intended to deprive rebels of supplies needed to continue opposing Norman rule, more it deprived the common folk. If men, women, and children did not quickly make their way south and take refuge, they might die of exposure to cold and starvation. Hence, many deserters had pronounced the campaign wicked and barbaric.

That Maël would not argue, nor had his youngest cousin who was threatened with imprisonment when he refused to lead a contingent to wreak those atrocities. William had relented, likely more because Theriot was a D'Argent than that Maël cast off his habitual indifference and defended him.

Thus, the young chevalier was charged with searching out pockets of resistance as his brother, Dougray, had done before the harrying. He had agreed, and yet in all the weeks since, no word nor sight of him.

Some said he had deserted the same as other cowards and weaklings, but it was not true. Maël was not Theriot's brother by birth, but raised alongside him, he knew his cousin well. Ill had to have befallen him.

Thus, as much as possible before William led his army west to extinguish the Cheshire uprising, Maël had sought an answer to the missing D'Argent. Finding none, he had sent word to his other cousins upon Wulfenshire, and great the hope they had succeeded where he failed.

"Vitalis is far worthier than the Aetheling and his advisors," the king said. "Could he be turned, he would serve me well, but after what the resistance forced me to do…" He shook his head. "Never could I give him my back."

Tempted to remind him he *had* given Vitalis his back and yet he stood here rather than face down in a pool of blood, Maël set his teeth.

"You are to hold this close," William said.

What of Vitalis and his rebels? Maël wondered. Would they hold close a tale that could rekindle a rebellion nearly reduced to ashes, proof of it a piece of the extravagantly embroidered mantle the king had worn to his coronation?

"I assume Vitalis took the cloth with him," Maël said.

"He did. Would that I had donned my simple mantle this day."

Which was of lesser weight and warmth than this one with its fur collar. Had he worn the other that was unremarkable but for exceptional wool in which many a noble indulged, Vitalis would not possess great proof the piece was taken from the king.

"Best I wear it now." William stepped toward the horses draped with blankets. None but Maël would know he exchanged one mantle for another to prevent any from questioning the ruin of the first. It would be assumed abatement of the storm caused the hearty conqueror to cast off excessive warmth.

A moment later, the king broke stride and turned. "Though it offends Vitalis makes of me a messenger, curiosity bids I pass along words he asked be delivered to you."

Maël tensed. "Your Majesty?"

"He said I should tell the captain of my guard he shall continue to watch for him."

That did not surprise. During their last encounter, one rendered impotent by the need to save the life of the woman his cousin, Dougray, later wed, Maël had warned the leader of the Rebels of the Pale he should keep watch for this Norman. Though that truce was forced on Maël and he would not as greatly begrudge it now, still he would do William's bidding.

Within godly reason, added a conscience so desperate to survive it clung to him as if it were the last of his humanity.

Regardless, Vitalis was surely laughing. He had kept watch as warned, and for it could have slain the conqueror.

"Explain the meaning of that, Sir Maël."

"It is the warning I shouted at the Battle of Stafford when I could not get near enough to engage him at swords."

"During the battle, you say?"

Afterward, and there the lie. "Oui, my liege."

The king shrugged his mouth again. "I am thinking you should make good that warning and retrieve what Vitalis stole from me."

Then once more he would detach his captain of the guard from his side, entrusting him with matters beyond the protection of his person.

Maël would not argue. Not only was he eager to give teeth to his warning Vitalis keep watch for him, but there was no settling of one's soul in the company of the man who had commanded unspeakable acts these past months.

William tapped his temple. "A plan forms, faithful chevalier."

"I await your orders, my liege."

Hours later, the front rank of the dispirited army appeared in the distance. Upon catching sight of the Normans at the base of a hill gently rising toward a cave's mouth, they ceased trudging and quickened their pace.

Rest here for them—providing William, who assured Maël he would think on making camp, was sympathetic following his own shaming.

He was, though it was dusk before he gave the order for his army to set their fires and make their beds.

"Doubtless, more for his comfort than those of whom he demands the nearly impossible," muttered the second in command of the king's guard who had come alongside Maël after aiding quaking soldiers in erecting the royal tent.

Maël glanced at the chevalier who was not kin, though he was kin to Maël's illegitimate cousin, Dougray, then returned his regard to the king and saw he berated a nobleman beneath a canopy that kept lazily drifting snow off the anointed one's head. It did not reflect well on William that one of his esteemed companions had brought up the rear of the army despite being astride.

"But then, he himself has not fully recovered, has he?" Sir Guy said somewhat slyly.

Maël looked at the one who would assume charge of the king's guard when William revealed his plan to recover what had been taken from him. "What say you?"

The chevalier cupped gloved hands over his mouth and warmed them with his breath. When he lowered his arms, his chapped lips curved. "I but confirm what you suspect. I saw the mantle ere he shoved it in his pack. What I do not know is how so prized a garment was ruined."

Maël had hoped his fellow Norman's ignorance was not feigned when he returned from scouting the area just as William removed that mantle, and surely the king hoped the same.

The chevalier's report of glimpsing snow tracks in the distance that seemed of a sizable animal, if not a man, had been received with little concern though William and Maël knew who was responsible and the tracks would dig deeper when Vitalis exited the cave's outlet to return to his horse and men. Hence, of no use to give chase since the rebel leader's numbers were likely greater at that time.

"Certes, the captain of the king's guard is not responsible," Sir Guy said, then jerked his head toward the cave. "Are there bears in these mountains?"

Maël nearly laughed as he would have done before being ruined in this godforsaken country, instead told himself there was nothing humorous here. Still, he could not entirely suppress a smile nor words that wanted off his tongue. "I *know* there are bears here. I just never expected they would be red of fur."

The chevalier's smile broadened, causing his upper lip to crack and a line of crimson to appear. "Red, hmm? I hear those are the most ferocious. Hence, quite the miracle our liege lives."

His eyebrows rose. "What I would give to know how he found such favor with God."

As would Maël who, not for the first time, considered that if such a man *had* found favor with God, he might himself.

Was redemption possible? If so, surely not whilst he served one who was more terrible than great.

CHAPTER TWO

Lillefarne Abbey, Wulfenshire
Spring, 1070

*S*he had thought she understood Gytha's hatred of Normans, but what she had felt when last she saw her grandmother hardly compared to what dug deeper with each arrival at the abbey. And more so this day.

It was not that this morn's refugees numbered more than expected now the passing of winter saw fewer Saxons fleeing south. It was that they were children lacking an adult to aid in their journey until the day past when, blessedly, they were overtaken not by Normans but the Saxon warrior who delivered them here.

Not all were orphans, some separated from families during their flight from the devastation ordered by the one who so coveted England he had risked being burned alive to gain a crown. But even if the parents of some of these children yet lived, orphans their sons and daughters would become were it impossible to reunite the families.

The woman who had mostly shed the person of Mercia of

Mercia these three years shifted her forehead against the cold stone floor. Spread before the altar and the simple wooden cross that had replaced the gilded one when William the Tyrant ordered raids on monasteries and abbeys to fill coffers from which to pay his army, she resumed her prayers. And once more strayed in marveling at how many were answered considering the lie of Abbess Mary Sarah, next bemoaned how many were ignored considering how great her people's suffering.

"Cease," she hissed and beseeched the Lord's forgiveness for disrespecting the audience granted her. "Almighty, I am tired," she rasped. "Tired of broken and stolen lives. Tired of questions I cannot answer. Tired of being what I am not and never wished to be. Tired of tidings that deliver much pain and little relief."

Again, her thoughts drifted, this time to news of William's most recent victory. Just as his rule had been strengthened by his devastation of the North, stronger he was for ending the latest uprising in Cheshire.

"Where are You, Lord? On the road back to us? Or does that road not exist? Will You forever keep Your face turned from us?" Chest pained by the sob held there, she gasped, "Amen," and flipped onto her back.

Opening her eyes, she searched the rafters for the bird who had flown in days past and had yet to find its way out though doors and windows had been opened. If not for the bread she left near the chapel's entrance alongside the font of water, the little thing might have expired. Hopefully, soon it would escape God's house.

"As I cannot," whispered its abbess.

There—a blink of light. The drab little bird roosted just off center above dust-scattered sunshine that lit an eye which seemed to return her stare. Then it spread its wings and flew toward a corner too dark to follow its progress.

It was silly to feel abandoned, but Mary Sarah did, and for a moment as abandoned as when the two Saxon women upon whom she most depended to aid with the refugees had departed England to journey to Normandy with their husbands.

That was silly as well since less and less she required help beyond that given by nuns, novices, and convent residents. Too, it was past time Lady Aelfled and her babe met their in-laws and made their home with them alongside her husband, Cyr D'Argent. As for Em who had wed Dougray D'Argent last December, once he reconciled with his sire, the two would return to Wulfenshire—for a short time only since lands awaited them in Derbyshire.

Still, she would have the aid of Chanson and Nicola of Stern Castle, as well as Lady Hawisa of Wulfen, though long the latter had cast a suspicious eye on Mary Sarah who assumed the position vacated by the aged abbess following the Battle of Hastings.

I am not alone, she told herself and wished it were true. One who played a part—who deceived no matter the reason—could never be well enough known to feel as if she belonged among others.

"Accursed Normans," she whispered. "Every one of them spawned by—"

Not every one, she corrected. Like pearls to be found in one of a thousand shells pried open, there were some good Normans among them, as proven by many of the D'Argent family—ladies Chanson and Nicola, and brothers Cyr, Dougray, and Guarin, the latter the husband of Lady Hawisa. As for the other D'Argents, surely the odds were against them the same as the Godwines.

Had not King Harold's treacherous brother, Tostig, contributed to the Saxons' defeat at Hastings? He had, so much it was likely his betrayal handed the victory to the Normans. But even before then, great her hope Tostig was not the one her grandmother would reveal had sired her.

Returning her thoughts to other D'Argents of silvered dark

hair, she considered Theriot who had accompanied the tyrant north last autumn in answer to the resistance taking the city of York and slaying its three thousand Normans. Also at that devil's side, and even nearer for being the usurper's captain of the guard, was one she knew better—in a manner of thinking, since she was more acquainted with Maël D'Argent than he with her.

When first she had looked upon him and his ruined face at Westminster, she had seen him only as a nameless Norman who aided the duke in taking their country at the cost of thousands of their men folk. But when he allowed the two women to depart the way they had come, preventing them from being exploited by William, the one then called Mercia had been unable to match her grandmother's hatred for him though he had not known how great the kindness shown them. Worse, something in the weak of her had reached out to something in the emptiness of him. Blessedly, the certainty she would not see the chevalier again had allowed her to mostly banish him from her thoughts—until he rode on Lillefarne a year and a half later and demanded its abbess send out one of the convent's residents accused of collaborating with the resistance.

Standing atop the wall, Mary Sarah had lost her breath when she recognized the handsome face disfigured one side of it and known beneath his mail coif was the silvered dark hair of a D'Argent.

Though fairly certain at the coronation he had been unable to look as near upon her as she had looked upon him, she had kept her chin up and, peering down her nose, refused to send out the one he was to collect for his cousin. Had not Aelfled herself yielded under threat to her grandmother, the chevalier and his men would have had to force their way into the abbey to take her.

In that moment of being bested by Maël D'Argent and fearing for Aelfled, Mary Sarah had tried harder to hate the tyrant's man as Gytha would deem proper—and might have succeeded had she not been doused with fear over her own fate when he asked if they had met before.

She had ignored the question, and though she assured herself he had not seen enough of her that Christmas Day to place her as one of the women he aided, it was false assurance. As he had peered up at her, something had returned him to that balcony in the chapel though he might not realize it was there he had gone.

Was it her voice? Unlikely. Since arriving at Lillefarne, she had put much effort into projecting strength and authority when she spoke as she had not at Westminster while buildings all around burned.

How peculiar Mary Sarah had felt when Aelfled departed with Maël D'Argent—both afeared for the young woman and relieved to see the chevalier's back. Surprisingly, concern for her charge had been unwarranted, the young woman gaining the protection of Cyr D'Argent and shortly thereafter wedding the Norman.

The same as all happenings of import upon Wulfenshire, Abbess Mary Sarah had sent word of their union to Gytha by way of the wine merchant who paused at Lillefarne twice a month to receive and, less often, deliver a missive.

Her grandmother had raged over tidings that Saxons upon Wulfenshire were making peace with Normans through marriage. As commanded, Mary Sarah had burned that missive as she did all of Gytha's correspondence, but she remembered its contents and, most painfully, the final words.

To save an old woman of no use to our cause, you whored away a Saxon of much use. Tell, you who are unworthy of my blood, of what value placing you at Lillefarne if you cannot prevent something so easily prevented? Time and again you neglect to prove yourself strong of mind, body, and spirit and true to the blood, the bone, the marrow.

If that you cannot do, shed the habit and ever remain ignorant of the one who sired you.

Mary Sarah breathed deep, mused bitterly, "Still I am ignorant." She had tried to make it right, but little of import came into her hands, and ever Gytha demanded more than could be given since her granddaughter lacked great influence on this Norman-controlled shire.

She was a woman confined to a habit and the walls of an abbey, not a lady like Hawisa whose warrior skills, lineage, and reputation permitted her the reach of many a man. And even if now Mary Sarah found a way to aid in restoring England to Saxons, there was naught she could do with it. For the past six months, all she knew of Gytha were the same rumors bending the ears of all—most recently that King Harold's mother had fled to the court of her kinsman, King Sweyn of Denmark.

Had she truly exiled herself, abandoning all hope of placing a grandson on the throne? Or was it a ruse to catch the Normans unawares? Three and a half years had passed since Harold and two of his brothers lost their lives on that bloody meadow. Three and a half years, and the conqueror's grip on England continued to tighten. And the harrying...

That savagery seemed the slamming of a lid on the coffin of Saxon-ruled England.

Abruptly, Mary Sarah sat up and turned onto her knees before the cross. "We have lost, have we not, Lord? 'Tis over, and we but shame ourselves in believing otherwise."

Another sob trying to force its way up her throat, she swallowed hard. Regardless were she the daughter of a king or an earl, she would not yield to tears of less use than spit on a muddied shoe.

"I am born of a son of Godwine," she rasped. "I am more than the refuse grandmother believes she left behind." She raised her arms, and when her sleeves fell back, laced her fingers and pressed her hands against her mouth. "Lord, if You wish me here, show me how to make right my deception. If You would have me go elsewhere, send me there, whether on my hands and knees or toes and heels. I..." Her voice caught. "I know You are here. Pray, remove this dark from my eyes and weight from my heart."

She stared at the cross, imagined her savior nailed there, then sank onto her heels.

And heard the flap of wings when only ever she heard the flutter.

As she dropped her head back to search out the bird in flight, she realized the sound came from behind and twisted around. The winged one was not a bird but a young woman whose mantle flapped as she hastened toward the door left ajar for the trapped bird.

Heart thudding so hard she felt it in her wrists, Mary Sarah leapt to her feet. "Lady Nicola!" she called to the youngest D'Argent sibling whose black hair shot with silver easily identified the Norman who had blundered in on a one-sided conversation that boded ill for the Abbess of Lillefarne.

Nicola squeaked, something to which she was given whether joyously surprised or horribly shocked. "Abbess!" She came around, clasped and unclasped her hands, then spread her arms as if in apology. "I did not mean to listen. Truly, I did not." She made a face. "I did mean to, but I thought... Well, I believed it just the prayers of a holy woman who would not mind me learning how to be nearer God. And as well you know from the words that sometimes pass these lips and how I chafe at authority and..." She shrugged. "...exaggerate or tell not the entire truth, I am in need of godly guidance. Certes, 'tis as my aunt tells as well as her husband who..." Her eyes widened further. "I like him—I do!—but he makes few allowances for me being a D'Argent. Time and again, I tell him I am made this way by four brothers—five do you count my cousin, and Maël ought to be counted since ever he has been in my life."

Mention of that D'Argent caused Mary Sarah to falter in her advance.

"I do try to be better," Nicola continued, "but 'tis never enough for Father Fulbert. Methinks the only thing of which he will approve is if I don the habit. And you know what grave misfortune that would be for a community of holy women." She frowned. "You do, do you not?"

Mary Sarah halted before her, and as ever lightened by the younger woman, smiled though fairly certain Nicola D'Argent had heard and deciphered prayers meant for heaven alone. "I know, just as I know that if you give your word what I spoke to the Lord will remain between the three of us, I will rest well this eve."

Exaggeration, the same as Nicola was given to. Sleep would be hard-won, not only over worry of what was learned of her this day, but how best to aid the refugee children.

The young lady breathed deep, replenishing air expended on that river of words. "The three of us." She gave a nod, stepped nearer, and said low as if others were present, "I do not understand all of what I heard, but enough I am pleased to know you better than before and have more questions. Might you tell—?"

"I will not," Mary Sarah said. "As is necessary, more and more I accept my past is of no consequence."

"Of no consequence? But what of your future? You are of the House of Godwine."

Hoping her secret would be easier kept were it revealed her parentage was of less account, Mary Sarah said, "I am misbegotten."

"Oh," Nicola mouthed, then shrugged. "Still…"

"It changes naught, Nicola. Thus, I fear my future is set at Lillefarne."

"Fear, Abbess?"

Abbess. Blessedly, she had not given the young woman cause to question that. "I misspoke, Lady Nicola."

"I do not think so. Had I to guess, I would say you are as unhappy giving your life to the Church as I would be."

Mary Sarah straightened her head covering. "I thank you for coming—and so soon. I thought I would not see you for several days." This Thursday, to be exact, as the young woman had said it was then she would return to aid those taking refuge at the abbey. And a far better day it would have been than this considering who was in the abbess's apartment.

The young woman grimaced like a girl told she must cease playing with her doll to gain her rest. But in the next instant, she was all smiles. "Of good fortune, I found myself with an accommodating escort and decided I would come early." She swung away. "Come meet him."

Accommodating, Mary Sarah mulled as she followed Nicola from the chapel into sunlight and a cool breeze she wished for the little bird. Did the young lady refer to her last escort, a chevalier caught staring at a lovely convent resident who tried not to be caught staring at him?

It must be that one, though Mary Sarah could see no reason for a formal introduction—unless he sought permission to court one whom he would not be allowed near, the lady's family having sent her to Lillefarne to keep her out of reach of Normans lest they plunder her the same as England. With firm words, the abbess would set him aright.

However, before the two women came within sight of the great doors alongside which one of Nicola's escort was permitted to await her while the others remained outside the walls, the lady gasped, "Mercy, I err!"

Mary Sarah looked sidelong at her and marveled over sunlit silver strands amid raven tresses.

Nicola grimaced. Though the expression contorted her features, still she was lovely. "Already you have met my escort."

Only if Mary Sarah's eye contact ladened with disapproval qualified as meeting another.

"What was it? A year and a half past?" Nicola nodded. "It was then my brother, Cyr, sent him to retrieve Aelfled. You recall Sir Maël, do you not?"

CHAPTER THREE

*U*ndone for having so recently revisited memories of the man once denied entrance to the abbey, and more undone by who else had entered earlier this morn, Mary Sarah stumbled. "Old slippers," she blurted as Nicola steadied her. "I must see them fit with new soles."

No suspicion about her green eyes, Nicola said, "And soon!"

Hoping she truly was unaware of how affected the abbess was at learning Maël D'Argent was inside her walls, Mary Sarah said, "I do remember your cousin, but why is he here when he should be keeping watch over—?" As ever, it was difficult to name that tyrant a king, but Nicola spared her.

"Le Bâtard." The young woman gave a huff of disgust. "And I mean that in all ways beyond the circumstances of his birth. Of course, never can it be spoken in the hearing of any but those worthy of trust, hmm?"

As Mary Sarah was to believe she could trust Nicola not to reveal the circumstances of her own birth. "Never," she agreed.

Nicola grinned. "Though I know not the details, weeks past Maël's liege relieved him of his duty as captain of the guard and sent him and a contingent on a mission of great import."

Mary Sarah moistened her lips. "One that delivered him to Wulfenshire. That is…curious."

"Though he told he paused at Stern only to visit his mother, I think it more. As I was hunting rabbit when he arrived, I know not what he revealed to Aunt Chanson and her husband. Whatever it was, the joy of a mother reunited with a son over whom she worried during the harrying should have been greater. And now that he has delivered me here, he is to continue on to Wulfen to tell Guarin and Lady Hawisa what he believes unfit for these ears."

So tense was Mary Sarah over her impending meeting with Maël D'Argent, it required much effort to attend to Nicola's chatter.

"But I talk too much, Abbess. Come renew your acquaintance with my cousin. Perhaps he will tell you something you can tell *me*."

"Hardly an acquaintance," Mary Sarah corrected as she was drawn forward. "I met him only once when he forced Aelfled to leave here, and great distance there was between us since I was upon the wall and he was mounted and coifed below."

Too much protest, she silently warned. *It sounds the lie it is.*

"Well then, this day you shall look nearer upon my cousin and see how handsome he is regardless of that cruel scar."

As if it mattered what Mary Sarah thought of him. Such was for ladies with whom Nicola hoped to see him matched, not her.

"I must warn he is a brood-y one, though only since…" Nicola made a sound of distress. "Forgive me, there is no light to be made of that ungodly battle, and I know it sounds as though I do. Our family's losses do not compare to those of your people, but ever the D'Argents will carry those wounds. I just wish you to make allowances for Maël who once was tenfold more charming than the man now given to glowering and few words."

Though tempted to further delay their meeting, Mary Sarah knew it was unworthy of a Saxon who must be strong of mind, body, and spirit. "Allowances will be made, Nicola." Confirming her veil permitted no glimpse of hair, including that which peaked on her brow, she continued forward, acknowledging Lillefarne's residents with nods.

When the two women rounded the stables, Mary Sarah saw Maël D'Argent before he saw her. Though memories of the chevalier at Westminster struck her with the longing to linger over him, she averted her gaze from the nearly unspoiled side of his face. Unfortunately, only so much interest could one believably feign over ground pocked by last eve's rain.

Out of the corner of her eye seeing him peer across his shoulder where he stood before his destrier as if conversing with it, she raised her chin higher and met his gaze.

No falter in her step. No flutter of lashes. No forced smile to disguise unease. And much gratitude Nicola had prepared her.

"Maël D'Argent!" she called in the commanding voice adopted when one too young to earn the position of abbess was disrespected by the older nuns—and was still disrespected by some, though more because she had yet to permit novices to make their profession, none aware the false of her lacked the authority to elevate them. "At last, you find a way inside my walls."

His eyebrows rose, the arch of the right broken by the upper end of the scar which had been more unsightly when first she looked upon him. It had healed much these past years, but not enough to balance the whole of his visage, which seemed all the more tragic for how handsome one side remained.

As she halted three strides distant and Nicola did the same, he lowered his hand from the horse's muzzle and, absent the ring of chain mail, turned. "I am pleased entering here proved less difficult than expected, Abbess." Though his accent was nearly as pronounced as the last time they spoke, his Anglo-

Saxon was clearer, the words better ordered and nearly without falter.

"And you have me to thank for that, Cousin," Nicola said.

A corner of his mouth creased. "Lacking desire and the need to enter here, that is so."

It was a threat worthy of regard. Doubtless, he was as capable of stealing inside Lillefarne as his cousin, Cyr, had done the night he captured Lady Hawisa's rebels whom the young abbess was not to have known Aelfled hid inside the outer wall. Of course she had not been ignorant, as was her duty to Gytha.

Returning his regard to Mary Sarah, Sir Maël scrutinized her.

Do not see Mercia, she silently appealed as this time he looked down *his* nose at her.

"I am glad we meet again under better circumstances, Abbess," he finally spoke.

That was the wrong thing to say, but she was glad since his words set her aright. He was no longer the Norman at Westminster who had drawn her to his emptiness when he aided two Saxons who were where they ought not be. This man had become more than a vassal to the detestable William. He was the captain of the king's guard, at the tyrant's side throughout all the ill worked upon her people.

Mercia tried to hold her tongue. And failed. "Better circumstances?" Disbelief pitched her voice above the range of one in command of her emotions, but though she saw surprise in the chevalier's eyes and heard the catch of Nicola's breath, her tongue would not be quieted. "Forgive me for believing you were privy to the terrorizing of innocents by your king. I was unaware you were out of the country."

Color rose in his face. "You know I speak of what goes between this one Norman and this one Saxon—what is required of each of us regardless of our wishes."

"Nay, what I know is that still refugees come, and this day

little ones—fatherless and motherless, and so starved we can feed them only spoonfuls at a time lest they sicken further and die."

His breath on her face, more than the greater sight and scent of him, alerted her a woman of God aggressed so brazenly his shadow covered her. And yet she could not retreat. Though she was to love even were she not playing this part, she wanted to hate him for not being a D'Argent like the others. More, for continuing to aid Le Bâtard.

"Hence," she continued, "these circumstances are far worse than when first we met, Chevalier."

His green eyes bored into hers, a gleam in their depths that should have prepared her for his response. "When exactly was that, Abbess Mary Sarah?"

As if he felt the suspension of her breath on his jaw, he smiled, grim though that curve of the lips. Would he now confront her over being an uninvited guest at his king's coronation? If not, because still he was unable to place that first encounter? Or because he liked such games?

Anger over the latter restored her breath, but once more she ill used it. "When first did we meet? Sometime between the atrocities you committed at Hastings upon Saxon warriors who sought to defend their people and your more recent barbarism in the North."

His smile lowered, and she was so pleased she did not heed the inner voice warning her to clutch victory close and hasten away. "You know what you and your kind are? You are mons—" She snapped her teeth on a word surely as offensive to him as *Le Bâtard* was to his liege. But too late, as told by a muscle jerking in his jaw and a whimper at her back that reminded her they were not alone.

"You are not the first to name me a monster, Abbess."

"I refer not to your face!"

Once more, the broken eyebrow rose. "Now you do. But

again, you are not the first nor will you be the last—just as you will be neither first nor last to say it is my due. And on that I agree more than I do not." Noting her surprise, he added, "Aye, monster, but there are more dangerous monsters than I."

Though she knew she ought to retreat, she could only stare.

"Heavenly Father!" Nicola exclaimed. "It is like watching a dog circling a cat—or is it a cat circling a dog?—knowing any moment one shall spring upon the other and naught can be done but wait to see who emerges the least bloodied."

Her words dropped Mary Sarah onto her heels, and though she balked at further retreat, she stepped back until no longer covered by the chevalier's shadow. And was thankful his eyes upon her did not reflect satisfaction. Still, something flickered there which, oddly, appeared relief.

"Forgive me, Nicola." He looked to the young woman alongside whom Mary Sarah halted. "I forget myself, which is irresponsible for one in my position and disrespectful of my training." His eyes returned to Lillefarne's abbess, and she knew he gave her space in which to own to the same.

"Apologies, Nicola," she said. "And now we ought go to the infirmary. Godspeed your journey, Sir Maël."

"There is a matter I wish to discuss with you, Abbess."

Struggling to mask alarm and fear over what should not surprise since he had not departed following delivery of Nicola, she looked back. "Would that I had the time, but I am long gone from the children who arrived this morn following a brutal journey across scorched earth."

"How many are there?" Nicola asked.

"Eleven, the youngest barely four years of age."

"Poor little ones." Nicola looked to her cousin. "Perhaps you could speak with the abbess in the infirmary."

"Lady Nicola!" Mary Sarah snapped. "It is not for you to invite a man to move among a community of women."

"Forgive me. I thought...well, since I know my cousin to be honorable, and other men enter here—"

"Others trusted by me," Mary Sarah said, referencing those who supplied the abbey with necessities and repaired what its residents could not, those of God who sought verification Lillefarne maintained its standing as a house of God, the physician who tended serious illnesses, and the one who had fallen asleep in her apartment.

"But in this matter," she continued, "of greatest concern is exposing traumatized children to a man whose Norman appearance and speech will further frighten them."

Nicola gasped. "I did not think there. Now I am the one who seeks forgiveness." She looked to her cousin. "I believe the abbess is right."

He inclined his head, and once more Mary Sarah thought she glimpsed relief. Hopefully, here evidence he still possessed enough humanity to be discomfited by the prospect of looking close on those whose suffering was dealt by the tyrant he protected. "Aid the abbess," he said. "Afterward, I shall speak with her."

Mary Sarah nearly screeched. "You will not, Sir Maël. Godspeed." Resuming her course, she called, "Come, Lady Nicola."

Now to set her mind on the children, of little difficulty once she entered the room lit with few candles and whose curtains were drawn to encourage its occupants to sleep and heal. Many of the youngest ones did so, but few of the youths who had suffered more for sacrifices made to ensure survival of the most vulnerable among them.

It proving necessary to shear lice-infested hair and scrub vermin from their scalps, it was difficult to tell the difference between boys and girls attended by novices who moved pallet to pallet offering spoonfuls of soup and sips of milk. Too, since it was also necessary to burn what remained of their clothes, all wore oversized shifts.

"Where shall I begin?" Nicola said.

"The wee one fretting in the corner." Mary Sarah nodded at where he—or she—snuffled around a thumb.

The young woman hesitated, said, "I know I overstepped with my cousin and did not think well on how the children would react. Aunt Chanson is right—I am impulsive. Will you pray for me?"

Glad Maël D'Argent prepared to ride to Wulfen Castle, Mary Sarah said, "I do pray for you, and just as you are in need of prayer, so am I. I hope you remember me when you go to the Lord."

Nicola smiled. "I shall pray for both our futures—more, these children."

The Abbess of Lillefarne nodded, then veered toward a novice in need of relief.

A while later, hearing Nicola soothe the little one with a song, she looked to where the Norman noblewoman sat with her back against the wall, in her arms a Saxon whose thumb was no longer sucked, freeing both hands to play in the lady's hair.

Nicola was impulsive and, at times, improper, but Mary Sarah envied her that. She was the clay Gytha could have molded into what was demanded of her granddaughter who was to be a Saxon strong of mind, body, and spirit. Instead, one born of a fierce Godwine warrior had feared furthering her audience with the chevalier, and not only because of the rebel who had delivered the children to the abbey.

Had she another opportunity to give ear to Sir Maël…

I would and be done with him forever, she told herself. And hoped she was done with him regardless—that never again his shadow covered her.

CHAPTER FOUR

The inner door was where Cyr had told he found it the night he scaled the wall to ensure rebels hidden in the passage were not let into the abbey to claim sanctuary. Thus, the Saxons, including Vitalis, had been trapped inside.

With less bloodshed than expected, Dougray, Maël, and their men had brought out the rebels the way they had entered— through the outer door concealed by a garden near the abbey's wall.

Now having moved aside empty barrels stacked in a shed erected against the inner wall, Maël lowered to his haunches before an iron door barred this side to allow the keeper of Lillefarne's secret to control who entered here. That long ago eve, the keeper had been Aelfled, but who was it now? Abbess Mary Sarah? Her alone?

Of greater import, at this moment were rebels on the other side? With William's men hunting them out of the North, it was very possible. But if rebels hunkered in that narrow passage, it was unlikely the one Maël sought was there. Still, one might know where Vitalis could be found.

Seeking the vibration of movement between inner and outer

walls, Maël splayed a hand on the cool iron, slowed his breath, and listened. Naught. He leaned in, pressed an ear to the door, and closed his eyes. Still naught, though that did not mean none were in the passage. Unfortunately, he did not possess the unnaturally keen senses of Theriot who would have known if prey dwelt within and been fairly accurate in determining their number.

"Theriot," Maël rasped and, opening his eyes, drew back. At Stern Castle he had been dealt a blow when, seeking assurance from his mother that the youngest of his male cousins had been found, he was met with surprised silence.

Tidings sent of Theriot's disappearance had not reached Cyr nor Dougray before they departed for Normandy, nor Guarin at Wulfen, meaning Maël's messenger had met a bad end in riding the same direction as Saxons fleeing William's solution to the resistance.

Theriot lives, Maël assured himself, chest tightening over time that would be better spent searching for him than retrieving a piece of cloth to preserve the king's dignity. At every place Maël and his men paused in following leads of what remained of the Rebels of the Pale, he had asked after sightings of a young Norman of dark silvered hair, but much more could have been done.

If not that Guarin would organize a search for his youngest brother as soon as he learned of his disappearance, Maël would keep his word to his liege later rather than now regardless of the opposition of men chosen to accompany the king's captain of the guard, among them a Saxon nobleman all the more distasteful for his fanatical support of the conqueror over his own people.

The D'Argents remained loyal to the man who had longer been their duke than their king, but now mostly because of oaths given and the value William placed on their vassalage that permitted Maël's family to stand more firm in their beliefs than most when things were demanded of them for which many a Norman would answer to God.

The creak of the shed's door sounded, then sunlight sprang between the barrels, striping him, the iron door, and the stone wall.

The arrival of the woman who hated him did not surprise since he had not stealthily gained the shed, instead turning the heads of residents who might have once paused over his silvered hair but now over a terribly scarred face.

Hearing her footsteps over the dirt floor, he straightened and turned to where she would appear in the gap of displaced barrels.

A moment later, she halted so abruptly her skirts flared, permitting a glimpse of shapely ankles. Too, her head covering was askew, gifting him with one more piece of the woman he was fairly certain he had encountered in the year and a half before Cyr sent him to Lillefarne to collect Aelfled. Above wide eyes, dark hair peaked on a brow no longer beautifully smooth as when she had stood before him earlier.

He inclined his head. "Abbess."

She stepped into the space one would not know was clear of barrels had Maël not moved two aside. "You trespass, Sir Maël!"

"Necessary since you refused me further audience."

She glanced at the iron door. "Of what use verifying the existence of a passage that once offered sanctuary to my charges should they find themselves attacked inside the abbey the same as they have been outside it?"

Knowing she referred to the ravishment of two novices in the wood whilst a portion of Wulfenshire lands was held by the mercenary Dougray had recently defeated at Wulfen Castle, he said, "Unfortunate that, and duly avenged by those of the resistance who made use of the passage far more than your charges."

Her chin rose higher. "I am aware of only one occasion

rebels entered there without my permission, and as you and your cousins put finish to that, Norman knowledge of the passage renders it useless to the rebellion—indeed, any Saxon fleeing the thieves and murderers overrunning our country."

It would be easy to take offense but wrong, especially since the harrying.

"And so I ask again the reason you trespass on holy ground, Sir Maël."

"I seek Vitalis."

He hoped blunt honesty would afford a glimpse of alarm, evidencing even if the rebel leader was not in the passage, others were. And she did not disappoint, fleeting though the fear in her eyes and soft the catch of her breath.

"How you reach, Sir Maël! I cannot believe such desperation worthy of a chevalier charged with protecting the man who perches on England's throne."

Again, easy to be offended, in this instance because the attack was personal, but he said evenly, "Not desperation, Abbess—diligence, tedious though it is. Hence, I must verify no one is on the other side." He nodded at the door that would require he bend low to pass through it. "Now if enough time has passed to permit any who lurk inside to unbar the door to the garden where I have posted men, I would have you deliver me a torch."

Now *she* was offended, but there was smugness about her smile. "I shall not be long," she said.

Shortly, she returned and thrust a torch at him. He thought an ember leapt onto his hand when he took it, but the stinging heat was delivered by soft skin across which his calloused fingers traveled.

So quickly she snatched her hand away, it was possible she felt it too—and wished to feel it no more than he who knew what it was though he had not been moved to attraction since taking up residence in the cold place inside him following

Hastings. Could she identify it as well? Or was her reaction that of a bride of Christ resigned to never knowing the touch of a man?

Giving him a dismissive look, she stepped to the barred door.

Saxon women! he silently denounced, then turned that frustration on himself. Years from now he might once more open himself to the allure of the fairer sex providing he had cause to pursue marriage, but not now. And never a Saxon as his—

Banishing that memory, he turned his thoughts to his cousins. Three had fallen prey to women of this country, sacrificing and suffering for infatuation. He would not. Still, he could not deny he was relieved the abbess was committed to the Lord.

The scrape of metal returned her to his regard, and he saw she had set back the bar.

He would have opened the door more cautiously than she, but were rebels there, they would not harm the one harboring them.

The abbess peered over her shoulder, causing her veil to shift further off center and reveal a slender neck sloping into an ivory shoulder. "Come see I speak true," she said and ducked to clear a rusted iron lintel.

Stripes of sunlight and the torch's glow entering the passage with her revealed a dirt floor and the lower wall opposite.

Certain a representative of God would not lead him to his death, Maël started to follow, but an inner voice warned, *She is of the Church of England that was in such need of reform the pope gave William his blessing to wage war. And godly though she is meant to be, she does not hide her hatred of Normans.*

He drew the D'Argent dagger, thrust the torch inside to confirm a single occupant, and straightened before the abbess.

She glanced at the blade. "As told, the passage is empty, Sir Maël."

Certainly true of this section. And from the silence that fell between them and confirmed by his senses, likely true of the section around the corner just as he, Cyr, and Dougray had left it the night they cleared it of rebels.

"So it appears, but again, due diligence."

She gestured for him to precede her. Were she a man, he would not allow her to keep company with his back, but though a woman, still he kept an ear turned to her lest she trouble him in the slightest.

The passage, strung with webs that would be more intricate were their spinners left in peace, narrowed halfway down its course. As he knew from when last he was here, further it narrowed around the corner.

When he turned it, a scuttle sounded and he tensed in anticipation of abandoning the torch to bring his sword to hand, but the light revealed the last coursing of the passage was clear except for rats bustling toward whichever gaps in the stones they could squeeze through.

The abbess expressed no dismay over vermin surely glimpsed beyond him. But then, neither did she seem afeared of being alone with one who, were he dishonorable, would prove more dangerous than rats. Because of his family's reputation and her interactions with Nicola and others? Or might her confidence be credited to an encounter with him at a place other than Lillefarne which she neither acknowledged nor denied?

Ahead, the creatures went from sight, and shortly torchlight revealed greatly gapped stones at the farthest end of the passage. "For a wall recently constructed, there is much settling," he said.

"To fend off Normans who think naught of attacking houses

of God, the wall had to be raised quickly," the abbess said. "Hence, in places it is not as solid as we wish."

He halted before the door whose bar was in place, proving none had departed the passage since his discovery of the shed.

"All is as told, Sir Maël."

"You spoke true, empty but for rats and other vermin. *This* day."

"*Every* day," she said, then, "As you know, the garden is beyond. And your men as well?"

Only if those awaiting him outside the walls were moved there by boredom or a need for privacy in which to relieve themselves. He had considered setting men to keep watch over the garden but determined in the unlikely event rebels were here during the day, it was better he deal with them than reveal the abbey's vulnerability to those who had yet to earn his trust. Too, he would have none come between him and any who could yield word of Theriot.

"My men as well," he said as he peered past the frame made of her veil into a uniquely pretty face with large eyes, snub nose, wide mouth, and slightly cleft chin. Guessing she was aged five to eight years beyond twenty, he returned his gaze to hers.

"It appears we are done here," she said.

He slid his dagger in its scabbard. This time as he traversed the passage at *her* back, he looked closer on the stone walls.

Blood having been cast against them, in several places he glimpsed crimson gone brown that had escaped scouring. Though no mortal wounds had been dealt here, that nearly changed when the rebels assembled in the garden to be bound and marched to Stern.

Harsh words had been spoken between Dougray and Vitalis that became fists which could have killed had not the two been dragged apart. And yet, less than six months past, something of a truce was declared between them—all because of the rebel, Em, who had also bewitched a D'Argent.

Upon reaching the inner wall's door, the abbess turned. "Curiosity bids me ask—why do you search for Vitalis?"

He settled into his heels. "Curiosity bids *me* ask—why so curious? Are you acquainted with the leader of the Rebels of the Pale?"

A corner of her mouth jerked. "I know little of him other than he was Lady Hawisa's housecarle before the great battle, took charge of her rebels when your king wed her to your cousin, and made warriors of the men and women bent on resisting Norman rule. As for my curiosity, I understand his rebels disbanded following the Battle of Stafford. Hence, as he is no longer a threat to William, for what do you hunt him? Vengeance, though the Lord claims it as His own? Or does your liege yet fear Vitalis—one man alone?"

The Rebels of the Pale had *mostly* disbanded. Though scores had returned to their homes and accepted William's rule, a dozen willing to give their lives even in the absence of hope had remained with Vitalis. And Maël would not be surprised if she knew that.

"It is not for me to question the king's motives, Abbess. I but follow orders."

Her eyes glittered. "Were you not a D'Argent, more I would believe you ignorant of William's motives. Blessedly, they are of no consequence to those of Lillefarne. As told, curiosity bid me ask. Now allow me to see you to your destrier so you may resume your journey."

Not curiosity alone, but it was past time he start for Wulfen.

She bent low to exit the passage, and as she stepped into the shed, gasped as if someone was present who should not be.

Once again, his hand was on his dagger, but as he drew it, he saw the cause of her distress was a matter of modesty.

On the other side of the door, she reached to the head covering snagged on the rusted lintel. He caught hold of it first, the drab linen between his fingers soft from much wear and many washings. Unlike some of the Church, the Abbess of Lillefarne did not indulge in fine trappings whose coin was intended for those with far less than she.

However, when he exited after the torch, he saw there was one thing in which she indulged though the cost was paid with time. And felt the pound of his heart as he looked upon what one would never know was beneath the veil she snatched from him.

Her gleaming dark hair was not loose like that of a maiden nor bound tight to her scalp or simply braided, and when she swung away to fit the veil, he saw the back was as lovely as the front and sides. A multitude of beautifully worked braids draped and looped, and yet their tails hung low enough that when their crossings were undone, the crimped hair would venture past her thighs—might even skim her calves.

Were there any doubt she was noble, none now. Only a woman of high birth would be permitted to keep tresses which could not have been more than trimmed since she was a girl. Of course, that she held a position almost exclusive to experienced, aged women also bore witness to nobility which granted unearned privileges. Since the conquest, many landed Saxon families had hidden heiresses inside abbeys to keep them out of the hands of Normans who wanted more than the reward William promised for bringing England to its knees.

Was Mary Sarah an heiress? Since she would have been required to make her profession to attain her high office, thereby binding her to the Church for life, likely not. But she was beloved enough for her family to pay for a position of great esteem, power, and influence.

"Never would I have guessed what could be found beneath a simple veil," he mused.

With jerks and tugs, she continued fixing it in place.

Maël did not understand why he wished to provoke a greater response as if he were still the young man of Normandy who teased many a maiden determined not to show interest in one who lacked lands, but he felt lightened as he had not in years.

Before he could think better of it, he said, "Is it possible I have been misinformed? That beneath the veils of all nuns and novices can be found hair fashioned to delight men who will never see nor touch it?"

Dropping her arms to her sides, she turned. Though the veil was off center, it covered her hair. "Most inappropriate, Sir Maël."

"I speak only of hair, though it *is* a great tempter of men, and for that married women keep it covered outside the bedchamber, as do maidens in want of a proper chaperone."

Her nostrils flared. "You test my godliness. Lest regret for words spoken finds me long repentant upon my knees and negligent of my charges, 'tis time you continue your journey to Wulfen Castle."

Halfheartedly suppressing a smile, he said, "Now that I have verified the one I seek is not here, I shall." He extended the torch and noted she avoided contact with his fingers.

After he had secured the iron door and returned the barrels to their places, Maël followed the woman whose stern bearing was at odds with glorious tresses he should not want to draw through his fingers.

As they exited the shed into sunlight dampened by the appearance of clouds that could see him and his men drenched during the journey ahead, silently he warned, *Beware, Maël D'Argent who will never take a Saxon bride, you are at risk of bewitchment by one who will never take an earthly husband. Gird the Norman who came to conquer and the D'Argent of your sire who would berate you for wanting such.*

As they came within sight of his destrier, the abbess intercepted a nun heading opposite and passed the torch to her.

"I thank you for granting me further audience, Abbess," Maël said as he drew alongside.

"As it could not be helped, gratitude is not due me."

"True." Seeing her jaw shift, he wondered if she had pretty teeth and a smile fit for hair likely no man other than he had looked upon since her profession.

As such musings portended he was at greater risk of beguilement, he lengthened his stride and was soon astride.

"Good day to you, Abbess," he said and took up his horse's reins.

"Hold!" cried one whose voice he would recognize even were it absent its Norman-French accent.

Skirts raised higher than acceptable outside the abbey, Nicola ran from the infirmary, waved at two novices who feigned disinterest in their abbess and her male visitor, and halted alongside the destrier.

"I seek the abbess to relate something of interest, and still you are here, Maël." She looked over her shoulder at that woman. "So kind of you to speak further with my cousin though your duties are many."

Seeing wariness in the abbess's eyes, Maël prompted, "What you seek to tell her must be beyond interesting to drag you away from the children."

"It is, though I would have waited had I not put my wee one to sleep."

"What so excites?"

Her smile was coy. Though less in charge of her life than she would be were she a man, her thoughts and words she could control. "Naught that concerns you, Cousin." She patted his arm. "I am merely glad to see you one last time ere you depart. And I would remind you to deliver my gift to Lady Hawisa."

Her creation of two tiny caps was not to be forgotten, though not for how beautifully worked they were. When he had complimented her for ensuring one or the other was appropriate regardless were the babe a boy or girl—the band of one embellished with a flower, the other a dagger—she had said she did not like the needle well enough to waste time better spent on other things. And one of those *other* things was that of which he should not approve.

Her training at arms had begun in Normandy when Guarin instructed his little sister in the flight of arrows and the wielding of daggers not only to calm the restlessness of a girl surrounded by males but afford her a measure of defense. However, it had not ended there. Nicola now received training from Guarin's wife at Wulfen. No warrior was this cousin, but pity the man who thought to do ill to one believed helpless beyond running, screaming, and biting.

"I shall deliver the caps this day, Nicola." Shifting his shoulders beneath his mantle, he moved his regard to the abbess. He meant only to nod in parting, but recall of her vanity made him consider again how far her loosed hair would fall, and he said, "I am glad to have furthered our acquaintance and to know though you don the habit and veil, you are yet of this world, Abbess."

Seeing more than hearing her swallow, feeling more than seeing Nicola's interest, he added, "Until we meet again." Then he touched his cousin's shoulder. "The Lord have a good care for you, Nicola."

She smiled. "Godspeed, Maël."

He turned his mount toward doors opened by nuns who appeared as if summoned.

Do I feel the abbess's gaze? he wondered as he and his men spurred away in an attempt to outrun the rain. *Or are her eyes upon me merely imagined?* Regardless, he hoped they did not meet again.

~

"Heavenly Father, I am not certain I saw what I saw, but methinks it possible."

As the nuns secured the doors, Mary Sarah turned to Nicola. "What is possible?"

"What I saw—or think I saw."

Great the temptation to walk away, but greater the need to know what had so captured Nicola's interest she had searched out Lillefarne's abbess. "Of what do you speak?"

"Maël."

Inwardly, Mary Sarah sighed. Outwardly, she raised her eyebrows.

"He saw you, Abbess."

"Of course he did."

"Not in that way. In the way of seeing a woman as once he saw women."

As Mary Sarah tensed over what she suggested and the realization it had naught to do with whatever caused Nicola to depart the infirmary, the young lady continued, "I was not so young then that it escaped me—well, once I turned an age to know when a kiss wants to be given."

Mary Sarah gasped. "You scandalize, Lady Nicola!"

"I am aware, but I must ask, did *you* see him the same?" She made a face, raised a hand. "Not that you can do anything about it since you are of the Church."

Struggling against revealing how unsettled she was by the possibility Sir Maël had looked upon her as might a man who wishes to be intimate with a woman, telling herself had he done so it was only because of her unveiled hair, Mary Sarah said, "Such ponderings do a lady no credit, Nicola. Now tell, what was of such interest you came for me?"

The young woman blinked away dismay, then gasped, "Ah, that. Most interesting and, I believe, best spoken outside my cousin's hearing. You know of the rebel leader, Vitalis, do you not?"

～

ON ONE HAND, gratitude was due the Lord that Nicola had been more discreet than expected. On the other hand, questioning was due the Lord for allowing the young lady to be privy to the whispering of youths who pondered the identity of the red-headed and bearded warrior who delivered them to Lillefarne.

The same as the boys, Nicola had questioned if their savior was the leader of the Rebels of the Pale who strove to protect his people from the invaders.

Mary Sarah had said she had spoken with the one who escorted the children here and, having looked upon Lady Hawisa's former housecarle years past, was certain this one was not the same.

Sensing Nicola was not entirely convinced, she had lightly scolded her by pointing out red hair and formidable build was not a rarity among Saxon men. Not a lie, though few were as tall and broad as Vitalis.

Now, pausing on the stairs to her apartment, she raised a head lowered by weariness and worry, confirmed her veil was secure, and pressed her shoulders back.

Upon entering the outer room where she conducted the abbey's business, she closed the door firmly, slid the bolt, and said, "Unseemly though 'tis, best you pass the night here."

～

Wulfen Castle
Wulfenshire, England

AS EXPECTED, Guarin would himself search for his youngest brother. Having departed the hall to begin provisioning warriors to ride north at dawn when, hopefully, they would do so beneath tear-spent skies, he had left Maël with the Lady of

Wulfen who was displeased at learning the reason there were king's men outside her walls and one inside.

"Thus, that rumor finds me returned to Wulfenshire," Maël concluded.

Hawisa stared. Once their disdain had been mutual, the lady so disrespectful and defiant over Norman rule that the king's messenger had liked her no better—even momentarily hated her for naming his sire a coward—but no longer. Much cause she was given to feel and act as she had and much redemption granted her in saving the life of the cousin feared lost at Hastings. True, she had bewitched Guarin, but her love for her Norman husband seemed genuine.

She pushed up out of the chair before the hearth and settled her hands atop a belly so great it raised her skirt enough to show her slippers. Were she yet six weeks from delivering the first of the Wulfrith-D'Argent line, a very large son or daughter she would place in her husband's arms—did she survive its birthing.

"I see," she said. "What I do not see is why *your* king concerns himself with a man no longer of threat to him."

There was venom in her rejection of William as her liege, and for that Maël was glad Guarin had permitted only his cousin to enter here. No longer begrudging her what once he had, only one who was cast of stone able to ignore the abomination recently perpetrated against her people, he said, "I do not doubt even were Vitalis in yon solar you would feign ignorance, and I could not fault you."

Disbelief narrowed her eyes.

"I am not here to ask you to betray him, Lady Hawisa. I am here to inform you my men and I must search your lands to do our duty to William, as well as give you my word we shall do so with the least amount of disturbance to your people."

"Generous," she said with less sarcasm than expected. Then with more generosity than thought possible, she added,

"Though your men must make camp outside our walls in consideration of the boys and young men whose training is entrusted to us, I shall have a chamber prepared for you."

He inclined his head. "One night, two at most. Now I will join Guarin to aid in preparing for his departure on the morrow."

"I shall see you at supper, Sir Maël."

He started to turn away, but the removal of her hands from her belly reminded him of a promise. He drew forth the pack slung over the shoulder of his rain-dampened mantle, tossed back its flap, and removed a bundle. "May I?"

She nodded for him to approach, and he set the gift in her hand. "Before I left Nicola at Lillefarne, she insisted I deliver this."

The lady plucked at the ribbon binding it and folded back the cloth. As she examined the caps, her eyes moistened and mouth began to tremble. Was she remembering her first child slain during the great battle? That Maël's sire was believed to have put through the boy, possibly in retaliation for the boy putting through him?

In that moment, Maël accepted words needed speaking, but before he could think how best to express regret over her loss, she returned her regard to him and smiled tremulously. "Our Nicola is gifted, as much with the sharp of a needle as the sharp of a blade—and forget not her tongue."

Half-relieved her departed son had receded, half-regretful what must be done would have to be done later, he returned her smile, possibly the first genuine one afforded her.

"She *is* a D'Argent," he said and dipped his head. "Until supper, my lady."

CHAPTER FIVE

Lillefarne Abbey
Wulfenshire, England

*H*ere one whose absence she had not missed, and great the temptation to refuse him admittance—not because their stores of wine were sufficient. Nay, for that other thing of which she did not wish to take delivery. And so averse was she, had she a choice between once more facing the chevalier who departed two days past and this man, she would choose Maël D'Argent—even absent her veil.

She pressed her shoulders back, then signaled for the other door to be opened to allow the merchant to bring his wagon inside, and only that. As ever, the mounted escort who ensured he was not set upon during his deliveries would await him outside the wall.

As she started for the shed in the back right corner where last she had been with the chevalier who hunted Vitalis, she heard, "Abbess!" and looked to the young woman on the infirmary steps.

Nicola jutted her chin at the merchant whose horse pulled the ladened wagon inside. "Shall I join you?"

After all that had transpired these past days—the arrival of starving children, Nicola's untimely appearance, the encounter with Maël D'Argent, the man who remained in her apartment, and now evidence the Abbess of Lillefarne was not forgotten by the woman who sent her here—Mary Sarah was so tense it was difficult to remain composed.

Knowing she ought not be annoyed with Nicola for seeking to relieve her restlessness over spending nearly every waking hour with the children, she called, "I thank you, but the merchant and I have matters of pricing and delivery to discuss. As he has much to answer for, it is best done in privacy. But rest a while longer, else walk in the cloister."

That last lightened Nicola's disappointment. "I shall, Abbess."

Mary Sarah resumed her course and reached the shed before the merchant who had to go the long way around, his wagon unable to negotiate the narrow spaces between buildings.

As she opened the door wide to allow him to roll in barrels of wine she did not need but which provided cover should a resident become overly curious about his visit, he arced wide as he drew his wagon near, turned, and brought it parallel to the shed. But rather than rein in as usual, he turned sharply alongside the door, causing the wagon's backside to swing around and the barrels beneath taut canvas to scrape against one another.

Easier to unload, Mary Sarah guessed, and confirming none of the residents showed undue interest, stepped into the shed as the merchant jumped to the ground.

"Abbess." He dipped his head.

"It has been a long time," she said. "I began to think I would not see you again."

"As did I, but then this from all the way across the sea." He drew a rolled parchment from a pouch on his belt. "It seems you might yet be of use to her."

Of use...

With a trembling hand, she accepted it. Much was required of her to administer Lillefarne, but more stressful it was with her grandmother heavy on her shoulder. Though she had begun to think herself abandoned, she did not overly resent it.

Except for when coastal raids on England were launched from Ireland by Gytha's grandsons who had been born of Harold and the handfasted wife he set aside to wed a noblewoman deemed worthier of being his queen, Mary Sarah was likely the only Godwine left in their country. As this was not the life she wanted, she had hoped one of the missives sent her would end the ruse. But now she almost hoped this one, so long in coming, did not. Almost...

It was possible Gytha finally accepted those of her blood would never reclaim the throne, was it not? It was possible she wished to make good whatever she could of her remaining years and do so with her granddaughter at her side, was it not?

"Whilst you read, I shall unload the barrels," the merchant said.

She nodded, then turned to the side to cast light come through the doorway onto the missive, broke the seal, and unrolled the parchment.

Though the handwriting appeared inked by trembling fingers, it was familiar enough to confirm who had moved the quill.

My dear Abbess, it began, *this Saxon noblewoman, bereft of all sons and lands, has arrived safely in her kinsman's country and been kindly received.*

Mary Sarah looked to the bottom for the name taken for the writing of this missive—Lady Edelwine. Never the same, and ever details to be interpreted by what was known of the old woman and what was rumored.

Returning to the top, she resumed reading.

I know not if my niece remains within your walls, but if she is yet in your care, I would have you deliver glad tidings I have secured a good future for her. The noble family who has taken in this lady seeks a wife of godly character for a second son of good character.

Mary Sarah—or was it Mercia?—identified not as a granddaughter but a niece, caught her breath. If she interpreted this correctly, Gytha referred to Canute, the second son of King Sweyn of Denmark who had sent an army last autumn to aid the Saxon rebels in ousting William. Instead, the rebel and Danes' victory over York had led to the harrying. But before Le Bâtard set that evil plan in motion, he had paid the Danes to withdraw their support from the resistance and permitted them to remain in England until spring when it would be safer to sail home.

All these months later they had yet to depart, and it was speculated they awaited the arrival of their king who intended to assert his own claim upon England's throne.

"What do you, Gytha?" Mary Sarah rasped. Had the old woman abandoned hope of returning England to her family's rule? Did desperation move her to gain the crumbs from Sweyn's table by aiding in gaining Saxon acceptance with marriage to a Godwine? If so, it would require Mercia be acknowledged as the daughter of one of Gytha's departed sons.

She drove her teeth into her lower lip. Did the King of Denmark know the truth of her? Though Canute was illegitimate the same as she since all but one of Sweyn's score of children were born out of wedlock, he was second in line to his father's throne. Lest one day the crown came to him, surely Sweyn would wish one of Gytha's legitimate granddaughters for his son's wife—*were* the old woman willing to part with one. But she was not, even though one day that young woman might be Queen of Denmark.

"What manner of man are you, Canute?" Mary Sarah

whispered. Might he not be worthy of even the least precious of Gytha's blood? Rather than a good future for this unacknowledged granddaughter, was she to be a sacrifice?

Hearing the merchant grunt, she looked across her shoulder and saw he stood at the top of the ramp he had fixed to the wagon's backside down which he would roll the barrels. As he shifted one in preparation to ease it onto its bulbous side, she returned her attention to the missive.

Hence, Abbess, I entreat you to make haste in preparing my niece to be delivered to her betrothed who shall soon arrive in England.

Once more, Mary Sarah's breath stuck. Was Canute already upon these shores? If so, was he in the company of his sire who had determined it was time to take the crown? And was that even possible? So strong was the conqueror's hold on England now nearly all resistance was ended, no matter how formidable King Sweyn's army, likely he would fail.

Then of what use a Godwine bride? Mary Sarah wondered. *What will become of the one who casts off the name Mary Sarah to reclaim Mercia? Am I a coward to wish to remain here? Though I did not choose this life, I have been a better shepherd than I thought possible and much I care for my charges. This is familiar to me and as acceptable as possible knowing I offend God in playing a holy woman. Now to become the chattel of a foreign prince...to have no say over my days and nights...over my body...*

She startled when the panting merchant rolled a barrel past her, breathed deep to calm her heart, and returned to the missive.

As it is imperative she begin her journey without delay and I would not further impose on the abbey's hospitality, all arrangements have been made. Thus, you have only to remind my niece of the duty owed her family and that she is to be strong of mind, body, and spirit, then give her into the care of those with whom her betrothed has entrusted her safety.

As the merchant strode past to unload another barrel, Mary

Sarah mulled that last. Did Danes come for her? If so, how would they present at Lillefarne and when? Soon, it sounded. A day? A sennight?

She shook her head and read the last.

Do this, Abbess, and when next we meet, your place in my affections will be secure. ~ By God's grace, Lady Edelwine

Mary Sarah closed her eyes and entreated the Lord to straighten her thoughts so she could determine what to do—were there anything to be done.

~

NICOLA KNEW BETTER. She knew she knew better. Was certain she knew better. Of course she knew better. Still, she did what she ought not.

What moved her off the bench where she had perched to consider the far shuttered window overlooking the cloister was a feeling bolstered by Lady Hawisa's misgivings about the abbess. But what sent her up the stairs was what she had witnessed last eve.

Though fatigued, after much tossing she had risen from her pallet, slipped out into the night, and checked on the children. Assured by two nuns all slept well, she had started back to the dormitory.

Lady Hawisa having impressed on her the importance of being aware of one's surroundings, Nicola had seen the abbess before she herself was seen and nearly called out. But in the woman's stride was what seemed urgency tempered by stealth. And Mary Sarah carried something close to her chest like a babe sheltered from rain.

Not yet proficient at stealth herself, though more so than the abbess, Nicola had followed at too great a distance to make sense of what was conveyed to the apartment. Drawing around her the shadows of the cloister, she had tipped her head back and watched the unshuttered windows for movement but gained only glimpses of Mary Sarah in the outer chamber where she conducted the business of administering a house of God.

But then light appeared in the partially unshuttered window of the inner chamber where the woman was to keep company with herself alone—and from which words sounded so low they were nearly unheard. Though no sense could be made of them, from the pitch and rhythm, Nicola had been fairly certain it was the abbess who spoke. Had she soothed a babe? Conversed with one not a babe? Or was it the Lord she addressed?

Nicola had told herself it was the latter and withdrawn. But this day, so greatly was she gripped by this feeling, she assured herself the abbess would be long occupied with the merchant, ascended the steps, and quietly opened the door.

Daylight all about the outer chamber revealed no one was behind the desk nor perched on a chair or bench where visitors were invited to take their ease. The only occupant was that which pooled in the chair before the brazier—a thick coverlet as if the abbess, also unable to sleep on the night past, had settled there to think on the day gone and the day to come. Else find her rest in less comfortable circumstances than usual...

Leave, warned a voice so small it had little to recommend it, then with measured steps she moved toward the inner chamber, wincing each time floorboards with whom she had only a passing acquaintance revealed which nails were loose.

Excitement, tempered by fear that Lady Hawisa said was more strength than weakness, trickled down her spine. Like the small voice, it urged her to turn back. Like the reckless Nicola her eldest brother named her, she did not.

Halting before the door, she touched the cool handle. This time fear tempered by excitement coursed her, and she had to tell herself no one was inside before she could bring herself to open the door. But even then it was not possible.

It was locked. From the inside or outside? she wondered, then accepted she would never know.

"And so your great adventure ends, Nicola the reckless," she muttered and turned away.

A click brought her back around. Snatching her dagger from its scabbard on her girdle, she stared at the door soon to be thrown open. But it was not.

She was certain she had not imagined the turning of the lock, just as she was certain Lady Hawisa would tell her to run —and more angrily her brothers. She should, but the click of the lock was no coincidence and, clearly, an invitation to enter.

Did the one inside—more plausibly one of the abbess's charges than a person of great interest—think her Mary Sarah? Likely, and when the abbess did appear, it would be reported someone had tried to enter her private chamber.

Already I am had, Nicola reasoned. And here the excuse to satisfy her curiosity—and apologize for disturbing the occupant. *Were* they harmless…

Keeping hold of her dagger, she abandoned stealth that had been of no use across the floorboards and thrust open the door.

The outer chamber's light swept inside, falling brightest on an unoccupied bed with a single pillow, blanket, and sheet Nicola was certain would not be as soft as her own at Stern Castle. But of greater note was the state of the bedclothes absent the coverlet seen in the outer chamber. They were tousled and hung to the floor on one side as if whoever had slept there did so poorly.

Standing near enough the threshold she could view the greater portion of the chamber that evidenced whoever was inside was either beneath the bed or to the right or left of the doorway, she said, "I know you are here—as you know I know." She suppressed a groan over those last words. "Show yourself!"

No response.

She strained to catch sounds of movement, but there were none. Because the person inside was very ill?

Might it be one of the displaced children whom Mary Sarah cared for separate from the others? If so, was the little one terribly diseased? Perhaps dying? What if he or she had collapsed after turning the lock and was on the floor behind the door?

Suppressing the impulse to lunge inside, she called in more precise Anglo-Saxon, "I enter. Be assured, I mean you no harm."

She took a step inside, looked sharply left into dim depths and right past the angled door. And nearly choked on a gasp that sent saliva down the wrong way.

Though the man sitting forward in a chair beside an unlit brazier was mostly in shadow, he was of formidable size. Too, he was so familiar she would wager his long hair and beard were red.

The abbess had lied.

"As thought," he said in a voice that sounded rusted, "'tis only the termagant." As she stiffened at being named harsh-tempered, he mused, "I wonder, does she still wish to kill this Saxon pig?"

It *was* as she had threatened to do—and named him—when he delivered Guarin half dead from the rebel camp to Stern, at that time unaware he was more ally than foe to her brother though long he had charge over his captivity. Hardly had she cast those words at the rebel than one of her cousin's men snatched her off the drawbridge and carried her back inside the walls.

"I..." She cleared her throat. "...thought you responsible for my brother's injuries."

"Not directly, Lady Nicola," he said as movement drew her regard to his forearms on his thighs and large hands past his knees drawing a piece of cloth through his fingers.

Absently or with thought? she wondered and wished the

light more generous so she could look near on what suffered a warrior's calloused fingers.

"But responsible enough that had your brother died, I would not begrudge you an attempt on my life."

His choice of words indicating an attempt was all it would be, she longed to demonstrate how accurate her dagger's throw, but what was the sixth lesson—or was it the seventh?— impressed upon her?

Let not pride show your hand before your opponent shows his.

A mistake at this time, but he would learn how great her facility with a blade if he attempted to take her only weapon that should not have been permitted inside the abbey. It was no meat dagger, as well the abbess knew, but the woman had ignored the relatively long scabbard above whose neck a wire-wrapped hilt jutted.

"Still, it is a pleasure to meet you again," he broke the silence, "and more so since these circumstances put me in mind of a recent victory when I played David to—"

"David?" she interrupted.

Was that a smile amid his beard? "Of the Bible, ere he became King of Israel."

Nicola deepened her frown.

Misinterpreting it, he said, "Aye, this Saxon is familiar with God's book. Though you Normans name my people heathens to excuse the heinous acts perpetrated against us, we are not. Thus, I do not think I would be remiss in claiming most Saxons are more Christian than those come across the narrow sea."

"It is true once I believed Saxons godless," she acceded, "but no longer, and after what our king—" She snapped her teeth. This warrior needed no reminder of what William had done nor that he was her family's liege.

"Continue, Nicola."

Telling herself his familiar use of her name unsettled only because it offended, assuring herself she longed to step nearer only to deliver a slap, she ignored his prompt to elaborate. "You read my confusion wrong, *Vitalis.* I did not question the depth of your faith nor knowledge of the Bible. My confusion sprang from you equating yourself with David who became king as it is highly doubtful you shall become."

"Nor do I wish it. Had you not interrupted, you would know I spoke of an encounter David had with one who *was* king." He flicked a hand, causing her to jump back and what he tossed at her feet to land short of her skirt.

By the light come through the doorway, she could see the cloth was of a size upon which she could place both hands side by side, was woven of fine wool, and worked with embroidery. As only one edge was finished, the others frayed, it had to have been cut from a larger piece. A lady's gown? A fine mantle? An exquisite coverlet?

"For you," Vitalis said.

Rebuking herself for ponderings that would have rendered her vulnerable had he moved against her, she said, "Why?" as yet oblivious to the tale he referenced and just as oblivious to what use the cloth was to her.

"Much gratitude you will gain from your cousin do you deliver that to him, perhaps even respect do you exaggerate how you came by it."

"Exaggerate?"

"Doubtless a woman who thinks naught of threatening a warrior is capable of embellishment."

He mocked her. "What would Maël want with a piece of cloth?" she snapped.

"The biblical tale I spoke of...'tis why he hunts me." He jutted his chin. "He is tasked with retrieving the cloth."

Rather than delve that, Nicola asked, "You know he was here —that he escorted me to Lillefarne?"

"I do, and because I lingered to speak with the abbess after delivering the children and fell asleep in a chair before her desk, I found myself cornered."

Nicola frowned. "It is two days since my cousin departed. Why are you still here—and in the bedchamber of a holy woman?" It was said more sharply than intended though she could not believe anything untoward had happened between Mary Sarah and Vitalis.

"Initially, the abbess insisted I remain to ensure the king's men long gone." He pushed up out of the chair.

Again, Nicola retreated and, seeing the true size of him up close, would have further distanced herself had he not earlier foregone the opportunity to overwhelm her. Too, still she had her dagger and the doorway was near.

Though she had heard Vitalis compared to Goliath the same as her aunt's husband and thought it exaggeration, the leader of the Rebels of the Pale was just as tall and broad as Father Fulbert. At the realization he likened himself to David rather than the giant that future king had slain with a stone, she almost smiled.

As he moved slowly into the light as if he feared frightening her, she saw he wore undertunic and chausses and the red of his beard was darker than that of his hair which was as tousled as the bedclothes.

He halted and reached to retrieve the cloth. When he straightened and stepped further into the light, she had the answer to why he had not departed Lillefarne.

"You are ill!" Her heart pounded over how drawn his face, sunken and red his eyes she had not known were brown, and dry his lips.

"Relapse only," he said gruffly. "With much gratitude to the abbess for her care, soon I shall depart."

Certain what Mary Sarah had carried to her apartment were items to aid in his recovery, Nicola was also grateful to the abbess—as compassion for a fellow human being demanded, she told herself.

Vitalis handed the cloth to her, and she noted he avoided contact with her fingers.

He fears his touch could pass his illness to me, she told herself, the alternative being he found this lady of Norman blood repugnant.

"Whatever tale you decide on, see this into your cousin's keeping," he said. "He knows the truth of how it was obtained."

Then she would have that truth from Maël. "I shall." She started to turn aside.

"Vixen."

She halted. "What say you?"

"Methinks *termagant* too harsh for Nicola D'Argent. More the fox you are—sleek and elegant, curious and cunning, sharp of teeth and claw. And let us not forget protective."

As she had been of Guarin. Though Aunt Chanson would believe it criticism what this Saxon named her, Nicola smiled over what she embraced as praise—even if Vitalis did not. "Much better," she said.

That should be the end their conversation, but it was the opening to ask what she had not. "Why did you let me in?"

"For the interest you showed in the window of the abbess's bedchamber—so much you could hardly sit still."

Then he had seen her in the cloister below, either through a crack in the shuttered window or an unshuttered window of the outer chamber.

"You knew it was I who entered the apartment."

His lips curved. "I did and unlocked the door so I might look nearer on a girl who appears to have become a woman since last I saw her."

It was fear not excitement coursing her, she assured one who should want naught to do with the Saxon rebel.

"Since your cousin and his men are long gone as soon I shall be, I saw no harm in satisfying your curiosity alongside mine. Now, lest dread grow into deception as it is wont to do the longer one delays confession, I advise you seek the abbess and tell her what passed here."

Or he would...

"I shall. Godspeed your journey and healing, Vitalis." She stepped into the outer chamber, and hearing the door close and the sound of metal on metal, returned her dagger to its scabbard.

Shortly, she secured the outer chamber's door and considered the cloth worked with many-stranded black thread shot through with a strand of gold. She touched the embroidery Vitalis had touched, brushed the frayed edges he had brushed. Then having no pouch in which to tuck it, she slipped the cloth down her bodice.

Guessing the abbess's business with the wine merchant neared its end and feeling dread that could, indeed, tempt her to deception were there no possibility Vitalis would reveal their encounter, Nicola decided to be done with it.

Were the abbess still at the shed, privacy would be had there in which to confess, earn displeasure, and be forgiven.

CHAPTER SIX

y final delivery to Lillefarne." Slapping his hands to remove the grime of a half dozen barrels unloaded from his wagon, the merchant halted before Mary Sarah and smiled as she had never seen him smile, revealing a broken front tooth. "Though it has been profitable, I will not miss supplying this abbey with wine—too far out of my way, you know."

She did not know. What she knew was she paid the price of superior wine, which his was not, and Gytha paid him for carrying and delivering messages. Though Mary Sarah assumed he was not privy to the contents of those missives, this day he knew enough that he bid her farewell.

"I thank you for your service." She pushed off the wall she had leaned against during the last reading of the parchment. "I shall meet you at the gate to deliver your coin." As ever she did after composing a response were one required.

"No charge this day."

She blinked. "That is generous, but—"

"Not generous, *Abbess.*"

Emphasis on her title turning her wary, she said, "Then?"

He glanced at the purse on her belt whose bulk evidenced Gytha's missive that she was to burn as soon as she reached her apartment. "Over and again you read it. What is not clear?"

Its seal had not been broken when he gave it to her, but it sounded as if he knew its every word, and that alarmed as much as his tone that was no longer respectful.

Determined to be strong of mind, body, and spirit though she wanted to hasten opposite, Mary Sarah stepped nearer. "Pray tell, what is clear to *you?*"

"As Lady Edelwine told, her niece is to begin her journey without delay. *This* day. *This* hour. *This* moment." He jerked his head toward the wagon. "Get in."

Feeling punched in the chest, she said, "It cannot be this day —not even this week." *If ever,* she dare not speak what dread over becoming more of a pawn made her consider. "To ensure the stability of this house of God, I require a fortnight to put all in order."

His brow grew more lined. "I have my orders and my honor, both of which have been bought. You depart now." He grabbed her arm and thrust her toward the wagon.

She stumbled, and as she regained her balance, saw the canvas move. Then that portion gone flaccid following the removal of barrels was tossed back to reveal three men—two fairly young and one of good age. Of greater note, they were Danes.

For this, lest she protest her departure, the merchant had positioned the wagon so that little could be seen of what went between its rear and the shed.

The last time she had been this frightened was at Westminster when her grandmother and she faced Maël D'Argent, a Norman given much cause to reveal them but had not.

Abandoning the Saxon of her who, in this moment, could not be strong of anything, she lunged left and evaded hands that snatched her veil from her head. However, in the next instant she halted at the sight of a nun and novice and several convent residents scattered left and right, as yet unaware uninvited men were inside their walls—wolves who, were they revealed, might not be content with taking only one lamb.

Fearing her resistance would be token only and others would suffer for it, she swung back and raised her hands. "I yield!"

The two Danes coming around the rear of the wagon halted so abruptly they sprayed her habit with dirt. And smiled. Triumph, she first named it, but the gleam in their eyes revealed something else—appreciation.

And she did not doubt it was due to her unveiled hair. Had she let go of that last bit of Mercia as she told herself she must after Maël D'Argent witnessed her vanity, these men might appreciate her face despite hair cut to a modest length but not as much as they did now.

Lest they entertain thoughts beyond appreciation, she enlisted the only weapon she possessed. "I would be surprised if your prince approved of you looking upon his betrothed in the manner of one preparing to undress a harlot."

She could not know how versed they were with a language similar to their own, but the youngest Dane understood enough that he blinked away what offended. As for the other who held her veil, appreciation yet shone from his eyes, but it was tempered by what seemed amusement.

Hearing a chuckle, she looked to the merchant who stood where she had left him. No need to give chase when he had younger, fitter men to force her into the wagon.

Knowing the longer they lingered, the more likely they would come to the notice of the women she sought to protect, Mary Sarah dropped her arms to her sides. "Make haste ere you are seen and word is delivered to the Wulfriths that Danes are at their abbey."

The youngest knew that family's name as told by widening eyes and how quickly he turned back.

Lord Almighty, Mary Sarah sent heavenward as she followed the Danes around the wagon, *keep my charges safe. And have mercy on me, reluctant servant though I have been.*

Once more out of sight of those who strolled the rear of the abbey, she eyed the merchant as he strode to the opposite side of the wagon and bent to exam the rear wheel.

A hand thrust toward her moved her regard to the young Dane. Ignoring his offer to assist in her ascent of the ramp, she raised her skirt and walked her slippers up the incline to where the other two straightened the canvas their hasty exit had caused to go aslant.

It was then she saw where they had concealed themselves at the front of the wagon in the space between barrels on each side where more barrels should have been. Since the merchant had unloaded six of ten, greater comfort would be had during the journey ahead—more than enough space so there was no reason to draw inappropriately near the woman in their midst.

The older Dane who was wiry, of unremarkable stature, and had long hair and beard gone mostly silver, motioned her forward. "I be Ingvar, Lady Mercia. Come."

She was shocked to hear her birth name spoken, but more that she was granted a title as if she were legitimate. Was it mere assumption on his part or his king's? Or had Gytha made it so, formally acknowledging her misbegotten granddaughter as a Godwine?

"Come, Lady!" he said with greater urgency.

Telling herself she must once more think of herself as Mercia, Mary Sarah bent to go beneath the canvas. However, her veil tucked beneath the belt of the amused Dane made her pause. It looked a trophy, just as had been made of hair shorn from two of her novices ravished by Normans.

"That is mine." She reached for it.

He caught her wrist and chuckled as if she sought to make a game of it. "Now mine. The betrothed of Canute has no need to cover her pretty hair." He reached with his other hand as if to test how silken those strands.

She knocked it aside. "Dare not touch me, you—"

"Unhand her, fiend!" cried one whose voice sang a song not of England.

Not her, Lord, Mary Sarah silently entreated though it could be none other than the young woman whose conquering people these Danes had come to conquer in turn.

Looking across her shoulder at Nicola whose fine gown was as detrimental as her accent, marking her as a lady not of the Church—and an unwed one as told by loose hair and ringless hands—Mary Sarah said sharply, "This does not concern you. Go!"

Nicola swiped her dagger at the young Dane who stepped near. "And allow these vermin to abduct a holy woman? I will not!" She bared her teeth at the one who gripped Mary Sarah's wrist. "Loose the abbess, else I will stick your little friend."

"Such spirit," said the amused one. "She must be in want of a man."

Again, Nicola swiped at the young Dane. "I said loose her!"

"'Tis only a misunderstanding, Nicola," Mary Sarah entreated. "I will deal with it. Now leave."

"We cannot have the Norman lady give warning," said the young Dane with mock sorrow. Then with what looked a smile of apology, he added, "Sleep sweet, my lady."

The wine merchant, whom neither Nicola nor Mary Sarah saw circle from one side of the wagon to the other, brought a stick down on the young woman's head.

As Nicola's eyes rolled up, the amused one clapped a hand over Mary Sarah's mouth and caught her cry in it. Thus, she could do naught but watch the only sister of the D'Argents collapse at the merchant's feet.

The young Dane bent near, then looked up at the one holding the Abbess of Lillefarne. "I like this silvered Norman lady."

A snort. "Of course you do. Put a blade in the hand of a pretty woman and she will put it in your heart. Every time, Bjorn." The amused Dane shifted his regard to Mary Sarah. "My cousin never learn. I say he ought to wed a godly woman of good face and figure, but does he listen to one older and wiser?"

Above the hand pressed to her mouth, she glared at the man who made himself sound a dozen years beyond the younger one though he could not be aged more than her own twenty and six.

He sighed. "He wants what he wants—spirit in bed and outside it. Me? Plentiful sons and daughters of good blood." He winked. *"My* lady."

IT HAD NOT GONE AS PLANNED, all because of Nicola D'Argent. *Blessedly,* because of that vixen.

Had she not resisted as the wagon departed the abbey—tossing back the canvas, pulling the abbess with her, screaming and cursing as the two were dragged back—the nuns who opened the great doors for the merchant would not have known he had brought Danes inside and exchanged barrels of wine for a Saxon abbess and a Norman lady.

Unfortunately, all had transpired too distant from the abbess's apartment for Vitalis to catch sight or sound of it and immediately pursue the miscreants. More unfortunate, it was two hours before he heard tale, and only because nuns entered the outer chamber. It did not take long to make sense of the crisis that required a missive be composed for the Baron of Wulfen.

Terribly improper though it was for Vitalis to reveal he occupied the abbess's private chamber, the alternative was to allow the abductors more time in which to work greater ill on the women. Thus, grateful he was fully clothed in anticipation of departing the abbey, he had shown himself and so scandalized the nuns it was necessary to raise his voice and use his intimidating size to quiet them.

Saxons themselves and long enough at Lillefarne to know him from when he was Lady Hawisa's housecarle and next led the Rebels of the Pale against their enemy, they had begun to calm. More they had calmed when he explained the arrival of the king's men had forced him to remain in the apartment after delivering the children to the abbey and that a relapse of illness had prolonged his stay.

Still their disapproval was great, but he gained the tale of abduction by the merchant and three others—Danes, they were certain from the voices of those who pulled the abbess and Lady Nicola back beneath the canvas. Just as they were certain it was the latter they had come for and their abbess was taken as well during her attempt to protect the D'Argents' sister.

Whether it was Lady Nicola they came for or the abbess, the only sense to be made of the abduction of a woman who was not an heiress was that one had come to the notice of a Dane determined to make her his own.

Greater youth, beauty, and opportunity to catch the eye of one of the allies who had failed the Saxon resistance favored Nicola. But there was something more to it, Vitalis was certain, whether the *more* was of Mary Sarah or Nicola.

He straightened from the edge of the ravine over which the wagon had been sent to break on jagged rocks fifty feet below— all splintered wood, bent iron, and spilled wine. No bodies, and from the trampling of spring grass, the occupants of the wagon were now astride and in the company of others who had awaited them in the wood.

"How many, Zedekiah?" he asked of the warrior advancing

on him who was all that remained of his rebels after the final disbanding following the encounter with William at the cave.

"Ten horses, mayhap twelve, and not all departed the same direction. A lone rider—likely the merchant—headed southwest, while one group went north and the other northeast." The stocky Saxon halted. "Had I known something was amiss, I would have followed."

Instead he kept vigil in the wood where he had been ordered to remain while the children were given into the care of Lillefarne. He had seen the arrival of the king's men with Lady Nicola and their departure absent the lady. As the hunted Vitalis was also absent, he had concluded either his leader had determined it was not safe to depart, else he was once more taken by the flux to which all his rebels had succumbed weeks past.

That sickness of the gut thought due to contaminated water had afflicted Vitalis least of all, though it weakened him sufficiently he had believed it possible he would bleed out his life had he challenged William to swords in the cave. In the days thereafter, he had improved the same as the others—until Zedekiah and he happened on the children.

But he was better now as he must be to pursue the Danes who had taken a Saxon woman of God and might do her great harm. And of course there was his lady's sister-in-law to recover. Much he risked since the missive sent by the nuns might see not only Guarin D'Argent—now Baron Wulfrith—give chase but his cousin, Maël, if that chevalier remained upon Wulfenshire.

Vitalis nearly laughed over how greatly he exaggerated what he risked. Though pockets of resistance remained across England, the harrying had accomplished what Le Bâtard intended. No longer were Saxon rebels a viable threat to his rule. Now threat came from Danes whose king would soon arrive had he not already. Even then, from what Vitalis knew of

William into whose back he had been tempted to thrust a dagger, Le Bâtard would find Sweyn an unworthy opponent the same as the Danish king's brother who had refused to meet the conqueror in battle after aiding Saxon rebels in taking York—a city once more in the hands of Normans.

Truly, little at risk, Vitalis amended. His country belonged to Normans. His family's lands belonged to Normans. The future he had imagined for himself belonged to Normans. The woman long he had loved belonged to a Norman. The child she would bear belonged to a Norman.

Albeit a worthy Norman, he silently acknowledged what once would have been a lie. Hoping should his quest to free the abbess and the vixen cause him to cross paths with a D'Argent it would be Guarin who no longer bore that family name, Vitalis returned Zedekiah to focus.

"I will go northeast and you north. Likely the Danes will regroup in two days—three at most—once assured they are not tracked, then we shall meet again. Between now and then, we must ensure neither Abbess Mary Sarah nor Lady Nicola is handed off and watch our backs lest the king's man is at Wulfen upon receipt of the missive from Lillefarne."

The man who looked as much a warrior now as he had a smithy when first he joined the rebels, grunted. "A good plan, my lord."

The title annoyed as if mockery was made of one whose future no longer portended such responsibility and honor, but mockery Zedekiah did not intend. Since becoming the last rebel to remain at his side, he had insisted on naming Vitalis that and would not be moved from it, just as he refused to go home though Lady Hawisa would welcome him back. Henceforth, he had declared, even were he Vitalis's only man, ever his man he would be.

"Aye, a good plan." Zedekiah confirmed, then added, "But good only if you are well enough recovered."

"I am. Now let us ride."

After the two clasped arms from atop their mounts, they went in search of those who, while awaiting the arrival of the king they believed could topple Le Bâtard, made sport of defenseless women.

Rather, *mostly* defenseless. Vitalis would not be surprised if this moment they rued having taken the vixen captive.

～

Wulfen Castle
Wulfenshire, England

"Lord, 'tis not to be borne," Lady Hawisa rasped so low that were Maël not seated beside her at supper, he would not have heard nor seen her splay a hand on her belly after dropping the missive delivered during the meal.

If not that the messenger insisted the tidings from Lillefarne were urgent, likely she would have waited to read it in the privacy of her chamber.

"My lady?" asked the housecarle seated on her opposite side.

Maël leaned in. "What is it, Lady Hawisa?"

She dropped back in her chair. "We are set upon on all sides. First Theriot, now this." She shook her head. "And Guarin is gone from Wulfen."

So he was, having departed yestermorn to search for his youngest brother as once Theriot had searched for him.

Though both Maël and Ordric reached for the missive fallen atop the table, the king's man brought it to hand. The tidings were succinct. Nicola and the abbess had been abducted by Danes smuggled into the abbey by the wine merchant. Though the younger woman must be the intended victim, it was believed the abbess was taken as well to quiet her after interceding on behalf of a D'Argent.

Every tooth and muscle tight over fear for Nicola who truly was as a sister to him and the holy woman who despised him, Maël stared at the name of the one who had signed the parchment—Sister Rixende.

"To me!" Ordric reached for the missive.

Maël started to pass it but drew back when he caught sight of a stroke of ink above the curled end. Unrolling the parchment in its entirety, he revealed more words written in a hand different from the first. There was naught precise about the bold letters, and after reading them, he was certain they were inked by a man.

My lady, having escorted displaced children to the abbey, I was at Lillefarne when your sister-in-law and the abbess were taken. Most unfortunate, I remained unaware for two hours. I set out now and, God willing, shall restore both to you.

No signature, but since a sighting of Vitalis near the Wulfenshire border had drawn Maël and his men here, likely the rebel leader had inked the lower parchment. Possibly, he had been at the abbey when Maël delivered Nicola there, but for what had he returned two days later? Having learned the king's men searched the demesne for what remained of the Rebels of the Pale, had he sought refuge within the hidden passage?

Believable had this day's search been near the abbey, but it was the eastern portion Maël and his men scoured, including the abandoned rebel camp tucked in a ravine where Guarin had been held captive for two years and which had been converted to a refugee camp when the harrying began last December.

What was now a permanent community was the first place Maël should have gone, but whilst aiding Guarin in making arrangements to search for Theriot, his cousin had asked that the village be searched last so his wife could prepare the northern Saxons for the king's men. Though Guarin had admitted some of the resistance were among those displaced Saxons, he had assured Maël they were rebels no longer, having submitted to William's rule in return for resuming their lives.

Maël had believed him, and though he knew it possible Lady Hawisa made more of the camp than her husband knew, he had given his word he would search elsewhere first though the delay could see Vitalis warned away.

"Sir Maël?" The Lady of Wulfen touched his arm.

Certain the missive's last words had escaped her, he said, "There is more written here. Your man, Vitalis, was at the abbey."

Her breath caught, and he relinquished the missive before she could snatch it from him.

Though by word she neither confirmed nor denied the writing was of her former housecarle, as her eyes darted over it, she exuded such relief it was confirmation enough.

Passing the missive to Ordric, she looked to her husband's cousin. "Not Vitalis," she sought to protect her man, "but blessedly, one loyal to the House of Wulfrith."

Maël pushed his chair back and rose. "I think it best I assume it is of Vitalis, for which you ought to be glad since continued pursuit of him by a good number of the king's men increases the chance of recovering Nicola and the abbess unharmed."

She opened her mouth as if to object, then sighed. "I will not begrudge you that, and shortly I shall send a messenger to alert Guarin he must now search for two D'Argents."

"I think that wise, my lady. Now as every minute is precious, my men and I will depart this eve rather than the morrow." He bowed. "I thank you for the hospitality. If possible, I shall send word of my progress in taking back what was stolen from our family and Lillefarne."

She inclined her head. "Think well on making use of the man loyal to me ere exercising loyalty to one undeserving of it, Sir Maël. And forget not that first, in between, and in the end, you are a D'Argent."

CHAPTER SEVEN

Lincolnshire
England

*T*his was not how she would have chosen to escape
God's house. Were she yet a bird amongst the rafters,
less harrowing that than being forced to depart the abbey as she
had. In the end it might not prove intolerable for her, but for
Nicola who continued to challenge the Danes…

*Dear Lord, I am responsible for the ill done her and what might be
done does that young man do more than look longingly at her,* Mary
Sarah silently appealed where she stood behind a shoulder-high
hedge exchanging her habit for the fine garment sent by Gytha
—a gown the amused one had warned he would himself see her
into if she offered further protest.

"As you will not long have eyes about you, stare your fill,
Dane!" spat the youngest D'Argent who remained astride, one
side of her head matted with blood from the blow that had been
of just enough strength to render her unconscious a few
minutes. "Aye, stare hard so I haunt your darkness after King

William digs the sight from your sockets for abducting his noble subject!"

The one named Bjorn who had paused in setting a fire to once more look upon her called, "Soon he who wears the crown will be too desperate to keep it on his head to bother with Bjorn and his woman."

A yelp of outrage gaping her pretty mouth, Nicola wrenched at the rope binding her hands to the saddle's pommel and jerked back and forth, causing her tethered mount to sidestep.

"Cease, Lady!" Bjorn hastened forward. "The rope will scratch your delicate wrists."

"They are not delicate!" she cried when he halted alongside, then thrust a foot against his chest.

As the four Danes erecting canopies against impending rain sniggered, the young man regained his balance and raised a hand. "I mean no harm, would only—"

"The D'Argents are many, and when they come for me, you will wish it were King William who but took your eyes."

He went still, then threw back his head and laughed. At the end of the jovial display that caused Nicola to quiver with anger, he said, "Oh lady, when I saw silver in your hair, I hoped you a D'Argent!"

"That I am, fool who laughs when he should be shaking in boots put to flight."

More laughter. "I know your cousin, Sir Dougray."

"Not my cousin. My *brother,* and he will—"

"Why does he not have your silvered hair the same as Sir Maël?"

Nicola glared.

He shrugged. "Mostly I like Sir Dougray. He gave me scar worthy of a warrior. You like to see?"

"The only scar I wish to see upon you is the one dealt when he puts you down for taking us from Lillefarne—if it has a chance to scar. I am thinking best not, *Dane.*"

"Finish setting the fire, Bjorn!" the amused one shouted.

The young man told Nicola he would make her a bed fit for a lady, jumped back from another kick to the chest, and returned to a fire more smoke than flame.

Reaching behind, Mary Sarah began to tighten laces she wished were worked into the sides to more easily fit the bodice. A moment later, she released them.

Though she was to cast off the abbess of loose garments and modest carriage to once more become the possibly marriageable granddaughter of Gytha of the House of Godwine, the single tug of laces that drew in the bodice in anticipation of hugging her every curve seemed wrong. Not because it would make her feel pretty again, because it was meant to present her as something desirable. Though that had appealed years past when she hoped to be valued enough to make a good marriage despite her birth, now...

She did not wish to give her life to the Church, but neither did she wish to give it to Gytha who, to better her lot and those more dear to her, would give Mercia to a man who regarded her as a means of gaining Saxon support, satisfying lust, and birthing babes. Though the part played at Lillefarne had been forced on her, there had been gratification in no longer being powerless and in engaging mind and hands to give to those in need of guidance and aid. In some measure, she wanted that still.

"For what do you take so long?" asked the amused one who no longer sounded amused.

"I am nearly done." She fastened her belt around her waist and paused over the bulky purse hung from it, the culprit being Gytha's missive that would have been put to flame were her granddaughter not taken from the abbey.

Not necessary now, she thought as she drew her habit off the bush over which she had draped it.

"That is no longer you," said the man who came around the

hedge and snatched it from her, causing her protesting hands to grasp air. As he tossed the garment onto muddied ground, he ran his gaze down her. "It was told you are fine of figure. I see it not. Turn around."

She stood taller. "I will not!"

"I shall do your laces."

"I prefer the gown loose."

"Not I." He reached to her.

She jumped back. "Do not touch me!"

"Leave the holy woman be," Nicola shouted, "else all the more the Lord will punish you."

"She is not a holy woman," he snapped, then caught Mary Sarah's arm and, as he dragged her from behind the hedge, caused her to tread on the habit as a final insult to that which had falsely clothed her all these years.

The other Danes having paused in their labors to give curiosity its full reach, their smiles contrasted with Nicola's bared teeth past which she called, "Bite him, Abbess! Scratch! Kick! Between the legs is good!"

It sounded she believed this tool of the Godwines was the same as a D'Argent who could, at the very least, make it difficult to hold her. Instead, the amused Dane who had yet to name himself the one she halfway hoped he was for his fairly mild manner, relative youth, and good build, had her entirely under his control.

He halted alongside Nicola's mount and pulled Mary Sarah forward. "Tell this Norman lady who you are, *Abbess*—more, what you shall become."

Hoping the young woman read the apology in her eyes which Mary Sarah had spoken before they were pulled from the wagon and it was pushed into a ravine, she said, "Lady Nicola knows I am of Godwine."

A surprised silence, then, "But does she know you spoke no vows ere donning the habit?"

Nicola startled.

He chuckled. "As told, no holy woman. Does the Lord punish any, it will not be me."

Does He punish me now? Mary Sarah wondered. *Is this but the beginning of worse to come?*

"Surely he does not speak true, Abbess," Nicola entreated.

Feeling bared to the skin, she swallowed. "I am not a holy woman, the name Mary Sarah but required to…"

"…be the eyes and ears in Wulfenshire for Godwine," supplied the man at her side. "Of aid to rebels."

"Of very little aid," Mary Sarah said.

Never before had she seen the young woman's mouth turn so opposite a smile, but it did now and tears brightened her eyes. "Then you never liked me."

"I was a Saxon then the same as I am now, Nicola, and ever I have liked you. I but sought to stay true to my own the same as you to yours."

The young woman glanced at the Dane. "Who are you to him?"

"First and ever, I am Mercia of Mercia," said Gytha's granddaughter who must refamiliarize herself with the name left behind. "And I have been given to wed a Dane."

"This Dane?" Nicola scorned.

"I do not know."

"This Dane," he said.

There was some relief in confirmation he was her betrothed, but it barely eased the pound of her heart.

"Who are *you,* Dane?" Nicola demanded.

"I am Canute who will be King of Denmark after my sire's passing should ill befall my brother who stands ahead of my claim."

Nicola looked satisfied rather than surprised, as if she but sought confirmation. Also of credit to her wit was she did not question him as to the suitability of a bride made of a misbegotten Godwine. *That* she held close the same as Mary Sarah who could not know what tale Gytha told and hoped her betrothed would reveal it.

"You would add England to your kingship, *Dane?*" Nicola said.

"For that, we cross the sea and increase the army my sire sent last year."

"This time he will come as well?"

"Aye, the mighty King Sweyn."

"Forgive me if I do not believe you." A tilt of her head caused moonlight slipping past the clouds to jump blood-matted hair and streak silver strands amid dark. "After all, he dared not accompany his men last year, and did he join them now, surely word of his arrival would fly across England."

"He is not yet ashore, but—"

"Then it is the same as last year. Just as the Danish army slunk away following the fall of York, allowing Saxons to pay the price when the resistance's allies refused to engage King William in battle, next accepting a bribe to return home—"

"A bribe?" Canute looked around. "Of what does she speak, Bjorn?"

A nervous smile flitted across his lips. "Nonsense, Cousin."

"Nonsense?" Nicola exclaimed. "You told you know Sir Dougray, and it was he our king sent to negotiate with King Sweyn's brother, the earl."

"With winter setting in, a cessation of hostilities both sides was negotiated with my sire," Bjorn said. "That is all."

"Hostilities *both* sides? Ha! So frightened was the earl after York that his efforts were spent on staying ahead of William's vengeance. And just as he allowed others to fight—and lose—his battles, no doubt the cowardly King Sweyn will do the same."

The son of that king released Mary Sarah, lunged, and gripped Nicola's thigh. "You will not speak—"

"Get your filthy hands off me!"

"Cease, Cousin!" Bjorn called as Mary Sarah tried to think what to do.

Canute stepped nearer. "I care not you are Bjorn's, you will not speak ill of my sire."

"I am not Bjorn's, and ever I shall speak as I find!" Nicola tried to kick him.

Knowing Bjorn would not reach Nicola in time, Mary Sarah grabbed Canute's arm. "Do not harm her!"

He rounded on her, and it was his betrothed he would have struck had she not released him and lurched back. As if delivered a backhand, she lost her footing, landed on her rear, and was nearly trampled by Bjorn.

"Coward!" Nicola flung at the Danish king's son. "Muck between my toes! Stink upon my heel!"

Fearing he would injure the D'Argents' sister, Mary Sarah startled when she was swept upright and saw the hand upon her belonged to Canute rather than Bjorn.

"Forgive me," he said as his cousin sought to calm Nicola who continued to sling slurs though her target had turned his back on her. "I have a temper."

Which had nearly seen Mary Sarah struck. Had he been jolted back to good behavior by the sight of her toppling or remembrance she was a Godwine?

She snapped her mouth closed, and when next she opened it, raised her voice to be heard above Nicola. "A temper, indeed— unbecoming for a man who thinks to one day rule people who will time and again test his patience."

She glimpsed resentment in his eyes a moment before he looked across his shoulder. "Get your lady down, Bjorn. We are soon for food and sleep."

The younger man nodded, and as Canute turned Mary Sarah toward the nearest canopy whose poles were fixed in moist ground, called for the Dane named Ingvar to aid with the lady's dismount. The earl's son might yet wish Nicola for his own, but he was learning she would be no easy conquest.

Beneath the canopy, Canute released Mary Sarah. "I want this less than you, but I do what my sire commands, Lady. As your grandmother told, a Godwine bride will sooner bring your people to accept Danish rule when we take the throne from our common enemy."

But what of a Godwine born out of wedlock? More greatly she longed to know the answer now she had seen a temper mere words spoken against his sire caused to surface.

Of a sudden, he smiled, but unlike most who were more attractive with a show of teeth—providing they were well cared for—he was not, the spread of his lips too large in a narrow face peaked by a long nose.

"I know what you think," he said. "If you tell your sometimes ill-tempered betrothed you were made on the wrong side of the sheets, he will defy his sire and free you."

Then he knew of the circumstances of her birth and it mattered not? Because Gytha would publicly acknowledge this granddaughter? Likely, though surely only because the old woman refused to risk a legitimate granddaughter in allying her family with one who might prove unable to take the throne.

"Unhand me!" Nicola cried.

Canute looked around, and past him Mary Sarah saw the young woman pulled from the horse. Wrists remaining bound, arms gripped on one side by Bjorn, the other by Ingvar, she was drawn forward.

"Were *that* one my betrothed," Canute said, "I might defy my sire. But you are mostly biddable."

Meaning weak...easily bent to his will...his wishes met ahead of hers...

As if her face reflected turmoil that made her mind work in the direction of escape, he said, "Your grandmother warned you might claim illegitimacy so I would reject you."

Then Gytha told it would be a lie if she revealed she was misbegotten?

"You *think* you are not legitimate," he read her again, "but what if ever your truth was a lie, hmm?"

Dear Lord, Mary Sarah beseeched, *what tale did Gytha weave to ensure I not thwart her?*

Deciding it best she hold her words, she looked to Nicola. Rather than suffer the indignity of being carried, the young woman moved her legs beneath her.

"Gytha is cunning," Canute continued. "Once we reach the Humber and my father joins his brother there, you will be told which son sired you."

Mary Sarah's heart leapt. At long last she would know who she was? Both sides of her? Might she even discover her mother lived?

"That is, providing no ill winds fill the King of Denmark's sails," Canute added somewhat emotionlessly. But since death upon the sea was common among those who habitually crossed the great waters, it must be an accepted part of life.

Returning to the truth long withheld from her, it struck Mary Sarah it might merely be a means of controlling her should she prove difficult. Certes, she had given her grandmother cause to believe it possible since time and again she failed the old woman, though only because what was asked of her was impossible for an abbess to deliver, whether something was out of reach or lest it endanger her charges.

As her betrothed turned away, he added, "Then the rest beyond that will be told."

That to which he alluded—the possibility she was well born. Determined to leave it be for now, she said, "Canute?"

"My lady?"

"You said you want this less than I. Is there another you wish to take to wife?"

"Assuredly, there is."

Then for this and that she was only a means of securing a more peaceful reign, he had assigned another Dane to carry her upon his saddle.

"Though she holds my heart in hers, is younger and prettier than you, and gave me a son, I must wed one of benefit to my sire. Thus, I do my duty as you shall do yours."

She did not believe he meant to scrape raw her feelings, and he did not since she had no care for him, but it stung knowing she might spend her life with a man who would long for one younger and prettier. And likely he would keep the woman denied him, and their child—perhaps children—would be raised alongside those legitimately born.

If I give him children, Mary Sarah thought. Since next she would be twenty and seven, she was not beyond childbearing, but more so than his lover. And considering the offense dealt the Lord in playing a holy woman, He might not bless her with babes.

"Worry not, my lady," Canute said, "my love and the children made with her will be kept elsewhere."

"Generous," she said with sarcasm of a strength sure to offend.

He shrugged. "What it is, it is," he said, then strode from beneath the canopy and called, "Bjorn, once we settle to our rest, see your lady's ankles are bound the same as her wrists."

Moments later, the Danes released Nicola's arms and she sprang toward Mary Sarah.

"I shall bring water and cloths to tend your head, Lady Nicola," Bjorn said.

She held her back to him, and when Ingvar and he departed, muttered, "Vile, grasping invaders." Trembling with the strain of trying to part her roped hands, she continued, "They come and take what they want, having no care for the wrong of it in the sight of man and God. Then they—"

"Attend, Nicola!" Mary Sarah gasped. "Though the Norman

is all about your voice, your words are the same spoken by Saxons against your people for near on four years."

She ceased abusing wrists dotted with blood drawn by the coarse rope, then said with desperation, "Do you think ever it has been and ever it will be this way, Abbess? The conquerors conquered, the oppressors oppressed, no peace for those who but wish to live and love so their children may do the same?"

The answer making Mary Sarah's heart ache, she said, "I fear so, that more than anything, envy is evil's greatest weapon against good." She breathed deep. "And as now you know, the title with which you honor me has never been mine in truth. My given name is Mercia, and that is how you should call me."

Nicola nodded. "This Canute does not know you are misbegotten, that you are no lady?"

Mary Sarah glanced at where the man who might one day wear a crown lifted his packs from his horse. "He said my grandmother warned I might claim illegitimacy to gain my release, then suggested what I believe of my birth is a lie and said he will reveal all when we reach the Humber where King Sweyn is to join the earl."

"He but seeks to control you!"

"This I know, and yet I believe he is entrusted with knowledge long denied me. Aye, it may be falsely spun by Gytha, but..."

"What, Abb—er, Mercia?"

"Ever I have longed to know which of her sons made me and who birthed me."

"Then given an opportunity to escape wedding that man, you would remain with the Danes?"

She would. Still, she tensed over the disbelief—possibly condemnation—in the younger woman's voice. "It is not for one legitimately born, loved, and raised by both parents to ask that of me nor sit in judgment. Ever you have known who you are, Nicola D'Argent, and if you will not try to understand this hole in me, think of your half brother, Dougray, who has finally found his own blood father and been blessed with healing. No matter which of Gytha's departed sons gave me life and that he is forever lost to me, still I wish to know. And if my mother yet lives, I would be reunited with her."

Nicola was silent a time, then stepped alongside Mary Sarah and considered their captors. "I am sorry, but I must question the price you may pay for knowledge that could prove a lie." She narrowed her eyes at Canute. "He would have struck me, and nearly he dealt you a blow."

"This I know."

"My sire says except in extreme circumstances, such as the need to protect a woman from herself or others she endangers, never should a man raise a hand to her—that it makes him less than an animal which, at least, has the excuse of base instincts and little wit."

"Canute apologized—admitted he has a temper." The moment the words left Mary Sarah, she hated that her defense of him made her feel a young woman to an older, wiser one.

"Then all is well!" Nicola's derision was sharp. "A fine and godly husband he will make—*when* he is in a good temper."

Mary Sarah caught her breath. "Much you overstep in matters that do not concern you."

Nicola raised her chin. "You are wrong, Mercia of Mercia. This became my concern when my bid to aid you ended in my abduction."

Her words dumped Mary Sarah back to earth. Regardless of what came of Gytha's plan for her granddaughter, it *did* concern this Norman lady. "I wish you had run, Nicola—that you did not suffer for me—but here we are until I find a way to return you to your family. And I will. No matter what is required of me, you will gain your release."

Nicola raised her bound hands and touched Mary Sarah's arm. "We shall both be freed. Do not think my thwarted attempt to escape out the back of the wagon was for naught. Certes, word has been sent to my family and they come for us."

Including Sir Maël and his men? Mary Sarah wondered, then pushed the chevalier to the back of her mind.

After attending to Nicola's injury that had begun to scab across a sizable lump, the two ate a meal of biscuits and dried fish washed down with wine. As a guard was being set around the camp, Mary Sarah and Nicola settled on the pallet Bjorn fashioned for them from blankets tucked around grass and leaves.

Though he had been instructed to secure Nicola's feet as well, instead he bound Mary Sarah's wrists and joined them to the younger woman's, surely more effective since one could go nowhere without the other and they would have to do so with bodies turned toward each other. Lacking speed, stealth—and a miracle—escape would be impossible.

As Bjorn straightened from draping a blanket over them, Nicola snapped her chin around. "Knave!"

He wagged a finger. "But honorable as your brother told after he bore witness at York that never Bjorn force himself on a woman."

She gasped. "At York, you say—following that city's fall to Saxons and Danes?"

He nodded vigorously. "Great our victory over Normans, possible only because Danes are the most fearsome warriors."

"So you say, but I will not argue that again. I ask because methinks the woman you did not force yourself upon is the same now wed to Dougray."

His eyebrows jumped, then he slapped a thigh. "The rebel, Em! For that the chevalier so protective of her. He liked her, too."

"He *loves* her, as she loves him."

"So the Lord make all right by giving me the sister of the man who took my woman."

A growl erupted from her. "The Lord did not give me to you! And never will I be your woman."

"Fear not, my lady. Until you come to love me, no relations shall we enjoy."

"Then never will you know me beyond that of an enemy who must be bound to remain at your side."

"You will think different soon. I am very charming. And honorable."

Whatever shone from Nicola's eyes appeared to have no effect on him. He exaggerated a bow, pivoted, and whistled as he strode to the canopy beneath which his cousin and he would sleep until patrol of the camp passed to them.

Nicola turned her face to Mary Sarah who was surprised by the lady's bright smile. "He *is* charming, but not enough man for me."

"Nicola!"

Her smile flashed more teeth amid the dim. "I begin to enjoy this. Far more interesting and challenging than spinning wool and needling cloth."

"And more dangerous!"

"True, but all the sweeter it shall be when we escape. Hopefully, we can do so ere my family overtakes us. No helpless women are we, hmm? And if I can make good use of the skills taught me by my brother and his wife, all the better."

Mary Sarah knew she should scold her further, but that was for an abbess to do, not a woman of deception. Too, Nicola's attitude gave her some small hope.

Seeing a tress of silvered dark hair slip into the lady's eyes, she reached to sweep it back—and took the young woman's hands with her own.

Nicola giggled, Mary Sarah grimaced, and together they cleared the hair from her brow.

"Your hair is a mess, too," Nicola said, "but still more lovely out from beneath the veil than I would have imagined."

"Vanity—time and effort spent on myself that was owed my charges and those to whom we minister." Mary Sarah sighed. "Ever my hair has been the most remarkable thing about me, causing many a man to look twice where otherwise they would not look at all."

"Then blind they would be. Even though fit with veil and habit, ever I knew you to be lovely, Abbess—as did my cousin who, I vow, looked upon you as I have seen him look upon no other woman since before Hastings."

Refusing to dwell on how he might have looked at her for how much it disturbed, even if only because of her hair, Mary Sarah said, "As told, no longer abbess. I am Mercia."

"Mercia," Nicola repeated. "My sister-in-law has wondered over you—said there is something untrue about the Abbess of Lillefarne."

This did not surprise since oft Lady Hawisa's mistrust and wariness were felt.

"Oh!" Nicola gasped. "You know what occurs? As you are not truly of the Church, mayhap you can save Maël."

Mary Sarah frowned. "Save him?"

"Heal him the same as Em healed Dougray—and he healed her."

Realizing she spoke of this Godwine matching her life to a heartless Norman, Mary Sarah said, "Cease such talk, Nicola. As the morrow's ride will be long and arduous to ensure our captors stay ahead of your family, best our time spent falling to prayer and sleep."

The young woman blew breath up her face. "I do not know I can sleep, but I shall pray."

A quarter hour later, she slept.

Mary Sarah's own prayers at an end, she eased onto her back. Left arm straining across her chest, that hand and the other bound to Nicola's, she stared at the canopy and wished she were not beneath it despite rain pecking at it. Though clouds obscured the night sky, she longed to see past the canvas since ever she felt nearer the Lord when she looked upon His heavens.

"Foolish Mary Sarah," she whispered, then grunted. As Lillefarne was lost to her no matter what came of Gytha's plotting, she was Mercia of Mercia again.

"I must think myself that, answer to that," she breathed. "Mercia of Mercia henceforth and..."

Not evermore. If she did what was required of her, whether out of loyalty to a family who had little care for her or to keep her promise to return Nicola to the D'Argents, Mercia would become Mercia, wife of Canute. And perhaps one day she would be Mercia, wife of King Canute. A queen raised above legitimately born Godwines.

She tried to find satisfaction in that, but it was not what she wanted which was...

"To be where I wish to be, to live as I wish to live," she whispered, "to be with whom I wish to be, to be loved as I wish to love."

Poor Gytha, she thought, *you put me in a position of authority and influence and left me there too long. Once I learn what Canute and his sire know, I will do all I can to escape marriage to a man I want less than he wants me. Do I succeed, one of your beloved granddaughters will have to be sacrificed. Not Mercia of Mercia, even if she is Mercia, daughter of King Harold.*

CHAPTER EIGHT

Of those under Maël's command, surely few believed he pursued the Danes foremost to do his duty to William. The majority were right. More than apprehending the rebel leader, he sought to recover his cousin and the abbess. If that delivered Vitalis into his hands, all the better, but it was secondary.

Not surprisingly, it appeared four of his men sought to profit should their leader's priorities cause him to stumble. They might think Maël oblivious to the narrow-eyed regard of those who conversed among themselves, but observance had been pounded into him. Though as a boy and youth, he had not appreciated how great a weapon it was alongside blades capable of severing lives, well before he followed William to England, he discovered it was, indeed, powerful both offensively and defensively.

The one who stirred his men was the least trusted—Aiken who had been present at William's coronation and among the first English thanes to embrace the conqueror and be greatly rewarded for betrayal of his own. The man had coin aplenty and was among William's military advisors due to extensive knowledge of the land and its people, but elevation to the status of *companion* to the King of England yet eluded.

That William held out of reach and likely would forever, even if the Saxon was the one to deliver the leader of the Rebels of the Pale. Aiken's son, who numbered among the four disaffected men, also aspired to something beyond his reach. As told by Sir Guy who overheard Daryl's drunken boasting months past, he would be captain of the king's guard—and soon, he had assured the ale woman perched on his lap.

William could be indiscriminate in rewarding those who served him, but not where his safety was concerned. Though Daryl was well versed in arms, having received his training at Wulfen before the conquest—thereby acquainted with Vitalis—he was too given to drink as once Maël had been. But of greater detriment, if ever William had been receptive to elevating the conquered to positions of great influence, years of rebellion had changed that. Time and again, Saxons pledged to him returned to the other side when it appeared the English resistance would prevail. Thus, when finally Maël was released from William's service, a Norman would replace him, likely Sir Guy.

And when I am no longer duty and oath bound to the king, when there is naught to hold me to this troubled land? he mulled as he and several of his men awaited the return of others gone to the wood to water their mounts. *Shall I return to Normandy? Seek my fortune in Paris? Mayhap Flanders?*

He grunted. Where did not matter as much as when. God willing, once he secured that scrap of cloth, gratitude for preserving the king's dignity would see him released.

Moving from the hopeful future to the unsettled present, Maël returned to a matter of greater import. Since mid-morning, his men and he had been on the trail of a half dozen riders heading north across Lincolnshire, of note since Saxons working the land reported two of the horses carried women in addition to men. Both had been dark of hair, but none could say if one was silvered.

Since Nicola was of too few years for those glinting strands to be of such quantity they defied distance and speed, Maël assured himself the riders were Danes, just as he had been certain the camp whose fire yet smoked was where those men passed the night. And likely Nicola and the abbess had slept beneath one of the canopies whose poles left deep holes in the ground.

He prayed it so, that neither suffered the attentions of men given to the belief whatever they laid hands upon became their possession.

"There!" The middle-aged Norman at his side jutted his chin at where something fleeting also caught his leader's regard.

"What do you make of it?" Maël asked.

"A single rider, if not very well fed then well-muscled, and of no great height."

Also Maël's impression. It could not have been Vitalis, but perhaps one of his men—better, a Dane fallen behind or scouting ahead.

"Await the others," Maël said and moments later rode the edge of a wood whose sparse growth allowed him to delve its depths.

Near where he had glimpsed the rider, he turned his mount inward. Moving diagonally, he searched ahead and to the sides and saw little of note beyond scurrying and flitting woodland creatures. Then once more, great movement that as quickly disappeared as it appeared. Now the direction was confirmed, and providing the sound of the prey's flight masked the pursuer's, an increase in speed would see him intercepted.

Shortly, Maël sighted the man again. Seeing he had a sword on his belt and another fixed to his saddle, he drew his own blade.

As if his prey sensed steel come into light, he snapped his

head around. It was the rebel Maël had last seen after the Saxons' defeat at Stafford when the formidably stout man accompanied Vitalis to the D'Argents' camp to give the injured Em into Dougray's care.

Certain Zedekiah's presence in the wood was proof Lady Hawisa's man was near, Maël shouted in Anglo-Saxon, "Halt, Zedekiah!"

The rebel spurred his mount faster, but when it proved no match for Maël's, drew his sword, came around, and charged. "Out! Out!" he gave the Saxon cry that had resounded across the meadow during the great battle.

Thrice the warriors charged and crossed swords. Though the rebel's greatest strength was the jarring power behind his swings, his weakness was quickly apparent. Not only did his muscular bulk slow him, it reduced the range of his swings. Too, he was unprepared for Maël to change tact.

During their next charge, the king's man did not strike center of their raised blades but used his greater height to land his sword near the tip of Zedekiah's. It unbalanced the rebel, and his refusal to release the hilt tipped him sideways out of the saddle.

Were he lighter and had he landed on muddied ground rather than packed earth, the breath would not have been knocked from him and he might have gained his feet before his opponent reached his side. Instead, Maël brought his boot down on the wrist of Zedekiah's sword arm and set his blade at his neck. "It does not go well for you, Zedekiah."

After much effort to feed his lungs, the rebel rumbled, "No matter the end, no dishonor in...refusing to lie down for a Norman."

"As I would have done the same, I feel something of a kinship with you," Maël said. "However, now we have established the victor of this contest, I am eager to engage my next opponent. Where might I find him?"

Zedekiah laughed, wheezed, gulped. "Do you speak of the mighty Vitalis, I cannot aid. As you know, the Rebels of the Pale mostly disbanded after Stafford, and those who remained have now gone their own way."

"If you speak true, I wager the final dismantling was after your leader met with mine in a mountain cave following a snowstorm."

The big man's grin showed yellowed teeth. "Met? Is that the word Le Bâtard used to describe their encounter?" He snorted. "I suppose I would myself were I, of fierce and cruel bent, utterly humiliated by a Saxon ill of body."

That gave Maël pause. Due to illness, had Vitalis left William in possession of his life? Though more easily he could have slain the king than cut away a piece of the royal mantle, in view of what Maël knew of Lady Hawisa's man, he was not one to put a blade in a man's back. Thus, it made sense he had been ailing. Were he in full possession of his health, surely he would have challenged the conqueror at swords.

Ever, it seemed, the Lord favored William, which made one question the mind of God who surely knew the man who had taken England's crown was more given to wrong than right, especially these six months when thousands of Saxons paid for rebellion in which they had no hand.

"Le Bâtard may call it whatever soothes his slashed pride," Zedekiah said, "but we both know 'twas no meeting." His grin broadened. "Was it his wife who fashioned that fine mantle? Stitched those flourishes and the letters *W* and *R?*"

Of course he knew of the piece cut from it. Because it had been shown him afterward? Or had he been in the cave with Vitalis? Though William had indicated there were others there, he had named only the rebel leader.

Deciding it was of no import in the moment, Maël said, "I read the missive sent Lady Hawisa that told of the abduction of my cousin and the Abbess of Lillefarne, and to which Vitalis added words of assurance he would pursue the abductors. So I ask again, where is he?"

Zedekiah's brow beetled. "The abbess was abducted, you say? And your cousin as well? You speak of Sir Theriot?"

He knew it was Nicola, just as he knew of the abduction. "You waste time better spent bringing the knaves to ground. As Vitalis surely has a care for the well-being of Lady Hawisa's sister-in-law and the head of the abbey founded by her family, the sooner I find your leader, the sooner the women can be retrieved."

Zedekiah shrugged. "If Vitalis pursues the Danes, methinks the women better served by his efforts than those of William's men."

Now Maël grinned. *"Danes,* Zedekiah? I did not name the men who took Lady Nicola and the abbess. With great purpose, I did not."

Those discolored teeth went behind the rebel's lips.

"At this time, Vitalis and I want the same thing, Zedekiah."

"But you want more," he growled. "You would see the worthiest Saxon in all of England dropped at the feet of the least worthy Norman."

As was Maël's duty, and though he ought to shrug the same as Zedekiah—and could have before the harrying—he could not now.

"You surprise," the rebel said.

Belatedly, Maël masked his face.

"You do not like the task given you, do you, king's man? You know what I think?"

"I care not what you think, only what you know. Where is Vitalis?"

"I think there is enough of your cousin, Sir Guarin, about you that if you joined forces with Vitalis, sooner the women would be rescued."

It was the same as Lady Hawisa suggested before reminding

him his loyalties lay first with the D'Argents. Though tempted to scorn Zedekiah, Maël said, "Ere such an alliance could be formed, first I would have to be told where to find your leader."

"Unfortunately, I know not his whereabouts." Zedekiah sighed. "Now, what will you do with me? Cut that vein?" He shrugged his mouth, reminding Maël of William who often did the same as if his shoulders were too weighted to raise them though swift their fall. "Likely for the best."

Maël knew he ought to agree, but the cold of him that had become almost comfortable was increasingly afflicted by soft spots like those of a summer apple struggling to make it through autumn without going to rot ere winter.

He would not take this rebel's life, but what was he to do with him? Relieve him of his every weapon and release him? Set men to follow him in the hope he sought out Vitalis?

A moment later, the first consideration became unsustainable. Peering across his shoulder, he confirmed his men rode toward him and his captive.

"I do not mean to sound a coward, Sir Maël," Zedekiah said, "but if those of the usurper think naught of torture to discover what I do not know, cut that vein now."

"No torture," Maël said. "But I will make bait of you to bring Vitalis to heel."

"You assume I am of value to him. But, alas, my rebel days are over—as are his. Disbanded all."

Maël glanced at his approaching men. "I have a lesson for you, Zedekiah. When your gut tells you to cease speaking, heed it lest too much protest reveals the lie."

The man hiked his upper lip.

"What have we, Sir Maël?" called the one who tried hard to be a Norman, including forsaking his own language. Though his imprecise accent revealed the tongue of the conquerors was not his own, he grasped it better than most Saxons.

Maël increased the pressure on Zedekiah's wrist and took

the sword from resistant fingers. "What *I* have, Aiken, is one of your countrymen." He stepped back and looked around as that one and the others reined in. "A Saxon the same as you."

The man snorted. *"Not* the same. That is common at best"— he jutted his chin—"and as often you forget, and to which my loyalties attest, I am also due the title of *Sir."*

Maël returned his sword to its scabbard and slid Zedekiah's beneath his belt. "I do not forget the title given you, just as I do not forget it was awarded for reporting your father-in-law supplied rebels with food and drink, resulting in forfeiture of his lands."

Aiken glared, as did his son whose grandfather, uncles, and aunts had been reduced to the ranks of the peasantry. It had to be a blessing his mother passed before the invasion so she not bear witness to her husband's betrayal of her family.

Though tempted to further needle the two by stating neither did he forget Aiken was denied the forfeited lands, he let it be. "I cannot be certain this Saxon is one of Vitalis's men," Maël began the lie, "but too much he resembles one I fought at Stafford to allow him to go free." He shifted his regard to the man's son. "Daryl, choose two to aid in getting Zedekiah of Wulfenshire bound atop his horse."

Though such service was believed beneath one who thought himself due greater consideration the same as his sire, he would do as told.

As Daryl called for others to assist, Maël strode to Zedekiah's mount, removed the scabbarded sword affixed to the saddle, next the packs. As expected, one held the personal effects of a man whose home was the countryside over which he traveled and included a mantle, tunic, and chausses. As not expected, besides dried food, the second pack held garments, but not those of a man nor ordinary woman.

Heart pounding, Maël turned toward the rebel who remained unmoving though Daryl commanded him to stand.

As if awaiting Maël's gaze, Zedekiah raised his eyebrows. "Surprising what one finds in an abandoned camp, eh?"

Maël glanced from the habit in one hand to the veil in the other and knew the rebel had first discovered that place where the Danes passed the night. That Abbess Mary Sarah was shed of these portended ill, not only for her but Nicola. But there was hope in the holy woman's habit being left behind absent their broken or dead owner—that it was merely exchanged for another garment which would draw less attention.

"Surprising," Maël agreed, "and quite the coincidence you happened on that for which the man you deny following searches."

"The formidable Vitalis seeks a nun's habit?" Zedekiah made a face. "Not the warrior I knew."

Maël ground his teeth, then ordered, "Get him up and secured."

Daryl kicked the rebel. "On your feet!"

Slowly, Zedekiah rose. Despite rough handling, he proved less easily humiliated than Daryl. Though tightly bound and an attempt made to put the rebel over the back of his horse, the young Saxon who showed no good regard for his countryman was dealt an elbow to the face. So vicious was it, Daryl was knocked onto his back and further angered when Maël refused to allow him to retaliate and ordered Zedekiah to sit the saddle.

During the ride that followed, often Vitalis's man grinned when he looked to Daryl whose lower face swelled and bruised. He flirted with fire, but even if he fell to its flame, Maël believed the man's only regret would be he had not done worse to the traitorous Saxon. And again, Maël felt a kinship he ought not.

Rather than protection of a rebel whom Lady Hawisa would welcome back amongst her people, he must set his mind on the Danes and Vitalis—and freeing Nicola and the abbess before what was done them accelerated and no amount of blood satisfied the longing for justice.

CHAPTER NINE

*M*ore rain, hopefully of sufficient strength and duration they would pass what remained of the day and coming night sheltered by the rock ledge they had hastened beneath an hour past. The longer it took to reach the Humber, the greater the chance of Nicola escaping.

So little was spoken between the women since awakening and departing camp that when restlessness finally moved Bjorn out of hearing distance, Nicola spilled words as if they had been backed up for days. "At last! You know not how hard it has been to wait until we could not be overheard."

Mercia, who had put herself to sleep last eve by whispering her given name over and over, sank deeper into her mantle in search of greater warmth. She liked her slender figure that permitted quick and efficient movement, but in this moment wished more fat on her frame.

Spring had warmed the land, but as she had become damp before Canute yielded to Bjorn's petition they take shelter for the sake of the women, she could not entirely cast off the chill as Nicola seemed to have done. But then, this quivering was not all from the rain. The further north they progressed, the greater the evidence of Le Bâtard's harrying. Blessedly, though the absence of life in burned and abandoned places was sinister, the Danes avoided riding near them, even it if meant going the long way around. Thus, Mercia was spared looking upon whatever death would be found there.

Nicola scooted nearer. "In the excitement of all that transpired yesterday, I neglected to tell what delivered me to your side when Canute abducted you."

Mercia had assumed she simply refused to accept the rejection of her offer to accompany the abbess to the shed. "What was it, Nicola?"

She glanced all around, wiggled nearer, and opened one side of her mantle to reveal a swatch of cloth. "Look upon this, Abb —er, Mercia. I had it down my bodice." She gave a little laugh. "I am curious if that would offend or amuse the one who entrusted it to me."

Wondering who that was, and why she had been given a scrap of wool, Mercia said, "Pray, explain."

She opened her mantle wider, and greater light revealed intricate embroidery worked with thread nearly as dark as the wool but for a single strand of gold. "You have not seen this before?"

"I have not. For what would you think I have?"

"Because the one who gave it to me is known to you." Nicola bobbed eyebrows above bright eyes and a mischievous smile.

"You speak of Sir Maël?"

The young lady snorted. "Nay, though he is the one to whom I am to deliver it."

"Riddles, Nicola," Mercia bemoaned. "I am too worn and chilled to unravel them."

She leaned in. "Late one night I saw you carry something to your apartment, and curious me in the cloister below heard your voice through an open window. It sounded as if you spoke with someone."

Mercia tensed.

"Thus, when you accompanied the wine merchant to the shed, once more I yielded to curiosity, for which I have yet to repent—though I shall—and entered your apartment." She drew breath. "He knew it was me and let me in your bedchamber. Though I was shocked to find him there, he told the reason, and methinks I believe him." Another nod. "I do, just as I believe you would do naught untoward though you are not an abbess in truth."

Mercia cleared her throat. "I appreciate your faith in me, but I am confused. Answer this and no more so I may think what to ask next—why were you to deliver the cloth to your cousin?"

"Vitalis told it is for this the king's man hunts him—that Maël is tasked with retrieving it and—"

Sharply, Mercia shook her head, silencing Nicola. "Of what import a piece of cloth cut from... What? A gown? An altar covering?"

She shrugged. "He said my cousin would know the truth of it."

"Then he gave no indication of what that truth is?"

"He did, but I could not work it through. Vitalis spoke of an encounter the biblical David had with one who was king before him, then tossed this at my feet and said my cousin would be grateful were it delivered to him."

Mulling the stories of David, King of Israel, Mercia bent her head to the cloth. The wool with its one finished edge and three frayed sides was exceptionally fine, as was the embroidery that included the paired letters *W* and *R*. If these letters stood for that which the Norman king titled himself—William Rex—this had been cut from the same lavish mantle he wore when he entered Westminster to claim the crown.

Though her interpretation of the riddle was nearly unbelievable, it seemed at some time Vitalis made even more an enemy of William by doing to him what David had done to King Saul.

Of course Le Bâtard would want this back, so distinctive was it his enemies could humiliate him by presenting proof of how it was taken unbeknownst to the wearer of the mantle. Had it also happened in a cave the same as King Saul? Under similar circumstances?

"Have you unriddled it, Mercia?"

"I believe so." She returned the cloth, and when the lady put it down her bodice, related that tale of David.

Nicola beamed. "That story was distant to me, either because I was quite young when I heard it, else my mind was adrift, but now I make sense of what Vitalis did." She blew out a breath. "So bold! How it must have enraged King William, and yet he ought to be grateful he lives. To draw near enough to do that, Vitalis could have made lethal use of the blade. I wonder why he did not."

"Because he is not a murderer," Mercia said sharply, causing Canute and Bjorn to look around where they and others stood back from rain streaming off the ledge. When they returned to their watch of the wood, she continued, "Not all men who seek to end a murderer's reign are well with themselves becoming murderers to achieve that end. Alongside courage, Vitalis has honor. Were there more Saxons like him…" Her voice broke.

Nicola set a hand on her knee. "I am sorry for what my people took from yours, but if the Danes can be kicked back across the sea, surely what continues to ail these lands will heal."

Would it? Or would that hope be doused like all other hope? Would it become worse for the English? Would it be better to place a Dane on the throne? And was that even possible? If not, the attempt to eject William would end in more bloodshed. Likely so much the Saxon race would not survive.

"It was obvious Vitalis was unwell," Nicola returned her to

the present, "and for that he told he lingered at the abbey. With what was he afflicted?"

"A relapse of the flux that struck him and his men weeks earlier."

"Dysentery," Nicola gave it the name by which she better knew it. "Terrible that." It was said with genuine sympathy, the lady having tended refugees laid low by belly cramps, muscles aches, loose bowels, and fever. She frowned. "I understand why Vitalis would be loath to put a blade in the king's back—honorable, aye—but perhaps here the answer to why, after humiliating William, he did not challenge him at swords."

Mercia also found it difficult to believe he would have been content with shaming the persecutor of their people when it was possible to forever end Le Bâtard's cruelty—albeit only his.

Since the great battle, the Normans had become so firmly entrenched it was unlikely the death of their king would remove the yokes from Saxons—even if the Danish king took advantage of unrest among Normans who sought to succeed the conqueror. And quite possibly among those contenders would be William's brother, Bishop Odo, who had fought at Hastings and proved an equally brutal leader each time William left England in his care to return to his duchy of Normandy.

"Do you not think illness the reason Vitalis allowed the king to depart unscathed?" Nicola asked.

"I do."

The young lady nodded, opened her mantle, and examined her wrists. "The rope chafed. You as well?"

"It did. Blessedly, we are not bound here."

"Because all are awake and it is not possible for us to steal away." Nicola smiled. "But perhaps this eve."

"Likely, they will bind us again," Mercia said and shifted on the damp ground, drew up her knees, and wrapped her arms around them.

"Ah, but I have a plan."

"Tell," Mercia said wearily.

"A woman's wiles."

"Wiles?"

"Surely you have them, Mercia—must only pull them out from behind the abbess's back."

Though Mercia was fairly certain of what she suggested, she said, "Speak clearer."

"Remember I told I transformed the rebel, Em, into what appeared a lady so she would find favor with the king and release from slavery?"

"A memorable tale," Mercia said. As though she were as young as the one who told it, she had been enthralled with the means by which Sir Dougray won a bride denied him—by the sword, the aid of a man whose blood coursed his misbegotten son's veins, and a woman's wiles.

"If it moved a shrewd, conquering king," Nicola said, "surely it will move a young, thieving prince."

Mercia was less certain, but even if whatever she proposed merely delayed the Danes' journey, it would allow their pursuers to draw nearer and sooner return the noblewoman to her family. And, hopefully, move Mercia closer to her truth.

"I pray I do not regret this," she said, "but do with me what you will, Lady Nicola."

CANUTE, second in line to the Danish throne, knew how to smile beyond mere amusement. To Mercia's surprise, she did not shy away from shows of teeth that appeared following suggestive sidelong looks.

He sees me, she thought as she raised the flask he passed to her. *He sees me the same as Nicola said her cousin saw me.*

Such would not please Abbess Mary Sarah, but it pleased the Mercia of old who had hoped one of the young, attractive Saxon nobles whose attention she captured would seek Gytha's permission to court her. Had they ever, naught had come of it before, during, and after her grandmother gave her in service to the one who became queen of the King of England, albeit brief that distinction.

"I am glad you seek to please me," Canute said.

Did he suspect her of motive beyond pleasing him? she wondered as she slid cool wine between her lips. She did not think him a fool, but since he held himself in high regard, it seemed more possible he saw Nicola's beautiful arrangement of the former abbess's tresses and the snug lacing of her gown as a means of attracting rather than escaping.

She returned the flask and smiled as learned mostly through observation during her short stay at court. A teasing smile. A look-near-upon-me smile. A think-upon-kissing-me smile.

She moistened her lips as also observed of other women. "Though I never wished to be of the Church, I was so long inside those walls the world outside became foreign. And now to be given no moment to even think on returning to the living..." She sighed. "Pray, be patient, Canute. I will grow accustomed to it."

He tipped the flask to his own lips, then dragged the back of a hand across his mouth. "I make allowances for you, and one is Lady Nicola." He looked at the young woman who sat on the opposite side of the fire in the camp raised several hours after the cessation of rain allowed them to resume their northward journey.

Nicola did the same as Mercia, feigning interest in Bjorn who sat near, smiled, and touched her hand.

"I do not understand how Lady Nicola is an allowance made for me," Mercia said.

"Bjorn needs a soft woman, and that one will command him as he ought to command her. But so you are not lonely, I give him what he thinks he wants. For now."

That last worried, but lest she rouse suspicion, she did not question him. "You are considerate."

"I will make a good husband."

"As I will make a good wife."

He turned thoughtful. "Since you are not much more a young woman, you will have to be quick to birth children. I want four boys and one girl—though she should be born last."

He offended, and yet she nearly laughed over expectations he believed she could meet merely because he voiced them.

A frown creased his brow. "You think it funny?"

"I do not," she lied. "I think it worthy of happiness. I feared being childless, and now I am to be the mother of many children—mostly fine boys."

He nodded. "Likely one will be king after me."

She donned her best smile. "I am glad you came for me, Canute."

His eyes flicked over her face, lingered on her hair. "As am I."

When he reached to her, she leaned toward him rather than away.

Setting a hand on her jaw, he slid his thumb over her cheek. "I can kiss you?"

Reminding herself to follow Nicola's plan, she said, "You are my betrothed. But I beseech again, be patient. I am unlearned in such things."

"I will teach you." He pressed his lips to hers.

She felt neither pleasure nor distaste, surprising since she ought to feel something for all the talk overheard of kisses both wonderfully passionate and terribly disappointing. His breath and pressure on her mouth was all she felt—until heated by embarrassment over the other Danes' expressions of approval.

Canute drew back. Appearing annoyed by the attention, he said, "As told, I will teach you, and I will like it better."

Not if the plan unfolds well, she silently countered, then glanced at Nicola who discreetly inclined her head.

"I look forward to your next lesson, Canute. Now, as the ride was long for one unaccustomed to the saddle, will you see me to my pallet?"

"I shall, my lady." He rose. As she set her fingers across his palm, he looked around. "Bjorn, it is time Lady—"

"Ah nay, let the young ones enjoy their time together," Mercia beseeched.

He grunted. "A half hour, Bjorn, then she must gain her rest."

"I thank you, Cousin." The young Dane returned his attention to the one he believed he charmed.

Shortly, unbound as hoped, Mercia lay on the pallet. A blanket pulled up to her chin, she prayed Bjorn would also trust Nicola enough to allow her to sleep unfettered. If not and Mercia was not awakened to be fastened to the other woman, the plan must be altered as Nicola insisted and her fellow conspirator feared.

If naught else, the escape of Gytha's granddaughter would slow the Danes who would seek to recover her, giving their pursuers a better chance of overtaking them and freeing Nicola.

And that was as it was to be, Mercia accepted when Canute reminded Bjorn to bind Nicola—this time hands *and* feet so Mercia's sleep was not disturbed.

When it was darkest night and the campfire burned low, Nicola rasped at Mercia's back, "Go now. All sleep but the patrol."

The progress of which Mercia had followed. Thus, she knew there would be no better time to slip away than while the men were most distant. "I fear leaving you, Nicola."

"I am not afraid. Not only does Bjorn think I return his affection, but this Norman cannot be faulted for being abandoned by a Saxon, hmm?"

"But—"

"The sooner you go, the more time my family has to save us both."

Once again, Mercia felt she was the younger one, but she would not allow pride to ruin what might be her only opportunity to remove the D'Argents' sister from danger.

Lord, she prayed, *quiet my feet and turn them in the right direction.* That of the monastery glimpsed an hour before Canute made camp. Help and safety were within those walls, and more so if she identified herself as the abbess abducted from Lillefarne.

"Godspeed," Nicola whispered as Mercia eased from beneath their blanket.

"Be wise, Nicola," she rasped. Then bending low, she set a diagonal course between the patrolling Danes.

Though she heard no hue and cry raised over her disappearance, she did not pause until she was a league distant, and only then realized she had neither drink nor food to sustain her should she lose her way.

All the more reason I do not, she told herself, and rather than search out a stream to moisten her mouth, continued in the direction of the monastery—or so she hoped.

CHAPTER TEN

*W*ere not the monks equally comprised of Saxons and Normans and had not the abbot been replaced with one from Normandy, Maël might have questioned their assurances no Danes had been sighted near the monastery.

Still, he was certain his prey had been in the vicinity. Yesterday's rain made it difficult to track, but each time the trail was lost it was found again, surprisingly once when Zedekiah commented it only appeared to disappear.

In response to Maël's disbelief, the rebel had said he had no care for the Danes who betrayed the resistance by refusing to engage William in open battle and accepting his bribe to provide no further support to the rebels. Too, it was right he advise foreigners on how to read the land of his birth the sooner to retrieve the abbess and sister-in-law of the Lady of Wulfen.

Maël had heeded his advice and, shortly, the trail that had gone cold warmed again—as it must this day in the absence of a sighting.

As he guided his horse past the door in the wall a tall monk opened for him, he looked ahead to where he had left his men. They numbered only six, including Zedekiah.

Though instructed to water their mounts at a nearby stream, all should have returned by now and be ready to depart. Had those absent encountered Danes?

The door hinges whining, wooden planks groaning, Maël urged his destrier forward and reached his men before the bar dropped into iron brackets to secure the monastery.

"Where are the rest of my men?" he demanded.

"When the last group did not return, I sent Daryl with two others to rouse them," Aiken said, "but still naught. I had just decided to go myself when you came out."

Maël looked to the others, momentarily pausing on the thickly muscled rebel in whose hand he almost wished he could place a blade. "Arm yourselves," he said, then drew his sword and spurred away.

SHE HAD CHOSEN her perch well, albeit with little thought. It was the nearest tree with branches low enough to catch hold of and sparse enough her mantle and skirt did not become entangled in grasping fingers as she stepped one branch to the other like rungs on a ladder until the narrowing trunk began to bend beneath her weight.

As evidenced by one of those circling below who had tried to climb the young oak after her, causing each branch he set foot on to snap, the only way to get to her was to starve her down or take an ax to her refuge.

What had happened to two of her novices who but enjoyed a walk in the wood on a spring day would not happen to her—at least, not without far more effort than what had been expended by the enemy who ravished those women and sheared their hair.

"Come down!" called one of the three who, a quarter hour past, joined those who had sent her up the tree. "We will not harm you." Unlike the others who passably addressed her in her language, his speech marked him as one of her people. Like the others, he was close-shaven.

Fearing confirmation she was a Saxon would sooner make her prey to their perversions—one or more dulling his sword in reducing it to an ax—she stared at them where she held tight to the trunk with one hand and with the other gripped the branch whose crook she sat in.

When first she had heard horses, great her hope the riders were of Wulfen, but she had not waited to confirm it where she knelt at the stream. As revealed by their appearance and accents, those who first gathered beneath the tree she climbed were Norman. Thus, the only hope left to her was these were Sir Maël's men, but it was not to be, the one who could free Nicola not amongst the first arrivals nor the next.

Forcing breath in and out of her quaking body, once more Mercia silently appealed, *Lord, if not for the sake of this deceiver, aid me for Nicola.*

"Come down, come down, little bird," her countryman called.

"Traitor," she whispered, then wishing she were in the chapel's rafters, trapped but ever out of reach, she closed her eyes and recalled being on her back there before her fractured world began to buckle.

"Come down, little bird of glorious plumage!" called a Norman whose accent made Saxon words sound obscene and her long for the head covering to conceal her vanity. "Come—"

Of a sudden, he quieted. She did not care what made him do so, was simply glad something had, allowing her to feel again the cool stone against her back, look upon the light in the eye of the bird overhead, and follow its flight out of sight.

More riders, she acknowledged the pound of hooves. Surely

Normans, and possibly among them one eager to sacrifice the keen of his sword to make plunder of her. Though she feared that, more she feared being unable to keep her promise to Nicola.

Hearing more enemy voices, she tipped up her face and, staring into the dark behind her lids, silently counseled, *The rafters, Mercia. Look there, not below. Go there, remain there. The shadows will shield you for a time, perhaps long enough for the Lord to intercede.*

"It feels we have been here before, Abbess."

The words soared into the rafters and strode into the shadows, not because they lacked a Norman accent—indeed, much they boasted one. Because here was a familiar voice. Because here was a memory to fit his words. Because here was a prayer not answered as she wished, but answered better than feared.

He had come, meaning those who sought to coax the vain bird out of her tree *were* his men.

Still she kept her chin up and eyes closed. She was not ready to look upon the chevalier in this vulnerable, powerless state that was far from that other time he remembered when she denied him entrance from atop Lillefarne's wall and he asked if they had met before.

This day, might he place her at Westminster? Recognize the younger of the women whose identity she had recently reclaimed?

"Surely you err, Sir Maël," one of his men said. "That looks no holy woman."

Of course she did not, garbed in a lady's gown, albeit soiled, hair plaited and looped, albeit disheveled.

"I see it not," said the Saxon who first tauntingly named her a bird. "No holy woman I have glimpsed has hair like that."

Since most, if not all, he encountered surely covered their

heads, his reasoning tempted her to shower him with scornful words.

Ignoring the men, Sir Maël called, "As the tree will not bear my weight, you must come to me, Abbess."

Her quaking having begun to subside, Mercia opened her eyes upon the blue above the tree's thin branches and searched for a bird. In the distance one careened as if at play, so high it need not fear a stone's throw nor arrow's flight.

"Abbess?"

Uncertain if it was concern or annoyance in his voice, she reminded herself she was still Mary Sarah to him and looked down.

Sir Maël having remained astride, his silvered dark head tilted back and a shaft of sunlight full upon his face, she saw first the scar that coursed the right side beginning just above and to the side of the eyebrow it divided in two.

Yet still he is handsome, she acceded and tensed over thoughts she wished were all the doing of the young lady who said her cousin had *seen* Mercia and believed one not an abbess in truth could save him.

"Nicola!" Mercia gasped, fear for her own fate and surprise over Sir Maël's appearance having caused her to forget his cousin was alone in the company of men surely angered by the escape of Gytha's granddaughter—perhaps so much the smitten Bjorn would be unable to protect the woman he wished for his own. "I escaped the Danes who abducted us, but Nicola was bound and I could not—"

"Abbess!" Sir Maël said sharply, "your seat is precarious. Secure your hold and descend slowly. We shall discuss my cousin once you are down."

Unaware of having loosened her grip and shifted forward, now she felt the branch beneath her rear rather than thighs, relaxation of her hands, and the sway of the tree.

Holding tighter both sides, she said, "I shall come down."

"Slowly," he repeated.

She jerked her chin, causing the settling tree to unsettle. Praying she would hold firm, she released the branch she sat on and, turning swiftly, slung that arm around the trunk above the other arm.

"King's men!" Sir Maël commanded as she slipped off the branch. "Stand well back."

She thought he feared for their safety should she crash down on them, but when cool air swept up her skirt as she set her feet on the nearest branch, she realized he sought to preserve her modesty.

Chest tight to the trunk snagging her bodice as it had done during her ascent, she peered down. Seeing now she blocked the sun that had lit the chevalier's face, she was struck by the realization her shadow covered him as his had covered her at the abbey. A silly thing to note, and yet it felt…

Naught, she rebuked. *It feels naught.* Then she called, "'Tis just as unseemly for you as your men to be directly below me, Sir Maël."

"Agreed, but one of us must catch you if you fall."

"From atop your horse?"

"In all our years together, in and out of battle, he has endured far more than the weight of a slight woman. And if you are concerned where I place my eyes, I vow I look only near enough to ensure you land in my arms."

Norman though he was, she believed him.

"I will not fall," she said and began working her way down, once more making rungs of branches, once more catching her braids on branches. She did not realize how near she was to the chevalier until he gripped her waist.

"Let go," he said as his men began murmuring and making sly comments. "I have you."

Wondering why *his* accent did not make her language sound obscene, she released the branch. As he lowered her to the saddle between his thighs, so relieved was she to be out of the tree and in his company, she nearly sank against him.

Looking across her shoulder and around one of her braids into dark green eyes, she said, "I thank you, Sir Maël. I feared…"

"This I know, and I regret you had cause. Unfortunately, few of my men were chosen by me."

"One is a Saxon."

"Two—Daryl and his sire, Aiken."

"Traitors," she hissed.

"As they have been since the beginning to profit from aiding my liege."

"The beginning?"

"Both were present for William's coronation at Westminster —among the few who remained throughout the ceremony though surrounding buildings were set afire."

"Not by Saxons," Mercia murmured, recalling smoke seeping into the chapel, its haze and scent rising to the balcony where this chevalier had confronted two Saxon women, then the flight with her grandmother through streets thronged by looting invaders and fleeing Saxons. "It was the—" She closed her mouth.

Suspicion narrowed his eyes. "You heard right. Mercenaries mostly, though some of William's liegemen were also roused to destruction and looting."

"You were there?" she asked, then wondered what so afflicted her she could not let the matter die.

"I was. Were you, Abbess?"

"Nay, I was en route to take up my post at Lillefarne." *A lie by a few days only,* she told herself. A lie all the more necessary now Gytha had put her pawn in play far beyond being the Godwines' eyes and ears upon Wulfenshire.

Much Mercia had pondered her situation these past days, and one thing was clear. That she was to be used as a weapon against Le Bâtard in King Sweyn's bid for the throne made her valuable to the enemy should they learn of her lineage and role in gaining Saxon support and acceptance of Danish rule. If she fell into William's hands, she could be locked away the remainder of her life or forced into marriage with a Norman to effect the opposite of what Gytha and Sweyn wished. Possibly worse. Were it known whom she served during King Harold's reign and were it believed she knew that one's whereabouts, she might be subjected to torture to tell what she did not know.

Pray, Lord, she silently beseeched, *once I learn who sired me, help me escape the yokes of all.*

"Are you hungry, Abbess?"

Guessing her stomach had grumbled, she said, "I am—and thirsty. Lest the stream is fouled, I drank little." Though tempted to add such fouling would be a result of the harrying, he did not need to be told. Too, of a sudden she was more fatigued than in want of food and drink, her nightlong journey having permitted little rest.

The chevalier settled an arm around her waist and nudged his mount forward. "We shall find a place to sit, and once you are refreshed, you will reveal all I must know to retrieve my cousin."

All but that it was for me the Danes entered the abbey rather than the abduction of the D'Argents' sister, she thought.

"Settle in!" he called to his men. "There is a tale I must needs hear ere we resume our hunt."

CHAPTER ELEVEN

*S*he did not reveal all. There was something she held close that would explain why, in seeking to prevent Nicola's abduction, she was not simply knocked unconscious or quickly bound. Considering how often she averted her gaze when he pressed for details, he was certain she feared he suspected her deception.

Of greatest interest was the revelation King Sweyn's misbegotten nephew, Bjorn, was among those who came for Nicola. And yet the young man Maël had met during Dougray's negotiation with the King of Denmark's brother last autumn was not the one who led the Danes that had divided into two contingents following the abduction at Lillefarne.

"As you do not know the name of the leader, can you describe him, Abbess?"

Continuing to pick at a biscuit, she shrugged. "Long hair and beard the same as most Danes."

"As well as Saxons," he said. "What age? What color hair? How fine his clothes?"

She raised her chin, causing one of several looped braids to shift off her shoulder, slide across a breast, and settle in her lap

—and him to tense over imaginings of drawing it through his fingers. "Does it matter?" she asked.

He moved his gaze to hers and saw the widening of her eyes through which wariness entered. Cursing himself for appearing a predator, he said, "As unbelievable as it is, I question if it was Bjorn's sire, the earl, who aided his son in abducting a bride. Not that I can make sense of Nicola being that bride since she can have had no contact with Danes to bring her to Bjorn's notice."

After a long moment, she said, "The leader was not as old as that. I am thinking…"

"What?"

"Perhaps in seeking a wife for Bjorn and knowing there is a convent within our walls, the Danes bribed the wine merchant to take one of our women and chose the first lovely maiden who was not clothed in a habit."

"Possible, and yet also they took a holy woman rather than subdue her."

She touched the braid that entranced him. "As once more I lost my veil, likely vanity is responsible for my abduction."

Believable since she was relatively young and lovelier yet wreathed with such hair, and yet not believable. As the Danes were also of the Christian faith, surely they would have deemed it more forgivable to quiet her than abduct her. Of course, in the moment they could have yielded to base instincts.

"It is possible," he said. "So how old the leader?"

"Mayhap a score and ten, hair dark blond and naught special about his garments."

"You did not hear his name spoken?"

She popped a piece of biscuit in her mouth. After slowly chewing and swallowing, she said, "It must have been, but when camp was made, your cousin and I were kept distant from most, and it was Bjorn who tended us."

"Smitten pup," Maël muttered, then once more struck by

what he wished were unimaginable, said, "It is true neither of you were…"

"As told. Though I feared violation when I was ordered to exchange my habit for this gown, we were not defiled." She glanced down. Her bodice and skirt were snagged and soiled, but their ruination could not disguise the garment was fine enough to have been fashioned for a noblewoman. "'Tis strange to once more appear to be of the world outside the cloister. I—"

A curse rendered in English moved her gaze to where Zedekiah remained astride though the king's men had dismounted to eat and stretch their legs.

As Maël pondered what went between the rebel and Daryl who held the halter of the man's mount, the abbess asked, "Who is the Saxon bound to his saddle?"

"I wondered how long ere he came to your notice."

"Almost as soon as I was out of the tree."

Since she had said naught of Zedekiah, he had thought her too shaken and weary. Had she delayed in asking after the rebel to prepare herself to deny knowledge of Vitalis's man? Or was he truly unknown to her?

"You say you do not recognize him?"

With something of a smile, she said, "Our country is not as large as France, but of the English there are hundreds of thousands."

Maël might have returned her smile had she not added, "At least there were ere your kind came." Briefly, she closed her eyes. "So tell, who is he? And for what was he not slain where captured?"

Knowing he had no right to take offense, Maël said, "His name is Zedekiah."

As if she knew the name, a glimmer appeared in her eyes.

"He was captured on the day past when I thought him in too great a hurry to allow him to ride on without being questioned. Had he not seemed familiar when I took him to ground, and had he a believable explanation, he would have gone free. But he was familiar, and in his pack something that revealed he and I have much in common."

"What have you in common?"

"You. He happened on the Danes' camp before us, and there found your habit. Since once he was of the Rebels of the Pale and remains true to Vitalis, I believe he will be of use in delivering to my king what is required of me."

She looked to the biscuit that was now mostly crumbs. "If what is required is of such import, I wonder why you bother with me—even your cousin—when you should be hunting Vitalis for your beloved William."

"The sooner I overtake those who abducted Nicola, the sooner I shall lay hands on the rebel leader."

"I do not understand."

"Because you do not know what I know."

"And that is?"

"Sister Rixende sent a missive to Lady Hawisa alerting her Nicola and you were taken. At its end was a message from he who delivered the refugee children to Lillefarne."

Her eyes widened.

"I know not when exactly Vitalis returned to the abbey, but he told it was two hours ere he learned of the abduction and that he would set out to retrieve Nicola and you."

Breath shuddered from her.

"Though Lady Hawisa denied the handwriting was Vitalis's, since a sighting of him upon Wulfenshire delivered my men and me there, I do not think I am wrong in saying she lied to protect her man. Now let us try this again—did you harbor the king's enemy whilst I was at the abbey?"

Measuredly, she said, "No men are allowed inside our walls beyond deliveries made by those who have our trust, and even they are not permitted to linger."

"That does not answer my question, especially since the

wine merchant you trusted conspired with Danes to abduct my cousin and you."

"Just because someone earns my trust does not mean one day they will not spend it upon something that could harm those of the abbey." She closed her fingers around the decimated biscuit, flung her hand out, and opened it to scatter crumbs. "Much I regret trusting the one whose betrayal endangers Nicola. Unfortunately, all I could do was follow her plan to use our wiles on the Danes in the hope they would loosen their watch over us. Last eve, they did, but though I was left unbound, Nicola was fixed hand and foot. Thus, I gave her my word I would go for help. Obviously, it was not you and your men I hoped to encounter but those of Wulfen who Nicola was certain would come for us."

He inclined his head. "It would have been Baron Wulfrith and his men had not I delivered tidings his youngest brother went missing during the harrying. As he set out immediately to search for Theriot, he was unaware of his sister's abduction— and may yet be unaware if the messenger sent after him has not found him."

"Heavenly Father," she breathed, "the D'Argents are set upon on all sides."

"Lady Hawisa said the same."

"Be assured, Sir Theriot will be in my prayers." She nodded. "'Tis good you were at Wulfen when Sister Rixende's missive was delivered."

"And that Vitalis also sought to recover you. Otherwise, I would have few men to aid me."

She frowned. "You would disobey William—cease searching for Vitalis if he did not also seek to overtake the Danes?"

"Though it may prove to my detriment, Nicola is my first concern."

She drew her lower lip through her teeth. "You are not entirely without heart, are you, Sir Maël?"

The observation, as much as the fullness of her mouth making him uncomfortable, he said, "My sire would name it loyalty and honor, and that is what I aspire to though often I fall short. Sometimes disastrously."

"Disastrously, Sir Maël?"

That last he should not have spoken. "Disastrously," he said.

Though interest was in her eyes, she said, "What will you do if you find Vitalis?"

"Take him prisoner."

She was silent a while, then said, "I know what happened in the cave."

The warrior who ought to be better at masking his emotions jerked.

"Nicola and I unriddled that which was given into her keeping," she continued, "and I believe it is what you seek as much as the man who entrusted it to her."

"What was given her?" Maël asked tautly.

"Vitalis was at Lillefarne when you were there, though as you know, not in the hidden passage. Since he was ailing, he recovered in my apartment." At his widening eyes, she snapped, "Naught untoward, Sir Maël, simply Christian charity alongside the need to protect a man I believe as honorable—if not more— than the best of your family."

"Continue."

"Nicola became suspicious and went to my apartment, and there she and Vitalis spoke. After he told her he played David to William's King Saul, he gave her a piece of cloth and instructed her to deliver it to you." She touched Maël's arm. "He is not your enemy, and as should be obvious from his disbandment of the rebels so they not uselessly spend their lives on what cannot be won, he is not even your king's enemy. He humiliated William, aye, but he made no weapon of that piece of cloth."

"Wise of him."

"More than wise," she said with what sounded desperation,

causing him to question if the holy woman had forbidden feelings for Vitalis. Of course, because something was not permitted did not mean she and the rebel leader had not succumbed to temptation. Vitalis had been in her apartment the day she revealed to Maël the vanity of her hair. Perhaps time expended on her tresses was for the rebel leader.

That bothering as it should not, he told himself it was only because she looked lovely despite her disarray and what he had discovered when she came out of the tree. Though at the abbey, briefly he had pondered what figure she possessed beneath the habit, there was no reason to ponder further after helping her onto his horse. He had glimpsed the shape of her calves, felt the small of her waist, seen the flare of her breasts above and hips below, and known the curve of thighs settling between his.

Mere attraction, he named it, then beseeching the Lord to aid him so he not suffer the bewitchment of a Saxon woman, rose from the fallen tree. "As best you can, Abbess, point me in the direction from which you fled, and men I trust will return you to Lillefarne."

"Nay!" She jumped up, lurched forward when her foot caught on her hem.

Gripping her arm, Maël wondered if her sharp breath had more to do with being a holy woman or with the woman she set aside to make her profession.

Once steadied, she drew back. Color striping her cheeks, all that was rigid and severe about her became soft and uncertain as if a mask had dropped, but even when she fit it back in place, he could see where it gapped against the truth of her.

And what was the truth? he questioned, glancing at his men who feigned interest elsewhere. From which of the noble Saxon families did she hail? Considering the position she had attained, it could be no minor family—at least, not before the conquest. Since most of the great Saxon families that survived the loss of their men and lands were sharply in decline beneath William's rule, likely it was the same with her kinsmen.

"For what do you stare?" she asked.

He moved his gaze from hair peaked on her brow to dark braids, large eyes, long lashes, a good nose, and lovely lips. And at long last, he placed her.

But was it truly Abbess Mary Sarah who had been mostly in shadow upon the balcony at Westminster? Or did she merely resemble the granddaughter of that angry old woman? Certes, then she had not worn a habit, and if this was the same woman, she had lied in telling she had been en route to take up her post when William was crowned.

"Why do you stare?" she repeated.

He looked to his men. "Prepare to depart!" he called, then said, "I question who you are, Abbess, and what you hide."

"I hide naught." She raised her chin higher, and its dimpled center cast doubt on her being the woman at Westminster. However, as it had been dim and the cleft was slight, it could have gone unseen.

Great was the temptation to ask if she was that woman and, if so, when she had made her profession. Had she been of the Church then and but eschewed the habit that day? Or had she spoken vows before beginning her journey to Wulfenshire?

"Who are you?" he asked again.

"As well you know, Abbess Mary Sarah."

"So you say, and yet a holy woman who ought to be more concerned for the Saxon women and children inside Lillefarne than my Norman sister whose captors are pursued by the king's men does not wish to return to her charges."

Though she did not avert her gaze, he sensed her struggle. "As told, it was your sister's plan that allowed me to escape, and I gave my word I would see her returned to her family."

Not for the first time struck by how beautifully precise her speech, especially now it called to mind the woman at

Westminster, he said, "Your word you shall keep by pointing me to the Danes."

"As I have every faith Sister Rixende and others of the abbey will care well for my flock during my absence, that I shall do—whilst in your company."

He could force her to accept an escort to Lillefarne, but there was much here, not the least of which was confirmation or rejection of this woman as the one who persuaded him to allow her and her grandmother to use the hidden passage one last time.

"Very well, you shall accompany us, *Abbess*."

Relief nearly bowed Mercia's shoulders. What he could not know was she was the best means of Nicola finding her release with the least amount of bloodshed providing a trade could be effected. Too, no matter what happened, the abbey was now consigned to her past.

"You will ride with me," Sir Maël further unsettled her. But as there were no extra horses, she could not argue it. Too, so impressive was his mount that even with her added weight, they would keep pace with the others.

"Mount up!" he called and started toward his destrier.

As she followed, the rebel shouted, "King's man, I am flattered by Sir Daryl and Sir Aiken's confidence in this Saxon's superior ability to control bladder and gut—perhaps better even than their king who surely must pause and make use of trees, hedges, even *caves*—but as I am not fully recovered from the flux, I may prove as inconstant as my traitorous countrymen. And that would be unpleasant and inconvenient for all."

"Aiken and Daryl," Maël D'Argent shouted, "Zedekiah *is* a fearsome Saxon, but surely together you can get him behind a bush without risk to your lives."

Shame caused their faces to darken. Did they not do as commanded, it would be seen by the others as confirmation the Saxons-turned-Normans did fear one rebel.

As they assisted their bound captive in dismounting, Zedekiah's rumbling taunts landed well, resulting in rougher handling.

"They hurt him, Sir Maël," Mercia said as they neared his destrier.

"They do, and yet Vitalis's man enjoys himself." He halted. "As long as I lead, no real harm will be done him."

Once again struck by how handsome that other side of his face—more, how much she longed to explore the damaged side, she pressed her fingers into her palms and permitted herself a moment's pondering as to whether he *did* see her as Nicola told. Then she said, *"As long as you lead,* meaning he is dead should your men determine not to follow you."

"A possibility, but that would require more of those under my command go the way of the few."

"They might."

"I am aware, Abbess. Now let us get you astride."

"If you relieved Zedekiah of his mount and released him, I need not share your saddle."

"I will not release him."

"Then I shall sit behind you."

"That would require you truly go astride, which is cumbersome in a gown."

"But not impossible. And better you can control your mount if I hold to your back rather than you hold to me."

He eyed her. "I am thinking you have never ridden in that manner for a long distance at good speed. But we can begin that way."

"And end that way," she said, determined not to suffer again the cramped and awkward fore of a saddle and arms of a man as she had with the Danes.

"As you wish." He swung into the saddle and reached to her. When she set her hand in his, she kept her chin down lest the heat sweeping her showed in her face.

With what seemed little effort, he boosted her up, and further she warmed in providing a show of woolen hose up to her calves and the bunching of her gown between her legs as she settled behind him. It was unseemly, but the alternative was perching between his thighs, the thought of which disturbed more than having done so with Ingvar who had shared his saddle with her.

Not until Sir Maël adjusted his seat did something forgotten come to notice. Tugged slightly forward, she saw he sat on the lower edge of her purse whose bulk was nearly all her grandmother's missive.

You should have tossed it on the fire—else buried it, she rebuked as she snatched the purse from beneath the chevalier and shifted it across her belt to her hip. Though Gytha's words spoke of one in the abbess's care, with all that had transpired, sense could be made of it.

"Draw nearer and fit your arms around my chest," the chevalier instructed as Zedekiah was heaved back atop his horse.

Mercia did as told, and when her forearms and hands came into contact with muscles felt through his garments, thought she might have erred in insisting she sit behind. She knew little of intimacy, but it was very possible the shiver moving through her was how the dance between men and women began.

"Lean in, Abbess." At her hesitation, he gripped her arms and pulled her forward, pressing her breasts against his back.

"Sir Maël!"

"Abbess Mary Sarah!" he mocked, then said, "I assume you wish to stay astride."

"Aye, but 'tis not necessary I be so near."

Peering over a shoulder, he presented the barely ruined side of his face. "You will lose the saddle otherwise, but if you are uncomfortable, reconsider my arms around you rather than yours around me."

She raised her face higher. "I will make do with this."

Rather than turn forward again, he looked to her lips, then lower.

Her chin wanted down, but she kept it up. "Should we not ride, Sir Maël?"

"We should," he said but continued to scrutinize her face.

"Just as your men grow restless, the Danes grow more distant, Sir Maël."

A corner of his mouth tugged. "Still I try to place where first we met."

"That was when you rode upon Lillefarne to do your cousin's bidding."

He looked to her chin again. "Mayhap you but resemble someone I encountered years past."

More than ever fearing he did not believe her, certain her hair and clothing were responsible, she said, "It will be good to don habit and veil again," then told him the direction they ought to ride.

Smile slight, he turned forward.

With each league that carried them northward, more tightly Mercia clung to him. And more shivers she suffered.

CHAPTER TWELVE

*L*ike it or not, the stubborn woman would sit the saddle's fore, though more for her safety than his comfort.

These past hours, often she had relaxed against him as if sinking into sleep. Each time he tightened his arms against her arms and closed a hand over hers to better secure her, she had returned to wakefulness. But this time she did not, and against his back he felt the slow rise and fall of her chest and warmth of her exhales.

Maël raised a hand to rein in his men, then peered over his shoulder at the woman who held to him only because he held to her.

Her dark head was down, the side of it pressed against his lower shoulder, and so deeply she slept that when he shifted around to move her to the fore of the saddle, she was unresponsive. Doubtless, she had not rested since escaping the Danes.

She did not stir until she was seated before him, legs over one side, and only when his attempt to shift the purse wedged between her hip and his abdomen snapped its leather thong.

Her eyes sprang wide upon his face above hers, then she

snatched the purse from him. "You dare!" She pressed the leather pouch so near her chest the parchment within crackled.

Interesting on two fronts. Her haughty rebuke was the same as that of the old woman at Westminster, and the parchment—or something else—was so precious she was more concerned with it than him moving her to the saddle's fore. Precious how?

"I but ensure your safety, Abbess, which was questionable with you asleep against my back. Whilst adjusting your purse to make both our seats more comfortable, its tie snapped. Now if you would look upon the land and confirm we continue toward my cousin, we can resume our ride."

She stared, huffed, sat forward. And caught her breath. "Aye, we came this way on the day past, the charred field far left, the village…" She shuddered. "We did not draw so near."

He rebuked himself for being unprepared for her reaction to the harrying. Though not as evident nor unsightly here as it would be nearer the Humber, an increasing number of homes had been abandoned by Saxons who feared perishing if they clung to what could take years to recover—and farther north what likely would take generations before the land was able to sustain communities again.

Though the abbess turned her face toward him, she kept her eyes lowered. "Now that I am awake, once more I can sit behind you."

Hearing ache in her voice, certain she concealed tears, the seams of the cold place inside him strained. "As we have few hours of daylight remaining, and we can make better progress with you seated before me, it is best you remain here." *And I hold you as I have not held a woman in a very long time,* he thought. "Now secure your purse, return to your rest, and if an inn can be found ere nightfall, you shall sleep better so we may ride harder on the morrow to overtake my cousin's captors."

Sensing argument, he shouted for his men to ride and spurred forward.

After fumbling with a purse too bulky to slip down her bodice and too precious to return to her belt lest he relieve her of it again, she knotted its severed ties and slid the loop onto a wrist.

What did the missive tell? he wondered. And who had inked it? A foul-tempered old woman? Possible, meaning the deception the abbess had owned to regarding Vitalis being present at Lillefarne could prove greater yet.

Over the next hour, she remained silent and rigid, but when they passed near scorched fields and the carcasses of slain animals, a groan escaped her. And when they approached a village of such grand size there was no doubt its inhabitants had prospered and of such devastation it appeared entirely abandoned, the stiff went out of her.

There being no way around it, the harrying widespread and including the bodies of villagers unable to escape with their lives, Maël was grateful when she turned her face into his chest.

Feeling her every breath—long, slow draws evidencing the stern Abbess of Lillefarne struggled to calm herself—once more his seams strained, and not for the first time he cursed William for resorting to ungodly measures to stamp out the rebellion. Measures all the more tragic seen through the eyes of this woman whose exposure to the harrying before her abduction was word of mouth and the living victims who sought aid at the abbey.

Her shoulders jerked, and her attempt to contain sobs which he would not have believed her capable of started her trembling.

More straining of Maël's cold seams, but though determined to hold against speaking words of comfort, he lowered his mouth to her ear. "I am sorry you saw that. More, that it will get worse throughout our ride."

Though he expected her to rebuke him, she nodded.

Encouraged, he tightened his arm around her waist. "Keep your chin down and eyes closed, Lady."

He did not mean to title her that though surely she was noble, but in this moment it was a better fit than naming her an abbess as done the day he first rode on Lillefarne.

"Sleep if you can," he said gruffly.

She bobbed her head, but a sob moved from her chest to his, followed by another and a murmured apology, then she slid her arms around his waist. Holding tighter to him than he to her, over the next quarter hour she cried so softly he knew it only by her quaking and the damp felt through his tunic. Then her arms around him eased, and she slept again.

Thereafter, for how often Maël looked upon her, he felt almost the youth he had been when first he found favor with a woman other men wanted. Not that this one sought his attentions, abbess or not.

Or not, he mulled, then let it be, telling himself he was no longer the entranced youth amazed to discover how easy it was for one of attractive form and face to fill his arms with those of the fairer sex.

So far was he from that young man, it felt as if he had been more observer than participant, intense training having bettered his form and Hastings having ruined much of his face.

Less than my due, he reminded himself, then set his mind on the ride.

Though no sighting was had of fellow travelers resembling Danes, Maël and his men made good progress across land and past homes as ravaged as he had warned the abbess. Thus, he was grateful she continued to sleep, even when they halted before the inn he had hoped to find just as dusk heralded approaching night.

Though only a quarter of the structure was burned, it appeared abandoned by the innkeeper and his family who had likely fled had they not perished.

"We pass the night here," he called and ordered two men to confirm the premises were vacant and four to scout the area.

145

"And the tyrant wonders why we oppose his rule," Zedekiah said as he nudged his mount alongside the king's man.

Maël had not been oblivious to his prisoner's witness to the means of ensuring the opposition lacked supplies to sustain efforts to oppose William, but he had told himself Zedekiah had seen worse farther north, and it was true. What was not true was the rebel would be mostly unaffected by devastation on a lesser scale.

"I do not wonder, Zedekiah. I understand. Just as I understand it is not for lack of courage nor ability Vitalis disbanded his rebels. It was for this, Stafford, York, Exeter, Hastings, and all between."

The man considered him, then the abbess. "Careful, Chevalier, unlike three of your cousins who gained more than land in invading my country, already this Saxon woman is wed."

What he suggested offended. Even were Mary Sarah not a bride of Christ, he would not want her. A far different path he walked from that of Cyr, Guarin, and Dougray who had fought side by side in the great battle until separated by chaos.

"You mistake courtesy for emotion, Zedekiah."

"Possible, but that does not mean there is not some truth to it."

As Maël struggled against rebuking him, one of two chevaliers exited the inn and called, "Clear!"

"Its furnishings are abused and stores stolen," said the other, "but it will provide shelter should it rain again."

When two scouts returned from searching the area and reported there were no signs of Saxons nor Danes and the other two would begin the night's watch, Maël returned his gaze to the woman seated before him, the hand to which she had bound her purse lax in her lap.

If not for Zedekiah, he might delve the purse's contents. "Awaken, Abbess."

She drew breath, sighed long, and sank deeper against him.

Not until he called forth two of his trusted men to aid Zedekiah in dismounting did she sit up and look around. Suspicion narrowing her lids, she drew her purse-bound hand against her chest.

Here again the abbess. Wishing he did not miss the lady who had cried herself to sleep, as much in his arms as he was in hers, Maël said, "More and more I am curious as to what you hide."

"Naught," she said, then as if to prove it, dropped that hand back to her lap. As if to make a liar of her, the parchment rustled.

"Abbess," acknowledged the rebel whose hands were being loosed from the saddle.

"Zedekiah, is it not?" she asked.

"'Tis."

She inclined her head, moved her regard to the inn. "Normans were here before you, Sir Maël, doubtless in so great a frenzy to slay fleeing Saxons they did not entirely return this fine establishment to the dust of the earth."

It was said with accusation directed at him for being of the same race as those who committed the atrocity, but it did not ring true. Guessing she sought to wipe from memory the lady who had grieved in his arms and strangely unwilling to let her go, he said, "I fear you are right."

She hesitated, then peered across her shoulder. "Rather than agreement, Sir Maël, I almost wish reproach—even a lie—fallen from your tongue."

As did he, the cold place within more comfortable for how familiar it was and how great the distance it placed between him and this woman. "Tempted as I am to accommodate you, I see what you see and know this is the least of my king's anger."

He glimpsed brightness about her eyes a moment before she turned forward again. "We shall pass the night here?"

"We shall."

"Did you sight Danes during the ride?"

"Nay, meaning they are many leagues beyond us."

"You cannot be sure of that."

Hearing fear in her voice, certain it must have been terrifying for a virtuous woman of God to be taken captive by plundering Danes, Maël said, "Be not afeared. You are safe with me and my men. To ensure we are not set upon, two chevaliers will patrol the area at all times. Now let us get you inside." He glanced at the heavens. "Rain soon, methinks."

Rain whose fall may mask the sound of Canute and his men coming for me, Mercia thought and wished she could reveal the likelihood Danes were near. Bjorn wanted Nicola and had her, but more King Sweyn wanted Gytha's granddaughter and no longer had her. Thus, were it necessary to slaughter William's men to reclaim her, it would be done.

"What so troubles?" Sir Maël asked.

If only I were, indeed, a mistress of deception, she silently bemoaned. Hoping a veiled warning would cause him to increase the patrol, she said, "As Saxons learned of Normans, one should be overly cautious where those from across the sea are concerned. Thus, would it not be better to double the patrol?"

"It is not believable the Danes would not go directly to the Humber to gain reinforcements for defense against Nicola's kinsmen."

As he did not know it was for Mercia they had come, he had no reason to exercise greater caution, but she dare not reveal the truth. Even if she could trust him with her identity, not so his men whom he did not entirely trust. Thus, were it learned this *abbess* in the hands of Danes could endanger Le Bâtard's rule, a trade for Nicola would not be made.

"It is just a feeling I have, Sir Maël."

"Noted," he said and swung out of the saddle and reached to her. At her hesitation, he said, "You will be stiff."

Though she wanted to refuse his aid for how comforting

the enemy's words and how welcome the strength of his arms after looking near upon the harrying as she had hoped never to do, she leaned toward him. Shivers shot her sides as he gripped her waist, next her hands when she fit them to his shoulders.

He did not delay in setting her to her feet and releasing her, but as if he felt her response to their hands on each other, he considered her visage before looking lower.

It was one thing for him to note the heat in her face, another he should see the rise and fall of her chest made all the more obvious by a fitted gown.

Pivoting, he cast over his shoulder, "Follow me."

"Sir Maël?"

He looked around. "Abbess?"

"I think it best I don my habit."

"As Zedekiah is no washer woman, it is as muddied as when he found it. Though you may rinse it out on the morrow when we water the horses at a stream, unless we make camp again ere overtaking the Danes, there will no time to dry the gown before a fire."

Resolved to wearing this traitorous, disarrayed garment, she followed him into the inn.

An hour later, the hunger and thirst of all were satisfied and beds made on the lower floor where once sturdy tables and benches caused weary travelers to press coins into the innkeeper's palm.

"You are recovered?" Sir Maël asked as Mercia settled beneath the blanket he gave her.

She looked up at where he halted before the corner in which she would pass the night. The unspoiled side of his face mostly in shadow, she wished the terrible scar over which flame flickered so thoroughly repelled that never did she have to make sense of what he caused to move through her. But it did not repel. At all.

He raised his eyebrows, a reminder he had asked after her recovery.

He referred to her reaction to the destruction—and death she had been nearly close enough to touch which had led to weeping and clinging. Though she was not recovered, neither from the horror of this day nor the shame of behaving a child, she said, "Be assured, I am better than those given no chance to recover."

Sensing what might be anger though it did not look it, she expected him to walk away, but he lowered to his haunches. "Much I regret what you saw, Lady."

Once more able to see the whole of his face and feeling ache in fingertips that should not miss what they had never touched, she said, "What I *saw*, Sir Maël? Is that all you regret?"

"It is not."

"Yet still you serve one such as that. Why? And how?"

Silence, then, "The king has my oath. Thus, for a while longer I must protect him and do his bidding."

She pushed onto an elbow. "For what did you give him your oath? Though he did not award you lands stolen from my people, you could have—"

"He did award me lands."

She startled.

"And the hand of a Saxon heiress. I declined both."

"Because the lands were stolen?" she said and winced lest she sounded as hopeful as she felt.

"Nothing as lofty as that, and it had naught to do with the lady."

"Then?"

His nostrils flared. "As I do not seek a confessor, my reasons shall remain private." He started to straighten. "It grows late and—"

She caught his hand. "What of your reason for remaining in

England to serve a man whose actions it seems you disapprove of?"

He looked to where she held him, and when she did not release him, said, "Since ever the D'Argents have been well-regarded by their liege, William wished me to be captain of his guard. As it was more command than request and a man must earn coin to pay his way through the world, that I became."

Certain there was more to it, she said, "For what else?"

Darkness flashed across his face, but as if to make light of what she glimpsed, he said, "Mayhap I deserve no better, hmm?" Were not his response a poor fit for what she knew of him and had not bitterness slipped through, she would not have persisted.

"I do not believe that of you."

"You do not know me," he said, then curled his fingers over hers and loosened her hold. A moment before he released her, instead of ache in her fingertips, she felt a thrill as though a promise were made that she wished fulfilled.

Dear Lord, is this desire? she sent heavenward. *Might it be lust?*

"I will be near until the patrol falls to me," Sir Maël said and, rising, jutted his chin at his bed. "Then Sir Anselm shall watch over you." He indicated the relatively young chevalier who had lost most of the hair on his crown, making him appear a tonsured monk. Though she had spoken no word to the one trusted by the king's man, she liked him for his easy smile.

"When do you begin your patrol?" she asked.

"Third watch, three hours hence."

"The middling of night."

Maël inclined his head. "Good eve, Abbess."

Hoping it would be, that rather than fall to slaughter in the night, the king's men would overtake the Danes in the light of day and by negotiation—a trade—win Nicola's release, Mercia set about her prayers as the other occupants settled to their rest.

~

REGRET. His greatest was, indeed, for the harrying and what the abbess had witnessed of it, but regret also for defending his service to William which he had no cause to do. Rather than withdraw, Maël had felt compelled to explain his actions, more to set aright her belief he had not fought well enough at Hastings to gain great reward.

As much as he proved unworthy of his family that day, he had proved worthy of his king, cutting down swaths of Saxons intent on cutting down him and his fellow warriors.

When Mary Sarah pressed him to explain why he declined to become a landed noble and he refused to answer, he should have left her. But as he struggled not to be moved by her touch, she had pried further into his reason for serving William. What he had told was true, but more true was what he sought to disguise by making light of it—that he deserved no better. Worse than that it sounded more self-pitying than teasing was that her refusal to believe it of him had caused warmth to seep into his cold place. And made him long for greater warmth.

Maël opened his eyes and looked to the woman who lay on her side, lids lowered, lips parted.

Once more craving warmth not his due, he rebuked himself for not sooner turning from her. Why had he not?

Because this woman makes you feel again, came the answer he did not wish. *Because she causes you to think and hope outside this cold place. Because she makes you want what you have not wanted in a long time. Because you weary of this existence. And more. So much more.*

He closed his eyes, thanked the Lord a Saxon he did not want was unattainable, and went down into sleep.

CHAPTER THIRTEEN

*D*anes. How had she known the enemy would steal upon the king's men, spreading out across ground dampened by a drizzle come and gone?

Since they numbered at least eight, if they were the same ones who abducted Nicola, the two contingents had become one again. And if Maël read this right, they risked confronting Normans for one reason—the abbess.

Silently cursing himself for ignoring the lesson reinforced with a thrust to the chest that dropped a young man of ten and five to his back, he heard again Hugh's words.

If the Lord did not bless you with the instinct to listen well when the pit of you warns something is amiss, I certainly did. Heed it, pretty boy, else die the least of the D'Argents—less even than that baseborn cousin of yours. If not to make me proud, do it for your mother so she not soak our bed with worthless tears.

Maël had hated him then, though not for long. Never for long. He had wanted to be what was required of him and for years strove to become the best of those his sire trained, but though he excelled in many areas, in others often he was bettered. It did not reflect well on Hugh D'Argent, but eventually the renowned warrior adjusted his expectations of the son he deemed too fine of face and grudgingly accepted if Maël could not be the best, he would be among the best. That he had become to honor his sire, ensure his mother did not bear responsibility for birthing an unworthy son, and not disappoint Uncle Godfroi who gave as much time and prayer to his nephew as his own sons. And all the easier it was once Maël learned to use his sire's goading to unwind the anger that enabled him to run faster, swing swifter, and strike harder— anger he might need this eve.

What felt like string wrapped around his emotions beginning to loosen in preparation for its unwinding, Maël looked to the wood on the other side of the road opposite that which he patrolled.

When Aiken raised a hand, acknowledging his position half concealed behind a tree, Maël signaled him to advance ahead of Danes who intended to surround the inn. Then, absent chain mail that allowed him to more stealthily patrol the area, he set his own sword before him and began moving tree to bush, bush to tree.

Certain if he could stretch his lead of fifty paces to one hundred before raising the hue and cry to rouse his men, there would be space and time aplenty for Aiken and him to defend the inn's occupants before the enemy abandoned stealth, Maël began reciting lessons.

Evade moonlight, Chevalier!

Sixty paces.

Use your enemy's advance to mask the sounds of your own.

Seventy paces.

Hunker low and move slow outside of shadow.

Eighty paces.

And that was all. Whether Maël or Aiken came to the enemy's notice or impatience won out, the Danes lunged.

As did Maël. "To arms, king's men!" he bellowed ahead of the Danes' war cries.

When his eighty pace lead was reduced to sixty, the inn's door banged opened and his men sprang outside with swords in hand.

Since they were not fully up out of slumber and needed time to don the warriors, Maël swung around. But the one who was to join him as the front line of defense was nowhere to be seen. Though possible a Dane had taken Aiken to ground without a cry of protest, it was unlikely.

Marking his first opponent as the bearded, blond-haired warrior at the fore, Maël reached his legs longer.

Forty paces.

Twenty paces.

He arced his sword up. Steel crashed on steel, spinning both warriors to the sides—of little concern for Maël's opponent who had sufficient time to recover before the king's men joined their leader, of great concern for Maël now in the path of another whose sword rose to deliver a blow.

He shouted as taught him to release tension and allow blood to course fast and hot, then twisted, and with his blade turned aside the Dane's.

As his new opponent stumbled back, Maël recognized the youthful face. Here the misbegotten Bjorn who had attended his sire's negotiations with William's representatives last autumn, the one who thought to take a D'Argent bride.

"Sir Maël!" he exclaimed almost jovially, while his leader shouted for his men to attack those running from the inn, then leapt and brought his sword down where Maël stood a moment before.

"Hold, Canute!" Bjorn cried. "Here Le Bâtard's captain of the guard—a D'Argent of silvered hair."

Having recovered his balance and pivoted toward Maël,

Canute snarled, "An ugly D'Argent and soon dead! Leave this one to me, Bjorn. Get her!"

As thought, they came for the woman Maël was further convinced was the same he had aided at Westminster. Regardless whether she was truly an abbess, she was of import to this Dane. Thus, Nicola was the one taken for interfering with the abduction.

Accursed, deceitful Saxon! he silently rebuked. *Accursed, unworthy D'Argent!*

Swords ringing out behind and to the sides as Normans engaged Danes, Maël beat back their leader with the ferocity required in battle when facing numerous opponents. But Canute was formidable, so much he could be the celebrated second in line to King Sweyn's throne.

Whoever you are, Mary Sarah, Maël seethed, *you have much to answer for. Fight me, but I shall see what is in your purse.*

A shout of pain to the right evidencing were it not first blood drawn it was of such quantity the injured might not rise again, Maël took a chance on his next stroke, momentarily exposing the side of his neck to land a blow to Canute's lower thigh.

The Dane roared and lurched away from the bloodied blade. Cursing Maël in the name of pagan gods of old, he continued backward to gain space in which to recover.

Maël followed, hopeful the leader's capture would end the encounter and the man could be traded for Nicola. A glance at the other battling Normans and Danes confirming the injured warrior on the ground was not one of his own, Maël ran at Canute.

"Halt!" the Dane bellowed. "I have Nicola D'Argent!"

Maël faltered and ceased his advance.

Stance defensive, Canute said, "You want your little cousin? Bjorn will not like it, but I shall pay that price for the *abbess* so no lives are lost."

His emphasis on Mary Sarah's title suggesting he believed she deceived not only the Normans but God, Maël's anger surged as much against her as his sire's gullible son.

Canute nodded. "Good trade for all, Sir Maël."

Much like the trade two years past when Maël was forced to yield Cyr's wife to Saxon rebels in order to save the life of Guarin who had been nearly beaten to death. Though as captain of the king's guard he was responsible for those under his command and some lives had been lost these past years, they were warriors and, as he did all he could to ensure their safety, it did not feel as if he played God with their lives. But this did, causing bile to stir, as when he had traded Aelfled for Guarin.

This is different, he told himself. *Though surely Nicola is yet hale, I have only to trade a deceitful Saxon to preserve the lives of my men and ensure my cousin is not borne across the sea.*

No matter Mary Sarah's value to the Danes, it *was* a good trade, and all the better since Maël knew the enemy's destination. Once Nicola was en route to Wulfenshire, he would continue his pursuit and, between here and the Humber, reclaim the *abbess.* Whatever her tale, he did not believe she wished to go with the Danes. Too, he had told Lady Hawisa he would recover her.

Keeping his sword before him, Maël said in Anglo-Saxon which all his men knew well enough to understand, "Agreed. Command your men to stand down, and I shall do the same."

Placing greater weight on his uninjured leg, Canute said, "Danes, fall back!"

Maël gave the same order, and soon enemy eyed enemy. Noting all his men were accounted for except Aiken who either remained among the trees or had fallen, Maël called, "Show me Lady Nicola."

"Nay, this time you first, Chevalier. Show me—"

"Canute! What do you?" Bjorn cried. Standing before an

opponent whose sleeve was bloodied, he was the Dane nearest the inn.

"We make trade," Canute said. "A better wife we shall find you, Cousin."

Though obvious Bjorn wished to argue, he set his teeth.

"He is young and foolish," Canute said. "Easily drops in and out of love. Now let me see the abbess."

"Sir Anselm, bring Abbess Mary Sarah to the door!" Maël ordered.

The chevalier stepped back from a Dane as bloodied as he and entered the inn. Though the woman might not wish to go with the Danes, when she appeared, she did not look frightened nor wary though she must have heard of the trade.

Guessing for this she had insisted on remaining with the king's men—to gain Nicola's freedom—Maël said, "Now my cousin."

Canute whistled.

Shortly, six riders appeared on the dirt road, trailed by the horses of those who had failed to steal upon the inn. By moonlight, Maël saw a gagged Nicola rode center, the Dane directly to her left of good age, the one to her right not a Dane at all.

Exceedingly tall and broad, of long red hair and darker beard, Vitalis aided in escorting Nicola forward.

What is this? Maël silently demanded. *And which direction does Vitalis turn? Toward Lady Hawisa whom he told he would aid in recovering her sister-in-law? Or once more toward the resistance who joined with Danes to take the city of York?*

"The one you hunt like a dog for defending his country surprises, eh?" Canute said.

Maël narrowed his gaze on the Dane with whom he shared as many years. "Your alliance with Saxon rebels was dissolved last year after my king paid for your warriors to return home."

"So I am told, but as King Sweyn's brother did not have the

authority to bargain, that silver is lost to England. But fear not, Vitalis does not want to fight. He but seeks the protection of his Danish allies, and he is only one man." His eyebrows jerked. "Nay, *two*. I ought not forgot the promise made him I would spend Lady Nicola on both the abbess and the rebel you captured. What is his name?"

Then Vitalis *had* turned from his lady?

"Zed..." Canute grimaced. "You know of whom I speak."

Maël looked again to the riders drawing near and curled his hands into fists when he saw how tightly gagged his cousin, the cloth cutting into the flesh beneath her cheeks. It had to hurt, though surely it had been necessary to keep her from shouting a warning. "Bring out Zedekiah, Sir Anselm!"

"Aye, that is his name," Canute said. "Hard one. Of the Bible, eh?"

Ignoring him, Maël ordered a young chevalier to collect the rebel's horse from the stable.

"Sir Maël!" Daryl called. "Surely you do not waste your trade of the abbess on your cousin when it is the murderous traitor we came for?"

Amid murmured agreement from those least trusted, Maël thought well on his response, but before he could deliver it, Vitalis said, "Murderous traitor, *whelp?* Methinks you mistake me for you and your sire."

"England is William's now," Daryl snarled, anger further deforming a face bruised and swollen on the day past. "You are the traitor."

Vitalis chuckled. "Five years gone, and still I see the sly boy deemed unworthy of defending his country. For lies and thievery, I sent you home. And there you should have remained beneath your sire's skirts."

Maël would not have thought it possible to be amused in that moment, but he was. Often Aiken boasted of his son's training at Wulfen Castle, telling it ended because of the conquering. A lie, the youth cast out before Hastings. Were Aiken alive, he struggled to keep himself hidden.

"You are dead, Vitalis!" Daryl's face was so dark it appeared he suffered apoplexy. "And you, Sir Maël, betray William in making this trade when we are here for Vitalis."

Maël raised his eyebrows. "Though sacrificing a woman to work vengeance may be the way of barbarous Saxons, it is not the way of Normans. In such circumstances, first the king would deliver a lady from danger."

Not all exaggeration. Before rebellion after rebellion kicked William over the edge of patience and the humiliation dealt him in the cave gave those tar-black wings more lift, he would not have yielded Nicola to gain Vitalis. Confident the next time he and his adversary met, he would take that man's hands and feet —perhaps his head—the trade would have been made quickly to draw nearer their next encounter.

"I do not believe that," Daryl said. "What I know is you place your family ahead of your king."

Maël felt his anger rise further, but he kept control as had been more difficult in his youth. "Close your mouth, Saxon who will never be a Norman even do you sacrifice your children as your sire sacrificed your mother's family, else I shall close it for you."

Daryl swept up his sword. "Where is my sire? Did you slay him? Is that why you chose him to patrol the wood with you?"

"If the one who should have stood my side has fallen, it was to a Dane. Does he yet live, cowardice put him to flight."

"Ah!" Canute crowed. *"That* is who I saw. Boy, I am grateful your sire lacked stealth and courage, but worry not, he is somewhere out there." He jutted his chin, then sighed. "This is entertaining, but too long my journey is delayed. Come, Abbess. Come, Zedekiah."

Acknowledging he would have to watch his back closer around Aiken and Daryl, Maël nodded at the place halfway between road and inn. "There I will deliver them, and you shall deliver Lady Nicola."

Canute patted his bloodied chausses. "I am injured," he said, then called, "Vitalis, bring the lady to the middle ground. Warriors mine, this side."

The Danes backed away, including the most seriously wounded who made it to his feet. Once they were past Maël and spreading out on either side of Canute, Maël motioned for his Normans to do the same, then crossed to the inn where Mary Sarah and the rebel stood, Sir Anselm behind them. "It seems the man you no longer follow still has need of you, Zedekiah."

"I am all surprise, Sir Maël." He raised his bound hands.

Maël sliced the D'Argent dagger up between his wrists, then nodded at the young chevalier who led the rebel's mount forward. "The middle ground," he directed Zedekiah as the stocky man took the reins and moved toward Vitalis who alone guided Nicola's mount forward.

Maël looked to the woman he would never again think an abbess even had she taken vows. Finding her eyes lowered, he considered mussed braids she had named her vanity, then a figure shapely despite loose laces.

"I sought to warn you," she whispered.

"Is that your apology for endangering my men? The only defense available to a deceitful Saxon?"

Her eyes met his. "Because of who you are, what you are, and to whom you answer, I could tell no more were I to keep my word to Nicola. As now you must realize, she is not the one for whom Canute stole inside Lillefarne."

"Indeed. So of what import are you to the Danes?"

She hesitated, and when her gaze shifted to the ruin made of one side of his face, he resented the heat rising up his neck. "Though Nicola gave her word she would hold close my secret, Sir Maël, methinks she will tell if you reveal knowledge of the name by which longest I am known."

"As you are known by the old woman at Westminster?"

Her lashes fluttered. "I feared you drew near that truth."

"Truth not only hidden behind veil and habit but spoken and unspoken lies."

She swallowed. "Just as you serve a man you do not wish to serve, I serve a family out of obligation and…" She shook her head. "Obligation only."

More deception, but Maël said, "Which family?"

"That Nicola also knows, and it is best you not at this time."

Might she be of Godwine, a daughter of the fallen King Harold? Non, those young women were accounted for, as were the sisters of Edgar the Aetheling, a young man who had more right to the throne than had Harold and had once more fled toward Scotland when his alliance with the Danes failed. It must be another prominent Saxon family to whom she was obligated, but of those not yet divested of all, did any possess power enough to threaten the king?

"Your real name?" he asked.

Her tongue clicked off a dry palate. "Mercia of Mercia."

"Your sire's name?" he pressed again.

Smile sorrowful, she whispered, "Unknown to me, the same as that of my mother."

"Baseborn, then."

"I am." It was said with what he might have believed pride if not for brighter eyes and flared nostrils.

"And yet of great value, it seems," he said.

"I question that, but I am assured all will be explained."

Once more, he considered her head to toe. "You do not belong in a habit, do you, Mercia of Mercia?"

Her cheeks spotted. Though he preferred to believe it the heat of anger or hatred, this seemed shame. And it should be. "As you see me now, gowned and unveiled, is as ever I should have been."

The only surprise was she owned to it. "If the Church learns the truth of you, your punishment could be grave."

"Certes, and more so now England's houses of God are under the fist of Bishop Odo."

It was true. William's brother was a man more ungodly than godly, making his power painfully felt amongst the Saxon clergy —and beyond. "I wager you are more guilty of aiding rebels than Aelfled was," Maël submitted.

Amid her hesitation, Canute called, "You keep me waiting!"

Maël looked around. "I but assure the abbess her charges will not be long without a *godly* woman's guidance."

He snorted. "You lie. Let us finish this."

Maël looked back at Mercia. "Did we not meet again, I would count it a blessing. Unfortunately, as I am not done with Vitalis, I am not done with those who aid him."

She stepped near and with urgency said, "As told, Nicola has the piece of William's mantle—"

"We keep Canute waiting." Maël took her arm and led her forward.

As they advanced on the middle ground, he met his cousin's wide-eyed gaze above the gag. Anger bounded from her, but also pleading. Knowing her well enough to translate that last into concern for the false abbess, he shifted his attention to Vitalis.

There was nothing smug nor triumphant about him. What he exuded was the confidence of a man accustomed to prevailing against his opponents.

"I thank you as I could not earlier," Mercia said low.

"For?" Maël rasped.

"What you did for my grandmother and me at Westminster. It was a great risk to use that passage, but she would not be dissuaded. She wished to see it for herself."

"Your enemy's coronation."

She jerked her chin. "A painful day for my people, one of many come before, after, and yet to come."

Though not of a mood to reassure her, he said, "God willing, once the last of the rebellion is stamped out, England will heal."

Her eyes widened. "Heal? If this island kingdom is now and forever your king's, England is dead to Saxons. As you must know, what is dead cannot heal. It rots, falls to pieces, becomes dust under the boots of those who slew it."

Her ache was so genuine, he felt what was cold within him warm further. Thus, he was glad their exchange ended when he halted alongside Zedekiah where the rebel stood ten feet distant from Vitalis and Nicola and several times that from Canute.

The red-headed warrior who met Maël's gaze was formidable as ever, but there was a cast about his face evidencing he was not entirely healed from what had caused him to linger at Lillefarne.

"I have watched for you, Maël D'Argent," he said loud.

"I have watched for you, Vitalis!"

"Alas, for naught. Though you and yours steal my country, never will you know it as we do—its hills, plains, marshes, rivers, mountains, and forget not caves which are particularly useful under the right conditions. Thus, a wise king would learn them as best he could else avoid them altogether."

Maël inclined his head. "You may be right."

"I am, and I believe Le Bâtard would agree."

"Enough!" Canute snapped. "Fight by blade not tongue, else be done."

As Maël led Mercia forward and Zedekiah followed, he expected Vitalis to smack the rump of Nicola's mount, but the Saxon urged both horses ahead. When the parties neared, he raised the reins, indicating he would pass them to Maël.

Unnecessary, as if he but wished to draw nearer. For what? If not that his sword remained sheathed, Maël might think he meant to work ill on the one tasked with delivering him to William. Still, Maël kept his own sword at the ready.

"Go, Mercia." He released her. "Go, Zedekiah." As the two

moved past, he held his gaze to Vitalis. When the rebel leader halted both mounts and extended the reins, Maël adjusted his grip on his sword and stepped forward.

"That is Bjorn's horse," Canute called as Maël accepted the reins. "See it returned to him."

Nicola growled against her gag and, eyes bulging, jerked at wrists bound to the saddle.

"I would wait on loosing your little cousin," Vitalis said low, causing her to whip her head around and struggle to work her tongue past the bulky cloth dampened by saliva. "Though the vixen is safe now, we must needs keep her so."

Maël needed no one to tell him it was best to remove her from the immediate area. The trade was made, but still armed enemy faced armed enemy, neither of which had all they wanted—Bjorn desiring Nicola, the king's men desiring Vitalis.

"Sir Anselm!" Maël called and, when the chevalier came alongside, passed the reins to him. "Once you are well distanced, aid in my cousin's dismount and send the horse back. But leave the gag."

Nicola's scream of frustration would be piercing were her mouth not stuffed.

As the chevalier led her away, Canute called, "She is trouble, your cousin, more than this one."

Maël looked past Zedekiah who had mounted his horse and accepted the sword Vitalis passed to him. The abbess—rather, Mercia—appeared to hold her breath where she stood alongside Canute. And when the Dane pulled her against his side and kissed her hard atop the head, Maël was tempted to once more engage him at swords.

"Ill timing," Vitalis murmured, and Maël resented him for thinking this Norman was rashly moved to aid that Saxon. "Do you have a care for her, Sir Maël, be assured—"

"You wily like your grandmother, my love," Canute laid claim to one who was baseborn the same as he. But there was more to those words. Though it had seemed unlikely Mercia was of those born of Godwine, the pieces came together when Maël recalled the old woman at Westminster. She had been imperious, callous toward the younger woman, and of an age to be the mother of King Harold and all his brothers now buried.

It had to have been the rebellious Gytha, and as Mercia's illegitimacy made her of little account to such a family, it made sense she was unknown to most. However, were she acknowledged for her Godwine blood, she could be of use to King Sweyn should he seek England's throne in earnest. Wed to Canute, it was possible the beaten Saxons would rally again, adding their strength to the Danes.

"But I shall be patient in teaching respect," Canute continued, causing his men to laugh, though not Bjorn whose gaze was fixed past Maël on the woman denied him.

"Ill timing, Chevalier," Vitalis rumbled again, and Maël felt his hand on his hilt. "And all the more ill for the dissension in your ranks. Not only that of Daryl, but his sire who surely watches. He longs to take me, likely as much for ending his son's training at Wulfen as to win your king's favor. Had he bow and arrow, he might put a shaft through my chain mail, perhaps even set a *stray* arrow upon you."

Maël narrowed his lids. "You make it sound we are allies. We are not."

"Not yesterday nor all the days before, but this day and perhaps the morrow."

Before Maël could look close on that, Canute called, "Make haste, Vitalis! We ride!"

Maël nearly smiled. The Dane believed they continued to posture, trading insults and threats. Was it as Vitalis wished? For this had he taunted Maël and drawn nearer? "What do you propose?" Maël asked.

"The son of King Sweyn believes this hunted man, bereft of country, wishes to make Denmark his home," he confirmed

Canute's identity. "It was a consideration but methinks not possible after this day." He opened his mouth to say more, scowled. "Pray, Sir Maël, buy me another minute by cursing and threatening me."

It was not in Maël's nature to spew emotion he did not feel, nor was he comfortable acting a part as Mercia of Mercia had done at Lillefarne. However, he raised his voice as well as his sword. "Coward! I shall deliver your head to King William!"

Vitalis laughed. "You will try, king's man. You will fail." Then as if to further the insult, once more he leaned forward. "Since I but joined the Danes on the day past after Bjorn vouched for me, I am not trusted enough to be privy to their plans. However, as Sweyn's son has come, methinks the father will follow with an army to add to the earl's that is anchored in the Humber. As must be obvious, there is an advantage to Prince Canute taking to wife the abbess who I begin to think no abbess at all. Thus, at the first opportunity, Zedekiah and I will gain her release and return her to Wulfenshire."

Before Maël could respond, movement behind and to the sides drew his regard to the impatient Canute who signaled his men to withdraw. Keeping watch on the Normans, all but Bjorn moved toward the horses and Danes farther down the road.

Maël looked to Vitalis. "Surely you do not think I will stand aside, not only allowing the one I hunt to escape but yielding a woman who can further Sweyn's ambitions?"

"You will have to trust me in this, Sir Maël. You have your cousin back, do you not?" Vitalis looked toward the inn, and the smile hitching his mouth made Maël glance around.

Nicola should be out of the saddle to allow the horse to be sent back, but she remained astride—and angrier as evidenced by high color as she glared at Sir Anselm who raised a hand as if to calm her.

"Out of hearing of Bjorn," Vitalis continued, "I persuaded Canute to trade her for Mary Sarah should stealth fail to catch the king's men unawares—saving lives both sides. If that advice has earned me some trust, it will be easier to take Mary Sarah from Canute, especially now I have Zedekiah at my side."

Maël had no intention of waiting for him to prove himself something of an ally, but before he could reject the proposal, the one lurking in the wood determined withdrawal of the Danes made it safe to wreak vengeance and better his lot.

"Vitalis!" Aiken cried and ran forward with sword aloft.

Canute might have left the rebel leader to his fate had not three of Maël's men, including Daryl, surged forward as if to pursue the Danes. And then there was Bjorn who wavered between retreat and reclaiming the horse yet to be returned to him—likely, more the lady astride. The nephew of King Sweyn would not be left behind.

Except for Canute who dragged Mercia toward the horses, the Danes on foot turned back. With resounding shouts, they ran forward, causing the Normans yet answerable to their commander to meet aggression with aggression.

Reaching Aiken ahead of Vitalis and Zedekiah, Maël beat back the sword meant to slay the one who had humiliated King William. "Ride, Vitalis!" he shouted, hopeful if he fled and Bjorn was quickly recovered, the Danes would fully withdraw with no lives lost. But now Daryl and the two other faithless Normans swung blades at the mounted rebels who drove them back with sword stroke after sword stroke.

Continuing to fight off Aiken who was strong and fast despite little finesse, Maël snarled, "Cease, else greater your king's wrath."

For answer, the Saxon arced his sword up, forcing Maël back to keep the blade from his unarmored belly. Retaliation tightening the muscles of his sword arm, he started his swing— and faltered upon glimpsing a horse speeding past.

The mistake made in taking his eyes off his opponent to assure himself it was not Nicola sharing the saddle with a Dane nearly cost Maël his life, that glance behind at where his cousin no longer was and Sir Anselm now lay on the ground displacing the air beneath his jaw.

Giving over to anger at Aiken's betrayal that had lost Nicola, Maël lurched back to gain space in which to land his next blow. Whether or not it would have been enough he would never know.

Spurring his horse forward, Vitalis leaned hard to the side, swung his sword, and landed its edge to Aiken's back, ensuring the one who sought his death did not complete his next swing.

The traitorous Saxon shouted as the rebel leader continued past, then toppled. Unarmored the same as Maël, the slice to his back would be the end of him.

His son who had borne witness where he and his one remaining ally danced around Zedekiah's horse, tried to run to his sire, but the big rebel used the distraction to land a blow to Daryl's arm that sent him stumbling back and dropped him.

"This changes all!" Vitalis shouted as he brought his horse around.

Maël adjusted his stance lest his prey sought to do to him what he had done to Aiken. "Bjorn has my cousin," he said. "I will not wait on you."

Vitalis inclined his head. "As told, all changes." Then neither trusting Maël, he spurred wide around him, and with Zedekiah following, rode after Bjorn and Nicola who had gone through the wood rather than by way of the road. And there the Danes' cue to end the contest. Leaving behind two fallen countrymen, they ran.

"Regroup!" Maël commanded, and his men pursuing the enemy turned back, which was best for those whose opponents would soon be astride the same as Maël.

"See to the injured!" he called and ordered two men as loyal to him as Anselm had been—and would be again did he survive—to collect their saddlebags.

CHAPTER FOURTEEN

*A*s with each time she dwelt on all that transpired since being forced from the abbey, Mercia feared she would be sick, so disgusted was she by a return to helplessness mostly unknown to the Abbess of Lillefarne.

Here again the impotence of her childhood, youth, and attainment of womanhood. Ever dependent on the kindness of Gytha, she had feared failing the only kin to acknowledge her. Thus, upon gaining control of her life beyond answering her grandmother's missives and meeting as many of the old woman's demands as possible, she had known a measure of happiness and fulfillment that made abbey life tolerable.

Now she did not have even that, and worse in this moment. After tossing her onto the horse of the older Dane, Canute had lingered near the inn to see how many of his men survived the return to arms. While Sir Maël fought the traitorous Saxon, Bjorn had taken back what was taken from him. The trade having gone awry, once more the Danes had both women. Thus, if not that Mercia would soon learn who sired her, the sacrifice of her freedom would be for naught.

Upon departing the inn, again Canute had divided his men

into two contingents to lead pursuers astray, but Bjorn had not been amongst either. Doubtless, distrust of his cousin caused him to go his own way. Upon reaching the Humber, likely he would beseech the earl to grant him his desire, and since Nicola had feigned feelings for Bjorn, it was hard to begrudge him for reclaiming her.

Had she now disabused him of those feelings? If so, what would he do? Continue to the estuary in the hope of persuading her otherwise? Or might she embrace the adventure a bit longer? Possible, especially as Mercia was once more in Canute's hands. Or nearly so.

She opened eyes she had closed lest once more she fall to weeping over the harrying that worsened the nearer they drew to the Humber—burned villages and fields, scorched woodland offering little refuge for rebels and innocents, carcasses and the bones of animals who would have sustained their owners through winter into spring and, increasingly, more bodies of those unable to outrun the terror, among them children.

Though Mercia fixed her gaze on Ingvar who carried her sideways before him at a more sedate pace than earlier, she shuddered over imaginings of what she would see if she peered past him.

"Canute's woman cold?" he asked

"Nay."

He grunted. "Keep eyes closed. It bad and get worse."

Though she wanted to do as told, she scooted up in the saddle, set her teeth, and looked to the Dane ahead, the one to the left, then past them.

"Lord," she breathed. She had heard the Danish army that remained throughout the winter had suffered much, losing many to the scarcity of food and illnesses that preyed on malnourished men. Regardless of the weather and their king's orders, those from across the sea should have returned home, if not in winter then at spring's onset. Would they still be here come summer? Likely, since King Sweyn's plans were set in motion.

"Worry not, we kill Le Bâtard," Ingvar said. "Then King Sweyn make all right."

If she could believe that, unreservedly she would give herself to Canute, but she recalled Gytha raging over the belief held by her son, Tostig, that his enemy's enemy was a friend. For that and betrayal of his brother, Harold, Tostig had died before the great battle in a clash of his own making.

"Of course Sweyn will set all aright," she said what was expected of her.

The man of slightly bowed back and silvered brown hair sighed. "That the hope. Mayhap God have other plan."

As so often He has these past years, Mercia thought, then said, "You believe we will reach the Humber ere dark?"

"I do, mayhap ahead of Canute if Normans gave chase and follow his or Bjorn's trail."

Mercia did not doubt Sir Maël pursued them. Even had Nicola not been recaptured, still he would come, not only for Vitalis but her now it was known she was of value to men who sought to place their king on England's throne.

Settling against the Dane, once more she retreated behind her lids and prayed, *Lord, let it be Nicola and Bjorn whom Sir Maël overtakes, and let it be enough for him to return his cousin to Wulfenshire. No more blood shed over this misbegotten Godwine who ought not care who sired her. But does...*

THOUGH HOURS HAD PASSED since finally he spied three horses carrying four riders, still there was no opportunity to isolate the Dane with whom Mercia shared a saddle.

Had not Maël sent one of his two men a different direction when it became obvious the Danes split again, he would have made his presence felt, but even with the older Dane disadvantaged by sharing a saddle, Canute had chosen her escort well. The other two were young and of good build.

If necessary, Maël and the man who followed at a distance to watch his leader's back would challenge all before they drew near enough the Humber to meet up with other Danes.

A half hour later, Mercia's escort sought a stream to refresh the horses, drawing him nearer to retrieving her. Or so he believed.

"We are done with this game, Sir Maël!"

Maël's hand went to his sword hilt, but he left it there. This was not what he would call a game since the chevalier who watched his commander's back had not watched his own and likely lay dead or dying. Regardless, it was a game to the Dane behind—and played well against one who, unlike Dougray, did not excel at stealth, and unlike Theriot, did not possess senses beyond the natural to sooner alert the predator he was in danger of becoming prey.

Certain were it not an arrow trained on him, a dagger was ready to fly, Maël kept his gaze on the others who drew swords as they swung their mounts around. As the Norman in their midst was well enough concealed only movement would reveal him, they looked past him to Canute with what seemed surprise as though unaware he had followed—as did Mercia whose eyes searched the trees and bushes that provided Maël cover.

Heed the pit of you, he heard his sire again. *Heed it, pretty boy, else die the least of the D'Argents.*

Ashamedly, there had been nothing to heed beyond the voice urging him to exercise caution to avoid alerting the Danes he followed. Hugh was long dead, but it felt as if he stood near, questioning how faithful the wife who bore a son whose face reflected more her beauty than the ruggedness of his own.

"Go forth, Sir Maël," Canute ordered. "Let my men see how greatly they disappoint me."

Maël peered over his shoulder. The leader of these Danes was distant, but not so much he could not land the dagger held at an angle so it flashed sunlight amid what could be the blood of the Norman who first failed himself, next the king's man.

Just as when Maël patrolled the area around the inn, this day he had eschewed his hauberk, leaving it in his saddlebag to muffle iron links that might betray him the same as the chain mail of those he pursued. Unaware of being followed by Canute who also denied himself armor, better Maël had donned his hauberk and moved more cautiously.

The leader of the Danes waved his dagger. "Go."

Removing his hand from the hilt, Maël urged his mount into the open. Behind, he heard the advance of Canute who no longer moved stealthily but was wise enough to command forward the younger Danes.

Fight them! Hugh commanded from the grave.

Watch for an opening, Godfroi countered, and Maël recalled his uncle sitting at the high table, offering advice and encouragement. *When you see it, think on the odds. Life is too precious and easily severed for every threat to be answered with a blade.*

It was true, but great this threat with the blood of his man on Canute's blade and that Dane closing in behind and his men ahead.

Though the warrior of Maël urged him to draw his sword, he left it sheathed, knowing more than facing three opponents, the odds were against him for his lack of armor.

When Canute came alongside and his men reined in fifteen feet distant, Maël glanced at the bloodied bandage around the Dane's thigh, an injury that would slow him, then looked nearer on the dagger.

"Aye, your man is dead," Canute said. "Unlike you, I gave him no chance to give answer."

"You put it in his back," Maël scorned.

"Regrettably, easier and faster, but the end is the same—one less Norman." Smiling, shaking his head as if amused, momentarily he closed his eyes.

The odds having shifted, Maël gripped the hilt of the D'Argent dagger that more quickly cleared its scabbard than would his sword, launched himself sideways, and slammed his forearm against Canute's that wielded his own dagger.

The man yelped as the force of his attacker's body carried both over the side of the horse. Between saddle and ground, Maël twisted to ensure it was Canute who landed on his back— he who lost his breath.

The young Danes' hesitation gave Maël time not only to drag Canute onto his knees, but moments in which to relieve the enemy of his dagger, haul him to standing, and press the D'Argent blade against his neck.

As Canute's men jerked on the reins lest further advance see their leader's throat opened, Maël leaned in. "I also weary of this game, *Dane.*"

King Sweyn's son coughed, sucked air. "Should have put a blade in *your* back."

"And proven more a coward," Maël said, then walked him back several steps and looked from the nearest Danes to the one whose arm was around the woman who stared wide-eyed. "Here we are again, and this time a trade on my terms!" he called. "King Sweyn's son for Lady Nicola and Mercia of Mercia."

The Danes exchanged glances.

Maël shifted his blade higher and pricked the underside of Canute's jaw. "Tell them to arrange it, *Prince.*"

"Bjorn has your cousin, not I," Canute growled. "And Mercia... What kind of man would I be to yield the woman I love?"

Mockery, his only care for her being how she benefitted his sire and him.

"Alas, my dear," Canute called, "we are of no use to anyone without the other. Thus, we shall be together in death. Ingvar, cut her throat the moment Sir Maël cuts mine—and do the same to Lady Nicola when next you see her."

Though the young Danes grinned as if certain their leader had won, the older one remained unmoving.

"Your dagger, Ingvar!" Canute ordered.

With what seemed reluctance, the man unsheathed his blade and set it against Mercia's pale neck.

"Count of three," Canute ordered.

"You will not kill her," Maël said.

"As told, she is of no use without me." He chuckled. "But I have heard of the D'Argents. You will not let her die."

In that moment, Maël wished his family did not boast so honorable a reputation. Though not entirely convinced Canute would order her death, he balked against testing the man.

"So, Sir Maël, you let me live, I let her live. And you go back to William to fight another day."

Maël did not believe it was as simple as that.

Canute sighed. "Very well. Ingvar, here the count of one!"

"I will bleed you," Maël warned.

"He will do the same to her." Once more, King Sweyn's son raised his voice, "Ingvar, here the count of two!"

Maël shot his gaze to Mercia and saw she had closed her eyes.

"Now, Ingvar, here the—"

Maël swept his dagger aside, shoved Canute forward, and reached for his sword. But before it cleared its scabbard, one of the mounted Danes set a blade at his throat, the other at his chest.

"I change my mind, Sir Maël." Limping between his men's horses, fresh blood blooming through the bandage binding his thigh, Canute drew fingers across his neck and considered the crimson. "Do I let you go, it will make me look soft. And so death takes you this day."

"Nay, Canute!" Mercia cried. "You are not so dishonorable."

He looked around. "Hard things must be done to save England. Trust me, my love, this is for the best."

"If you kill him, I will not wed you!"

"Aye, you will—for England, your grandmother, and what you want told."

She shook her head. "Only if you release him as you said you would."

"I cannot." He stepped to the side and retrieved the dagger lost during his shameful dismount.

"But he is of value! As a D'Argent and captain of the king's guard, you can ransom or trade him for captive Danes."

Maël did not believe Canute would agree, but the man went still, then smiled. "You are of good wit, my love." His eyebrows pinched. "Or is it you like this Norman more than your betrothed?"

"What I am is sick of death! Do you slay him, then command Ingvar to do the same to me since *I* will be of no use to your sire."

He considered Maël, nodded at his men. "Take his weapons and bind him. We keep him alive. For now."

Maël did not resist, and once relieved of all blades and bound, Canute drew near and delivered a fist to the left eye. Maël heard Mercia cry out as pain and light flared through his skull, and again she protested when Canute struck his captive's nose, but Maël remained upright.

Blood running onto his lips and tongue, he brought the prince into focus. Though Canute was ready to strike a third blow, he lowered his fist, swept his gaze from the right side of his captive's face to the left, and said, "I like balance. Soon you will be ugly both sides and my Mercia will not like you so much."

Even were it true she had a care for this Norman whose sentence of death she had delayed, these were mere bruises and swellings. They would heal, unlike scars that served as reminders of his great betrayal.

The rope so tightly cutting into Maël's flesh it impeded blood flow, he raised his bound wrists. "So courageous, King Sweyn's son who attacks from behind with the throw of a blade and faces opponents only when they are bound by his men."

Dismay skittered across Canute's face. He was a warrior, his training likely worthy of esteem, but the same as Maël had done at Hastings, he behaved badly, thus of no credit to his sire.

"Get the chevalier astride," he commanded.

Shortly, the four riders that had become six resumed their northeastern journey, Mercia and Ingvar riding behind Canute, Maël and the two Danes bringing up the rear.

Hours later, with the sun moving toward its rest as they neared the estuary, the scent and salt of the ocean thickening, the Danish contingents became one again—as feared, absent Bjorn and Nicola.

~

The Humber
Northern England

MERCIA PACED, reminiscent of her grandmother though many had been Gytha's strides in rooms sizable enough to accommodate her angst and well populated with servants upon whom she could unleash anger for the slightest offense.

In the small cabin of the earl's great ship, its occupant had only enough space to stretch her legs three times side to side across the gently dipping floor, four times if she moved diagonally.

Somewhere in the hull beneath her feet was the one who had

yielded to Canute under threat to her life and lived because she, in turn, said she would not wed the Dane. Maël was safe, but would he remain so once she spoke vows with Canute? Was it enough the chevalier was of value to his family as well as the tyrant?

Groaning, she turned her thoughts to Nicola and Bjorn. She had expected to be met by one or both upon boarding the ship and being presented to the hard-faced earl. She was not alone in that expectation, Canute demanding to know his cousin's whereabouts.

The earl's disavowal of that knowledge had not seemed feigned, and concern for his missing son softened his face before his nephew told Bjorn must be found so the D'Argents' sister could be ransomed alongside her cousin. So what had become of the two, there surely no safer place for a Dane than where their forces anchored? Had they been overtaken by Maël's other men? Captured by patrolling Normans whose base was the city of York north of the Humber? Felled by Saxons who would deem a Norman lady and Danish warrior enemies?

"Lord," Mercia whispered, "let Vitalis be the one to gain on them. He will see Nicola restored to her family, perhaps even Bjorn returned to his."

The tap of boots brought her around.

Canute opened the door, ducked, and entered. The moment he set eyes on her, his brow lined. "Why did you not do as told? You cannot dine with my uncle and me looking a servant."

Though she had cleaned her face and hands and made simple braids of her hair, she had not exchanged the heavily soiled gown for another sent by Gytha. She had meant to but been uncomfortable with no means of barring the door against the Dane posted outside.

She ran hands down the gown that had replaced her habit days past, paused over the purse that held her grandmother's missive. "Methinks this suffices for now, especially as I am weary and prefer to eat my meal here."

His displeasure wavered then eased. "Remain and rest. On the morrow, don the clean gown so you not dishonor me."

"Dishonor?"

"The priest rows over late morn to wed us in daylight."

She caught her breath. "So soon?"

"My sire says we should begin making babies." When words eluded her, he continued, "As I make good on the bargain with Sir Maël's life, you will make good on yours."

Though there seemed no way to escape their union, she was not ready. Too, the longer she delayed, the longer the one given to changing the terms of an agreement—as Canute had done in refusing to free Maël—would keep his side of the bargain. But how was she to delay him?

"We will be husband and wife on the morrow," he reiterated.

"On the morrow." Though she nodded, hopefully between now and then she would devise a means of thwarting him. As he turned toward the door, she recalled their other bargain. "Who sired me, Canute? How is it I am not misbegotten?"

He looked around. "You will know soon."

"When?"

"Once we wed."

"Nay, I would know now."

"As told, my sire will reveal all when he comes."

"Then you yourself do not know the truth."

"I know it, else I would not wed you."

"Then tell."

"My sire says it best you learn from Gytha whose missive he carries across the sea."

"Then we shall wed when he arrives."

"Nay, the morrow."

"But—"

"The morrow, my love." He stepped outside, closed the door, and commanded her guard to keep close watch.

As his boots sounded a retreat, Mercia sank to the floor. Gripping her head in her hands, she whispered, "Lord, if Sweyn's coming does not give godly answer to my peoples' groans, deliver him not to these shores. Let me not be the cause of false hope—more suffering, more blood, more death." She drew a shuddering breath. "Even if never I know who I am."

CHAPTER FIFTEEN

his the Lord's answer? That she die?

Mercia fumbled the bucket onto its hook, then on hands and knees backed up to the wall where four days past she had spread her blankets beneath the hammock she eschewed despite assurances the ship's movement would be less felt. It was, and yet upon the floor she found more relief from the constant shift and bob. Though she could keep down very little liquid and food and sometimes slid across the floor, here she could toss and turn and that was the cost of her own movement as opposed to the slightest shift setting the hammock to swinging.

Then came the storm last eve whose wind and rain lashed at vessels anchored in the estuary. Lest she suffer injury from being slammed about the cabin, she had gone into the hammock and suffered its careening the night and morning through. Then an hour past, all calmed enough to allow her to once more set feet on the floor. God willing, the storm was nearly worn out so she would not have to return to the hammock.

Easing her rear onto her heels, stretching her arms out

before her, she pressed her forehead to the musty blankets thus far spared fouling by the contents of her belly.

"This your answer, Lord?" she whispered into the dusky dark that would be pitch black if not for a gap beneath the door that permitted light to crawl through.

By her second day aboard ship, she had thought herself miserable, so terrible had been the tossing of her belly, lightness of her head, and ache behind her eyes, but that was almost comfortable compared to this. If she did not keep more food and drink down, she would lose what remained of her strength. Of course, did she vastly improve, the priest who had visited several times would wed her to the man who came once a day to see for himself she was incapable of speaking vows.

Scornful of her reaction to what he called *a wee rocking,* ever Canute departed with the warning to be ready to keep their bargain as soon as the weather calmed, else the king's man would not be ransomed nor traded.

"Maël," she let fall from her lips the name of one who, unlike any before, set more value on her life than his own. Emotion tightening her throat, she slid a hand onto the floor whose rough boards pricked her palm. "Be here, be well," she rasped. "And forgive me, Maël. Pray, forgive me."

She eased onto her side and scooted back until her shoulders touched the wall. She knew she should drink from the wineskin, even if only to dissolve the bitterness on her tongue, knew she should nibble at the biscuit, even if only a few crumbs, but first rest whilst it could be had amid pattering rain and rocking that was now nearer swaying.

"Let the storm pass," she whispered. "Let it not be the death of me."

Be still, she heard as if in her ear. *Wait for me.*

That last opened her eyes. She thought she counseled herself, but no need to wait for someone who was present. Might that have been the Lord assuring her when she breathed her last He would be here to receive her regardless of deception worked as much on the Church as Normans? What of Maël? Would Canute put him to death?

Pushing to sitting with one hand, with the other she retrieved the wineskin, then pressed her back to the wall and tried again to force down what was needed to survive.

HAD she lost a day or did he come twice in one?

Awakened by the door's groan, Mercia narrowed her eyes against the light entering with the man who always deeply ducked though he could clear the lintel standing at full height. Were he taller than most men, it was not by much.

That thought surprised Mercia who had no cause for frivolous musings. And as her betrothed strode toward her with wrinkled nose and grim mouth expressing disgust over the scent of her sickness, she was struck by how settled her belly that had not rejected the biscuit eaten in its entirety nor watered wine that had made swallowing possible.

Canute dropped to his haunches and considered her where she sat beneath the hammock. "The storm moves inland, the wind now a breeze. You are better."

That last was a statement. Since she had been a bundle of misery during his previous visits, it was hard to argue the assumption. "Somewhat better, but still very weak."

"Then we wed on the morrow so it is done ere King Sweyn arrives."

She tried—and failed—to moisten her lips. "When will he come?"

"It could be days but no more than a sennight. Then you will know your truth."

Deciding argument against wedding on the morrow could save, she said, "A truth I am anxious to learn."

"But more anxious to make a good wife," he reminded. At her nod, he straightened.

"Canute?"

"My love?"

Her belly tossed, hopefully more over his mocking endearment than further sick of the sea. Though she knew she should not ask, she said, "How fares the king's man?"

He raised his eyebrows. "As Ingvar has not sent word otherwise, he must yet live."

Then the older Dane was his jailer—a good thing since he exuded neither hatred nor bloodlust. "Have you delivered a ransom demand to the D'Argents?"

"Nay."

"Le Bâtard?"

He shook his head. "I wait on Bjorn and Lady Nicola."

"Still they have not come?"

"Unless my uncle betrays again as he did in taking William's bribe, they are somewhere upon the land."

Did the earl hide his son and Nicola?

"I will send more food and drink," Canute said and departed.

Mercia set her head back against the wall. Regardless of how appealing the viands and improved her appetite, she would eat and drink only enough to begin restoring her health. Thus, she should be able to delay the wedding another day—perhaps two —without threat to Maël. Much could happen in that time, of greatest import the king's man and Nicola finding their release.

ONCE AGAIN, the silver-haired and bearded Ingvar set a shoulder against the iron bars, confident no harm would befall him as long as he did not keep on his person the key to Maël's cell. And he was right, it being of no benefit to the prisoner to reach through the bars and overpower his jailer.

"I hear Canute tell she better," Ingvar said as if delivering information for which he would see a coin flipped into his palm.

Feigning disinterest, Maël took another bite of dried fish that had only sustenance to recommend it and required much drink of poor quality to swallow it—both to be remedied upon King Sweyn's arrival with provisions, the older Dane assured him.

"Canute say he wed her on morrow, but I think not."

Maël took another bite, confident Ingvar would finish what roamed his mind as most times he did no matter how impregnable his prisoner's silence.

He heaved a sigh. "As told, she very ill—all this movement hard for one whose feet know only ground." He nodded. "It a few days ere they wed, then your duke go back to Normandy."

Another bite, another swallow.

When Ingvar did not retreat, Maël looked to the man who raised his eyebrows, indicating he required prompting for what he wished to divulge.

The light in the Dane's eyes indicating he knew something of value and required the payment of conversation, Maël said, "I am guessing you have tidings of my cousin."

He shifted against the bars. "Speculation more than rumor, but possible earl have Bjorn on another ship with Lady Nicola. Much he love that boy—give him anything, and since Bjorn want lady and lady want him..."

Maël suppressed the temptation to correct him. Though Ingvar said he had witnessed Nicola's affection for Bjorn and was certain she liked his kisses, Maël would wager she but bettered her chance of escape.

Ingvar nodded. "Methinks earl make it so Canute not interfere."

"Bjorn is fortunate to have a loving father, which few men

possess," Maël said and, hearing bitterness in his voice, once more raised the wineskin.

"It sound you not like your sire, Chevalier. He beat you?"

Maël took another swallow.

"My father beat me," Ingvar said, "but I lazy, so it deserved. It make me better warrior."

Another swallow.

"You not like sire?" Ingvar pressed. "Or just thirsty of a sudden."

That yanked Maël back to the warrior who had gripped his sword hilt, lifted his ruined face to the heavens, and vowed never again to use drink to numb anger nor sorrow.

Lowering the wineskin, he narrowed his eyes on the man several years older than Hugh would be had he survived the great battle. "Aye, my sire beat me the same as yours to make a better warrior, and much I deserved as well." He stoppered the wineskin and dropped it beside the pallet the Dane had provided for use when the waters were calm. "He was not affectionate, but I respected and defended him."

"Defended?" Ingvar made a face. "For what?"

Maël hesitated, said, "Lies spoken against him. Lies that were not all lies, I learned too late."

"What lies were not lies?"

Refusing to yield to memories of the night before Hastings, he said, "It matters not. What matters is the man I was four years past behaved a boy and for it others suffered."

More than I, and far more than I suffer now, he thought and looked down. By the light of a lantern suspended above the stout table beyond his cage, he examined his wrists. The rope binding them during the ride to the Humber had scraped the flesh, some places yet red, others scabbed, but they would heal enough that none would ask after unsightly scars other than those upon his face—unlike his cousin, Guarin, whose wrists bore permanent evidence of captivity by Saxon rebels.

"Your guilt heavy," Ingvar said.

Once more the Dane surprised as first done when he became Maël's jailer. The key to the cell given into his keeping, the others having departed, Ingvar had drawn near and assured the king's man he would not have cut Mercia's throat. Such days were well behind him, he had said—and much of the warrior. Now his value to his liege was mostly in the ghost he could make of himself among the enemy and the quick of his fingers among their treasures.

"Aye, Sir Maël." He nodded. "You need pray for forgiveness."

Was he a priest as well? Maël mused.

"Have you?" Ingvar asked.

Of course he had and continued to—and gained some relief. However, he had only to look upon the ones he had failed for his chest to become weighted again.

The Dane gave a grunt of frustration. "And you need ask for forgiveness from those wronged."

From his mother and cousins, but that would require he reveal the reason he needed grace.

"Next you accept forgiveness, Sir Maël, then air sweeter and brighter and you live again."

"You err in thinking to know me," he muttered.

"Possible, but you call to mind friend who die at York while taking city. He not fighting man, but wife angry over death of sons sent to resolve disagreement with his liege. At their graves, she tell him join earl and fight like a man else come to their bed no more. Now his bed English mud, and still his sons dead and wife made a beggar." He blew out breath. "Were there anything to forgive, better for all he content with God's forgiveness and his own and stay home."

Maël stared at the man it was impossible to dislike.

His jailer straightened. "You need anything, I get it for you, hmm?"

As ever he offered and delivered, which would displease

Canute were he to discover his captive was that only insomuch as he was unable to depart the ship. Far different from Guarin's captivity.

"As I am long without a bath," Maël said, "I would be glad for a basin of water and towel."

"This eve." Ingvar said and, eschewing his hammock, crossed to the table secured to the floor and dropped onto the bench fastened to the wall.

He was not long for sleep, and with naught to occupy his prisoner, neither should Maël have been. But though he stretched out on the pallet, over and again he heard the man's tale of his friend. And wondered how it would feel to forgive himself even if no others could.

CHAPTER SIXTEEN

*T*hree more days' reprieve, but this morn Canute had deemed her well enough to do a wife's duty and told she would pledge her life to him the next day.

With a long sigh, Mercia returned the breath drawn from the breeze, then propped her arms on the railing, leaned in, and settled her chin atop her hands.

The narrow sea beyond the estuary's mouth rippled with sunlight, no sign of further churning that would return her face to a bucket. Lowering her lids, she savored the warmth on the deck that was barely felt in her cabin and surely less felt in the hull.

For the hundredth time, she wondered how Maël fared. Through observation she had learned the location of the forward hatch that accessed the ship's bowels, but as someone was always set to watch her, there was no opportunity to steal down the ladder to verify the king's man was well.

Just because Canute said he must be did not make it so. Too, it was possible Maël had been moved to another ship—or none. In all these days, he might have been ransomed and was once more amongst his own. Else dead...

"Ships!" bellowed the man atop the mast.

As lookouts aboard other bobbing vessels sounded the alarm, Mercia straightened and swept her gaze over the sparkling sea.

Ships, indeed. Many ships.

Were they of Sweyn as seemed likely, Canute would be pleased the earl's nearly crippled fleet would soon be strengthened by hale, vigorous men, but also displeased at being unable to present Gytha's granddaughter as his wife.

"Much I have indulged you, Mercia," her betrothed said when he appeared at her side. "Now I shall look little in my sire's eyes. 'Tis an ill start to a marriage."

She raised her chin. "I would think him pleased to witness his son's momentous Godwine union."

His brow lowered further. "Fool woman! He is a king come to give war, not listen to a priest's ramblings." He motioned her guard forward. "Go to your cabin. Should the king wish to see you, I will summon you."

Swallowing a retort, she looked one last time to the sea and fearfully marveled at how quickly dozens of ships became scores.

When they were numbered, would there be enough to remove William from the throne? If so, would life be better for Saxons? The same?

Worse?

THE SOUND of boots were of more than one man.

After waiting all day to be summoned and now with the estuary dark beneath middle night, Mercia had eased into the hammock to which she was determined she would become accustomed.

Was this the long-awaited summoning? If so, why had

Canute sent more than one man for her? Or perhaps he did not. Though difficult to believe a king would come to her, those boots might belong to father and son.

When the door opened, she was out of the hammock, hands clasped at her waist.

Canute entered first, followed by an older man of similar face, height, and build, albeit loose around the jowls and thickening around the middle.

The introduction was brusque, then King Sweyn stepped near. "Mercia of Godwine blood and no stomach for the sea, regardless of your grandmother's spinning, you will not wed my son."

Torn between relief she would not spend her life on one she did not want and offense at being deemed inadequate, she stared at the man who had surely learned the falsity of whatever claims Gytha made about her granddaughter. It was of no event Canute was born out of wedlock, but of great event Mercia had been.

She looked to her former betrothed, and the relief on his face told he was grateful the storm had turned her belly inside out and her every groaning thereafter further delayed the exchange of vows.

Settling into her heels, she asked that to which she believed she knew the answer, "Lord King, for what am I set aside when you and your son were so eager to make a Godwine the bride of a prince of Denmark?"

His face darkened. "The machinations of a brother I trusted render you useless to my cause."

Then rejection of her had naught to do with the circumstances of her birth? All to do with the earl who accepted Le Bâtard's silver? "I am not sure I understand."

"You would not. You are a woman." He gave her his back.

She sprang forward and gripped his arm. "What of the truth I was to be told?" Ignoring Canute's rebuke and sidestepping so he could not catch hold of her, she placed herself in front of his sire. "Where is the missive you carry for me?"

"Nay, Son," the king said when Canute reached for her again. "Do I wish, I can myself swat this fly." As the younger man eased back, Sweyn narrowed his eyes on Mercia. "You are years from a girl, but not so old you cannot bear a man sons. Fortunately, you are lovely—more than Gytha's well-born granddaughters, she assured me. Thus, I believe your future will be tolerable."

"Tolerable? Again, I do not understand."

"All you must needs know is I shall do well by both of us." He removed her hand and stepped past.

"Canute!" Mercia beseeched as he followed his sire, but he closed the door between them.

"Of what do you speak, Sire?" his voice slipped through the gap beneath.

"Great our losses, my son. Hence, the ransoms of William's man and Mercia are a good beginning to seeing our war chests refilled, and more so raids along the coast as far inland as our warriors can steal."

Relieved over confirmation Maël lived, Mercia pressed an ear to the door's seam to make sense of words muffled by footfalls and distance.

"Then all we have done is for naught, Sire?"

"You have your uncle to thank for that. I but make us as whole as possible."

If she correctly interpreted that and what he had said to her, what Sweyn found upon his arrival had decided him against making a bid for the English throne. And just as Maël was to aid the Danes in recouping their losses, so would she—God help her.

Panic constricting her throat, she commanded herself to think. Was it possible to depart the ship unseen? As her guard left her door several minutes each time he had to relieve himself, the ship was anchored near the shore, and she could swim a little, she might be able to escape.

"And where would you go?" she whispered. Might the woman she served before King Harold's death give aid, perhaps allow her to resume her position? Possible, but only if Mercia could discover her whereabouts. Highly unlikely, but it was all she had to hold to in the moment.

Once more gaining the hammock, she closed her eyes, hopeful on the day she was to have wed she could distance herself from those who would make currency of her. But that day came too soon.

As dawn bled across the speckled black sky, she was pulled from her bed and across the deck by a Dane who refused to reveal her destination. When he halted before the hatch down which she had wished to go on the day past, she demanded, "What is this?"

For answer, he tossed back the door and ordered her down the ladder.

MUCH HAD CHANGED, and it required no great movement of the mind to fit this piece with that of the arrival of King Sweyn and his fleet.

Maël sensed it was Mercia before she came around the corner into the light of the lantern against which Ingvar knocked his head in his haste to rise. If not that her arm was gripped by a Dane urging her ahead of him, Maël might have thought she found favor with Denmark's king and had been sent to speak on his behalf, but she was no more in control of her person than he. And fearful, he saw when her eyes swept past where he stretched in his hammock and immediately returned to him.

Breath rushed from her as if she was relieved to see him.

Because she hoped to make him her savior again?

Her escort halted near Ingvar. The Danes conversed in a language similar enough to that of the Saxons that Maël understood what was required of his jailer—Mercia would occupy the second cell and there remain until King Sweyn ordered otherwise.

When her escort withdrew, Ingvar retrieved the keys and led her forward.

Mercia averted her eyes, allowing Maël to linger over a face that was thin but no longer gaunt as it must have been days past, hair simply braided and looped only once to restrain its length, and a gown different from the one for which she had exchanged her habit.

"Here, Lady." Ingvar opened the door fashioned of bars and handed her inside. "'Tis humble, but I see it fit as possible for noblewoman the same as Sir Maël's fit for nobleman. And I hang blanket to give privacy for…woman things."

He crossed to his hammock, and when he returned, passed one of his blankets to her. "Keep you warm."

She thanked him and, as he locked her in, retreated to the corner farthest from where Maël made his bed. Drawing the blanket around her, she eased to sitting beneath the hammock hung between the cage's back and a side wall.

"I return soon," Ingvar said and departed.

Maël swung out of his hammock and stepped to the bars between the cells. "As it seems you are not to be the wife of a king's son, Sweyn accepts never will he be King of England."

"You guess well," she said, chin lowered between the blanket's edges.

"More a conclusion based on what I know of William and what Sweyn did not know of the state of his brother's fleet."

"His own fleet is of great size."

"So Ingvar tells."

She looked sidelong at him. "It will wreak havoc on England

ere it returns to Denmark, but return it will, and with many riches. Doubtless, you will be ransomed, and I…" She closed her eyes, shook her head. "Much coin will be gained by delivering this Godwine to your king."

Here confirmation of what he had concluded of the young and old woman at Westminster.

"Thus, never again can any who oppose Norman rule attempt to use me to rally opposition." She sent her gaze around the cell, said barely above a whisper, "I begin to believe ever I will be caged, a bird flitting corner to corner, beating its wings against bars too tight to squeeze through." Her voice caught.

Maël felt an answering catch in the vicinity of his heart. And wanted to resent it. "Did you learn exactly how great your value to the King of Denmark? Was all explained as promised?"

Her laugh was bitter. "Sweyn refused me the missive from my grandmother I was told he carried. Hence, I know no more now than I knew at the inn." She turned her face to him. "Gytha's words will be of benefit in setting the price your king shall pay to render harmless the threat I present."

"Of what benefit?"

Her shoulders jerked. "I know not how true whatever she inked in her bid to avenge her sons' deaths, but she was to reveal what long she refused me—which of her sons sired me out of wedlock. *If* it is true I…"

"What?"

"Canute suggested I may not be ill-gotten, but more likely she wished to make marriage to the disposable granddaughter more desirable. But lies or not, I doubt I shall ever know what the missive tells since alongside me it will be sold to William, then destroyed. Perhaps the same as I shall be destroyed."

"The king does not execute nobles."

"Then in this Normans are more civilized than the English, though only if that *kindness* extends to those who have only the word of the enemy to attest to their legitimacy—more importantly, if one can be forgiven for deceiving the Holy Church."

Once more yielding to the need to reassure her, he said, "He will not kill you, Mercia."

"Just as it cannot be said I slew the exhausted bird that shall drop from the rafters of Lillefarne's chapel though my carelessness tempted it inside?" She shook her head, whispered, "Oh, to be forgiven my trespasses, to have been strong not weak, to have said, *I will not offend the Lord no matter I offend you, no matter your promise to tell what I ache to know. Better you turn your face from me than the Lord turn His face from a false servant.*"

Maël did not know what to say, though a fortnight past he might have spoken cutting words in answer to self pity. But then he had thought her merely a sly, disagreeable Saxon. Legitimate or not, this Godwine was more, and because of his cousin's suffering over his own illegitimacy, he understood why she had agreed to play an abbess.

She said no more, and when Ingvar returned with bulging sacks to make her captivity more comfortable, she turned into the corner.

The Dane entered her cell, placed a bucket on a long hook, another blanket and a towel in the hammock, and made curtains of thin blankets fixed to the upper bars between Maël's cell and hers and the bars facing Ingvar's station.

"You have only to pull them back and tie around a bar do you wish to visit with Sir Maël or speak with me, my lady," he said as he withdrew.

"I am not a lady."

Though Maël could no longer see her, her voice was not muffled, and he guessed she had turned out of the corner.

"Why you say that?" Ingvar's voice was firm as when he spoke to Maël of forgiveness. "You wish I assure that you a lady? Sir Maël say it too? Nay, I speak it already. Now you decide if lady or not."

There seemed surprise in her silence, then she said, "'Tis unlikely I am legitimate."

He grunted. "No say have you what mother and sire do, so not your sin. *You* decide what you are." Then came the rustle of the curtain being moved aside, the rasp of rusted iron, the key's scrape.

Stepping to the side, Ingvar peered at Maël. "Sleep now. On morrow, I learn more of what will be."

And would pass on much of it. Hopefully, Canute and others would never know that though Ingvar yet possessed the strength and skill of a warrior, if ever he had the heart and mind of one, it was barely evident. Here a man who should be sitting beside his wife before a hearth, his children's children begging tales of young Ingvar's exploits across land and sea.

One day might warriors in their prime think the same of Maël D'Argent who was not at home nor hearth because he had none?

More possible than not.

CHAPTER SEVENTEEN

*S*elf pity crippled.

She knew it the same as Ingvar who passed food and drink to her through the opening at the base of her cell door.

Curtained from the two men, Mercia paced her confines as Ingvar spoke and Maël responded with few words, the former sounding an ally as he told what was learned of the newly arrived Danes, confirming what Mercia had revealed and Maël concluded.

Sweyn had crossed the sea believing his men added to those sent last autumn would be sufficient to challenge William for the crown, and it might have been had not the earl withdrawn his support for English resistance in exchange for silver he was to have paid to Sweyn and a goodly portion quietly paid to himself. Thus, when William set to harrying the North, there was none of strength to oppose him, and while the earl counted his silver, the food and supplies required to sustain his men through the winter was mostly destroyed, resulting in starvation, illness, and death. The opportunity for Danes to conquer the conqueror no longer viable, the King of Denmark would recoup his losses with ransoming and raids and return home.

All that told, the sounds beyond the curtains suggesting Ingvar had settled down to eat, once more Mercia assured herself that no matter what happened, she could make a way out were she patient, strong, and watchful. She could be. Must be. Would be.

"This sunrise, it began," Ingvar spoke thickly as if around food, and once more she stilled. "While Sweyn send brother with many ships down coast to raid East Anglia, men ride to William to offer terms."

"How long?' Maël said.

"Until you free? As weather good for raiding, Sweyn patient. The longer he stay, the heavier his coffers. Too, his men need find your king to gain ransom. Could be weeks, could be months."

The latter, Mercia hoped. Though she hated this cage, more she would hate the one Le Bâtard and the Church fashioned for her. If a cage at all. Aye, better here than—

A sound of disgust parting her lips, she berated her selfish self who would prolong the chevalier's captivity and raiding to delay her punishment. "Lord," she whispered, "let William give answer soon."

"Have you word of Lady Nicola?" Maël asked, and once more she chastised herself, this time for allowing the young woman to slip her thoughts.

"Alas, nay. As angry as Sweyn is with brother, unlikely Bjorn keep your cousin if she found. She be ransomed too."

"For the best," the chevalier said. "Otherwise, your king and his kin will know the D'Argents better than they would like."

Ingvar chuckled. "And Wulfriths, eh? Your cousin of that family now."

"Guarin has taken his wife's name as commanded by King William, but ever first he will be a D'Argent."

"Good blood you have, Sir Maël."

"It binds us well, though no more than many other families."

Amid the silence of consideration, Mercia marveled over their exchange in which the chevalier contributed in nearly equal measure. Did he befriend Ingvar in hopes of making a hole in the watch over him?

"Nay, I not believe that," the Dane said. "Canute and brothers rivals first."

"Then warriors is all that was made of those crawling around Sweyn's throne."

"What else made of D'Argents?"

"Mostly, my sire trained me and my cousins into warriors. If not for my uncle, that is nearly all we would have been."

"Your uncle a priest?"

"Nay, a great warrior until battle stole the use of his legs. You have heard of Paul of the Bible who persecuted Jesus's followers—"

"Damascus!" Ingvar exclaimed. "Aye, Jesus come down and change him on that road. Then he become Apostle Paul."

Mercia heard Maël's chuckle, and that sound made her heart beat fast as she imagined it near enough to feel its warm breeze.

"You are a learned man, Ingvar."

"Nay, I but like stories of good come of bad. Tell me more."

"My uncle, Godfroi, was not a bad man before his injury, but a better man he was afterward. My aunt said his great loss was *his* road to Damascus. Though fairly well my sire bound his son and nephews with training at arms, tightly my uncle bound us with training in right over wrong. If either of those is in the blood, methinks it must be brought to consciousness before it can be given proper form and strength."

Mercia did not realize she pressed fingers to her wrist until she felt the coursing of her own blood. And that was all it was were the chevalier to be believed—of little form and strength, regardless were it Harold, Tostig, Gyrth, or Leofwine who sired her.

It matters not, she told herself, but still she longed to know the contents of the missive. Even if what Gytha told was twisted to her advantage, surely there was more truth there than Mercia had now.

"What think you, *Lady?*" Maël said as if she participated in the discussion. And she did if one counted she had turned over their words as if they were rocks beneath which a treasure might be found.

Though she bristled over his emphasis on titling her a lady, she was grateful he was aware of her presence, next regretful she must seem a self-pitying girl.

She crossed to the bars separating her from the chevalier and drew back the blanket. He was nearer than expected where he stood at the front of his cell across from Ingvar who sat atop the table tossing an apple.

Despite bruising of Maël's left eye, a reminder of the sacrifice of his freedom to ensure Ingvar did not slit her throat as Canute had threatened to do, so handsome was the side of Maël's face turned toward her, she stared.

Then he looked around.

Though she could not meet his gaze, she considered the whole of his face and was relieved the fist also delivered to his nose had not broken it.

"Have you an opinion, Lady?" he said, this time without emphasis on the title.

Having begun tracing his scars with her eyes, realizing just as she wanted to feel the warmth and breath of his chuckle, her fingertips wanted to follow the ridges, she tucked them into her palms.

"An opinion besides how ruined this visage," he prompted.

She flushed. "Better I would have to consider what is in the blood to give an opinion, Sir Maël, but my first thought is you are right. 'Tis not enough for a warrior and godly man to be in the blood. Such honorable character must be summoned forth and a bridge built between them."

He stared.

"Well you speak it," Ingvar said. "Does she not, Sir Maël?"

The corners of the chevalier's mouth tucked as if he might smile. "She speaks it well," he said and dropped the core of his apple on the platter near his feet.

Sidelong, she watched him stride to his hammock and settle in.

"I get you anything, Lady?" Ingvar asked.

She looked down at the platter of food more fine than what had been given her before Sweyn's arrival. Doubtless, the Danish king had brought provisions aplenty to feed men now set on raiding rather than battling.

"I need no more than this," she said. Rejecting the temptation to once more retreat behind the curtains, she hooked back the one between her and the king's man, secured it, and did the same with the one facing her jailer. Then she carried the platter to her pallet and feigned an appetite.

Being in sight of Maël was increasingly uncomfortable, not for feeling as if watched, though she guessed he must look upon her from time to time, but for the longing—nay, *need*—to thank him for giving himself into Canute's hands to save this deceitful Saxon. And she would thank him. Until then, better to think on how to escape Le Bâtard.

The day dragged and, discouraged to find each path her mind traveled to salvation blocked, she told herself, *I will be patient. I will be strong. I will be watchful.*

As if Ingvar believed she needed more than determination, there was something else besides viands on her platter that eve. "Borrowed from earl's trunk. He well down coast, so not miss."

Mercia stared at a psalter smaller and more beautiful than any she had seen. Encased in covers of embossed silver bound with silken cord to a leather spine, center of the front cover was a raised cross, at the intersection of which was a white gemstone beneath whose surface pale colors flashed like the scales of the loveliest fish.

Was this the opal her grandmother had bemoaned for how many slaves she would have to sell to attain one sizable enough to proclaim how precious and costly that which adorned her person? More importantly, might this be the psalter gifted by the ninth-century King Alfred to his daughter when he wed her to the Lord of the Mercians? Gytha had coveted one such as this said to be in the possession of a bishop who refused to part with it.

Mercia looked up. "Certes, the earl will miss this."

Ingvar shrugged. "If ever he return."

"You think he will not?"

He glanced at Maël who remained silent though Mercia was certain he questioned what need an ungodly woman had for a psalter.

"Canute say king think to punish earl bad. Mayhap exile." Ingvar looked directly at Maël. "Still no word of Lady Nicola. As all earl's ships searched, either she never on Humber else Bjorn get her off before king's men board." He raised his eyebrows. "That I think."

"Have you thoughts of where she could be now?" Maël asked.

"Earl slippery, and as I told, he love that boy. I say if she and Bjorn not on raiding ships gone south, earl send them to Denmark." He nodded. "Mayhap your cousin gone from England."

Maël muttered what sounded a curse, then said, "As warned, better the Danes shall know the D'Argents."

And I will be responsible for the blood shed to retrieve Nicola, Mercia thought. Feeling the chevalier's angry gaze, she said, "I am aware of my duplicity, Sir Maël, and I am sorry for it."

Leaving her supper, she returned to the pallet made beneath her hammock.

As the men satisfied their hunger and thirst, she slid her palms over the psalter and fingered leaves embossed in silver. She longed to open the book of prayers and delve words with which she had become fairly familiar during her youth when she resided at the convent where she had expected to live out her days. As the false abbess of Lillefarne, more familiar she had become with the prayers, and often they had comforted.

Would they comfort now? Though tempted to close her curtains to take in the word of God lest Maël mock her piety, it would be too dim to read. An hour later, Ingvar wrapped himself in a blanket and lay down. Shortly, the chevalier did the same.

She gave them time to succumb to sleep, then confirming Maël's eyes were closed, returned to the door of her cell where her meal remained and the light shone brighter. Clutching close the blanket drawn around her, she lowered into the corner between the cells. After picking at the viands, she opened the psalter.

Finding the inside cover and first page blank—no inscription to reveal its patron nor owner—she turned the page. The left side was also blank but not the right.

As she moved her fingers to the psalter's furthermost edges to ensure she did not sully precise, elaborate text and colorful illustrations, she concluded it was by thievery the psalter was among the Danish earl's possessions, the words of the first psalm written in her language. Had this not been the property of the bishop Gytha scorned, it had to have been in the library of a great house of God or that of a high English noble. Lillefarne had several illustrated psalters, all hidden away from grasping Normans, but nothing like this.

Mercia lingered over the single enlarged letter that began the psalm's first word. It was one-quarter the height and one-third the width of the page, its thick lines and curves inked in shades of blue. Filling its center was an illumination of a crowned and robed man seated on a bench and plucking a harp.

"Alfred," she whispered, guessing the artist depicted the great man who had worn England's crown two centuries past.

All around the psalm was a frame of vivid reds and glistening gold, and along the edges various animals, including a deer, rabbit, and boar, while in the bottom right corner of the page was a crowned lady holding a babe. But this was not Alfred's queen, the little one having a halo around his head. Here was Mary, mother of Jesus.

The page was beyond beautiful, but that was not what tempted her to look upon the others. It was dread of the psalm inked on this page that felt written for her alone as it had since first she donned a habit.

One page a day, no more than two, was all she would read, think, and pray on whilst here, she determined. As there appeared to be three dozen pages, they should last throughout her captivity—hopefully, well beyond.

Angling the psalter toward the lantern, she shone light on words small relative to Psalm One's first letter.

Blessed is the man that walketh not in the counsel of the ungodly, she read.

She was not blessed, having taken Gytha's ungodly counsel. As for giving counsel to her charges at Lillefarne, though she did not believe it ungodly, it had been given by one who was herself made ungodly by weakness, desperation, and deception.

"Lord, forgive me," she whispered but did not return to the psalm. That first portion provided enough to think and pray on. The rest would save for other days. Hence, if it took months for Sweyn and William to come to terms, she would not lack the sustenance of God's word and much reflection.

~

SHE WAS loveliest in sleep though few women were in Maël's opinion. The same as men, their faces became so slack and expressionless that even those boasting youth tended to sag. Not so Mercia of Mercia where she sat against the bars between their cells, head tipped to the side as if to return his gaze.

Whilst awake, her face was so stern its sharp lines and tension merely gentled in sleep. Were not her eyes now closed, he would think her relaxed rather than senseless—and easily coaxed to smile at which once he had excelled with the fairer sex.

She angered him, though more for Nicola's sake than his own. As done often between dozing and watching her stare at a single page in the psalter, he wondered what had become of Vitalis who rode after Bjorn and Nicola, as well as Guarin and his men who sought Theriot.

If Ingvar's musings were incorrect, was it possible the rebel leader had overtaken Nicola and Bjorn, slaying the latter to keep his word to Lady Hawisa to return her sister-in-law to Wulfenshire? Had the messenger who was sent after the Lord of Wulfen found him, and might Guarin now search for his sister as well as his brother? Was it possible he had found one or both?

Regardless, better prayers were spent on his missing cousins than forgiveness as urged by Ingvar.

Maël dropped to his haunches and looked to the elaborate psalter half open on Mercia's lap, just enough of the first page visible to identify the language of the Anglo-Saxons. Though he spoke it fairly well after all these years, he was far from proficient with its written form, something he would not have to remedy since he was determined his days in England neared their end.

As he started to withdraw, he caught sight of the purse on Mercia's belt. As noted upon her delivery below deck, it yet bulged, surely with what he had promised himself he would gain to learn her secret.

No longer necessary, Gytha's granddaughter, he mused, though tempted to reach between the bars and open her purse.

"That would awaken me had you not already," she said softly.

He swept his eyes to hers and wondered how long she had gazed at his ruined face. "So it seems," he said and settled more deeply into his haunches.

Mercia straightened from her slump. "As 'tis no longer of consequence, you have only to ask, and I shall salve your curiosity."

He realized he smiled only when her eyes dropped to his lips. Flattening his mouth, he reached between the bars. "May I, Lady Mercia?"

She set the psalter on the platter and drew forth her purse. Shortly, her fingers brushed his palm when she set the missive in his hand.

Her fleeting touch caused something of Maël's past to move through him, and not for the first time with this woman to whom he did not wish to be attracted. As she snatched back her hand, he wondered if she felt—and rued—it as well.

"I assume you can read my language," she said as he unrolled the parchment.

"A little." He turned the writing into the light. *Too little,* he amended as he struggled to decipher enough words to make meaning of the whole.

"Would you like me to read it?" she asked, then added, "As God is my witness, I shall leave every word intact."

He returned it to her.

After a glance over her shoulder at Ingvar who might only appear to sleep, she lowered her chin. But it was not the missive's words that passed her lips. "I thank you for sacrificing your freedom to preserve my life, Sir Maël."

He stared at the top of her head, and wanting to feel the soft of her hair, made fists of his hands. "Though now I know Ingvar would not have slit your throat," he said, "were Canute's threat real, the task would have fallen to one of the other Danes."

She looked up. "Truly, I am sorry for all. I do not deserve forgiveness, but I wish you and your kin to know I meant no harm."

Though tempted to remind her of all those affected by her deceit—foremost, Nicola—it did not compare with his own failings at Hastings and the many who suffered for them.

She swallowed. "This is what my grandmother sent with Canute to retrieve me from Lillefarne." She moistened her lips. "My dear Abbess, this Saxon noblewoman, bereft of all sons and lands, has arrived safely in her kinsman's country and been kindly received."

"She speaks of King Sweyn," Maël said.

Mercia inclined her head and continued, "I know not if my niece remains within your walls, but if she is yet in your care, I would have you deliver glad tidings I have secured a good future for her."

Written in such a way to protect Mercia should the missive fall into enemy hands, Maël interpreted.

"The noble family who has taken in this lady seeks a wife of godly character for a second son of good character. Hence, Abbess, I entreat you to make haste in preparing my niece to be delivered to her betrothed who shall soon arrive in England. As it is imperative she begin her journey without delay and I would not further impose on the abbey's hospitality, all arrangements have been made."

Mercia looked to Maël. "No delay at all, and that is what Nicola happened upon."

"Continue," he said.

"Thus, you have only to remind my niece of the duty owed her family and that she is to be strong of mind, body, and spirit, then give her into the care of those with whom her betrothed has entrusted her safety."

Maël grunted. "Your betrothed himself."

"I did not know it then," she said and returned to the writing. "Do this, Abbess, and when next we meet, your place in my affections will be secure. By God's grace, Lady Edelwine." Mercia looked up. "Just as ever I signed my responses *M of M,* ever she used a name not her own lest our correspondence was intercepted. And missives between us were, indeed, lost—some questions asked and answered again, others never asked nor answered at all."

"What did she ask of you and what did you report?"

"The goings-on upon Wulfenshire, of which I never knew enough and for which my grandmother rebuked me for taking my position as abbess too seriously. But unlike Lady Hawisa, I was raised to be protected by men—no training at arms, stealth, nor intrigue. Thus, all I could report was what was delivered to my ears—your arrival at Wulfen Castle to collect the tribute for Lady Hawisa to retain her lands, your cousin's arrival to take possession of a portion of her lands, how often Saxon rebels sought sanctuary inside Lillefarne's secret passage of which I was to know naught, and whatever could be learned of Norman armies crossing over Wulfenshire and the destruction they wrought."

She rolled the missive and returned it to her purse. "I know 'tis pitiful I should cling to this, but as I was ordered to burn every missive received, and it seems never will I possess the one Sweyn holds, this is all I have of my family—or nearly so."

She drew something else from the purse. When she folded back a piece of cloth, he saw a brooch too small to fasten a cloak closed. This one's only function was adornment.

Surprised she passed something so precious to him, he drew his hand back through the bars. As he turned the brooch into the light, the feeling of being watched made him seek the watcher.

Ingvar was on his side facing the cells. He met Maël's gaze, then lowered his lids as if to grant them privacy.

"My grandmother said my sire gave that to my mother the eve of my conception. 'Tis all I have of my parents and nearly all I know of them."

The brooch was masculine but beautiful. Wrought of silver, a thick letter G for Godwine was impaled down its center by a sword whose hilt and cross guard were gold and point was tipped with a triangular ruby.

"Costly," Maël said. "Regardless of who bore you out of wedlock, I wager your conception was no mere tumbling of an innkeeper's daughter. This looks a promise of more."

"I thought the same, but Gytha assured me it was mere foolishness."

"Your mother is dead?"

"I do not know. Ever my grandmother held that close the same as my sire's identity, but as I am in possession of the brooch, it seems a fair conclusion my mother passed." She looked down. "I know I should not put great store in who made me and I ought to turn from unraveling it—more so now I shall never see my grandmother's missive—but too long I have ached for the truth." She drew a deep breath. "I am resolved to let it go, and I will." She slipped a hand between the bars, and Maël relinquished the brooch. She returned it to her purse, and as she started to rise, said, "I shall wish you good rest."

"Alas, I am much awake now," Maël said, curiosity making him loath to see her close the door opened to him, especially as she might never again allow him to enter. "Tell me about your life before Lillefarne—that which delivered your grandmother and you to Westminster."

"For what?"

"As we are to live together a time, I am interested in knowing who you were before you took the name of Mary Sarah."

"It is already told. I am an illegitimate, unacknowledged Godwine." She straightened. "And therein my downfall—the wish to know who I was before Lillefarne so I might know who I am now."

Maël also stood. "You must know I do not speak of your parentage but of your days and nights, of where and how you lived ere you were sent to Lillefarne."

He felt her lean toward obliging him, but she shook her head. "I know 'tis the least due you, Sir Maël, but as it is not only my tale, I think it best not told. Good eve."

CHAPTER EIGHTEEN

a fortnight having passed since first she boarded the ship and over a sennight since being caged below, she believed herself accustomed to the hammock's sway, even its swing when a wind come off the sea whipped against the hull and played chase among the masts. And perhaps she was, but this fairly gentle rocking met with what awakened her—a bristling against the back of a hand and a glimmer in eyes— made her belly toss. Worse was what felt like teeth sinking into the side of her hand.

"Mercia!" Maël barked when she cried out.

"My lady?" Ingvar called.

She flung out her hand, and the vermin released and thumped to the floor. Reflex and an aversion to remaining in the place of her attack made her spring out of the hammock as if to give chase, and immediately she longed to climb back into the rope sling. And she would have if not for the burn rising up her throat that demanded the bucket.

"What goes, Mercia?" the chevalier demanded from the other side of the curtain.

One moment she moved toward the bucket, the next

sideways as the floor tilted opposite. She struck a shoulder against blanket-covered bars, dropped to her hands and knees, and as she began retching, the side curtain was torn down, letting in lantern light. Then the king's man thrust an arm between the bars, hooked an arm around her waist, and pulled her against their shared wall—just as the ship rolled again, which would have sent her to the other side.

"Rat," she croaked, and nearly retched again over the scent of sour. "I felt it…saw its eyes…it bit me."

Though she did not hear the key in the lock, she startled over the door's rusted protest as Ingvar entered with a lantern and stick. "I kill it, Lady!"

Providing he could find it. Several times she had seen or heard him put finish to kin of the one that awakened her, making her all the more determined to use the hammock for sleep though never had she glimpsed a rat inside the cells. But one had come, and where one came…

She shuddered.

"I have you," Maël said. "Now move away from the sick, lower to the floor, and turn onto your side."

Hardly had she set her back against the bars than the ship rolled again, causing Ingvar to grab hold of the cell wall opposite to steady himself and his lantern.

If not that Maël also lowered to his side, drew her nearer the bars, and cupped the back of her head with his free hand, she would have struck her skull on iron.

"Rat gone," Ingvar said as the ship shifted toward center. "Keep hold of her, Sir Maël. I clean up sick and bandage hand."

Though Mercia felt like a frightened child, she refused to be ashamed, certain a man would also react with considerable aversion to becoming a rat's meal.

"Slow breaths," said the one holding her, his words warming the top of her head and causing her scalp to prickle. "Slow, deep breaths."

She tried to do as told, but even after Ingvar cleaned the floor and set to tending her hand, she continued to shake and draw ragged breaths. Her pierced flesh stung, next burned when the Dane poured strong drink on it.

"Save some for me, Ingvar," Maël said. "The lady also draws blood."

Feeling moisture beneath fingertips digging their nails into the top of the hand he curved around her waist, she released him. "Forgive me, Maël."

Immediately he recaptured her hand and closed his fingers over hers. "Slow, deep breaths," he repeated, and this time his words warmed the air between her ear and neck.

Though no longer shaking, she quivered. Knowing it had less to do with fear and pain than being held by this man as a beloved wife would be held by her husband, she dug her teeth into her lower lip to distract her great awareness of him. But it was futile, her heart pounding so hard and fast she feared it would crack open.

"Hand swells, but salve sooth and draw out sickness," the Dane said as he bandaged it.

"I thank you," Mercia rasped.

"I light another lantern, Lady." He tied a knot at the back of her hand. "Should keep rats away." He pushed upright. "Now I help you into hammock."

She hesitated. Even with the bars between Maël and her, this was nearly sinful, but she did not wish him to let go. More, she longed to turn into him and, impossible though it was with the bars between them, tuck her head beneath his chin.

"Rat bother you in hammock," Ingvar said, "but still safer than floor, especially now curtain down and light get in."

She knew she ought to pull away from the chevalier as the abbess would have done, but she was no longer that woman. "If Sir Maël is willing, I shall remain here a while longer."

She did not know what she expected of the man behind, but

it only mildly surprised when he said, "Rest, Mercia. I shall watch over you."

"As you will," Ingvar said and secured her cell door, lit another lantern, and returned to his hammock.

Rest eluded Mercia the same as Maël she discovered a quarter hour later when he murmured, "I thought you unafraid of rats."

She went so still only then she realized her thumb stroked the outside of his.

"After all, you expressed no concern over those encountered in the abbey's hidden passage," he added.

And proud she had been of the Abbess of Lillefarne, a grown woman in a position of authority who had many times dealt with vermin that caused her charges to scream and scramble atop chairs and tables as she wished to do herself. Mostly, she had become accustomed to the vile creatures, but what had happened here was different.

"'Tis one thing to look upon rats from a fair distance," she whispered, "another to feel foul fur against the skin and find black eyes near one's own—worse, to be bitten." She opened and closed her bandaged hand. "It aches. Do you think...?"

"What?"

"I have heard a rat's bite can be deadly."

He tensed, causing her to peer over her shoulder—and her heart to jump as she looked upon the unspoiled side of his face. But it was imaginings of a slow, painful death that made her tremble anew and long for the psalter tucked in her pillow. "It is true, then?"

"I have been bitten by a rat, and I live. Of those who die, likely it is due to the wound being improperly tended."

Did he merely seek to calm her? she wondered as she turned forward again. "When were you bitten?"

Maël wished he had not opened that door, but prompted by protective instincts and the need to move her thoughts

216

elsewhere, it was as if he had taken her hand and led her to the threshold. He wanted to yank her back, but something felt right in this moment. And he knew what it was—an absence of great loneliness to which he was long accustomed, though somewhat less so since Ingvar became his jailer.

And so I am bewitched by a Saxon as I vowed never to be, he acknowledged.

"Pray, speak to me, Maël," she said and once more slid her thumb up over his.

Was it her pleading that moved him? Her familiarity with his name? Her caress of sword-toughened skin that should not be sensitive?

All that and more. As if told to take up arms ere fully recovered from a battle hard fought, he said wearily, "Shall we while away our captivity by telling each other tales, my lady? Salve curiosity and boredom with a trade of our own—you tell who you were ere Lillefarne, I tell you who I was ere Hastings?"

"It seems we have naught to lose that is not already lost, Sir Maël."

Not entirely true. Her secret was mostly known to him, but not his to her. But then, he did not have to carry his tale that far. "You called me Maël before," he said. "Just Maël. Let us remain there a time."

"It sounds we are to be friends."

It did, but it did not feel that way. So near were they, the warmth of her back against his front and curve of her waist in his hand, he could almost forget the bars. "For now," he said gruffly.

"For now," she said with what sounded regret. "Methinks I will like having a friend, so few have I had."

Then here upon a Danish ship on the Humber they would learn some of each other's secrets.

"How fares your belly?" he asked.

"It settles, as does my aching hand. I thank you for being so kind to ask."

"As told, it is only for now," he said and was surprised by what sounded teasing, of which his sire had disapproved and Maël had subdued in Hugh's presence and the absence of a great quantity of drink. The only way his sire would approve of his warrior son's exchange with Gytha's granddaughter was if it were strategy—a means of gaining information to better one's chance of besting the enemy.

"Would you share first?" she asked.

Bare himself ahead of her? Though he did not think she was given to strategy, he said. "Then I have not yet earned your trust, Mercia?"

Though it seemed a reasonable thing to put to her, she hesitated, but said, "As you have earned my trust more than I have earned yours, I will speak first. Pray, ask me a question."

Fairly certain Ingvar listened for how barely perceptible his breathing, Maël set his face nearer the bars and said low, "As I am aware our jailer may listen, you should be."

She shrugged. "Once my past may have been of great interest to King Sweyn and your king, but my grandmother has made it known to the former and the former plans to make it known to the latter. Thus, what I reveal is of little account. Too, I do not believe our jailer inclined to carry tales."

Neither did Maël, but still one ought to be cautious. "Begin at the beginning with who first you knew yourself to be," he said.

"That is very far back, but I remember my grandmother being nearly young, though it would be many years ere I knew she was kin. Until the age of four or five, I was raised in her home by Sarah who was first my nursemaid. There were many people about, and though rarely was I permitted to move amongst them, oft Sarah hid us in places where we could watch. Thus, by sight I knew Gytha's sons and daughters, their wives and husbands. Sarah told me tales of all, especially Harold and Tostig, and though they thrilled, I was lonely for the company of little ones. Still, I must have been happy. I smiled, laughed, and danced, and I recall how hard it was not to when the countess visited our cottage near the stables. She seemed unhappy, but providing I behaved well, she was kind to me and Sarah."

She swallowed. "All changed the night I awakened to a great din and heard Sarah cry out to me. I ran to the door and a man snatched me up and pressed my face hard to his chest. Sarah beseeched the countess not to do something, and as I was carried outside, I heard a slap and a scream. I…"

Where Maël cupped his hand over hers at her waist, he felt hers bunch, but as if now it was her own flesh into which she dug her nails, she splayed her fingers. And gasped when he slid his between hers and curled them into her palm. "You were frightened as never before," he prompted.

"Not only for myself but Sarah who was as near a mother as I had." She swallowed. "The man took me onto a horse and away from my home, and that eve he pushed me through the small door in the abbey's gate. I do not know what he said to the abbess, but she told I must cease crying and settled me on a small bed in a great room where many girls slept. Henceforth, they would be my sisters and she my mother, she said, and one day I would don robes like hers and wed Jesus. I remained there fifteen years, I believe, and from time to time Gytha visited. Though never did she stay long, she was kind and brought small gifts. I was twenty and two when she revealed she was my grandmother and gifted me the brooch she said one of her sons had given my mother whom he bedded and left with child. She said it was good I showed no passion for becoming a bride of Christ since she had arranged a better life for me. Grateful for the chance to live in the world, I departed the abbey. And that set me on the road to being here with you."

"What better life did she give you?"

A curt laugh moved her back against his chest. "Methinks twenty and two years enough of me for now. What of you?"

Maël thought himself prepared, especially since he meant only to relate his training into knighthood, but his muscles tightened. "Sleep beckons. Let us save my tale for another night."

She pulled away. Though he wanted to assure her he would keep their bargain, he was hopeful something would happen between now and then to render it unnecessary.

"I am disappointed," she said as she stood and gripped a bar to steady herself against what was now gentle swaying. "But since you have proved more principled than the false abbess, I trust you will reveal who you were ere Hastings. Tomorrow eve?"

He stood, inclined his head. "Tomorrow eve."

Both gained their hammocks, this time without a curtain between them, allowing light into her cell to keep the rats away —and allow one to look upon the other if desired. And too much Maël desired that.

Blessedly, a return to sleep came easy. But the same as each time his mind let in memories of what followed the tale due Mercia, they carved into him vivid sounds and images of lunging, swinging, and thrusting warriors, of iron striking iron, flesh, and bone, and of cries of triumph, defeat, and death.

And then came the great regret and shame of betrayal.

CHAPTER NINETEEN

$\mathcal{T}$he curtain hung again, now it was closed only when the modesty of one of the cell's occupants demanded its due.

Though night and day were mostly the same in the hull, the passing of hours was marked by meals. This being the third, were it not yet dark outside, soon it would be.

Having lingered over his food and drink at the front of his cell where he had conversed with Ingvar over the Danes' history with England, Maël looked across his shoulder at where Mercia sat beneath her hammock. Feet to the floor bracing her against gentle rocking, with her bandaged hand she drew her hair over her shoulder. The same as her speech, her movements were gracefully precise as she worked that great length into a thick braid.

Maël dropped a crust of bread and a rind of cheese on the platter at his feet, finished his cup of ale, then pushed the platter through the opening. "I thank you, Ingvar. As ever, I appreciate fare too fine for a prisoner."

"I have my ways—make king think on how it pinch do you

or lady fall ill and die. Nobody pay ransom for dead body." He grinned, retrieved both platters, and looked to Mercia.

Though she appeared intent on finishing the braid with one of the ribbons Ingvar had given her, surely she listened.

The Dane knew it as well, stepping near enough the bars that, were Maël of a mind to harm him without benefit of release, he would succeed. "Keep your word to her, Norman," he murmured. "I be a time learning day's tidings."

Tidings thus far absent William's response to paying the ransom of his captain of the guard and the wardship price of kin to his fallen enemy.

When he departed, Mercia settled her back against the wall and picked up the psalter.

"Does it comfort?" Maël asked.

Only after finding her place among the pages did she answer. "It does. Do you find that hard to believe of one who but played a holy woman?"

"No longer." It was true, and more so now he knew of her past. "What is this eve's psalm?"

"Thirty-one. You know it?"

"Not by number, though likely by word. My uncle's doing, not my sire's."

Her mouth curved. "Of which you will tell this eve?"

"I shall."

"Then I will be quick here so you may begin."

Maël pushed off the bars and strode to the back corner of his cell. "Will that not offend the Lord? Glancing over His words to sooner attend to mine?"

She grimaced. "You are right. Hence, when the Lord is done with me rather than I with Him, all my attention you shall have."

"As I have nowhere else to be, you are assured of my patience."

She started to lower her chin, said, "I could share the psalm with you."

It being many years since he more than received the Lord's word in passing, he did not think himself ready, but before he could decline, she said, "Draw near me, and I shall draw near you," and began repositioning her blankets in the corner of their shared wall.

One incapable of being bewitched is bewitched once more, he thought and lowered to his haunches.

"First, look upon this illumination." She raised the psalter and turned the page toward him. But he was struck not by beauty made of mere words, rather her soft smile. This was not the stern, Norman-hating abbess who refused him entrance to Lillefarne. This was Mercia who had done her duty to family that acknowledged her only insomuch as she benefitted them.

Her smile lowered, and he raised his gaze. Finding her eyes wide upon his, he shifted his regard to the left-hand page.

The large initial letter beginning the psalm was embellished with yellow and orange leaves outlined in gold, and along the outer edge of that page was the slender oak from which the leaves sprang. Set all around the other edges were the colorful figures of a kneeling lady, an enthroned king, and various beasts, most of which were mere imagination—including a unicorn.

"I have never seen such," he said.

"As told Ingvar, this will be missed."

"*If* the earl returns."

"If," she agreed and turned the psalter toward her. "In thee, O Lord, do I put my trust." She paused.

Thinking she awaited a response and having none, he said, "I listen. Continue."

She raised her eyebrows. "That is much, do you not think? To trust in the Lord above all else?"

Such sincerity and enthusiasm had she for so few words, it jolted when her expression fell.

"Mercia?"

"It is much," she whispered, "and for that often I fail."

As did he. Against his own good counsel, he said, "I recall an argument between my uncle who told we must trust in the Lord above all else and my sire who said in matters of great import a man cannot simply bury his head in his arms and wait on the Lord to deliver him. My uncle silenced him with agreement and the proviso one's trust in the Lord be that which guided a man's actions."

She opened her mouth, closed it.

"What do you not speak, Mercia?"

"It has to do with your story at which we are soon to arrive."

"Tell."

She lowered the psalter. "When you crossed the channel to make war on Harold and his people—my people—were you trusting the Lord to guide you in spilling the blood of fellow Christians?"

He deserved her every accusation though there was more sorrow about her than anger or bitterness. Because this was Mercia of the convent, he realized, not Mary Sarah of Lillefarne.

"Pray, do not turn from me," she said as if fearing he would drop the curtain between them. "If you cannot answer, we shall return to the psalm and from there venture to your life before the conquest."

Though the man he had become following Hastings protested, words slipped from him like a traitor crossing a battle line to join an enemy he believed would win the day.

"I can answer, Mercia. I told myself I trusted in the Lord to guide me, that I was but a tool to save the heathens of England, but I half believed it only. And that half was corrupted by the other half longing to prove worthy not only of my sire but great reward. I wished to become a landed noble as was not possible serving my family in Normandy. Thus, I did not entrust myself to the Lord's guidance. My decision to join Duke William was far more in accord with my sire's beliefs than my uncle's. For it…"

This time he did not cross the battle line. Nearly as much as he dreaded what his family would think of him, he dreaded what Mercia would. Were they friends in this moment, no longer would they be though his betrayal had surely saved Saxon lives.

"I am thankful for your honesty," she said. "You are secretive, but methinks you less inclined to deceit than I."

Strange how reflexive the impulse to defend her, he thought.

"As told, one verse is much to think and pray on." She set the psalter aside.

Maël knew what was now expected of him, and though it was no easy thing to reveal who he was before Hastings, it seemed of less account after revealing that greed for approval and land was the reason he was here with her. Shifting from his haunches to sitting, he said, "I shall begin with my earliest complete memory."

She tipped her head against the wall and waited.

"My uncle having lost the use of his legs in battle, he summoned his twin brother home to aid in training his young sons into warriors. Despite rivalry in their youth at which my uncle prevailed, and which saw him awarded the family lands, they cared for each other. Thus, my sire, who had earned great repute selling his sword arm, brought home his wife and son. I recall sitting on the fore of his saddle and him commanding me to look near on the fortress. He said as it belonged to his brother and would one day pass to Godfroi's son, it would never be his. Thus, if ever I wished to set my feet firm in one place and rule rather than be ruled, I must be better than my cousins, even my own sire. I must become the greatest D'Argent. I vowed I would, but my mother said I was too young to make such promises and warned her husband against sowing envy. It was brave of her, for he could be difficult."

"He abused Lady Chanson?"

His mother's name on Mercia's lips jolted as if never had Hugh's widow and she met. But in a way they had not. It was Abbess Mary Sarah whom Chanson had known, not this woman come out from beneath a habit.

"Did he beat her?" she pressed.

"He did not, but he was demanding and distant when displeased and did not have as great a care for her as she for him." *However,* Maël silently added, *Hugh had enough care that his son believed he had been faithful to his wife despite rumors otherwise.* A belief proven false.

"She loved him?" Mercia asked.

Pulling back from memories of clashes with peers who spoke ill of his sire, Maël said, "My mother did love him and was a good wife. When we arrived at my uncle's home—"

"Losing him at Hastings must have been very difficult for her."

Tempted to anger over Mercia shifting his tale to the aftermath of the conquest, he said, "It *was* difficult, but she is wed again and seems happy."

"I like Father Fulbert, but I fear for their marriage now England's priests are to be denied the comfort of wife and children."

That also concerned Maël. Though he had disapproved of his mother wedding Fulbert, he hated the possibility of her losing another man she loved. "My mother and he wed ere that was decreed. Hopefully, what is done will remain so. Now what else would you know of who I was before Hastings?"

"Your relationship with your cousins."

He nodded. "As mostly I was raised alongside them, they are as brothers to me—Nicola a sister."

"Then you did not envy them, especially Guarin for being his sire's heir?"

"Some envy, though far less because of the title and lands he was to inherit than that he and Cyr were usually a step ahead of me in earning their spurs, which was difficult for how much I disappointed my sire. Often what had to be much trained into me required less effort from them. My mother believed warring was more in their nature, but Uncle Godfroi did not concur. He said I tried too hard to please Hugh, that in defending my life and the lives of those entrusted to me I must please myself first, gauging my progress and accomplishments by those of the day past, next those of the day to come. And ever holding them up to God."

Maël paused in remembrance of the man one would not know was no longer a warrior when they stood before him where he sat high, broad, and confident in his chair, a blanket over wasted legs.

Godfroi D'Argent, believed to have died in battle, had returned to his wife as what others named half a man. But he was more man than most fully in control of their bodies, so great his confidence not only in himself but the Lord. Unlike his brother, he was capable of great affection and unashamed of expressing it. And at forgiveness, he was unequaled.

But not always, Godfroi quickly corrected any who named a sinner a saint. The cruelty of his great loss had embittered him for a time, but with the aid of a godly man and much prayer, he settled into what he had rather than what he had not. Though it was rare he spoke of that transformation, believing better his actions than words testify, much honor he was accorded by his family, even Hugh who had chafed under his authority.

"He sounds a good man," Mercia drew Maël back to her. "Methinks you love him like a father."

He nearly reminded her he had a father and needed no other, but Hugh was long gone—if ever he had been halfway present for his son—and Godfroi had aspired to be to his nephew what he was to his own children.

"He was as a father to me whilst I dwelt in his household," Maël acceded, "and much I care for him."

"When last did you see him?"

"Ere departing Normandy with William who, dissatisfied with being merely a duke, sought a crown."

"Then you did not yourself bring your mother to England following your sire's passing?"

Once more moved where he did not wish to go, he shifted his jaw. "I did not."

"Because you became William's captain of the guard?"

He was tempted to grasp that handhold, but he would not lie. "Though I had accepted the position with King William, I could have gained permission to escort Lady Chanson to Stern Castle, but I did not. Now let us return to before Hastings."

With obvious reluctance, she nodded. "I would know of the training of the young man who aspired to become a chevalier. Even if your cousins continued to progress ahead of you in some areas, you must have made your sire proud."

He had, though such pride was often short-lived. "His praises were mostly reserved for goading those who disappointed him by raising high those who disappointed less. But as I grew into a youth, he adjusted his expectations, allowing that I number *among* the greatest of the D'Argents. Hence, more praise I earned—until I began attracting women less for my ability to wield arms than my appearance. Though Hugh found it offensive—as if a personal affront his son was best known for a handsome face—I continued to court ladies, even at the cost of my training, which led to a great argument before all."

"When I refused to desist in pursuing ladies, he said I wasted time with noblewomen since those of worth would never wed a landless chevalier. The insult to my mother was unintentional, but knowing how deeply it hurt one born noble but of so few prospects her sire accepted Hugh's offer of marriage, I struck my father. I hardly felt the pain in my knuckles, and certain he would retaliate for the blood running in his teeth, I determined to make it as difficult as possible for him to beat me to the ground. But he laughed and declared here further proof anger was the cure to my many shortcomings— even my beauty. Then he tossed his purse at my feet and said rather than spend time on noblewomen, better coin spent on…"

Pausing lest he scandalize the wide-eyed Mercia, Maël realized once more boundaries were being crossed, but before he could back away, Ingvar returned. Something in his eyes evidencing he bore grave tidings, Maël gave a slight shake of the head, hopeful Mercia would not be long in finding her sleep this eve.

As the Dane moved toward his bench, she said, "Better coin spent on easily used and discarded commoners—joy women."

"I was tempted," Maël acceded, "but seeing the horror in my mother's eyes and anger in my uncle's, I kicked my sire's purse back to him. I did not cease wooing ladies, but I did so with less enthusiasm, fully aware as long as I had only my sword arm to recommend me, I had no hope beyond flirtation, the touch of hands and feet beneath tables, and kisses when possible to slip into shadows unseen." He glanced at Ingvar who gave a barely perceptible nod. "And now you know as much of me as I know of you, Mercia of the Godwines."

He heard her swiftly drawn breath. "You should not name me that."

"As evidenced by the coin sought for you, you are of that family. A lady."

Staring at Maël, Mercia wondered if, given the chance, he would have pursued her with flirtation…the touch of hands and feet…kisses in the shadows…

In the next instant, she rebuked herself and said, "A lady only if the missive denied me is true."

"Still you wish to see it?"

He made it sound as if he had the power to secure it. "I do, and yet for what? To believe what may be a lie? To reject what may be the truth? Better my mind spent on finding a way to escape your king ere he can lock me away or worse." She sighed. "As you tell he does not execute those of noble blood, I can only hope he believes my grandmother's missive."

"I will not allow him to harm you."

She raised her eyebrows. "Will you not, loyal Norman, captain of the king's guard, one warrior amongst many?" As soon as the words were out, she knew once more she sounded the contentious, disapproving abbess. "Forgive me, Maël. I appreciate your attempt to allay my fears, but they are valid."

"Then we should both embrace Psalm thirty-one."

In thee, O Lord, do I put my trust, she silently recited as her heart strained toward a man who was not her enemy in this moment and perhaps none henceforth. But neither was he a friend. What had moved through her on the night past when he held her through the bars was something never before felt.

Is it love? she wondered, then silently beseeched, *Lord, let it not be. Let me not feel much for something so unattainable.*

"Aye, Psalm thirty-one," she said, ashamed she needed reminding.

He rose. "We should find our rest."

He thought her oblivious to Ingvar's unease. Had she entirely cast off Mary Sarah, she might have been, but years of great responsibility had rendered her observant more for the sake of her charges than herself.

Rising, she scooped up the psalter and blankets, but rather than retreat to her hammock, said, "What tidings do you bear, Ingvar?"

He jerked his shoulders. "Naught of import, my lady."

She forced a smile. "It is kind of you and Sir Maël to try to protect me, but it is a temporary measure."

He shifted his gaze to the chevalier.

Following it, Mercia said, "Pray, Sir Maël, do not grant him leave to further the lie. Since whatever he knows involves me as much as you, it is mine to hear as well."

He nodded slowly. "If you intend to share what you have learned, Ingvar, tell us both."

The Dane leaned forward. "It comes to pass, Lady, you shall aid in replenishing silver wasted on quest to oust Le Bâtard—providing what Sweyn tell of you is true."

"Then William was not sent Gytha's missive?"

"Only told of it. Once verified it from your grandmother, coin will be paid for it, you, and captain of guard."

"What if it is not believed Gytha wrote it?"

"Canute also ask, and Sweyn say he return you to old woman and she pay him for your keeping—more if he arrange good marriage with one of his nobles."

Then the inability to verify Gytha inked the missive was her only hope of not falling into Le Bâtard's hands, hope even were she wed to a Dane. And yet…

"When is the exchange to be made, Ingvar?" asked the one her thoughts had flown to as if he offered greater hope.

"At sun's rising we sail south to estuary between Lincolnshire and Norfolk."

"Not far from Wulfenshire," Maël said. "It is the king who comes?"

"Nay, Le Bâtard's brother."

The blankets slipped from Mercia's arms. Distantly hearing the thump of the psalter atop them, she looked past Maël who had turned to her. "Which of his brothers, Ingvar?" she rasped. "Bishop Odo?"

"That his name."

Closing her eyes, she sent up a prayer for the winds to

change, the rain to slash, the earth to move—anything to see Le Bâtard or his other brother make the trade—then looked to Maël.

He said naught, knowing the same as she the punishment for impersonating an abbess would be greater were she to stand before one of the Church—worst of all Odo who wore the robes of his holy office for personal gain and glory.

She retrieved the psalter and blankets and began making her bed in the hammock. Unless a storm delayed their departure from the Humber, ere this time on the morrow she would stand before a Saxon-hating bishop who professed the love of Jesus.

"Odo bad man?" Ingvar asked.

"Not a good one," Maël said darkly. He might be confident his liege would do her no great harm, but he did not believe it of the bishop.

A quarter hour later, whether or not they thought she slept, the two spoke so low that only had she strained could she have pieced together some of their exchange, but of what benefit? Better she strain to work a way out of a mess that would become more dangerous when she traded one captivity for another. And was parted from Maël whom she—

Do not think there, she chastised, then reminded herself of Psalm thirty-one. Still, her insides stirred as if to make fire of embers—until fatigue offered the only relief to be had.

CHAPTER TWENTY

The thump of feet awakened Maël. Narrowly opening his eyes, by dim lantern light he saw Mercia stood unmoving at the center of her cell, hands splayed to the sides as if listening to determine whether she had disturbed his or Ingvar's sleep.

Just as when Maël had quietly conversed with the Dane after she retreated to her hammock, he felt her angst and was tempted to assure her she would not fall into Odo's hands, but he could not guarantee that. Though he had sought to turn something of an ally into an ally, Ingvar had yet to give answer. However, as the stealthy, quick-fingered jailer had not outright rejected the proposal, there was more hope for Mercia than she thought. The morrow would tell.

She began pacing the confines, and he let her believe him at rest until she rasped, "Thirty-one."

As he swung out of the hammock, she hastened to their shared wall. "Forgive me for awakening you. I sleep poorly, and more often not at all." She reached to the curtain.

"Leave it, Mercia. Neither do I sleep well."

She went very still, then said, "I am afeared," and stepped nearer.

When his shadow ran down her and pooled around her feet, he nearly drew her to him. However, lest in holding her again he kiss her, as was possible with her facing him as she had not on the night past, he resisted.

"It is difficult," she whispered.

"What is difficult?"

"Being powerless when first we met at Westminster, holding power when next we met at Lillefarne, losing power when Canute came for me, regaining power in escaping him, now again entirely powerless. Mayhap forever." Her voice caught. "I wish an end to being tossed back and forth like a ball in the games of dangerous men and women. Though I do not want an extravagant life as Gytha thought to give me, I want a good life, and more than ever it seems impossible."

Choosing his words carefully, he said, "I do not believe that. Bishop Odo is a hard man, but—"

"It is not just him, not just punishment for impersonating an abbess, nor the Godwine in my veins."

"You fear retribution for aiding the resistance?"

"There is also that. Though I told I knew of only one occasion rebels hid in Lillefarne's wall, you knew it for a lie. However, as your king has mostly put an end to the rebellion, that is of less concern than what Gytha's missive could tell besides who sired me."

Maël reached through the bars and cupped her jaw. "What else have you done?"

"I—"

The creak of a hammock turned them toward Ingvar as he dropped his feet to the floor. "As could be your last night together," he said, "do you give word you not trick me, Sir Maël, I let lady in your cell and give you time alone."

The offer jolted for what it implied, and Maël felt Mercia's disquiet as well.

The Dane snorted. "I not think there. You chevalier, she lady. I but remove bars so you sit and speak comfortable. You want that?"

It was Mercia who answered. "I do."

As do I, Maël thought, *and therein the problem.* His attraction for her was more than a stirring of the body. It was the wish to know better her heart and mind as he should not.

"I get keys, Sir Maël?"

He knew he ought to reject the offer, but he said, "Aye," and moved to the back of his cell as further assurance he would work no trickery on Ingvar.

Shortly, Mercia was handed into Maël's cell. "You call loud do you want return to your own, Lady," the Dane said and locked them in. "I walk on deck but never far."

As he withdrew, Maël thought how small and uncertain Mercia looked and almost wished back the imperious abbess who had peered down her nose at him.

"Will you come to me?" he said. "Or is it better I come to you? Better yet we keep this divide between us?"

She moistened her lips. "I wish to draw nearer."

"Then come only as close as you trust me."

She took a single step, hesitated.

"What is it, Mercia?"

"I question how, in so little time, not only has my enemy become an ally, but something more."

As she had become something more to him.

She hesitated as if to give him time to confess the same, but when he did not, continued forward. "I trust you as far as this, Maël," she said and halted before him.

Struggling against the longing—or was it need?—to feel the soft of her cheek, dip of her waist, curve of her hip, and small of her back, he gripped his fingers in his palms.

She set a hand on his chest. "I do not believe this *could* be our last night together. I believe it is. Thus, I refuse to regret not drawing near enough to feel your warmth one last time. Near enough to tempt you to kiss me as I do not think I will be kissed again."

Had he a chance of winning the struggle to hold himself from her, it was lost when she leaned in and, toes touching his, tipped up her face. "Only a kiss, Maël."

Loosing his fingers from his palms, he put one hand around the back of her neck, the other at her waist. "A kiss," he rasped, "as much because you seek to tempt me as I need no tempting."

She swallowed. "Tell me what to do."

He drew her to him. "Only what feels right."

"This feels right," she said and melted against him.

Desire long packed away beginning to unfold and stretch, Maël pulled her onto her toes, angled his head, and touched his mouth to hers.

"This also feels right," she whispered.

Though he knew he should end it there, he deepened the kiss, and breath by breath it became as intoxicating as wine and as sweet as honey. Many women he had known thus, but had he ever wanted one as much as he wanted Mercia? Was this great pull merely born of the empty years between Hastings and now? Or did he truly begin to feel what he should not for a woman who was a Saxon—more, would soon be gone from him?

As what was only to be a kiss had moved beyond and might move further, he drew his head back, and when she opened her eyes, said, "Forgive me," and eased his hold.

She frowned. "For what, Maël? I asked this of you, and I do not regret it, just as I will not regret speaking what is in me." She breathed deep. "Canute and a kiss I did not like is my only experience with men, but ere *you* kissed me, I knew hereafter I would wish to be with you as we are now. Is that love or merely loneliness?"

Though he ought to assure her it was loneliness, he wanted to name it love—and be capable of returning such depth of emotion. But he was undeserving of such.

"Now I fear *you* suffer regret," she said. "That you are thinking—why did I not push her away?"

Uncomfortable beneath her searching eyes, he pressed her head beneath his chin and settled a hand atop the looped braids at the small of her back. "What I am thinking is best it not be love you feel for me, Mercia."

She stiffened, surely having hoped he would ease her fear, but then as if with acceptance, she sighed long.

The boat was so still, Maël was less aware of their captivity than the silken strands beneath his fingers and the temptation to loosen their crossings—until words spoken above deck wended downward. The exchange was too muffled to understand, but he recognized Ingvar's voice.

Lest their jailer return soon, Maël led Mercia to his pallet. "What other thing do you fear Gytha's missive may reveal?" he asked after they lowered and set their backs against the bars.

Mercia kept her profile to the man she had dismayed with what sounded a profession of love. Though something that momentous was deserving of much consideration before being voiced, the words had been so thoughtless one might believe she merely commented on the weather. Now, just as she knew he cared for her, he knew how much more she cared for him. But if her feelings filled even a corner of his emptiness, it was worth baring herself.

She moistened her lips, turned her face to him. "You recall I told my grandmother took me from the convent ere I made my profession, that I served my family out of obligation?"

"I do."

"It was not only obligation. The hope of learning more of my family made me do what I found distasteful. You are aware King Harold set aside his handfasted wife, the mother of his many children, to wed a noblewoman more acceptable as England's queen?"

"Alditha."

She nodded. "Gytha approved of the alliance, but as she had cause to distrust the lady and her family, she gave me in service to her daughter-in-law with instructions I report anything untoward."

"You acted as her spy."

"The same as I did upon Wulfenshire. Blessedly, there was naught of import to divulge, and even had there been, I do not know I could have, for much I liked the sorrowful Queen Alditha." And sympathized with the woman who, more egregiously than what had been planned for Mercia, was made a tool of powerful men. First wed to the King of Wales, next the widow was wed to Gytha's son, Harold, to whom had been sent her beloved's head.

"Is it true she bore Harold a son?" Maël asked.

Remembering the queen's belly ripening with a child sired by the man responsible for her first husband's death, once more Mercia questioned if the babe was a half brother or sister, then said, "Alditha was heavy with child when she received word Harold had died, and my service to her ended when her brothers spirited her out of London to keep her from William. Hence, thereafter all I know of her is rumor—that she birthed a son and both survived."

Maël inclined his head.

"As your king wishes to know the location of Harold's royal heir to extinguish that threat to his rule, if Gytha's missive reveals I served Alditha..." Mercia swallowed. "I have heard terrible things are done men and women to force them to reveal secrets, and though I wish to believe I would not betray the queen, I fear it is possible I would—*if* I knew where she could be found. Thankfully, I do not. Thus, death could prove the only end to my torture."

Maël set a hand over hers in her lap. "I shall do all in my power to keep William's and Odo's wrath from you."

Thinking no matter his family's reputation nor his value to Le Bâtard he would be unable to stop either man from abusing her, she nearly challenged him. But better she store up memories of their time together and make of it a place of refuge should she find herself amid utter darkness. "I thank you, Maël."

He eased her hands apart and set one atop his thigh. "The end of secrets," he murmured.

"*My* secrets," she corrected. "But though I wish to know you better, methinks it best I do not lest it cause me to hurt more than already I shall when I see you no more."

He was silent a long time, then said, "As I do not wish you to hurt, I will tell what I hold close so you not waste more emotion on an unworthy D'Argent."

"It would have to be very bad for me to think and feel different about you."

"It is, though what I did—and did not do—may have benefitted your people. You recall I said though I aspire to loyalty and honor, often I fall short?"

"Sometimes disastrously."

"Aye. As told, my sire was a hard man. Hard to love. Harder to like."

She frowned. "I have little experience with family. Thus, I do not understand how it can be harder to like than love."

"Though it requires more to love, I speak of it being easier to remain in a state of love than merely enjoying time spent in another's company. Whereas the roots of love go deep, wrapping around one's soul so the only way to be free of it is to rip out a piece of the soul with the roots, to like a person seems more immediate—more in the moment—hence, less tolerant and forgiving, often optional."

Mercia considered that with regard to her grandmother whom she could not say she loved but had grown more in that direction than liking the old woman who demanded things of Mercia she had not asked of her legitimate grandchildren.

"Shallow roots, if roots at all," Maël brought her back to him.

She stared at this man she loved as much as she knew how to love and wondered if his secret would pull out the roots of what she felt for him. Possible, since they had not years to grow deeper, and perhaps it was for the best. Tear them out while they were relatively near the surface, and the piece of soul they took with them might be small enough she would become numb to the loss.

"Pray, continue, Maël."

"Years ago, it was more than family loyalty and honor that made me defend my sire when rumors about him demanded a response. It was the belief they were only rumors. Thus, I beat those who carried tales of Hugh's infidelity, and on occasion they beat me. Only the first time did my sire ask after bruises and scrapes gained off the training field. When he pressed and I told him whence they came and assured him I knew he was faithful to my mother, he declared that before him stood the D'Argent long he sought to make me." Maël breathed deep. "I do not think he had ever been more proud of me, and I was so grateful I did not question why he did not confirm his fidelity."

"Then he *was* unfaithful?"

"On one occasion, likely many others—meaning it is possible though I am my mother's only child, it is not so of my sire."

"I am sorry."

His smile was forced. "As was I when I discovered his betrayal, though first I was so angry I hated him."

"When was that?"

"The afternoon ere the battle of Hastings, William bid his men to pray for the Lord to grant them victory and commanded the D'Argents to accompany him and his companions to a village church whose English priest had been replaced with a Norman. Some of us prostrate, others kneeling, the murmurings of our prayers swirled amongst us like a brisk snow. As we were there for hours, it was not unusual for men to pause in their beseechings to relieve themselves, but I remained vigilant as trained to do, aware of each one's departure and return. Though unlike Theriot, I do not possess a keen sense beyond the natural, what little I have urged me to raise my head only once, and I saw my sire moving toward the doors. I continued my prayers, and when he did not return, worried ill had befallen him, whether an enemy had stolen upon him or he was struck by dysentery which had afflicted some of William's followers."

"The same as Vitalis," Mercia murmured.

"But also I was suspicious since several times over the past days my sire had disappeared for hours. At first, I assumed the duke set him a task, but then William sent for him and raged over his absence. Hence, that eve I went in search of him. The village was quiet, the Saxons who had not fled their homes having closed themselves in for the night. I asked those on patrol if they had seen my sire, and all denied it—except one whose nose I had broken years earlier for spreading rumors of Hugh's infidelity. He said my time would be better spent looking where harlots aplenty could be found. Though tempted to do worse to him than break his nose, I continued my search. It was fruitless, and to prove him wrong, I went to the village tavern. And proved him right."

"My sire was in a dim corner—a nearly admirable attempt to be discreet. I heard the soft laughter of the woman who shared his bench, saw her lean near and Hugh kiss her, then they rose. Though they traveled the shadows to the stairs, they could not avoid torchlight on the upper landing. Thus, I glimpsed the comely Saxon slip into a chamber with a man who took pride in his son beating those who spoke true of the mighty trainer of chevaliers. I returned to camp as had the others with whom I prayed, but when my cousins asked after my sire's whereabouts and my anger threatened to spill on them, I determined that night I would confront the one who betrayed my mother and went back to the tavern. And yet..."

"Yet, Maël?"

"It was he who confronted me. Having seated myself near the door to await his reappearance, greatly I imbibed as oft I did when I disappointed him or he angered me. I do not know how many hours passed, but it was still dark and few patrons remained when he wrenched me to consciousness where I lay face down on the table. He berated me, called me a drunken fool, told I ought to be gaining sober sleep to ensure I did my duty to my family when dawn broke. I could hardly stand nor see straight, but I heard and felt his every word. And though slurred and broken my own, I made certain he heard and felt mine."

Once again, Maël was transported from the bowels of the ship to that filthy tavern. "All color left his face when I revealed what I had seen, then returned when *I* told him how greatly *he* disappointed. I said it was not with pride I claimed him as my father, that it was nothing more than fact, he was undeserving of my mother, and..."

"Tell me, Maël."

His ears hurt over remembrance of what he had said after deflecting Hugh's backhand. Had he not longed to save Mercia the ache of loving one undeserving of such, he would hold it close, but the sooner she knew who was behind this ruined face, the sooner she would turn from him and less she would hurt.

"I said I cared not if he fell in battle, that his wife was young enough to make a match with a better man who could easily prove a better father." Maël drew breath through his nostrils. "I saw that rarest of things in his eyes—pain—then it was gone, in its place disappointment, perhaps even hatred for a son he longed to beat."

"Did he?"

"Non. He told me to sleep off the drink, be at his side ere the march to meet the Saxons, and departed. I did sleep off the ale, but not before several more fills of the tankard. What next I recall is sharp pain in my neck that returned me to consciousness." He raised his eyebrows. "A rat, one of several crawling over me outside the tavern where the innkeeper dumped me."

Understanding lit Mercia's eyes.

"It was dark, the sky just beginning to lighten when I left the village. Since several times I paused to empty the sour in my belly, when I reached the camp, William's army had departed. My squire awaited me, and not only passed to me my horse but my sire's instructions that were to be delivered as spoken. With apology, the boy said, *You, a blot upon our name, break faith with the House of D'Argent in behaving a child. Get the man of you to the battlefield, even if the boy of you must crawl. Though there can be no great reward for my wife's son in William's England, perhaps a life can be made of selling your sword arm to those less worthy of the duke's good regard.*"

He breathed deep. "The remorse felt upon awakening and the determination to redeem myself threatened to scatter like fallen leaves. I *was* a blot on the D'Argent name, but to be told that by one more a blot for betraying my mother..." He shook his head. "Though I could hardly think right, I armed myself, got astride, and made it to the field before the battle commenced. However, so averse was I to being near my sire, I fought distant from him and my cousins. For a time, I kept them in sight, but my swings were sloppy, movements slow, and vision so cramped that to preserve my life and the lives of the Normans alongside whom I did fight, I had to set my mind on what was directly before me."

Looking to Mercia, he wondered why her eyes did not brim with disgust since she knew the losses the D'Argents suffered that day. "When the blade sliced my brow and nearly took my eye, my first thought was it would please my sire who hated that his son was so fair of face. My next thought was to slay the Saxon who sought to part my head from my shoulders, then the one intent on cutting my legs out from under me."

Maël kneaded the muscles of his neck. "Once the Norman victory was complete, this D'Argent was standing, the only price paid for his treachery a face over which women would no longer sigh. When I learned of Dougray's injury, my sire's shameful death at the hands of boys, and that Guarin might be among the dead, I was certain had not anger and disgust dictated alongside whom I fought, all would be different. Instead, I made my mother a widow, Dougray a cripple, and for two years deprived my uncle of his heir who was believed dead." He met Mercia's gaze. "So now you know this man you feel for is unworthy of such."

She rose and turned onto her knees to face him. "I thank you for sharing a burden so heavy it drags down your heart and mind, but I know no such thing of you who are with me now because you *are* worthy. What I know is, pained by betrayal, you were not thinking right. You drank much, and it affected your ability to defend yourself and others, but you cannot say it would have made a difference to your family had you fought alongside them. It could have proved of great detriment—a distraction with so much ill between father and son."

"Ill because of words I should not have thought, and certainly not spoken," he clipped, frustrated she made excuses for him. Because she truly loved him and love blinded her to his failings?

She set hands on either side of his face. "We all speak without thinking first, especially when confronted with truths that send us reeling. That night, what you learned of your sire knocked you backward and—"

"—set me to drinking though I gave my mother my word I would not yield to that weakness no matter what befell me across the narrow sea. I did not keep my word, Mercia. I lied, and that lie made her a widow."

"Not a lie. I know that sin, having donned the mantle of an abbess and fully aware of my deceit in the moment. That you did not do."

He grunted. "The result is the same. I failed my mother, my cousins, and my sire. Though I have gained control of my drinking, there is no remedy for a life lost and lives seriously altered by the refusal to fight alongside my family."

"But do you not see, Maël? If you failed them it was not by way of deceit, and you have righted your wrong by refusing to use drink as reprieve from the cruelties of the world. And so I say, accept the Lord's forgiveness, seek the same of those you may have failed, and no matter how you are received, be done with it. Live the life left to a man bettered by his failings. Cease looking behind and begin looking—" She faltered. "What is it, Maël?"

He reached up, touched her cheek. "At my side—near scandalously so—the Abbess of Lillefarne. Did you thus counsel your charges? Prying open their eyes to the benevolence of the Lord? To the righting of wrongs? To walking a new path?"

Her lashes fluttered. "I tried."

"Then the false abbess was not entirely false. Though she did not commit her life to the Church, she aided those who did and sought to do."

She sighed. "Unfortunately, here on earth it is not God who will judge me for what I did. It is Bishop Odo, and I do not believe he will see good in it." Lowering her hands, she sat back on her heels. "But let us not speak of what will or will not be come the morrow," she said as if she could not bear further assurance of hope. "Tell what happened after Hastings—how you came to be at Westminster that day."

Remembering, he said, "I did not intend to remain in England, but neither was I prepared to return to Normandy.

Not only did I hope to locate Guarin, be he alive or dead, but I could not bear facing my mother. And so Theriot and I remained with William, fighting alongside him as we made our way to London and the crown he meant to claim."

"You were not yet the captain of his guard, am I right?"

"I was not. After I left you and your grandmother, I aided in putting an end to clashes between the mercenaries who set fires and roused Saxons to anger. Thus, I was among those who delivered to England's new king the miscreants responsible for making a travesty of his coronation. When later he gathered men who had distinguished themselves at Hastings to reward them, he offered me English lands."

"You told you declined them as well as the hand of a Saxon heiress," Mercia reminded him of what he had revealed the night the Danes came for her at the inn.

He nodded. "Though better I would have fought had I not succumbed to drink the night before the great battle, many the Saxons I cut down to preserve my life and the lives of fellow Normans. But having failed my family, I proved unworthy of such reward and, thus, no longer wished a life in England."

"But you did not leave my country."

"When I rejected lordship of English lands, William offered the position vacated by the captain of his guard who was deemed lax in ending the chaos outside Westminster. Once more I declined, and he said it was an offer in name only. Though tempted to argue, it occurred it would give me time and excuse before I faced my mother. Too, being a position of great responsibility, it would allow me to redeem myself in some measure."

"And yet you brought Lady Chanson to England."

"Because of Theriot. He pressed me to deliver her across the channel for the sake of his brother whose lands he had been given to administer until Cyr returned from pilgrimage. He said he needed a Norman lady to set up the household of the castle raised upon Wulfenshire, and when I resisted, accused me of having little care for her and said she might as well be in mourning for her only child as well as Hugh. Accepting he was right, I agreed. Still, no matter how often I promised myself I would tell her all, ever I have sidestepped the truth, not only because of my hand in Hugh's death, but so I would not have to deceive her by hiding his betrayal of their vows."

"I do not know your lady mother well," Mercia said, "but methinks the truth will not undo her, especially if it returns to her the son she loves—and all the easier now she has a good life with Father Fulbert. Indeed, I believe she is as beloved as he. Since she wed him, the only shadows I have seen about her face are when Nicola speaks of you." Mercia touched his hand. "When next you are with your lady mother, tell her all. It may not make either of you whole, but surely more than you are now."

Was she right? Or would Chanson be less whole knowing he was behind her loss? Might she blame herself since Hugh had attributed their son's shortcomings to the soft of her?

"Promise you will tell her," Mercia said.

He peered into eyes nearly black for the breadth of her pupils. "You have my word."

"I thank you."

"*You* thank me?"

"Knowing you and your mother are reconciled, better I can accept my punishment when I stand before the bishop and—"

"As you said," Maël interrupted, "no more talk of what will or will not be on the morrow."

She shifted her gaze to the scarred side of his face. "Neither within nor without are you a monster, Maël D'Argent." She rose to her knees again, lifted a hand between them.

Knowing what she asked, he wanted to refuse, but he nodded. And tensed when she set fingers on his brow where first the blade had dug in before curving toward his eye.

"Have never been, will never be," she whispered and traced the path no other had done besides him and the physician. "Just as never have you been my enemy though once I believed it."

"As once I believed Saxon women the enemy," he said. "After our crossing of the channel, my sire warned those of your country are capable of bewitchment, thus dangerous to William's cause and our own. Superstition, my cousins and I named it, but after what I witnessed in the tavern, I wanted to believe it. Though no longer convinced rumors of Hugh's infidelity were lies, it was something of a balm to blame forces outside him for his behavior. And more proof was had when Cyr, next Guarin and Dougray, succumbed to English women."

"Not bewitchment," Mercia said. "Love both sides and surely with the Lord's blessing, for how better to heal England than unite Norman and Saxon with marriage, making one people of them through offspring?"

Knowing it was impossible to be united thus with her, he stared.

"I do not understand it," she whispered, "but when first we met, I felt your emptiness, and when you agreed to allow Gytha and me to depart, I near ached to fill that space in you with what little in me was not empty." She touched her lips to where her fingers had been. "I will miss you, Maël."

He ceased breathing, but the lack of air only intensified his longing for her, and more so when she began pressing kisses up the scar to his brow.

"Pray, remember me," she said, then set her mouth on his.

He let her kiss him until he could no longer bear receiving without giving back. Then leaning hard into the meeting of their mouths, he opened his on hers. As the breath returned to him became hers and hers became his and their hands began exploring the hollows and curves of necks, shoulders, waists, and backs, the fraying seams of the cold place where long Maël had dwelt gave. Warmth suffusing him, he felt the pound of a heart returned to life. It was glorious and—

Dangerous, his conscience struck hard.

Lest one more touch cause him to dishonor her, he set her back and, peering into her wide eyes, said, "I will not have us cross a line over which we should not set foot, Mercia. I *will* remember you, but as we are now, not with regret as shall be felt do we continue what can find no good end."

Her shoulders lowered. "As told, not bewitchment," she said. "As told, you are honorable and worthy. And so I shall sit beside you the night long do you allow it."

Though it would be best for Ingvar to return her to her cell, he said, "Sit beside me."

It was another hour before the Dane appeared and found her sleeping, Maël's arm around her, her head on his shoulder.

"Have you answer for me?" Maël asked low.

"Thus far, what you request is not possible, Sir Maël."

Then the Dane had not merely walked the deck and conversed with those on duty.

"Best chance when there much excitement over preparation to sail." Ingvar nodded. "Then I see if can make possible."

"Ever I would be grateful," Maël said.

"This I know." The Dane crossed to his station, lowered the lantern's flame, and climbed into his hammock.

Lord, help me keep Mercia out of Odo's hands, Maël silently beseeched as he drew her nearer, *even though it means returning her to that manipulative old woman.*

CHAPTER TWENTY-ONE

*T*hough tempted to linger over his ablutions in the cabin where first Mercia was taken to make herself presentable for King William's brother, Maël had quickly bathed and exchanged fouled garments for the clean ones provided him, which proved of good quality, including a green woolen mantle whose edges were embroidered with ivory thread.

Now, stepping onto the deck into sunshine long denied him, he narrowed eyes pained by the sparkling sea last he had sailed upon when he believed his future dependent on depriving the enemy of their own good futures.

"I not like if need go in after you, Lady," Ingvar called, turning Maël toward where the man perched on a crate behind Mercia.

Once more beautifully clothed, the former Abbess of Lillefarne gripped the railing, setting her face against a cool wind that made hair released from its braids lift off her back and flutter like a pennant across her far shoulder. Should the wind cease, that great length would drop and settle against her lower calves if not her ankles.

Looking around, Maël saw the Danes who worked the rigging divided their attention between keeping air in the sails and the woman who was to have been their prince's wife.

"You hear me, Lady?" Ingvar raised his voice though he was near enough she had to have heard.

Did she consider a leap into the sea a means of escaping Bishop Odo? Maël did not believe it, and neither did Ingvar who would otherwise have planted himself at her side. As the coast was too distant to reach even were she a strong swimmer and able to shed her gown before becoming entangled, only if she preferred death over severe punishment would she give Ingvar cause to go in after her. And the Dane would, regardless of whether Canute ordered it.

Maël did not have to look far to locate Sweyn's son. Richly garbed to reflect his station when he represented his sire who had remained on the Humber, he stood at the bow with legs braced apart. Here a prince of Denmark soon to take audience with the brother of the king whose lands he and his sire coveted, and sailing to the left, right, and behind seven other ships to protect against Norman treachery.

Far less a concern that would be were it William come to the estuary into which the Great Ouse river emptied into the sea, but it was to be Odo who had less honor than the man who ordered the harrying of the North.

Hopefully, Ingvar would give the bishop good cause to refuse to pay Mercia's ransom. If so, a safer life, though not necessarily a good one, awaited her beyond England's shores. Once Maël did all he could for her, he would aid in recovering Nicola were she yet missing, and have reason to do so in the eyes of his king—retrieval of the mantle piece.

"You look a chevalier again, Sir Maël!" Ingvar called, causing Canute to peer over his shoulder.

Maël acknowledged the prince with a nod, then strode toward Mercia whose attention remained on the coast. As he drew near, he looked questioningly at Ingvar to determine the man's success in accomplishing the task set him.

The Dane's face remained impassive, but if Canute yet looked this way, it was necessary to avert suspicion were something of great import soon discovered missing. Unfortunately, had Ingvar failed, little time remained to aid Mercia. Within the hour, the Danes' ships would turn west and drop anchor at the estuary's mouth. Soon thereafter, the ransoming.

Catching the scent of cloves that Mercia's washed hair shook into the wind, suppressing the longing to catch hold of it and sift it through his fingers, he halted on the side of her buffeted by stirred air.

As he did not expect her to speak more than she had this morn before being escorted to the cabin, he was relieved when she said, "I hold to Psalm thirty-one, over and over reciting it. Though still I am afeared, I am stronger for it—and for you being here with me." She set a hand atop his on the railing. "Will you remain until you can no longer?"

Not caring who watched, he turned his palm up and fingers around hers. "I will."

She turned to him, moved her gaze over his face. "Though it appears you are of a mind to make the facial hair of my menfolk your own, you do look the chevalier again."

He let his mouth tilt. "Unfortunately, I was not permitted a razor to scrape clean this jaw. You prefer it bearded?"

He should not have asked that, and more he regretted it when her eyes moistened. "'Tis not for me to approve nor disapprove."

She will be gone from me soon, Maël thought, and as what remained of that cold place beckoned him back inside, amended, *Gone unless Ingvar fails, and then...*

What? he demanded of the man who had given his oath to William. *How do you free her without betraying your king?*

Mercia raised her chin, forced a smile. "With sunlight running the silver of your hair, above all you look a D'Argent."

That he was—first, in between, and in the end. Were Mercia a D'Argent...

Impossible. Even if he wished it, he could not grant her the protection of the name of which he was unworthy. Were he given the opportunity to speak vows with her—and that would require a miracle—an enemy he would make of the king. Thus, a life spent evading William's vengeance could bode worse for her than what awaited her should Ingvar fail.

"'Tis most wondrous hair," she said.

Now Maël forced a smile. "Do you not think it makes me look aged?"

"At first glance, but at second it is as breathtaking as a moonless night when the stars shine brightest against the heavens." She averted her eyes. "Though it is wrong, I wish I had put my hands in it last eve."

Such honesty he had not expected despite what had passed between them, especially as she had hardly spoken this morn as if regretting kisses that had sought to move them to acts reserved for marriage.

Determined to be as honest as she, he said, "I wanted to loose your braids, but far too dangerous that for how it stirs a man." When she looked up, he nodded over his shoulder. "I wager there is not one aboard who does not long to wind the soft of your hair around his hand."

Her wind-flushed face brightened further. "It is immodest to leave it unbound, but it was the only way to ensure it is dry when I stand before the bishop."

He inclined his head, and once more she turned to the sea. After a time, she said, "Ingvar is a good man. I worry what might befall him if Canute discovers what I carry on my person."

Maël tensed. "He has given you something?"

"He told I should keep the psalter and bound it up in linen with the brooch and my grandmother's missive."

Catching hold of that last, Maël said, "You speak of the missive instructing you to leave Lillefarne with the Danes?"

She frowned. "As told, 'tis the only one I possess, and still I cannot bring myself to destroy it."

Disappointed, Maël said, "You have it on your person?"

"Aye, Ingvar instructed me to secure it beneath my skirts. He said should I require funds to deliver me from Norman wrath, it will bring more than enough coin to see me out of the country. Though I know it is of great worth, especially if it belonged to the daughter of King Alfred as I suspect, it is only of value if the one to whom I offer it has integrity enough to give service."

As it was possible it would be stolen from her—further endangering her—it was all the more imperative their jailer gain what was of greater value to her.

"Regardless, I would not have Ingvar pay a terrible price for his kindness," she said.

They fell silent until a shout alerted the Danes the estuary was sighted.

Holding tighter to Maël's hand, Mercia strained to see what the one atop the mast saw. And there it was...

"Go put your hair in order," Maël said. "A simple braid, perhaps two."

As she also thought best. The bishop might not be softened by the false abbess if she looked a humble lady, but he would be further hardened were she arrayed in elaborate braids that made her look a haughty Saxon.

Feeling great loss when she released Maël's hand, she crossed the gently rolling deck.

When she emerged from the cabin, hair fashioned into two plaits looped once and fastened at her nape to make their great length less obvious, clearly she saw the estuary beyond Maël who remained at the railing with Ingvar at his back.

Several sails having been lowered, the ship made for the wide mouth bordered on all sides by low-lying fens that discouraged stealth in daylight. Though the vegetation scattered near and far was of a height and breadth behind which men might take cover, they would not be able to do so in numbers great enough to present a threat to one shipload of Danes, let alone eight.

Now it was Mercia who came alongside Maël. "You think Bishop Odo will come this day?"

He turned his face to hers. "As word was surely sent him as soon as Danish ships appeared, methinks he will show soon. Have you a veil?"

She touched the one tucked beneath her belt. "I will don it when we are out of the wind so I not lose it to the sea."

Shortly, Canute gave the order to drop anchor and lower the rowboats that would carry them to land, then the tap of his hard-soled boots announced his approach.

"Now we make trade," he said as his captives turned to him.

"What will you tell my grandmother?" Mercia asked.

He shrugged. "That is for my sire to do."

"She will not like that I have been traded for silver."

"She will not, but she will understand the need to make good our losses and her need to maintain favor with the King of Denmark upon whose benevolence she depends."

Then Gytha did know that what remained of her life was to be spent in exile.

The prince looked to Maël. "Once we are on land, your weapons and purse will be returned. God willing, we will meet again one day so I may redeem myself in bettering you."

"God willing, so I may prove redemption beyond your reach, Prince."

Canute chortled, ordered Ingvar to keep watch over his prisoners, and departed.

"The Danes are not done with England," Maël said. "The same as their ancestors, they shall return."

"When?" Mercia asked.

"As their losses have been great, their ranks rife with treachery, five years, mayhap ten."

Will I be here to see it? she wondered. *If so, at what place? A tower room whose locked door makes me as much a prisoner of Le Bâtard as I have been upon this ship?*

More a prisoner, she realized, for Maël would not be with her. Throat tightening, she said, "Where will you go?"

"Much depends on this day."

She wanted to press for more, but he turned back to the railing and said, "Bishop Odo comes."

So he did. Upon the fens most distant to the eye appeared a dark mass, the only light about it the glint of silver evidencing armor and weapons.

"Psalm thirty-one," Maël murmured.

Struggling to keep from quaking, she turned her face up to his, and he set his mouth on hers.

Though the Danes were so occupied with preparations to disembark it was unlikely many witnessed the kiss, it was brief.

"Psalm thirty-one," Mercia said when Maël drew back. "I hold it close."

CHAPTER TWENTY-TWO

*S*eparate boats, two of a score lowered from Canute's ships, carried Maël and Mercia up the estuary and through branches of the fens to a place of firm, expansive ground where Bishop Odo and a force of one hundred fifty men were to trade chests of silver for the king's captain of the guard and the woman said to be of Godwine blood.

Unfortunately, Maël had been unable to converse with Ingvar before departing the ship and the older Dane had remained aboard. Thus, it was unknown whether Odo would pay Mercia's ransom. The only thing for certain was Canute was confident of returning to his sire with two chests of silver.

Maël's dagger, sword, and purse returned to him, he was flanked by Danes ordered to ensure William's man presented as a prisoner accorded honor, but not so well that the weapons on his person jeopardized the ransom paid for him.

At the far left where Mercia stood unmoving, from beneath her veil she stared at the Normans who had yet to send a representative to the middle ground where Canute's man had positioned himself.

At last, the bishop of two score years whose elaborate dress beneath a mail vest identified his high office, looked behind and motioned someone forward.

No mere representative this, but Guarin D'Argent now of the name Wulfrith.

Relief suffused Maël. As his cousin was so soon returned from the North, he must have found Theriot, perhaps even Nicola.

Odo and Guarin conversed, then the latter urged his mount forward and, meeting Maël's gaze, inclined his head.

Words were exchanged between the two representatives, then both withdrew to report what was required of the other.

Laughable formality, Maël mused. They knew exactly what was needed to make the trade.

After calling forth Maël and Mercia, around whom were set four warriors each, Canute tucked a wooden cask beneath his arm and began the march to the middle ground.

Odo did the same—or nearly so. As though beneath the bishop to sully his boots across marshy ground, he remained astride, his mount led forward by one who wore the garments of a simple priest. The two were accompanied by eight warriors the same as Canute, two of whom carried chests considerably larger than the one borne by the prince.

At a distance of twenty feet, both sides halted.

"Canute, son of Sweyn of Denmark," Odo called, eschewing the titles due father and son, "in the name of God's anointed one, King William the Great, sovereign of England and Duke of Normandy now and forevermore, the most holy, honorable, and high Bishop Odo greets you."

Canute snorted. "All know that holy peacock's plumage is dipped more in blood than ink," he muttered, then called, "Odo, *half* brother of William, in the name of God's anointed one, King Sweyn the Magnificent, lawful and beloved sovereign of Denmark now and forevermore, the courageous, honorable Prince Canute asks—have you the silver to redeem your brother's man and gain wardship of Lady Mercia of the House of Godwine?"

Pink sweeping up the bishop's neck and coloring his jaw, he jutted his chin at Maël. "As there the man I know by sight, I have the silver to redeem him."

Hoping if distaste for Odo showed in any measure, it disguised itself as disaffection with his captors, Maël inclined his head.

"As he appears to be in good health as promised," the bishop continued, "send him forth, and I shall send payment. Then we shall confirm wardship of the lady."

"Go, Chevalier," Canute ordered.

Feeling Mercia's gaze, Maël looked to where she stood on the prince's other side. Though her eyes were moist, her chin was up as if once more she played the Abbess of Lillefarne.

Hoping for her sake that never again would he be so near her, Maël set his teeth and strode forward.

One of the two Normans bearing a chest broke from the others and, moments later, Odo's man passed William's man.

"My side, Chevalier Maël!" the bishop called, and the warriors opposite the priest who held the bridle of Odo's mount opened a path for him.

In the Norman ranks beyond, Maël caught sight of Guarin at the fore. Beside him was Eberhard, his and Hawisa's adopted son. But of greater note than the squire who was now more man than boy were two noblemen on Guarin's other side.

The first was Hugh de Grandmesnil, a companion of William's greatly rewarded with lands in Leicestershire and entrusted with aiding Odo in governing England during the king's absence. The second was De Grandmesnil's son, aged ten and six, who had been named after the duke who became a king.

Maël halted alongside Odo. "Bishop."

William's brother flicked his gaze over him, then returned his regard to the Danes.

Shortly, the prince looked up from the chest he had been presented and dropped the lid. "As agreed, William's brother," he called.

"That is a great quantity of silver, Sir Maël," Odo said. "Though much you disappoint in being captured, the king is confident many times over you will repay it in service to him."

Maël clenched his hands. He had not considered what the ransoming would cost him. Now his service to the king could stretch years beyond retrieving the mantle piece. Though such captivity would be far different from Mercia's if she, too, crossed to this side, a captive he would be.

"Now proof the false abbess is a Godwine," Odo called.

Canute gave the cask to one of his men who carried it forward, passed it to Maël, and stepped back to await the bishop's approval.

"What think you, Chevalier?" Odo said when Maël turned to him. "Is she a Godwine?"

He had not expected to be consulted, but here an opportunity to sow greater doubt. "For a time I was imprisoned alongside the Saxon. Though she presents well at first, often the face of nobility slips. Thus, likely she is but a pawn of Harold's mother—not only set against our king but possibly Sweyn the unwise."

Odo chortled. "The unwise, indeed. Hence, I come prepared."

There was something almost ominous about that last. Were there a place near for forces of great number to conceal themselves, Maël would think an attack on the Danes imminent, but the bishop made other, less bloody arrangements to ensure he benefitted more than Canute.

"The cask, Chevalier," he said, and Maël handed up what he prayed was lighter than it should be.

"A pretty box of good construction," Odo mused as he

balanced it atop his saddle's pommel. "Ere these miscreants thieved it from a House of God, likely it held holy relics."

As such sacrilege was not unique to Danes, numerous English churches having been stripped of valuables to pay for William's army, once more Maël set his teeth.

Odo pulled the latch's chained pin and raised the lid. One moment his smile made him appear attractive, the next unattractive for how flat it fell—and more so when the corners arched downward to deeply groove his chin.

He snapped up his head. "Where is the hag's missive, son of Sweyn?"

Silently heaping gratitude on Ingvar who, hopefully, had found his way off the ship, Maël looked to the prince.

Face transformed by such genuine confusion few could believe it feigned, he called, "It is exactly where my sire placed it."

Odo scrabbled over the contents and lifted out a gossamer veil, hammered silver circlet, and a ring set with a purple gem. Doubtless, all sent by Gytha with the missive to quickly see Mercia wed to the prince.

"This is all it contains." The bishop thrust forward that hand while the other shook out the cask's emptiness atop the head of the priest on his other side. "Where is your proof the false abbess is a Godwine?"

Canute took a step forward as if to confirm the missive's absence, halted, then his eyes shifted wildly as if searching for sight of the parchment which was to have doubled the silver received for Maël.

"Ingvar!" the prince barked and pivoted toward Mercia.

The instinct to protect her nearly shouted down reason that warned Maël any attempt to aid her could endanger her more. Standing firm, he watched as Canute grabbed her shoulder and pulled her near.

"Did you persuade him to use those quick fingers of his to

steal the missive? Did you buy him with sexual favors, Gytha's granddaughter?"

"Loose me!" she cried.

Canute shook her. "Tell!"

To the surprise of those whose murmurings ceased as if to belatedly catch the sound of flesh striking flesh, she slapped her former betrothed.

He fell to stunned silence, then drew back a hand.

This time Maël's instincts shouted down reason, but hardly had he started forward than Odo commanded, "Do no harm!"

The prince faltered, looked around.

As Maël struggled to remain this side of the divide with his eyes on Mercia whose shoulders rose and fell with great breaths, Canute said, "She is deception, making me appear unworthy of my sire's trust in order to escape your king and join her grandmother in Denmark."

"As all men of good wit know," the bishop said, "more women are of Eve than of the blessed Mary. But fear not, even in the absence of proof of her blood, I may yet make use of her."

Though Maël had known Ingvar might bear blame for the lost missive, casting Mercia as an accomplice, he had not considered the bishop would part with coin lacking proof of her parentage.

"What do you propose?" Canute demanded.

Odo returned the veil, circlet, and ring to the cask, dropped the lid, and swept a hand to the man holding his horse's bridle. "Accompanying me this day is the Saxon priest, Jonas, who served as a clerk for Gytha of the House of Godwine. Though no longer possible for him to verify the missive was written by her hand, I would have him look close upon Lady Mercia to confirm she is the same who served the usurper's wife, Lady Alditha, and was in Gytha's confidence."

Then this what he had meant when he boasted he came

prepared, Maël realized—no coin given without some proof Mercia was of value.

Canute narrowed his eyes. "Does the priest say it is she, you will buy her wardship?"

"I will, though the price must be adjusted since it is not wardship of a Godwine I buy but that of a companion who may not prove useful in locating Alditha and her young son who are much in need of King William's protection."

The prince guffawed, expressing both disbelief over the queen and her child's fate should they be found and bitterness over acceptance of less coin. But he said, "Two of three portions is the price for Queen Alditha's companion."

"*Lady* Alditha's companion," Odo corrected. "And the price is one-third—*if* Father Jonas confirms she served that lady."

"One half," Canute countered. "No less will I take."

"One-third."

The prince gripped Mercia's arm and turned her opposite. "Come, Lady Mercia, the mother of King Harold will be pleased to make a good marriage for her granddaughter so one day the Godwines may reclaim England's throne."

"Hold!" Odo shouted.

Canute did not falter.

"I will give one half!"

The prince held his back to the Normans a long moment, then brought Mercia around. "Very good, Bishop," he said as if praising a dog. "Now begin counting out half that silver and send over your priest."

CHAPTER TWENTY-THREE

*M*ercia knew Jonas. Jonas knew Mercia. Not well, but enough that only were the priest's eyesight deficient would he need to look nearer upon her than already he had across the distance.

As she watched, he loosed the bishop's mount and, with a slight weave in his step as compensation for the twist in his spine, waded through the long grass.

Smooth of jaw and bald of pate, the man of thirty and five years halted before her. Regret shone from his pale blue eyes, but the Saxon man of God who now answered to a Norman bishop announced, "Here Queen Alditha's companion, keeper of the wardrobe and, on occasion, companion to King Harold's mother."

Thus, Mercia's fate was sealed, whatever that might prove in Bishop Odo's power—and Le Bâtard's if she survived punishment for posing as an abbess.

The prospect of the days ahead—be they few or many—making her long for Lillefarne where she had the honor and authority to do good for others, she sent heavenward, *Lord, You answered my prayers to escape that life knowing more I would regret this one. I know not what is left to me, but help me keep my trust in You. Let me not waver. Let me hold firm.*

"The deal is struck!" Odo called, and one of his men hefted the chest emptied of half its silver and carried it forward.

"Any words you wish delivered to your grandmother?" Canute asked as Mercia began the crossing alongside the priest.

She turned back. "Only that I wish her a good life and shall keep her in my prayers. And Ingvar... You shall believe as you will, but I asked naught of him that would cause him to betray you." And it was true, that bound to the outside of her leg beneath her skirt not asked of him and only of consequence had Canute been aware the earl possessed something so precious and thought to relieve him of it.

The prince frowned. "Mayhap it was not you who persuaded him to take the missive." He looked to the man she also suspected of gaining their jailer's aid. "Or mayhap Ingvar did not steal. But of all my men, he is best at it—without sound and shadow slipping in empty-handed, slipping out full-handed." He sighed. "I shall make you a promise. Should Ingvar be aboard when I return, I will give him time to convince me of his innocence."

Would he be aboard? Mercia wondered. Or had he departed knowing suspicion would fall heavily on him, thus requiring time to distance himself from royal wrath?

The latter, she determined, and all because he had done what Maël asked of him—unfortunately, to no avail. Hoping he would not pay a high price, Mercia started to turn away.

"Have you not a question for me, granddaughter of Gytha?" Canute said too low for the enemy to hear.

She considered his slight smile, and made sense of him. But though great the temptation to have him reveal who sired her, she was done begging for scraps. Too, even were she to look upon the words, they could not be wholly believed. In the hope of restoring the Godwines to the ruling class, Gytha had wanted a marriage between the Danish prince and her blood, and no lie was too big to secure that.

"You are too kind, Prince Canute, but as I find myself in untenable circumstances because of the desire to learn that which was long withheld from me, best I trust in the Lord to be my father than a man who never was and can never be now he is dead." Knowing she should find no satisfaction in his surprised disappointment, but finding it, she regained the priest's side.

As she moved her gaze from Odo high in the saddle to Maël standing tall alongside him, the priest said low, "Forgive me. I longed to save you from that bishop who is more a false warrior of God than ever you were in donning the robes of an abbess, but I strive to be a man of few lies."

His choice of words brought her head around. *"Few* lies?"

With a smile more crooked than his spine, he said, "After William gained London, here and there a lie told to preserve the lives and liberty of many, including Lady Gytha and you so you might escape the city. Among the greatest of my lies was that written under the direction of Harold's mother for a woman never did she tell was of her blood—she who was to become Abbess Mary Sarah of Lillefarne."

Recalling the missive delivered to the nuns of the abbey, Mercia shook her head. "It was Archbishop Stigand who named me the new abbess."

Jonas shook his head. "My quill, my ink, my parchment. Having gained Gytha's assurance it was in accord with his wishes and her word she would inform him it was done under her direction, I wrote it and set his name to it."

Mercia glanced ahead. Seeing they drew too near to long continue the discussion, she said, "Does Bishop Odo know this?"

"He does not, and I pray you hold it close lest I be tempted to another lie and further disappoint the Almighty."

"I will say naught."

"I thank you. Though I know not where Queen Alditha's brothers took her when they fled London, I would not fall under more suspicion than I do in having served the king's mother."

Mercia nodded.

"Upon much reflection, I believe you are of Godwine blood," Jonas continued. "Though Gytha thought to make use of you to advance her interests, it was obvious she was more fond of you than any of the ladies long in her service."

Mercia needed none to confirm Gytha's blood flowed through her, nor that the old woman was fond of her in some small measure, but it had not been enough to stand inside the circle of her family. For that, she was here now.

"I thank you for your kindness, Jonas, and I hold you blameless for whatever path I now walk. All I ask is you pray for me."

"I shall, my lady."

They halted before the bishop, and though Mercia ordered herself not to show any regard for Maël, her eyes were drawn to him. In his she saw disquiet. And something that could prove of great detriment to him—assurance he would aid her.

Only of comfort and hope did she not love him.

ODO WAS MORE GIVEN to games than William, and this day was no exception. No word had he spoken to Mercia when she stood before him as the Danes retreated. Only when her gaze wavered and her clasped hands began to tremble had he broken the silence by ordering the priest to escort the false abbess to where his army awaited them and commanding Maël to join his cousin.

Since there had been no delay in journeying to Wulfenshire

and the pace set to reach Stern Castle by nightfall was a rigorous one, no opportunity was there for Guarin and Maël to speak until two hours later when they paused at a stream to water their mounts.

Maël looked from where Mercia was aided in dismounting the horse shared with a chevalier to his cousin.

"Much has passed since we parted at Wulfen Castle," Guarin said as he yielded his horse's reins to his squire, Eberhard.

Maël inclined his head. "You have found Theriot and Nicola?"

Guarin's mouth tightened. "Finding and retrieving are two different things."

"Where are they?"

Guarin took a long draw from his wineskin and handed it to Maël. "Theriot is in Scotland at King Malcolm's court."

"Scotland?" Maël exclaimed.

Guarin jutted his chin for Maël to drink and after he did, said, "Several different accounts I have picked apart and pieced into one that halfway makes sense."

"That is?"

"Theriot was tracking Edgar the Aetheling and his men who fled the harrying to once more gain Malcolm's protection. Near the border, he was injured and captured."

Maël stiffened. "How badly injured?"

"Likely nothing serious. The men I sent into Scotland returned with reports of a young man of silvered dark-haired walking Malcolm's gardens with a lady."

Recalling the rumors Theriot had deserted William's service, Maël said, "The king has been told?"

"I pray not lest he make much of the tongue wagging that Theriot deserted."

"When will you go in after him?"

"As Cyr now makes his home in Normandy, Dougray has yet to return to England, and Nicola seems the more pressing concern, my reach is stunted. Thus, for now I leave Theriot in God's hands."

"You know what transpired at the inn when I sought to trade Mercia for your sister?" Maël asked.

"Sir Daryl gave an accounting, but a truer accounting I had from your other men left behind when you gave chase."

Recalling the Saxon-turned-Norman who lost his sire to Vitalis during the skirmish at the inn and himself took a blow from Zedekiah, Maël thought it likely Daryl would seek vengeance against his countrymen. "Then you know the earl's misbegotten son, Bjorn, took Nicola from there."

"I do, and that Vitalis followed and he is our greatest hope of retrieving her."

"She may have been borne across the sea."

"Blessedly not. The day before I returned to Wulfen Castle and learned Bishop Odo had paused at Stern en route to trade silver for you and Mercia of Mercia, my lady wife received Zedekiah who carried a message from Vitalis. It told Bjorn joined his sire in raiding down the coast as ordered by King Sweyn and Nicola remains with the infatuated Dane. He assured Hawisa she is in good health and treated well despite the frustration of finding no opportunity to escape."

"Where are they?" Maël asked.

"Possibly very near since Vitalis believes they intend to venture further inland to seize the town of Ely and set up a base there from which to raid the wealth of East Anglia."

"Word was sent to William?"

"Oui, and Odo warned as well. For that—lest his forces are set upon—he hastens back to Wulfenshire."

Maël nodded. "With Danes abounding in East Anglia, it was not necessary for Canute to bring so many ships to pay the ransom. Methinks he will send back one with the silver and he and the rest of his men will join forces with his uncle's, which could as easily benefit Nicola as prove detrimental."

"Explain, Maël."

"If she falls into Canute's hands, he will ransom her. If Bjorn is forewarned of his cousin's approach, he will run with Nicola, this time across the sea."

"I do not believe Vitalis will allow that," Guarin said, "but the sooner I take my leave of Odo, the better."

Once more, Maël looked to Mercia and saw she knelt at the stream sipping water from her hands. "I do not know what lies ahead for her, but I am bound to aid her, Guarin. Hence, as soon as possible I will join you in retrieving Nicola and Theriot."

His cousin's brow grooved. "How is it you are *bound* to aid a Saxon woman?"

Though pride kicked Maël as if to knock the truth back down him, he said, "There are things I must needs tell—answers never given of what happened at Hastings—and I will, but at a better time than this. Until then, I admit I care for her."

Guarin gripped his cousin's shoulder. "I am pleased, above all that such feeling bodes well for the return of one who has ever been more a brother than a cousin to me."

"I hope you will feel the same when you know all."

"I shall."

Discomfited by how much he wanted to believe that, Maël longed to turn the conversation, and there were several things that gave him cause. "One of my best men fell to a Dane the night Canute came for Mercia at the inn. Know you if Sir Anselm survived?"

"He did. Though his injury is serious, he was taken to a nearby monastery and there recovers."

Maël thanked the Lord, then asked, "How fares Lady Hawisa?"

"Greatly she tires, the babe so large the physician believes she will birth ahead of her time." Guarin breathed deep. "Much prayer for that."

Maël understood. The greatest danger to women of

childbearing years was bringing life into the world. Hence, the smaller the babe, the easier the delivery and more likely both survived—providing the child was nearly full term.

"I shall keep your lady wife and child in my prayers, Guarin."

"As I will keep Mercia and you in mine."

Maël looked to where De Grandmesnil conversed with Odo. Though he did not esteem this companion of William's, compared to others who kept close company with the king, the man was decent and capable of humor that made one think hard rather than entertain themselves at the expense of another's dignity.

"You question why De Grandmesnil is here?" Guarin asked. At his cousin's nod, he said, "Much speculation over the High Sheriff of Leicestershire's accompaniment, but none with merit enough to repeat."

Still Maël would hear it, but before he could press his cousin, the command was given for all to regain their mounts, which was done quickly as if to stay ahead of the enemy.

And quite possibly they did.

CHAPTER TWENTY-FOUR

Stern Castle
Wulfenshire, England

$\mathcal{L}$ady Chanson surprised. Though she had to know the truth about Lillefarne's abbess, the talk of Odo's men having revealed they passed last eve at Stern, the lady stepped from her son's side toward the woman who had deceived all.

Ignoring the bishop's sharp reproof, she continued forward, and when the chevaliers flanking Mercia attempted to block her progress, pushed past and wrapped her arms around one she ought not. And surprised again in a different way.

Unseen beneath her full skirt was a firm bulge. Maël's mother, of two score years, was with child. Cause for joy, but also fear since the delivery of a babe could be as dangerous for a woman approaching the end of her childbearing years as one just entering them.

Was Maël aware of his mother's state? Would she give him a brother or sister? More, how would he feel knowing this babe further distanced her from her first husband? Would it be of relief that she continued to rebuild a life lost and with what seemed a better man?

Guessing she would never know, Mercia closed her eyes and savored what felt a genuine embrace.

Chanson drew back, then clasping the false abbess's face between her palms, said for all to hear, "Praise the Lord you are returned to us."

"Lady Chanson!" Bishop Odo barked. "Already a fine line you and your husband walk. At greater peril, you stretch it and my patience thinner."

"And thinner yet when he learns a marriage of which he disapproves has produced a babe," Chanson whispered, then released Mercia and turned to the flushed man who stood at the center of the hall. "Forgive me, Bishop. It is difficult not to rejoice in the return of one taken by the Danes, and as you must know, it gives hope the Lord will also see my niece restored to us."

"I would not begrudge you the joy of that Norman lady's return," Odo said. "But as you know, this Saxon is the false abbess who made mockery of the Church, and likely under the influence of the unholy one."

Mercia's heart lurched. Refusing to look to Maël whose regard she felt, she beseeched the Lord to stand in judgment of her ahead of men who professed to be His representatives on earth. Were she accused of consorting with the unholy one rather than merely the departed king's mother, more likely death would be her end even had she proof of Godwine blood.

Though Mercia sensed Chanson wished to argue with Odo, the lady said kindly, "Yours has been a long journey, Bishop. Pray, take your ease in Stern's hall, and the drink and viands being prepared for you will be served."

His lids narrowed. "See it done soon, and the solar made ready for me."

"Of course. May I ask how long we shall be honored with your presence?"

"Only as long as it takes for this woman to repent."

Mercia wished she did not understand that, but better she was fearful than ignorant of what lay ahead.

"I give her into your care," he said. "Now take her from my sight."

As Lady Chanson drew Mercia toward the stairs, he called, "Her finery offends. When next I look upon her, she will be clothed in the garments of the lowly."

No longer could Mercia keep her eyes from Maël, but it was a good thing. Though Father Fulbert gripped his arm, her curt shake of the head settled him. Now was not the time to give aid. If ever again...

"WHAT IS THIS?" Chanson looked up from the packet Mercia had unfastened from her leg following removal of the fine bliaut.

"One item of great value to many, the others of value only to me." Mercia lowered the hem of the soft chemise Chanson had insisted she retain since the servant's gown was woven of coarse wool. "As it could bode ill were they found on my person, pray give that into your son's keeping."

Chanson arched an eyebrow. "He knows of this?"

"He does."

As Mercia had answered most of the lady's questions covering the abduction at Lillefarne through the ransoming, thinking here the end of their exchange, she looked longingly at the bed she was to share with Chanson whilst the bishop occupied the solar.

"He is changed," Maël's mother said softly. "Was it you?"

Mercia frowned. "Me?"

Chanson set the wrapped psalter on the table alongside the bed, stepped near, and swept from Mercia's eyes hair over which she had marveled when the veil was removed.

See what you have hidden from the world, she had said. *Has ever a woman worn a crown more glorious than this?* She had run her fingers over a braid. *A rope could be made of such hair, so beautifully strong and nearly as thick at the ends as at the roots.*

"Oui, methinks it you who changed him," Chanson said. "Much time you have spent with my son these weeks, and now he returns weighted by something different from what has burdened him since the great battle—pain not in the dark below but in the light above. I saw it in his eyes, felt it when he tried not to look upon you, saw it again when he nearly challenged the bishop for reducing you to a commoner."

Mercia was tempted to lie so she not further bare herself and Maël, but she lowered to the mattress and said, "I will leave it to your son to tell how first he saved me, but know though brief that meeting ere I took the name of Mary Sarah, and unbelievable though it may sound, it was then first I felt something for him that I more deeply feel now." She touched her chest. "Regrettably, it needs pulling the same as what he has come to feel for me."

Eyes moistening, Chanson dropped to the mattress and lifted Mercia's hand in hers. "You must be saved. I know not how, but you absolutely must." She set the younger woman's hand on her belly. "A child grows in this cradle where first Maël grew when I was little more than a girl. God willing, five months hence I will not look upon the babe born of Fulbert and me in the hope it fills the place of the son who has been mostly lost to me since Hastings."

Mercia swallowed. "Does Maël know you are with child?"

"Though brief our embrace, I felt him startle the same as you." She breathed deep. "As much good came of your administration of Lillefarne, I care not why you did what you did. I may sin in thinking first and selfishly of my boy, but what matters is that Maël and you have the chance to see where your feelings lead."

Emotion pushing past Mercia's constricted throat, she caught a sob behind her lips.

Then Chanson's arms were around her again. "Mercia," she drew out the name as if to set it to music. "A better fit than Mary Sarah."

As ever, the lady seemed too young to be the mother of an adult, but Mercia knew this was how it would feel had she been comforted by the woman who birthed her—and how she had told herself it would feel were she permitted inside the Godwine circle.

Turning her face into Chanson's shoulder, she yielded to tears as the lady stroked her head, rubbed her back, and murmured assurances the D'Argents would stand her side.

They would try, but more for their sake than hers, Mercia feared they would fail.

"Mercia?" Her name should not have been the first thing out of Maël's mouth, but there it was.

Rimmed in moonlight, Lady Chanson halted alongside her son who had departed the hall a half hour earlier to escape Odo's presence.

"Mercia sleeps," she said, and he saw wonder in her smile. "Strange she is so different from Abbess Mary Sarah. Stranger yet it feels I know her better as if ever I saw Mercia beneath the holy garments." She set a hand atop his on the wall. "She loves you, and do you not love her, I believe you will."

Though tempted to deny having feelings for her, he said, "You assume I will have the opportunity to grow into love with her."

"I do, but that is what I want for you, Maël—the blessings of love till death do you part." She glanced down. "As methinks you know, I am to be a mother again, making Fulbert a father and you a brother."

"I am happy for you."

"Though you care not for my husband?"

Turning his hand up, he closed it around her small fingers. "I am sorry I allowed you to believe disapproval of your marriage was founded on dislike of Fulbert, though it is true for a time I cared not for him."

A soft breath went out of her. "Then?"

Was now the time to follow the advice of Ingvar and Mercia? Or would there be a better time? Deciding the sooner told the sooner his mother could fully embrace the life she made beyond Hugh, he said, "I seek your forgiveness."

"*My* forgiveness?"

"For a broken promise, for what I took from you at Hastings, for cowardice born of shame that sealed my lips and raised a wall between us."

"Tell me and spare me no truth, my son. I am strong and all the stronger now I am one with Fulbert."

Over the next half hour, Maël related what he had told Mercia, sparing his mother no truth though more gently he presented each for having first revealed them to the woman who made him feel the heart he had doubted he still possessed.

Throughout, Chanson spoke little, but never did he sense anger nor disappointment. Only sorrow.

Where they had lowered and set their backs against a wall of wooden timbers, Maël said, "And there the truth of your son for which he seeks but does not expect forgiveness."

She looked from the ebony canvas above to Maël. "How could you not be forgiven? Oui, I was betrayed by your sire, and not for the first time as you learned that night, but so were you."

"You were aware he was unfaithful?"

Torchlight glanced off wet eyes. "The same rumors, for which you beat boys and men, reached me by more sly means. In the beginning, I did not believe what was told of the man I loved, but long ere I accepted he defiled the marriage bed, simply I did not wish to believe it. You erred, my son, but your sire gave you cause—"

"That does not excuse me. I was a man not a boy. I knew what I was doing and that I ought not."

She set a hand on his jaw. "Hence, you sought the Lord's forgiveness, and just as I believe He has granted it, I believe the truth of Hugh will move others to offer forgiveness as they would themselves wish to be forgiven." She raised her eyebrows. "You will tell your cousins, will you not?"

"I shall seek their forgiveness, especially that of Guarin and Dougray who suffered most when I did not fight alongside them."

She moved her hand to his shoulder. "No matter what comes of your confession, you must lean hard on the greatest giver of grace as I did in beseeching Him to return my son to me. And so He has—much, methinks, by way of Mercia."

"I do aspire to lean hard on Him, Mother."

She smiled wearily, sighed. "And now much I long to lay my head on a pillow."

"I shall return you to the donjon."

He drew her up beside him, and she hugged him fiercely and a small cry escaped her when he returned the embrace. However, almost immediately she set herself back.

"I nearly forgot!" She opened the purse on her belt. "As Mercia fears this being found on her person, she asked me to give it to you."

He knew what it was. Too large to fit in his own purse, he raised his tunic and tucked it beneath the waistband of his chausses.

"May I ask what it is?" Chanson said as he led her across the wall walk.

"All she possesses, including a valuable psalter."

They did not speak again until they stepped off stairs carpeted in moonlight and started across the bailey, then his mother said, "What will you do, my son?"

She spoke of Mercia who had not been made to stand before Odo this eve, though she would on the morrow. "I shall seek to deliver her from the bishop without him knowing of my hand in it."

"And when you have done that?"

Were the situation not dire, he would smile over how confident she was of his success. "I will get her to safety beyond England."

"Normandy?"

"Non. As the duchy belongs to William, better Flanders, Paris, even Italy."

"Flanders! My brother is there. He would aid you."

He nodded. "Once I have secured a good position for Mercia—"

"A good position?" So swiftly she stepped in front of him, he nearly trod on her. "You will not make her your own?"

Accepting that was what he wished despite being unworthy of her love, the dull ache at his center turned sharp. "No easy life could I give Mercia. Not only am I landless, possessing only my sword arm to support me, but—"

"No easy life?" Chanson interrupted. "As evidenced by how effortlessly your sire gained my hand in marriage, methinks few things easily attained are greatly valued. But not so those things which require us to reach deep inside and outside ourselves to gain them. They are precious, and more so when they must reach deep inside and outside themselves to gain *us.*"

Struck by words so impassioned they made him want even

more what he should not for how terrible the cost of openly betraying William, Maël said, "I believe you are right, Mother, but the king has my oath, and having expended much on my ransom—"

"Your oath! After what he did in the North, such loyalty is no longer due him. It is due a man of honor, and that William is not." She gripped his arm, in a more fierce voice, said, "Hear me, my son. As your uncle would tell, there is a difference between keeping God-honoring and God-defiling oaths. That difference is known to you. Pray, do not let guilt of which you have been absolved by the Lord and will be absolved by others cause you to stay the side of one whose atrocities ought see him denied eternal rest."

Then she thought aversion to betrayal—this time that of his liege, rather than his family—the reason he could not make Mercia his own. Though once it would have been, no longer. As his mother said, there was a difference between keeping God-honoring and God-defiling oaths. And it could not have been clearer now there was Mercia.

"Pray, Maël," Chanson rasped, "seek God's counsel and go where He would have you go."

Setting his hands on her shoulders, he said, "You are missing a piece of what I meant to tell, Mother."

She frowned. "That is?"

"Oui, the king has my oath. But of more concern than earning his wrath for leaving his service without permission, which will be greater for how much he has expended to pay my ransom, is earning his vengeance once word of my marriage leads to the discovery I am the one who stole his wardship of Mercia."

His mother's eyes widened.

"With such a name as D'Argent, it will not escape him," he said. "Hence, it would be exceedingly dangerous—even deadly—to make Mercia my own."

Her shoulders sagged. "You are right, and I know William

well enough you ought not have to tell me that. I just so desperately wish you to be happy, Maël."

God has been kind to me, he thought. *Unlike Mercia who has neither mother nor father, I have this beautiful lady. And what Hugh could not give me, Uncle Godfroi did.*

"Come, let us see your head upon that pillow," he said and urged her toward the donjon.

He led her through the silent, torchlit hall and up the stairs, and at the door to the chamber she would share with Mercia, kissed her brow. "God rest ye, Mother."

She started to turn aside, hesitated, then gripped his arm and whispered, "I am thinking there is a way for you and Mercia."

Then her churning felt since departing the bailey was more scheming than angst. "Mother—"

"Non, hear me," she interrupted again as was not in her nature. "If you can set aside your pride as Guarin did to gain Hawisa, that which is dangerous will be less so. Indeed, perhaps enough to make it worth the risk."

That he doubted, but he said, "I listen."

When she finished, he neither agreed nor disagreed with her proposal. Not only because of a slap to his pride. Not only because still there was enough risk it could end badly. Because of what he would lose, even were he unworthy of it.

Knowing how hopeful his mother was in spite of what *she* would lose, he assured her he would think on it. And so he did as he lay on a pallet in the hall—until he determined naught could come of it whilst Mercia was so firmly in Odo's power. But afterward...

Perhaps.

CHAPTER TWENTY-FIVE

*G*uarin was gone.

An hour ahead of dawn, a rain-drenched messenger from Wulfen Castle had roused Stern's occupants and announced Lady Hawisa labored to gift her husband their first child.

The scowling, bleary-eyed Odo had hesitated to grant Guarin permission to depart, but it was not asked of him. As the bishop spluttered, the Baron of Wulfen ordered Eberhard to gather their belongings and meet him in the stables.

Maël had followed, and as he aided in saddling the horses, reminded his cousin soon they must speak of Hastings. Guarin had not responded, but before he swung into the saddle, had embraced his cousin and said, "Soon."

Maël had wished him Godspeed, and as he watched Guarin and Eberhard go from sight amid slashing rain, beseeched the Lord to grant Lady Hawisa a good delivery and a healthy babe.

Now as he paced, the only thing keeping him from thrusting past the bishop's men positioned before the stairs was knowing his mother and stepfather were present for Odo's questioning.

Propriety demanded a man of the Church, especially one of

high office, not be alone with Mercia. Blessedly, though Odo's men could have borne witness, he had agreed to Lady Chanson's petition that she and her husband accompany him.

How long had they been abovestairs? It felt hours, but from the slant of light come through the hall's windows, an hour would be much.

Halting before the great doors, Maël looked around at the bishop's men crowding the hall and settled his gaze on De Grandmesnil seated upon the dais. On the night past, the nobleman had announced he and his son would depart this day and grumbled much this morn when the rain prevented them from doing so. Guarin had been right about the speculation over their accompaniment. No merit could be found in it, but it mattered not. As soon as the skies cleared, they would be gone.

Maël opened a door, stepped onto the threshold, and peered out across the walls at a wood that was little more than dark shadow beyond the curtaining rain. Did someone huddle there gazing upon Stern?

Hopefully, he did and would provide evidence of Mercia's lineage, the absence of which had failed to keep her out of Odo's hands and rendered her useful only if she told what she did not know.

"Psalm thirty-one," Maël murmured, then strode to his pack in the far alcove and retrieved his mantle. It was time to ride to the wood.

"No MATTER HOW many times you ask—softly or loudly, kindly or cruelly—I will say the same. I am Mercia of Mercia, misbegotten of the House of Godwine, Queen Alditha's companion and keeper of the wardrobe, the false abbess of Lillefarne, the cast-off betrothed of Prince Canute. That is all."

Once more Odo circled her, once more thrust his face near.

"That is not all!"

Ears ringing, gripping the rim of the stool so hard her knuckles ached, Mercia stilled her fluttering lids and swallowed against a dry throat. "I say again, I am not privy to the secrets of the queen who left me behind when she departed London. The same as you, I know only rumors—that she and her son are hidden in the midlands...they fled to Ireland...they joined my grandmother in Denmark..."

Nostrils flaring between ruddy cheeks riddled with tiny veins, Odo straightened. Then he circled again, so closely his robes dragged across her arms, back, chest, and face. Four times he did so, and with each circling she tensed further in anticipation of angry words, sour breath, and a spray of saliva.

"You lie, Witch!"

She startled hard despite being prepared, heard the catch of Lady Chanson's breath, and out of the corner of her eye saw Fulbert set a hand on his wife's arm.

"I do not lie," Mercia croaked.

A flash of red preceded the hand come at her. Light jumping between the facets of the large gem set in his ring, he thrust a finger between her eyes, this time so near she felt its warmth. "Liar!"

She stared. And gasped when he jabbed his finger against her forehead as not done before.

"Bishop!" Chanson protested.

"Silence!" He gripped Mercia's chin. "Repent of your lies, Heathen!"

"Bishop Odo!" Father Fulbert boomed in a voice that rose from depths many a man must envy.

William's brother released Mercia and swung around. "Speak another word, and I shall send you both from here."

"She cannot tell what she does not know!" the priest dared further, anger in his eyes and the jut of his jaw.

The bishop was silent so long Mercia thought he prepared to

cast off all pretense of holiness and attack Fulbert, but he jerked at heavily embroidered sleeves and turned back. "As I weary of this game of yours, a different question I shall ask." Again, he pointed a finger. "If you did know where the usurper's wife and son cower, would you tell?"

What he asked seemed a great vice of sharp teeth set to catch large game. However, it was little more than a taunt. Whether or not she lied or told the truth, still he would believe she knew what she did not. "As my God-given conscience will not permit me to endanger the lives and liberty of two innocents, did I know where the queen and her son are, I would hold it close."

Again he swung away, again came back around. "As I find Stern most comfortable, I shall give you time to grasp how severe the consequences of refusing to make restitution for your sins. Does it take days or weeks, you will tell what I wish to know, and in less comfort than thus far enjoyed."

Then she would be removed from the donjon to a cell in Stern's outer wall?

"Lady Chanson, Father Fulbert." Odo gestured for them to follow.

In passing, Maël's mother gave a smile that might have encouraged had not worry in her eyes outweighed the curve of her lips.

When the door closed, Mercia tried to find comfort in imagining Maël in the hall below but could not. His mother would tell him of the threat to the false abbess, and likely he would try to aid her. Futile since even had his cousin not departed to be with his laboring wife, the bishop's men numbered too many for Maël to overwhelm them. Thus, he could also fall victim to William's brother.

"Do not," Mercia whispered. "Leave me and live for both of us."

RATHER THAN REMAIN in the chamber that was ordered cleared of all but a stool, it would have been better had she been moved to a cell in the outer wall despite harsher conditions. Thus, more easily Maël could effect her escape should it prove necessary. And it might if the one who should have been in the wood did not soon appear.

Having been intercepted by Fulbert as he led his drenched horse into the stables following a fruitless search of the bordering wood, Maël had learned of Odo's solution to what he believed Mercia's lack of cooperation. Not only had the bishop made her prison less comfortable, but henceforth she would be isolated and provided minimal food and drink.

Jaw aching, Maël asked, "Has the bishop questioned her further?"

The priest nodded. "Twice this afternoon, and again my lady wife and I were present and no abuse did she suffer other than a battering of questions and accusations."

Then he had not laid hand on her again. "How well did she hold?"

"She sat the stool, kept her head up and eyes on his, and did not waver from asserting her ignorance."

That hardly comforted, this only the beginning of trials she would face as Odo grew increasingly impatient. If Maël did not soon provide proof of her lineage, much he would have to risk to bring her out of Stern.

A grip on his arm turned his head to the priest. But not just a priest, he told himself as anger and frustration threatened to fall upon one undeserving of either. *My mother's husband. The man she loves. The father of my brother or sister. My stepfather.*

"Lady Chanson asked that I remind you of a lesson imparted by your uncle," Fulbert said. "Seek the still of prayer that you may know yourself and make order of what is required of you."

Maël recalled it being taught him and Guarin, both youths having stolen away at middle night to explore the temptations of a tavern when they should have been patrolling the walls. Whereas Hugh had been mostly angered the fortress was left in a vulnerable state, just as greatly Godfroi was concerned over the vulnerable state of his son's and nephew's souls.

Maël nodded. "Assure my mother I shall."

"As she and I will do all we can to aid Mercia," Fulbert said and stepped past.

"Father." As Fulbert turned back, Maël wished he had added the man's name to his holy title. But it was too late to do so now without drawing attention to what might sound a claim to kinship. "I am pleased my mother has found happiness with you and a child is to be born of your union."

The one whose size rivaled that of Vitalis smiled so broadly he looked more a callow youth than a formidable man of God. "My heart is gladdened, my soul lightened, Sir Maël."

Maël did not attempt a smile, but said, "Henceforth, I am Maël to you."

Fulbert inclined his head. "Seek the still of prayer, my son," he reminded and departed.

So Maël would, but there was another lesson he must tend to which was given by Hugh when they set sail with William amid the grumblings of many who had begun to question the chances of taking the crown from Harold.

Given time to plot and maneuver, engage the mind ere the muscles, the aging warrior had said, *and all the more imperative should you lose favor with the odds.*

And that, it seemed, was in danger of happening now as it had at Hastings when the battle swung in favor of the Saxons before desperate Normans engaged their minds to once more find favor with the odds.

"Think first, act second," Maël told himself. "And pray you can make order of what is required of you if Ingvar does not come."

CHAPTER TWENTY-SIX

*T*wice more she had been questioned on the day past. Though Chanson and Fulbert were present and assured Maël she remained strong, this morn he learned the man-at-arms set outside her door had awakened her every quarter hour last eve. Only because during this day's first session Mercia had scorned the bishop for taunting her over how fatigued she looked, had those who witnessed their exchange learned of that cruelty.

It was not the torture many men suffered for refusing to reveal secrets, but though it left no visible marks on her body, hand in hand with little water and food, it could prove deadly.

Engage the mind ere the muscles, Maël reminded himself as he stared after Odo who, having announced the new Abbess of Lillefarne would this day arrive to testify against the pretender, moved toward the stairs followed by Chanson and Fulbert.

Two of the bishop's men stood on either side of the steps Maël longed to rush with sword in hand. It would be no great feat to cut them down, as well as the guard outside Mercia's chamber, but more than those three men stood between Maël and the woman he would not forsake. Not only did the hall abound with soldiers loyal to Odo, but the bishop was first a warrior—and a fierce one. Though the shedding of blood by a man of God was looked ill upon, he would use his sword or club to stop any who defied him. And of more concern was the possibility Maël's mother could be harmed in a clash.

Easing his hand from his sword, Maël determined it was time to depart for Wulfen as he had told the bishop he would do before resuming the task set him by the king.

Odo had snorted over concern for Guarin and his wife who had not yet sent word of their child's birth, hopefully due to the rain rather than tragedy. Concern for them did drive Maël that direction, but also the need to gain his cousin's aid if this day's search of the wood proved as futile as that of the day past.

Lord, let mother and child be well, Maël sent heavenward and crossed the hall.

Maël stared at answered prayer, miserable though it appeared wrapped in a wet cloak that would be long in drying though the pitiless rain had become a drizzle.

Ingvar stared back from alongside the tree he had come out from behind. "The lady, Sir Maël?"

As expected, he was aware the trade had been made. Guessing he had watched at a distance after stealing off the ship he dared not be aboard when Canute returned, Maël said, "For what are you so long in meeting me here?"

"You rode. When I not hiding from men Canute sent after me, I run and walk. So, the lady?"

"She is at Stern Castle." Maël swung out of the saddle and landed his boots on sodden ground. "Though denied Gytha's missive, still Bishop Odo wanted her for what he believes she knows of Harold's queen."

"Does she know?"

"Nay, and for that she shall suffer more do I not deliver the missive that tells of her Godwine blood. Hopefully, it will safeguard her a while." Maël halted and held out a hand.

Ingvar shook his head. "I dared not be caught with it."

Fearing it had been destroyed, Maël demanded, "Where is it?"

"If not taken from Lady Mercia, in her possession."

Maël frowned. "She did not tell you gave it to her."

"She not know. After I took it from Canute's cask, I bound it up in psalter I told her to hide beneath skirt."

Relief flooding Maël, he returned to his mount, took the packet from the saddle bag where he had secured it against rain, and unwrapped it beneath the shelter of his hooded mantle.

The Godwine brooch Mercia had shown him was inside the front cover. Inside the back, their bulk causing the binding to bulge, were two folded missives. The thinner one was that which directed Mercia to give herself into the hands of the Danes who would deliver her to her betrothed. The thicker one was of many words inked small to fit the parchment. Here the revelation long denied the misbegotten Godwine.

Maël looked to Ingvar when he came alongside. "You have read this?"

The Dane grimaced. "I try, but barely can I read my own language."

Though it felt a violation of Mercia's privacy to set eyes on words first she ought to know, it was necessary to be versed in them before yielding the missive to the bishop. Thus, Maël read it slowly, not only because he was less proficient at written English than Norman-French, but to find meaning beyond revelation of who sired the woman who was to have made the Danish conquest of England more acceptable to desperate Saxons convinced the rule of Sweyn would be better than that of William.

"Well?" Ingvar prompted as Maël returned the missive to the psalter.

"It is not possible to know if this is the truth of Mercia's birth since much her grandmother and her legitimate siblings have to gain from placing a Godwine near the Danish throne, but I believe it is enough to ease her suffering and, hopefully, make it possible to steal her away," Mael said, in that moment fully accepting what he must do, regardless of pride, risk of terrible punishment, and what he would lose.

Ingvar smiled. "I good at taking what does not want taking."

So he was, but there was considerable difference between thieving an easily concealed missive and delivering from an enemy of great number a woman not easily concealed.

"Worry not," Ingvar said. "I prove worthy of Wulfen."

That was their bargain—the Dane's aid for the opportunity to serve Guarin and Lady Hawisa. Maël knew he had no right to speak for the Lord and Lady of Wulfen, but he believed they would give Ingvar a chance to impart skills to their charges that could prove useful when they became England's defenders.

"Since the sooner I get Gytha's missive in Odo's hands, the sooner we free Mercia," Maël said, "it is time to lay plans."

HE HAD THREATENED to cut her hair.

It jolted her, but certain the Lord was with her the same as Chanson and her husband who watched from the doorway, Mercia had managed to hold the bishop's gaze, even when he set a heavy hand on her head and warned he would see her scalp scraped clean.

"And still I will not know what you ask of me," she had said for the hundredth time.

The third session this day had not lasted long, not because Odo accepted there was nothing to be gained. Because one of his men had entered and whispered something that made him smile and withdraw with the Lady of Stern and Father Fulbert.

Hoping he would forget to set a man to awaken her as done each time she began to drift, Mercia pushed up off the stool and aimed herself at the corner to the right of the shuttered window.

Though not yet the vulnerable, sniveling victim, she was weary, thirsty, hungry, and her eyes burned. It was tempting to let tears fall in her tormentor's absence, but if he returned soon, her reddened eyes would betray her and, encouraged by the show of weakness, he would press her harder.

Knees soft, she eased down in the corner, drew up her legs, and wrapped her arms around them. "Sleep," she rasped past lips beginning to crack.

Soon, she found herself in Lillefarne's chapel, and perched on a rafter above her was the bird her carelessness had trapped inside.

"There the door, little one," she called. "There near the bread and water I leave so you not be as hungry and thirsty as I."

It put its head to the side, causing light to glint in the eye turned to her.

"How can you not see it when you feed on the bread? Drink at the font? Are you blind? Dull-witted?" She frowned. "Or do I make it too comfortable and safe for you? Though much you long for freedom, do you fear it more? I did, pecking the scraps from Gytha's hand, telling myself it was worth the bondage for what one day she would tell." She raised a hand. "Come, I will carry you out, and you will see how blue the sky and how sweet the air you can only dream of in here. It is not safe, but it is no cage. You determine the bounds. You."

The door to the chapel banged shut, its meeting with the frame causing vibrations to shoot through her body. But when she turned that direction to rebuke whoever trapped the bird inside, she saw the door remained open, the blue sky visible above the convent's roof.

"Awaken!" demanded someone whose boot prodded her stockinged feet. As she realized she was being snatched from a dream, a rough hand pulled her upright.

Mercia blinked to focus on one of two men who followed the bishop's orders to deny her restful sleep, then drew back an arm to slap him as done Canute.

He knocked it aside and pulled her across the chamber.

"Where are you taking me?" she demanded, throat so dry each word cracked.

"The bishop wants you belowstairs," he said, his answer doing naught to allay fear of what judgment awaited her there.

Do not be present, Maël, she silently pleaded as she was drawn down the corridor onto the stairs, keeping her feet beneath her only because the man's grip was firm and his footing sure.

The light was brighter in the hall, an abundance of torches lit to burn away the shadows of another overcast day that continued to wet the land though with less enthusiasm than an hour earlier as told by the rain's assault on the roof.

As befitting such a day, the hall was crowded with warriors, none of whom was Maël. And neither was he one of those who sat at the high table on either side of the bishop, among them Chanson and Fulbert whose faces were grim. Unless Maël was in a corner or alcove where light barely ventured, he was not here.

Praying he distanced himself from Stern, she distracted herself by looking near upon the bishop's men who thought little of being showered by blood but were loath to be washed clean by a spring rain.

Or was it a summer rain? she wondered as she approached the dais. If not, then nearly so, meaning soon she would attain her twenty seventh year. *If* she survived the false bishop who named her the false abbess.

The one who had borne Mercia forward between tables where men conversed, drank, played games of chance, and dozed, halted.

As she expected to look upon Bishop Odo where he stood before the high table atop the dais, no surprise there. Surprise was for the woman beside him who Mercia would have sworn was not in the hall moments earlier, meaning perhaps fatigue caused her to overlook Maël as well.

She stared at Rixende who had been the first of the sisters to accept Abbess Mary Sarah at Lillefarne. Nearly a friend, the fairly young woman had shown kindness, genuine eagerness to do Mercia's bidding, and offered good counsel. Was she here only because the bishop wished to use her against the false abbess? Or to denounce the one who had deceived her and the others?

Odo called for silence, and when it fell, jutted his chin at Mercia. "You know this woman, Abbess?"

Mercia startled over Rixende's elevation to the position vacated by the woman she had served. Not that she was unworthy. Better than any she would administer the abbey and shepherd its good work, but unlike several older nuns who would have vied for that honor, Rixende was not noble either side and could have been tainted by her close association with the false abbess.

The woman met Mercia's gaze. "I knew her as Abbess Mary Sarah."

"Never as Mercia of Mercia?"

"Never. We were deceived all."

A great weight dropped through Mercia. She could not begrudge Rixende's sense of betrayal, but it hurt that no credit was given Mercia for what she had done to meet the needs of her charges and those come unto the abbey in search of shelter and aid. Of course, such had also been extended to rebels...

"Then you did not know this woman aided the enemies of our king?" Odo said.

"I knew not, Lord Bishop."

"And had you known?"

The weight within Mercia increased at the realization she was not the only one who must answer to the bishop. Regardless of Rixende's feelings for Mercia, she could not show any kind regard for the false abbess without endangering herself and her charges.

"Ours is a House of God, Bishop. Thus, its servants are charged with looking upon Jesus's flock not with the eyes but the heart, and that requires us to ease the suffering of all regardless of which side of a battlefield they stand upon."

His lids narrowed. "You say you, too, would have aided the king's enemies?"

"I say it not. As told, be it man, woman, or child who suffers, my heart would not see an enemy of the king but a child of God. Unless the scriptures long fed me are false, it is God's will I do." She frowned and, with what appeared genuine concern, said, "Tell, Bishop, do you think them false?" At his hesitation, she added, "Certes, you would know better than I."

Mercia nearly smiled, but lest it was noted by Odo, she was grateful those muscles were weary.

The bishop flicked a hand. "Let us return to the sins of the false abbess. I am told many are the professions of faith denied novices whilst Mercia of Mercia played a holy woman."

Rixende inclined her head. "Blessedly, their professions were made a sennight past, and many the expressions of relief by Christ's brides that she who called herself Mary Sarah did not yield to their grumbling and conduct the sacred service." She swept her gaze to Mercia. "Great the sorrow of all who admired and respected this woman for her guidance and good works after Lillefarne was set adrift following the death of our old abbess. For this, that never did she lead them astray though she be false, daily the good sisters pray to extend forgiveness born of pure hearts."

It was not what the bishop wished to hear, his mouth pinching, but he heard it as did all within the hall.

Mercia swallowed, winced at the sting of a dry throat. *Dear Rixende,* she thought, *I hurt you and the others, yet you grant me grace.*

"It is difficult," the abbess continued, "but all are determined forgiveness be given ere the work this woman began in placing dozens of children refugees in homes across Wulfenshire is completed." She sighed. "So many innocents dead and suffering that surely the Lord weeps. As I am certain one as holy as you weeps as well, Lord Bishop."

Mercia feared Rixende went too far, but before the flushed Odo could respond, a nobleman of middle years sitting with his chair tilted back and booted feet crossed atop the table said, "We all weep, Abbess, even our king who was forced to end the rebellion at the cost of innocent lives." When she looked around, he raised his eyebrows. "Now England can heal in earnest, and the children displaced by their self-serving countrymen will grow into men and women who embrace the peace and prosperity of Norman rule." He shifted his regard to Odo. "Do I not speak true?"

A corner of the bishop's mouth rose. "For the sake of those children, Lord de Grandmesnil, that is the hope."

Therein a threat, Mercia knew.

To the man who had delivered her belowstairs, Odo said, "Return the false abbess to her chamber and provide her an extra ration of water so more easily she may reveal what I tire of waiting upon."

Though Mercia's dry mouth moistened slightly at the prospect of drink, more she dreaded he would not be long in following.

"And you, Abbess," he addressed Rixende as Mercia was guided across the hall. "I give you leave to return to your abbey."

"I thank you, Lord Bishop."

Partway up the stairs, Mercia peered around one last time to search out Maël. He was not here. Hoping he had been ordered to resume the task his king set him, certain it was for the best though his absence made her ache, she started to look forward. But her eyes landed on the woman she would not see again. It was worth the slip of a foot and pain in the knee when she dropped to the step's edge. As her escort righted her, Rixende turned her face to Mercia and smiled softly.

No bitterness. Rather, much sorrow and sympathy.

Though given no opportunity to beg forgiveness, I am pardoned, Mercia marveled over what she would cling to when next she sat upon the hard stool and struggled to keep her head up and thoughts clear as over and again she denied the false bishop satisfaction.

"Mercia of Mercia!" Rixende called, her clear, authoritative voice quieting the many who had begun to converse.

With far less volume, Mercia answered, "Abbess?"

"The bird in the chapel whose plight so distressed you... The same day the Danes stole you away, it found its way out. Curious that, hmm?"

Warmth spreading through Mercia, she smiled. "Much that comforts, Abbess. I thank you." Then hardly feeling the sting of stretched lips, she resumed her ascent of the stairs.

CHAPTER TWENTY-SEVEN

*W*hat ill befell you that you should return hours following your departure, Sir Maël?"

Lord, forgive me the lies I speak in defense of Mercia, Maël silently beseeched as he strode past those languishing in the hall toward the bishop who sat in the high seat that had been moved to the hearth, the same as the chair in which De Grandmesnil sat low. A goblet dangling from one hand, legs stretched out before him, the heels of the nobleman's boots dug into the floor to keep him from sliding down further.

There was blood on the rain-dampened tunic Maël wore over his chain mail, not his own blood but Ingvar's—the Dane had insisted—and Maël saw the moment Odo noticed it.

"You were set upon?" he demanded.

Maël halted and, in a voice meant to carry, said, "Halfway between Stern and Wulfen." There the first lie, one for which his mother had been grateful when, discreetly summoned to the garden, Maël revealed to her and her husband the plans laid.

The bishop's lips curled. "Filthy Saxons. Is there no end to their evil?"

"It seems not," Maël said, "but these Saxons were of note."
The second lie.

Odo sat straighter unlike De Grandmesnil who merely uncrossed his ankles. "Speak, D'Argent."

"The three were the same I saw upon Canute's ship, and it was made known to me they serve the mother of Harold."

"For what did they attack?"

"They recognized me as I recognized them. And had cause to silence me." In preparation for the third lie, Maël removed the thick missive from his purse. "I found this upon the one I slew whilst the others fled. Certes, it was they who stole it from Canute, believing its absence would prevent you from paying Mercia of Mercia's wardship price and ensuring she was restored to her grandmother."

As Odo snatched the missive from Maël, De Grandmesnil sat up and gestured someone forward.

"You have read it, Sir Maël?" the bishop asked.

Here, in front of numerous witnesses as planned lest Odo attempt to discount Mercia's high birth in opposition to his brother who believed the nobility were closer to God than the common folk, Maël said, "In its entirety, Lord Bishop." He glanced at De Grandmesnil's son who halted alongside his sire. "Quite the bargain you made acquiring Lady Mercia of the Godwines."

A muscle jumping in his jaw, Odo unfolded the missive. "*If what is written here is true.*"

"It seems likely," Maël said, "else for what would those men risk their lives to retrieve a woman of little account?"

"You think they followed us to Wulfenshire to rescue her?"

"I do."

Belatedly, Odo commanded the onlookers to be about their business, then lowered his gaze. As he read the missive, he became more tense, as did the De Grandmesnils, causing what Maël had suspected and rejected several times to gain ground.

"Father Jonas," Odo called the man to his side. "Is it Gytha's hand?"

The priest carried the missive near his face, shortly said, "Lady Gytha of the House of Godwine set down these words."

Odo snatched the missive from him. "Even if what is written here is false, much use can be made of it. Thus, Mercia of Mercia is of import beyond what she knows of Alditha." He looked to De Grandmesnil. "Just as the Danes thought to calm the Saxons by wedding one of their own to a Godwine, so we shall by joining her to a Norman of high birth."

Face grim, the nobleman nodded.

"God's hand in this," Odo said. "He sent the rain that held you and your son here the sooner to see His will done."

Unseemly though it was, the youth *was* to be Mercia's husband, Maël acknowledged. For this, the king had sent father and son with Odo. Neither was pleased it should come to fruition, but they could not be as displeased as Maël would be had he not plans to take De Grandmesnil's betrothed from here.

SO SOON? Had even an hour passed since Rixende and she departed the hall? It could not have—unless she had slept as she did not recall doing.

Continuing to search backward, Mercia paid little heed to those within the hall who fell to murmuring as she was led toward the dais.

It has been less than an hour since last I was here, she told herself despite uncertainty. *This but further abuse that spills no blood.*

Drawn to a halt, she looked up. Though her lack of sleep caused Odo's figure to waver and edges to darken, she saw his wide sleeves covered hands clasped at his waist.

Looking down upon her, he said, "I have glad tidings that shall return you to comfort—indeed, greater comfort than any you have known, Mercia of Mercia. That is, providing you thieve no more of my time."

"I do not—" Her voice cracked, and though she tried to restore it by swallowing, her mouth was too dry.

"Lady Chanson!" the bishop called, and Mercia saw Maël's mother hasten toward her with a goblet in hand. Though much she ached to set her lips on the rim raised to her, she pressed them tight lest the lady was punished for ignoring Odo's rebuke.

"Drink," Chanson urged.

Mercia shook her head.

"Drink, Woman!" Odo commanded.

Certain she heard wrong, Mercia looked to him.

He jutted his chin. "Drink."

Then he had not rebuked Lady Chanson for seeking to quench Mercia's thirst. He had ordered it.

Mercia swept up her hands, cupped them over the lady's, and drew the vessel to her lips. A deep gulp of heavily-watered wine coursed tongue and throat, momentarily relieving parched tissues, but before she could further wet them, the lady lowered the goblet. "Slowly, else you will not keep it down, Child."

Argument over being denied what her body needed and offense at being named a child bounded onto Mercia's tongue, but Chanson's choice of words returned her to Lillefarne where she had said the same to refugees regardless of their age.

Amazing the power of desperation and helplessness, she had thought many a time. *It makes children of many.* As now it sought to make one of her. And more humiliating it would be if she fell to her knees to empty a mostly empty belly.

Mercia loosened her hands from Chanson's and the goblet.

"Remain strong," the lady whispered, "all will—"

"Stand aside, Lady Chanson," the bishop commanded.

Setting her teeth, Maël's mother turned alongside Mercia whose struggle against peering at the goblet's contents landed her averted gaze on two figures to the left of the bishop—an attractive, well-dressed Norman of middle years and one who might only now be called a man.

"We will not further argue Alditha's whereabouts," Odo returned her attention to him. "Though be assured, if she and her runt live, they will be found."

Be long and far gone, Mercia silently beseeched, *be it across the Irish Sea or the narrow.* She cleared her throat. "Your glad tidings, Bishop?"

He shook back a sleeve to reveal a creased parchment. "You see what this is?"

Likely tidings from Le Bâtard.

"Here that which reveals your parentage, Mercia of Mercia."

She knew she could make sense of that despite muddied thoughts, but he gave her no time.

"Or so goes the tale. After all, your grandmother is a mistress of falsehood."

She gasped. Then here Gytha's missive stolen from Canute?

"Regardless, it grants you privileges for which you ought to kiss my brother's feet," Odo added.

How had it come into his possession? What did it so convincingly tell that his cruel questioning was at an end? More, what would now be required of her to enjoy greater comfort?

She tried to moisten her lips, but the drag of her tongue over the cracks made her wince. "What must I do?" she rasped.

"You have only to wed a Norman, *Lady* Mercia."

There the answer that should have been close at hand—that just as the Danes had wished to make a tool of her, so did the conquerors.

Amid the murmuring of those gathered in the hall, Chanson stepped in front of Mercia and once more offered the goblet. One long sip was all Mercia permitted herself, and as it slid down her grateful throat, the lady whispered, "Maël—"

"You shall wed this day," the bishop interrupted the lady again.

Heart leaping, Mercia turned her face to Maël's mother as the woman resumed her place at the false abbess's side. Had she sought to assure Mercia her son would be the one to take a misbegotten Godwine to wife? Was he present as she had assumed he was not since he had been absent earlier? Unfortunately, even were the answer in Lady Chanson's eyes, it could not be seen with those eyes fixed on Odo.

"Who am I to wed, Bishop?"

To her great confusion, it was the boy barely a young man who was summoned forth. To his great distress, evidenced by the pale of his face and set of his jaw, the bishop set a hand on his shoulder. "Your lord husband is to be William, son of our king's esteemed companion, Hugh de Grandmesnil."

Staring at the Norman who had to be ten years younger than she, the murmurings all growing louder, Mercia's world began to tilt. She wished it were a great movement of the earth that forced her to widen her stance, but it was the disappointment of something she should not have been so quick to light her heart upon.

I am glad Maël is gone, she told herself, *and I pray he stays gone so he not be moved to make an enemy of the king's brother when I thieve more of Odo's time.*

"Lady Chanson will aid with your ablutions and see you properly garbed," he said.

She pushed her shoulders back. "For what, Lord Bishop?"

"As told, this day you wed."

She looked to William de Grandmesnil, offered him a thin smile that made her lips hurt. "I shall not wed this Norman."

The youth blinked, and she knew it was the light of relief in his eyes that displaced resentment. She was far from an old woman, but to one of ten and six she must seem of an age near his mother's, especially compared to the girlish maidens whose attentions he had surely begun to seek.

The bishop shouted for his men to quiet, then growled, "Do you test me further, it will go badly for you—and in the end, you will give what I want."

She moved her tongue around her mouth, but despite her attempt to sound courageous, more she sounded a frog when she said, "To test you implies there is room for negotiation. There is not. Never will I speak vows with this…" She nearly named him a boy, but he had done naught to earn her scorn.

Again, she cleared her throat. "I will not wed this Norman who deserves a maiden near his own years."

With a single step, Odo descended the dais, with another step, thrust his face near hers. So accustomed had she become to this form of aggression, she did not flinch when her nostrils were filled with the scent of perspiration poorly disguised by the herbs in which he bathed. "Methinks you forget the severity of punishment due one who posed as a holy woman!"

So she did, too weary and uncomfortable to think long on it these past days.

He narrowed his lids. "No matter how much *persuasion* is required, you will wed a Norman."

Her thoughts flew to Maël, and she said, "Do I wed one of your own, it will be a Norman I know to be honorable and of an age fit for my own."

The cessation of the bishop's breath on her face urged her to more closely attend to her situation, next the thoughtful silence lowering him to his heels, then a question asked kindly, "Have you a Norman in mind, dear Lady?"

Though a voice within counseled her to think well on her response, someone seemingly outside her said wearily, "I do."

∾

Non, Mercia, Maël silently entreated where he stood far right of the dais as commanded by the bishop before Gytha's granddaughter entered the hall. *Do not speak my name.*

As if Odo heard, unlike Mercia whose gaze Maël had sought since her arrival, the bishop glanced across his shoulder. He suspected—likely not only in this moment—what would make it more difficult for Maël to remove Mercia from his power. Not a bad thing were Odo inclined to grant her marriage to a Norman of her choice, but even were Maël landed, she would be of far less benefit to William than were she wed into the family of De Grandmesnil who possessed extensive lands worked by numerous Saxons in need of pacification.

"Speak his name, Lady Mercia," Odo said, "and mayhap it will be done."

Do not! Maël silently demanded of the woman who had only to look far right to read the warning on his face just as his mother did where she remained alongside Mercia.

Chanson's fear was the same as her son's, but neither could she do anything but hope the dearth of sleep Mercia suffered did not further loosen her mind and tongue to make meat of mere suspicion.

A sound of distress escaped Mercia, then her shoulders lowered. Swaying slightly, it appeared she might collapse—in this moment a good thing—but she said, "I believe Sir Maël D'Argent as honorable a Norman as his cousins."

Though Odo's face was in profile, there was enough satisfaction there to threaten the plans made with Ingvar.

"So Sir Maël is," the bishop raised his voice to be heard above his men who found it difficult to hold their tongues. "However, what you do not consider is that he is but captain of the king's guard—lacking title and lands."

She blinked as if to focus her eyes. "I care not he is landless, only that if I am bound to a Norman, he be..." Her lids fluttered. "...of good character."

Once again, Odo looked to the king's man.

Though it was hoped Mercia would follow his gaze and read the displeasure Maël fixed on his face, prompting her to do no further damage, she did not.

The bishop arched an eyebrow.

Maintaining a show of displeasure, Maël shook his head as if he believed it possible he, rather than De Grandmesnil's heir, would be forced to wed a Godwine.

Whatever was believed of his rejection of Mercia, the bishop said, "I might think you in love, Lady, were it not impossible to have the handsome of Sir Maël without the unsightly."

Maël stiffened. Such things the enemy had shouted at him in battles since Hastings, but of the Normans who dared, mostly it was done in whispers behind his back. That the fairly discreet Odo did so before all meant he sought to further unbalance Mercia to better learn her feelings.

She was unresponsive so long, Maël began to hope she had grown numb to Odo's baiting, possessing only enough consciousness to remain upright.

But she said, "Enemies though you and I are, Bishop Odo, I believed we shared the same God. How tragic we have not even that in common, you who are more a false representative of God than ever I was."

Lord, do You not quiet her, Maël sent heavenward, *her punishment may not be wedding a boy but losing her life.*

Knowing he was not the only one praying for the Lord's intervention, Maël looked to his mother whose eyes were closed and lips moved slightly.

"Tell me about *your* God, Mercia," Odo said with what sounded amusement.

"My God does not scorn the downtrodden, the outcasts, the imperfect. The same as His son who embraced the least lovely of creation, He sees the hearts rather than the forms that hold them. And loves them all."

Odo chuckled. "As it sounds you are almost as fluent in God as you are Norman-French, I begin to understand how you were able to deceive the sisters of Lillefarne. It seems they are not as foolish as thought."

Mercia stared.

He shrugged. "Then that is what you see when you look upon Sir Maël—his heart rather than the terrible scar one of your countrymen dealt him?"

"I do," she said, this time with what sounded wariness.

"And is it love you feel for him?"

Her throat bobbed. "Though I esteem him for his honor that will make it easier to tolerate spending my life with a Norman, never could I feel for him that which a wife should feel for her husband."

Odo glanced around at De Grandmesnil's son who remained pitifully hopeful upon the dais, looked back at Mercia, and called, "What say you, Sir Maël?"

She did not disappoint, startling and turning her head left and right, gasping when her eyes found the man she preferred to wed.

Odo watched the tapestry of emotions stitching and unstitching themselves across her face, then turned to Maël. "Were you landed, Chevalier, would you wed this Saxon of Godwine blood?"

Grateful to have become versed in concealing his thoughts and emotions these past years, Maël considered her—all the while constructing another lie since he was certain De Grandmesnil's son was the only match under consideration.

"Though I find Lady Mercia attractive and of good wit, and now I better understand how my cousins fell prey to Saxon women, great the compensation would have to be for me to take to wife one as deceitful as the false abbess. Thus, unless our king has plans to elevate me higher than my cousin, the Baron of Wulfen, I will but thank Lady Mercia for her kind regard and wish her and young William a blessed and fruitful union."

Knowing Odo gauged the veracity of his words, Maël was grateful the distance between them ensured his face was even less easily read—too, that it allowed him to shift his gaze a fraction to assess Mercia's reaction.

Whereas minutes earlier she had struggled to make sense of his presence, now upon her face was what appeared to be understanding. Hopefully, she grasped that just as she dared not profess any depth of feeling for him, neither could he show any for her.

"Alas," Odo said, "as I do not believe the king has such plans for you, Sir Maël, the lady shall wed William de Grandmesnil."

"I will not!" she exclaimed.

"Ah, but the alternative, Lady..." Odo shook his head in mock sorrow. "Strongly, I advise you to wed the Norman of your king's choosing so you may enjoy greater comfort and esteem than ever you have known. Do you not, never will you know the contents of Gytha's missive and you will give us no means of shielding you from punishment for your trespass against Church and God."

"I will not wed him," she said more forcefully and looked to Maël. "I am only as deceitful as you and your kind forced me to be to survive in an England ravished by barbarians. You may not answer now for your own trespasses against Church and God, but one day you shall—as shall you, Bishop."

Maël could not know if she was truly angry with him as she was with Odo, but that was good. Feigned or not, her reaction should alleviate some suspicion about their feelings for each other. But more was needed.

"My Lord Bishop," he called, "as further delay in completing the king's task will incite his wrath, with your permission I shall depart Stern."

"Granted," Odo said, then to Mercia. "You are very tired,

therefore not thinking right. Hence, you shall return to your chamber. Once you have rested, we will speak again, and you will see the wisdom of becoming William de Grandmesnil's wife."

Yield or not, just do not wed this day, Mercia, Maël silently beseeched as he strode across the hall. Already it would be exceedingly difficult to extricate her, but if she spoke vows with the youth, it could prove impossible—and once more bury the heart she had unearthed which had determined to risk all to make her his own.

CHAPTER TWENTY-EIGHT

This time he came alone, and more she feared him than before as she sat on the stool and wished Chanson and Fulbert present. But shockingly, the bishop was no more aggressive than before. At times, he was even charming in his attempts to persuade her of the merits of speaking vows with a boy who was of good temperament, handsome, easier to command than a full-grown man, and would make on her children of great privilege and standing.

Despite having been assured of rest before next they spoke, less than an hour had passed between her departure from the hall and the bishop's arrival abovestairs. Thus, over and again fatigue caused her thoughts to drift belowstairs and out the door in search of Maël. And ever she was snatched back up the stairs by a grip on her shoulder that steadied her on the stool.

Unable to recall Odo's last words, certain they could be little different from the others, she said, "I will not wed him," and looked to the shuttered window whose horizontal and vertical seams revealed the dull grey light outside had darkened further.

Did Maël ride through it, distancing himself from her? Or was he doing what she should not wish but selfishly longed for?

"Will you try to take me out of here?" she whispered.

"What say you?" Odo asked.

She opened eyes that had fallen closed and, for the first time, noted the tyrant's brother was a fairly attractive man. Fearing the observation was the result of a rattled mind, she gave her head a slight shake. "Whilst serving as the Abbess of Lillefarne, I found if I changed tact with a difficult nun or novice, oft I could bring her around, even were it by the long way." She swallowed. "Provide me drink, food, and sleep, and mayhap on the morrow my answer will be different."

It would not be, but as more and more she felt what might be cracks in her mind, it could be worth giving him false hope that would further anger him.

He straightened. "I will think on it, Lady Mercia." Then he was gone.

Slumping, she tried to make sense of the voices on the other side of the door. She could not, but a short while later she made sense of the key turning in the lock. Her guard needed to relieve himself, else satisfy hunger and thirst.

As his footsteps faded, she pushed up off the stool and unbalanced it. Leaving it where it fell, she crossed to the wall to gain sleep whilst the bishop considered her proposal.

So deeply she went down into that blessed quiet that she was surprised to see a platter alongside the door upon awakening. Atop it was a small candle that would be a puddle of hardening wax within an hour, a bowl of cooled soup, a hunk of bread, and a cup of milk.

"Thank you, Lord," she rasped, then with trembling self-control, sip by sip drank the milk and nibble by nibble ate half the soup and bread. It was no easy thing to leave the rest, but it helped that her body needed rest more than food.

Let me sleep through the night, she prayed, then curled on her side and clasped her hands beneath her chin.

~

THE BEST WINE was served during the evening meal, the Lady of Stern having ordered the opening of two casks held in reserve for a visit from the king and further ordered the servants to be as free with drink at the lowermost tables where Stern's household knights and garrison dined as at the upper tables claimed by Odo's men. Thus, most imbibed more than usual, as noted in the message Chanson left for her son beneath the altar cloth in the outer chapel, as well as instructions on how to contact his uncle in Flanders.

Something else had been beneath the cloth. From its size and weight, Maël had known that which was wrapped in linen was what he had refused years past. Though he did not believe he should accept Hugh D'Argent's dagger until he could forgive his sire, since it could be a long time before he saw his mother again, he had taken it.

Albeit excessive drinking by those within Stern aided in entering the walls undetected, next the donjon by way of a side door used by servants that should have been bolted, the risk of awakening one of those sleeping in the hall was not to be made light of.

In the event someone roused, it would fall to Ingvar to silence them. And were an alarm sounded, the Dane would distract all with what he called a *merry chase* to give Maël time to lower himself and Mercia by rope to the garden below her window.

As he moved through shadows toward the stairs, grateful for deep and whistled breathing, snoring, and restless shifting, Ingvar veered toward the curtained solar behind the high table. From there he would keep watch, near enough the sleeping bishop to take him hostage were it needed to escape Stern. God willing, it would not be necessary.

As Maël neared the stairs, he recalled his mother's warning.

Stay to the right the first four steps, then move center, entirely avoiding the last step before the landing. It creaks loud no matter where you set foot.

Maël adjusted his hood and carefully began his ascent. Though Odo's man posted outside Mercia's chamber might have imbibed as much as the others, if the relative silence abovestairs was violated, more easily he would be roused and sooner require subduing. However, when Maël eased onto the landing and peered down the corridor, he found the torch-lit stretch empty.

He tensed. Unbeknownst to Chanson, had Mercia been moved for her refusal to wed De Grandmesnil? Could this time have been better spent freeing her from a cell in the outer wall?

Testing his footing all the way, gnashing his teeth when the floor creaked, he continued to the door behind which he might find someone other than Mercia. And saw a key protruded from the lock. Hoping it proof she was within and had been left to her sleep with only a locked door to guard her, Maël turned the key.

The first thing he saw when he opened the door was the platter beside it lit by the remains of a candle whose wick was tipped by a shuddering flame above a pool of glistening wax. Alongside it was half-eaten food and an empty cup. The next thing he noticed was the toppled stool center of the chamber upon which, he had been told, Mercia was questioned, lastly a figure against the wall.

Maël lowered his hood and started forward.

In response to the groan of a board beneath his foot, Mercia rasped, "Lord, strengthen me."

Lest she loudly protest the disturbance of her sleep, he turned back, but as he eased the door closed, she said bitterly, "The stool. Aye, this I know."

Then she believed Odo came to question her again.

As Maël strode toward where she rose onto hands and

knees, she said more angrily, "Aye, the stool," and sought to get her feet beneath her.

"I have come for you," Maël said and swept her into his arms.

Her gasp was dry and grating, then her hand was on his jaw, eyes searching his face. "You should not be here."

"Then where?"

"As far from me as possible. You will lose all if—"

"If I fail, I will lose all. *You*, Mercia."

A sob jerked her body. "You love me as I love you?"

He would have answered her with a kiss if not that it would pain her parched lips. "These past days have been the longest year of my life, dearest Mercia."

Another sob, the last of it muffled when she turned her face into his chest.

There was more to say and assurances to be given, but they must wait until Stern was far behind.

Since no warning had sounded from Ingvar, they would depart the way he had come rather than out the window which, exposed to the light of torches, could catch the eye of one of the few men sluggishly patrolling the wall walks.

"Put your arms around my neck and speak naught until Stern is at our backs," he said.

She slid her hands up his chest and linked them at his nape.

Maël carried her from the chamber, but as he turned to secure the door, he saw a figure near the landing stood with a shoulder against the wall and ankles crossed.

Outside of a miracle, he—and Mercia—*would* lose all.

De Grandmesnil.

As Ingvar had given no warning, likely the Dane's life had been lost on the edge of the dagger that was the only weapon upon the Norman's belt. Not so Maël whose mantle concealed dagger *and* sword—one or both of which must be brought to hand were there any chance of taking Mercia from Stern.

"I need you behind me," he said low as he eased her to her feet.

She raised her head and, following his gaze to the man who was to be her father-in-law, whispered, "Dear Lord."

King William's favored companion straightened from the wall. Hands empty at his sides, slowly he advanced as Mercia stepped to Maël's back.

In preparation to draw a weapon on the warrior who, though proficient at arms, could not match his own skill, Maël elbowed aside his mantle to sooner bring his sword to hand. "Lord De Grandmesnil," he said when the man halted five feet distant.

The nobleman settled into his heels and considered his son's rival for a Godwine bride. "Though the bishop is uncertain as to how changed you are from the one who has long served his brother, Sir Maël, as I have spent some time in your company, I am less uncertain. Thus, though your dear mother was exceedingly generous with fine wine this eve, I satisfied myself with one pour the better to watch for your return. And you did not disappoint."

"Ingvar?" Maël demanded low.

"A problem in the beginning, but easily resolved."

"You slew him," Maël bit.

"Non, though that the bishop may do should he rise above his fourth pour of wine."

Maël frowned.

De Grandmesnil chuckled. "Clearly, your Dane was to keep watch, but he could not resist the plunder to be had on the other side of the curtain."

Maël's anger shifted toward Ingvar. And faltered. He could not claim to know the Dane well, but it was difficult to believe greed was responsible for De Grandmesnil cornering Mercia and him. And there was another thing more hard to believe. "Why have you sounded no alarm?"

De Grandmesnil raised his eyebrows. "Is it not obvious I want what you want?"

Just because something seemed obvious did not make it so. "I would hear it, my lord."

"I wish Mercia of the House of Godwine wed not to my heir but another." A corner of his mouth rose. "I am thinking you, son of Hugh D'Argent—*after* you leave England."

Maël considered the man who shared his departed sire's Christian name the same as De Grandmesnil's son shared that of the duke who became king. "I know I betray William in removing Lady Mercia from Stern," he said, "but do you stand aside and let happen what will, you shall betray as well."

De Grandmesnil inclined his head. "Though many my children, none do I love as well as my eldest. He is his family's great hope, and more I would betray him than his namesake do I not ensure our line remains Norman pure. Thus, give me the word of a D'Argent that no matter the outcome of your escape with Mercia of the Godwines, you will not name me a party to it, and I will give you the word of a De Grandmesnil none will know I witnessed it was you who stole her away. And one better I will do to decrease the chance Lady Mercia is recaptured and made to wed my son."

Maël waited.

"You reported two of the Saxons who set upon you fled," the man said.

A tale that, had he believed it, he no longer did, Maël mused.

"I am certain those who shall overwhelm me when I rise to relieve myself of much wine are Saxons and, ere I lose consciousness, will speak the name of Mercia." He nodded. "Certes, they took her and are bound for the coast to deliver her to her grandmother."

For so sharp and conniving a wit, of great value he has been to King William, Maël thought. *And now, the same as I, he risks all.*

"Have I your word, D'Argent?"

To attest to his vow, Maël set a hand on his sword hilt. "You do."

De Grandmesnil touched his dagger's hilt. "As you have mine." He stepped to the side, nodded for Maël and Mercia to advance, and added, "Methinks it will be less than an hour ere I am fit to raise the hue and cry. Were I you, I would make haste."

Though Maël believed the nobleman more than he did not, he pulled Mercia against his side and, firmly holding his gaze to De Grandmesnil, drew her past.

"One other thing," the king's companion said as they neared the landing.

Maël paused. "Oui?"

"Share our bargain with your cousin, Baron Wulfrith."

Once again, De Grandmesnil surprised. "My lord?"

"As I am much about the business of administering the lands King William awarded me, I have decided to send my son to Wulfen to complete his training. I do not ask he receive preferential treatment but that more be required of him than the others as he completes his journey to manhood."

Since De Grandmesnil was among the most courageous of the conqueror's men, it did not surprise he wished his son a worthier reflection of him.

"My William has the blood and desire to be a man of the sword," he continued, "but also the heart of his mother that sometimes causes him to hesitate when he ought to swing as if to part a man's head from his shoulders."

Maël's sire had said the same of his own son and gone to great lengths to correct his wife's influence. Mostly he had, rousing Maël to anger with taunts that could turn cruel if more was demanded of him than he thought he could give.

De Grandmesnil stepped nearer. "Tell the baron to attend to that weakness."

That Guarin would do, though he would not resort to cruelty. "I shall, my lord." At the man's nod, Maël turned Mercia toward the stairs. "You can walk?" he asked.

"I can."

"Then follow me, stepping where I step, avoiding the places I avoid."

She did so, and soon they moved through the hall.

Maël looked to the dais, and immediately a figure crouched between the high table and curtained solar straightened.

Ingvar had much explaining to do, but as now was not the time, no word passed between them inside Stern's walls. Indeed, none at all until well past the time De Grandmesnil was to raise the alarm.

CHAPTER TWENTY-NINE

*I*t having proved impossible for Maël to secure a second horse for Ingvar without drawing notice, his stepfather had arranged for the palfrey he rode to a nearby village late on the day past to be tethered in the bordering wood.

Hoping Fulbert was not forced to speak false to explain his return on foot and grateful only once between Stern and Wulfen was it necessary to rest and water the horses, Maël glanced behind at where he had settled Mercia on a rock. Pleased the newborn sun showed color in her face, he had left her there with drink and viands so he could confront Ingvar over abandoning his watch over the hall.

As he neared the man who hunkered before the stream, forearms propped on spread thighs, teeth wrenching at dried meat, Ingvar looked around. "Sir Maël, you must see what I took from Stern!" He stood and turned to his mount.

A bishop's ring? Maël wondered as the Dane rooted through his pack. The intricately embroidered belt Odo wore to further set him apart as a holy man? Whatever it was, Ingvar had left Maël and Mercia vulnerable in order to obtain it. Thus, it was not possible for him to serve at Wulfen and best they part ways now.

Ingvar swung around. "For Lady Mercia."

Maël stared at the folded parchment, then looked into sparkling eyes above a broad grin.

Though pleased Gytha's missive had been recovered so Mercia could herself read the tale, it did not absolve Ingvar of endangering them.

"For that you abandoned your watch?" Maël demanded.

The man's joy wavered, but without hesitation he said, "When I hear devil stir, I look behind curtain and see him sit up in bed. I stay shadows, steal behind, and hit back of head—not hard since not wish to kill. Then I bind so he not alert others if soon awaken." Ingvar shook the missive. "This on table by bed, and only this I take. Since made to look Gytha's men stole Lady Mercia, its loss believable."

So great was Maël's relief that Ingvar had not betrayed his trust, he stepped forward and put an arm around the wiry Dane. "I thank you, Friend."

Awkwardly, Ingvar patted his shoulder, then he stepped back and held out the missive.

Maël took it, but as he started to turn toward Mercia, the Dane groaned.

"Ingvar?"

The man puffed his cheeks, blew out breath, and reached into his purse. "I lie a little." He held up a ring with a wide gold band, perched atop it a many-faceted gem of deep red. A bishop's ring. "Only fool or Norman of great honor not take it," he said. "So see, must be hated Saxons who further humiliate William's brother."

Sound reasoning, even if self-serving, Maël acceded. "It cannot be found upon you, Ingvar, and best not sold in England lest Odo's men come pounding at Wulfen's gate should my cousin take you into his service."

"This I know." The Dane considered the ring from every angle, heaved a sigh, and tossed it in the stream. At Maël's look of surprise, he grinned. "It safe there."

"Indeed," Maël said, then strode to where Mercia had settled back on the rock over which he had draped his mantle.

Face turned to the sun, eyes closed, it appeared she slept, but as he neared, she rolled her head to the side and smiled though it would be many days before she did so without discomfort.

Reminded of that to which Odo had subjected her, Maël's own smile was not only for her but the ring at the bottom of the stream. By now, it was greatly missed, men sent to retrieve not only Mercia but the pride worn upon the bishop's hand. Thus, soon the journey to Wulfen must be resumed. Were it believed Saxons stole into Stern, all the more likely supported by De Grandmesnil's encounter with one, contingents would be sent toward the fens and possibly York to try to overtake Mercia's rescuers. But there was the possibility that just as De Grandmesnil had peered behind Maël's mask, Odo would peer behind that of William's companion whose beloved son could not hide his distress over a bride he did not want.

Hugh De Grandmesnil would not veer from his tale lest he fall out of William's favor as he had for a time while his liege was but a duke, but suspicion that landed upon him could merge with suspicion over Maël's feelings for the former Abbess of Lillefarne. Hence, a contingent might also be sent to Wulfen.

"Ere long we must ride," Maël said as he lowered beside Mercia whose thick braid stretched beside her. "But first look upon this."

As her eyes had been all for him, she gasped, sat up, and glanced at Ingvar.

"He retrieved it from the solar when it proved necessary to subdue Odo," Maël said.

"He did not betray your trust, then."

"He did not." Maël reached the missive to her. "Here that which I had him steal from Canute, believing its absence would cause Odo to refuse to buy your wardship. Unbeknownst to me, Ingvar hid it in the psalter to get it off the ship."

Her eyes widened. "Then I had the missive on me ere I asked your mother to give the psalter into your keeping."

"You did. When my attempt to keep you out of the bishop's hands failed, causing you to be regarded only as a means of learning about Alditha, I delivered it to Odo with a tale of taking it off one of Gytha's men who attacked me when I set out to resume my mission for William. Though I could not know how your grandmother's words would be received, I hoped they would sow enough belief Odo would see your value more as a tool for controlling your people than locating a long-gone queen, thereby ending the questioning and easing the watch set over you."

Smile small, she said, "And so it did. For that I am here with you now." She glanced at the missive which he had expected her to eagerly accept. "You have read it, Maël?"

"I have. And now it is for you to know its contents."

Mercia considered that whose inked words she had longed to hear. They would never be spoken to her now, but there they were, dark lines and curves slightly visible through the parchment's backside. She had only to take it, and she would know who she was—whether the daughter of a king and the half sister of a prince, or the niece of a king and cousin to a prince. Then…

What? she asked herself. *Of what import now? Of what import ever?*

"Ingvar's gift to you," Maël prompted, and added wryly, "His gift to himself, a bishop's ring."

Remembering how proudly Odo had worn that which flashed red during his questioning, she said, "Methinks the ring will be missed more than I."

"Very possible. For that, Ingvar cast it in the stream."

Relieved, she returned her regard to the missive. So great was the temptation to know what Gytha had written, she reached, but hardly had her fingers brushed the parchment than she dropped her hand to her lap. "Long I have rued not knowing who I am, believing it more important I learn the name of my earthly father than honor that of my Heavenly Father. It made me clay in Gytha's hands, and that made me a deceiver in a House of God. Now..." She looked up. "You love me, Maël? Truly?"

"I do."

"We shall make a life together?"

"We shall, though it will be beyond these shores."

As was necessary. Blessedly, leaving her country with Maël made her ache far less than had Canute delivered her to Denmark. "Then I do not need Gytha's words to know who I am."

His brow lined, but then understanding lit his eyes.

"Not only am I the Lord's beloved, I am yours, Maël. That is far better than Gytha's words, even if they are true—and more than I deserve."

He leaned in and touched his mouth to hers. "As I am your beloved, Mercia."

"I not like interrupt love," Ingvar called, "but we ought ride."

Maël raised her beside him, fastened his mantle around her shoulders, and led her to their mount. Before assisting her astride, he removed the psalter from his pack and tucked the missive inside. "Lest you think different, it is here."

"I will not think different. It is the present I shall live in, not the past."

He nodded but closed the missive inside the psalter and returned it to the pack.

She nearly asked him to destroy it, but she would prove

stronger than any temptation to read it. With Maël at her side, how could she not?

As he turned their horse toward Wulfen, Mercia tried not to worry over how she would be received by Lady Hawisa whose suspicions about the Abbess of Lillefarne were confirmed, though likely not in any way she had guessed.

Regardless of the Lady of Wulfen's feelings for the deception worked on all, Mercia was determined she would not further offend. Her tale would be told and forgiveness sought—providing the lady was able to receive her. God willing, she had birthed a healthy babe so she and her husband would not bear greater burdens than those of the missing Theriot and Nicola.

Mercia looked around. "What of recovering your cousins?"

"That needs discussing with Guarin. I will give aid, but first I must deliver you to safety."

"Where?"

"I will take you to my uncle, Godfroi."

"But his demesne is in Normandy and Le Bâtard his liege."

"Thus, we must be discreet and wise in all things, especially in pledging our lives to each other, which we will do as soon as we reach France. Until I am no longer needed in England, you will remain under my uncle's protection."

Mercia's heart hurt in a most splendid way. Of course they would wed, but to hear him speak it as if never was there a question they would be husband and wife was further proof she did not need Gytha's missive to tell her who she was. The same as Cyr's Aelfled, Guarin's Hawisa, and Dougray's Em, she was to be the wife of a D'Argent.

That last reminding her of a conversation with Nicola, she laughed, and when Maël frowned, said, "The need for discretion is not what amuses me, rather something Nicola said when she learned I was not of the Church."

His mouth curved. "I am halfway to understanding."

324

"She suggested I save you, healing you the same as Em healed Dougray. And he healed her."

Maël chuckled. "Of course she did. The reckless one, Guarin names her, and rightly so. But when she stills, whether out of curiosity, fatigue, or being given no choice, she delves what others barely glimpse. One would not think her observant, but she is, often seeing things that can be and should be."

"Only the good, then."

"So it seems. However, though long she has been shielded by her family, her life free of hardships, I fear much may have changed these weeks."

Whereas minutes earlier Mercia had savored happiness, now came regret and fear. "Because of me."

Maël shook his head. "Believing herself invincible, she went the way of the reckless. Had she not done so at Lillefarne, she would have elsewhere, and likely Vitalis would not have been there to keep watch over her."

"You think he does?" she asked as Ingvar drew his horse alongside.

"So it was told Guarin," he said, then nodded at the Dane. "Now we ride hard."

ERE WULFEN CASTLE was in sight, three riders came at them from out of the wood. After assuring Mercia the men were neither Danish nor of the bishop—indeed, not even men—Maël identified himself and his companions to the knights-in-training who quickly escorted them to the donjon.

Guarin greeted his visitors in the hall, and long he considered Mercia, then he gave his cousin a knowing look and ordered two squires to settle Ingvar at the hearth with food and drink. Once the Dane was distant, Guarin informed Maël and Mercia his wife remained abed following a difficult birthing.

There being an air of joy and pride about him rather than sorrow, indicating both mother and babe fared well, Maël congratulated him on the birth of their child and was about to ask after its sex when his cousin bid them wait.

Likely a son, Maël thought as Guarin went behind the solar's curtains. *The first of the line of Wulfrith-D'Argents.*

"He is happy," Mercia said.

As Maël intended to be with her. "He wed better than first I believed," he said, "as did Cyr and Dougray."

She set a hand over his on her arm. "I was thinking the same of Aelfled, Hawisa, and Em." When he smiled and drew her against his side, she asked, "All is well with you and your mother?"

Realizing there could have been no opportunity for Chanson to reveal to Mercia what had transpired between mother and son at Stern, he said, "I told her what happened the night ere the great battle—of my sire's wrongs and my own. She said it was not the first time Hugh strayed from their marriage vows. Thus, she was not surprised and surely far less hurt than she would have been had she not wed Fulbert."

"And your own wrongs?"

"Forgiven." He nodded. "It is well between us."

"I am glad, Maël."

He meant to tell her what else was discussed that night at Stern that led to Chanson's proposal which, though it decreased the risk of endangering both Mercia and him, would cause him to lose much, but Guarin reappeared and invited both to Lady Hawisa's bedside.

"You have naught to fear," Maël assured Mercia. "You may have misled the lady, but methinks your fellow Saxon will make allowances for your loyalty to Gytha."

"I pray so."

When they passed through the part in the curtains, Guarin and Hawisa's adopted son turned from the bed, in his arms a babe whose tiny head was fit with one of two caps Nicola had fashioned—this one's band embroidered with a flower.

Then the baron and his lady's first child was destined not for the training field but the administration of a household and gifting of children—that is, were the girl born of one other than Lady Hawisa, Maël amended. The training Nicola had received at Wulfen would pale compared to what this wee one would grow into.

"Come, Sir Maël," the lady called from behind Eberhard. "Meet our Abelard and Wynflaed."

Had he any doubt he heard right, Mercia swept it away with, "Dear Lord, the blessing of twins."

Maël's sire and uncle having been twins, he was pleased she was not of the belief a shared womb indicated the mother had relations with two men—all the more believable were the children not identical in gender and looks—and further pleased at the realization Nicola had anticipated twins. Then there was the irony of it.

Three years past, Hawisa had presented Eberhard, a slave bought at auction, as the twin of her departed son, and with good cause. In the absence of a half-Norman heir, England's new king would have tried to wed her to one of his noblemen as payment for aid in taking the crown. Now wed to Guarin, she had birthed twins in truth.

Maël halted and looked upon Eberhard's sister. Though tiny, there was good color in her round face and alertness in eyes that appeared to stare into his. Would the blue-grey become the green of the D'Argents? What of the strands of black peeking from beneath the cap? A dozen years from now, might silver begin to streak Wynflaed's tresses?

"She is beautiful," he said, then realizing Mercia had fallen behind, drew her forward. "Is she not, my love?"

Though the endearment was felt, voiced in the presence of others it sounded stilted. But then, there was naught spontaneous about it. Despite assuring Mercia all would be well, here his declaration—even warning if need be—this woman was under his protection. If Hawisa doubted Mercia was precious to one thought to have lost all heart, it mattered not. What mattered was it be known he would defend her.

"Beautiful, indeed," Mercia agreed and stepped around Eberhard. "You and your husband are to be congratulated, Lady Hawisa."

Following, Maël glimpsed surprise on the Lady of Wulfen's face as she looked upon Mercia whose gown beneath the mantle was visibly shabby. However, the long braid draping her shoulder, its bound end falling below her knees, was surely of greatest note.

"Forgive me for staring," Hawisa said where she leaned against stacked pillows, upon her chest the babe who wore a cap embellished with a stitched dagger. The bit of hair visible beneath it was dark the same as his sister's, but compared to Wynflaed, Abelard was far from tiny. The sleeping infant, bound to grow into a formidable warrior, had to have been the cause of his mother's long, difficult labor.

Hawisa reached to Guarin on her opposite side, and as he enfolded her hand in his, said, "It is just that you look much changed from the Abbess of Lillefarne."

"Because no longer am I that and never should I have been," Mercia said. "Thus, I beseech you—"

"Be assured, I require no explanation," Hawisa said. "As I found deception necessary in the England of William Le Bâtard, I understand why you did what you did, and all the more for the struggle against becoming your grandmother's pawn. Hence, there are only two things I would ask of you."

"I shall answer as best I can, my lady."

"Are your feelings for my husband's cousin—a Norman —true?"

Mercia raised her chin. "More true than any feeling I have known."

"You speak of love?"

After a thoughtful pause, Mercia said, "If love is deepest sorrow at the mere thought of being parted from this man, it must be. And you?"

Hawisa's eyebrows jumped, then she laughed softly. "You express well the heart's fear, Lady Mercia. Aye, I know it too."

Mercia's tension easing, she said, "What else would you know, my lady?"

"Where the abbey's wealth can be found. Sister—rather, Abbess—Rixende told you hid it when you learned William ordered the plundering of our churches to pay for his army."

"I did. Though I did not consult you when you paid for the wall to be erected around the abbey, I ordered a cavity built into the lower half where the inner passage ends just beyond the door to the garden. The stones there appear immovable, but they are less than half the depth of the others."

As realization struck Maël, she looked up. "The rats," she also recalled his inspection of that passage. "They know that hiding place well." She returned her regard to Hawisa. "When it is deemed safe to bring out the treasures gifted by your family and others, whether for display or to sell to give aid to our people, all can be found there except two silver sconces sold to replenish food supplies when Lillefarne was first overwhelmed by the great numbers fleeing the North."

"I thank you for protecting the treasures," Hawisa said, then gingerly shifted against the pillows, doubtless not only to avoid disturbing her sleeping babe but to ease whatever discomfort she suffered from giving birth. Once settled, she said, "Would you like to hold our Wynflaed, Mercia of the Godwines?"

Hearing her breath catch, Maël said, "As I have much to discuss with my cousin ere we depart England, if it is well with Lady Hawisa, I will leave you with her."

"I would be glad of her company," Hawisa said. "Eberhard, pass your sister to the lady and draw near a chair for her."

The young man slid the babe into the arms of one visibly uncertain one moment, in the next all wonder as she peered at Wynflaed.

Lord, grant us this, Maël silently prayed as he stared at the woman with whom he would spend his life. *Let us not only be husband and wife but father and mother—a family so no matter where we make our lives, we have others with whom to grow our love.*

As he started to follow Guarin and Eberhard from the solar, his gaze was drawn to the Lady of Wulfen, and he found her eyes awaited his. And knew the reason, it having perched on the edge of his thoughts since first he looked upon her daughter. As his sire was more responsible for the death of her first child upon the battlefield of Hastings than that young man was responsible for Hugh's death, words yet needed speaking.

"As my sire cannot beg your forgiveness for what he stole from you, Lady Hawisa, know how great his son's regret and sorrow that it cannot be returned."

Her throat convulsed and eyes brightened as if a thousand stars fell from the heavens to cool their fire in her tears. As she struggled for a response, Maël felt Mercia's gaze, but he did not look away.

Giving a nod too slight to tip a tear onto her cheek, Hawisa said, "Never shall I forget my beloved Wulf who took much of my heart with him. Blessedly, the Lord returned a goodly portion by giving me another son and husband." She glanced at Eberhard and Guarin. "Well they tend this pieced-together heart, and now the Lord further strengthens it by entrusting to me another son and a daughter." She nodded again, this time spilling a tear. "Though I thank you for speaking where your sire cannot, know I but wish relations better between us, neither holding the other accountable for what a father did to a son and a son to a father."

Until now, Maël had not realized how great the need to make things right with one long regarded as an adversary, in the beginning because she was a Norman-hating Saxon, then for her son having aided in slaying Hugh, lastly for bewitchment of his cousin.

"What say you, Maël?"

"I say what was wrong has been set aright, my lady. My only regret is the necessity of leaving England means there shall be few, if any, occasions to know each other better."

"My regret as well," she said, then frowned. "Do you recall what you asked of me at Darfield ere I wed Guarin?"

He did. *What is it about the women of England that so ensnares?* he had demanded, desperate to understand how both Cyr and Guarin had been captured by Saxon women. Her answer further frustrating him, he had said she and those of her ilk could prove the downfall of the D'Argents. Rather than be offended, she had suggested otherwise—that Saxon women would be their salvation.

"I recall, and though I did not believe it then, I do now," he said. "Salvation, my lady. Much-needed salvation."

She inclined her head. "Until we dine here this eve, I will keep your lady occupied with my new loves and share that tale with her."

Maël looked to Mercia, savored her smile, then the men left the women to their talk so the cousins could speak of a place being made at Wulfen for the quick-fingered Ingvar—but more, of the painful past, the uncertain present, and the hopeful future.

CHAPTER THIRTY

Castle D'Argent, France
Summer, 1070

*G*uarin would not forgive him and believed neither would Dougray, Cyr, nor Theriot. Not because they were incapable of extending grace, because grace was not needed, Maël's cousin decreed.

Albeit a poor decision, it was made under such painful circumstances that any of those trained by Hugh might have done the same, he had excused Maël's attempt to drown the fire of disillusionment and anger in drink, the failure of which caused him to distance himself from his family during the battle.

His understanding had lightened Maël, but greater peace was sought five days later upon his arrival at Castle D'Argent where he was greeted by his uncle and aunt, Cyr and Aelfled, as well as Dougray and Em whose return to England had been postponed. A good thing, Maël had thought until he learned the reason.

Three months pregnant, Aelfled had lost what would have been a brother or sister to the son made with Cyr. Thus,

Dougray and Em had remained so the latter could tend and comfort her sister-in-law.

It hardly seemed the time to deliver tidings that not only was Godfroi and Robine's youngest son still missing, but now their daughter. However, it had to be told alongside an explanation of the hooded one who accompanied Maël. He had drawn Mercia forward, and his cousins and their wives stared when she revealed the familiar face beneath her hood. Further they were astonished by revelation of her true identity, and more so when Maël announced they were wed.

Though Cyr and Dougray had asked for an accounting of that in its entirety, the watchful Godfroi had wanted more—to venture further back than Maël and Mercia's first encounter so he might understand why his nephew had not fought alongside his family. Thus, sooner than anticipated, once more forgiveness was sought.

Now as Maël stood outside the chamber in which Mercia and he would consummate their marriage, he traced the scar's path from off center of his forehead down to his right brow bone which the blade had jumped before resuming its course at the outer corner of his eye and ending it at his ear.

The flesh had ceased healing, leaving behind a discolored ridge to remind him of that for which he thought never to be forgiven. Yet he *was* forgiven, even by his cousin who might not have lost an arm had Maël been at his side. Before Dougray's own healing that had begun with Em, likely the most bitter of the D'Argents would have blamed his cousin for his injury. Instead, after less struggle than expected, much grace.

"Praise, Lord," Maël rasped, then moved his thoughts to the woman on the other side of the door being prepared for the wedding night it had seemed best to delay under the circumstances.

Though the journey from Wulfen to the nearest port, followed by the channel crossing, had been without incident,

Maël had wasted no time lest it was discovered he had not returned to his hunt for Vitalis and it was not Gytha's men who delivered Mercia out of Odo's grasp.

After arriving in Calais, they had met with Chanson's youngest brother who held lands in Flanders. Maël had not seen his uncle in a dozen years, but he whose prosperity was of his own making had aided in discreetly obtaining a legal alias for his nephew that was passed to Mercia through marriage. Thus, it was not Mercia of the House of Godwine who entered Castle D'Argent, but Mercia de Chanson—just as Maël's mother had proposed that night.

Since first, in between, and in the end, Maël was of the family D'Argent, before he could be known by the surname that afforded Mercia protection, he must aid in recovering Nicola and Theriot. Afterward, husband and wife of the family De Chanson would begin their lives in earnest far from William's reach. And therein the loss that was more regrettable than any slap to Maël's pride. Once he forsook the name of D'Argent, it would be dangerous to return to England or Normandy. Were he to see any of that family again, including his mother, likely they would have to come to him and Mercia.

Hearing a door open, he straightened from the wall as his aunt, Aelfled, and Em exited the nuptial chamber opposite. Feeling a youth for how great the longing to push past them, he said, "My lady wife?"

They halted, and he was glad Aelfled's smile was more genuine than earlier. He had known her reserve had much to do with the miscarriage, but also he was responsible since he had been unsympathetic when first they met, so much he had endangered her life. With good reason, he had believed. And been wrong.

"Your wife, Mary Sarah—" Aelfled snapped her teeth, shook her head. "Forgive me. Too long I knew her by that name."

He smiled. "I am certain you will become better acquainted with her birth name whilst I am gone from her side."

"A strange reacquaintance it shall be, so heedful was I of the stern Abbess Mary Sarah, but methinks we will be friends."

"I am glad. And..." He glanced at her hands clasped at her waist. "...I am sorry for your loss."

Her smile was tremulous. "Greatly, we have been blessed with one child. We ache for the one we shall never hold, but we hold closer and more precious what we do have than what we do not. That is my prayer for you and Lady Mercia."

Knowing she spoke of when it came time for him to take the name De Chanson, he said, "I thank you, Aelfled."

She inclined her head.

When his aunt set a hand on his arm, he peered into her beautifully-lined face. Though she was deeply concerned over the fate of Theriot and Nicola, as her faith was a good match for her husband's, there was no strain about her joy over this occasion.

"Your wife is ready to receive you, dearest Maël. Is she not, Em?"

Dougray's wife, whom Maël first encountered when she was a slave, said, "More ready she would be had she permitted us to loose her braids, but she insists it is for her husband to do."

Though Maël's beating heart urged him to hasten inside, he paused over the sparkle in Em's eyes. Of all the survivors broken by the conquest, she more than most should have been unable to recover. And yet she seemed at peace when her beautifully mismatched eyes were not upon Dougray, happy when they were.

Greatly the D'Argents were favored, and Maël did not doubt it had much to do with the faith Godfroi passed to all who had sat at his feet as children and respectfully bent the knee to him as men. More than the injury that deprived him of the use of his legs, it had set him apart from his brother, Hugh. And drawn his nephew to him when spaces a father ought to fill needed filling.

"It is your time to begin anew," Robine said. "Go to her, Maël."

He started to step past, paused. "My wife shall require no tending come morn."

The women exchanged looks, nodded, and when their footsteps faded on the stairs, he pushed open the door. And stilled at the sight to the left of a postered bed hung with sheer white curtains.

Mercia stood with her back to the brazier, its glow lighting the weave of her chemise to reveal her every curve. And of further distraction were the braids draping her shoulders she wished him to loose. And so he would, fashioning from them a mantle to warm them both.

He stepped inside, closed the door, and halted near enough her to breathe in the scent of lavender. "I am told Lady Mercia de Chanson wishes her husband to undo her braids."

She peered up at him through her lashes. "I do not believe I am wrong in stating long Sir Maël de Chanson has wished to do so. But first..." Her smile parted lips that no longer thirsted, inviting more than the brush of his mouth. "...the kiss."

He drew her to her toes and closed his mouth over hers.

She sighed, slid her hands over his chest and around his neck, and pushed her fingers up into his hair as if to prevent him from ending the kiss. But there had to be an end to it, though only this one.

The barriers between them needed shedding, and so they were—not frantically but with lingering caresses as, layer by layer, their clothes fell to the floor until all that remained were her braids. Only two, and simply crossed unlike when first he saw beneath her veil. Vanity or not, he was glad of what appeared thick, silken ribbons upon the loveliest of packages.

Turning Mercia to the side to cast the brazier's light between their bodies, he stepped back.

Breath quick and shallow, she lifted her lids.

They stared into each other, and it was her eyes that first strayed as his longed to do.

"All of you is beautiful," she whispered, then said in a rush, "Am I truly here with you? If I am not, tell me I am, and I will not drift back to the abbey...the ship...Stern Castle. I will remain here with you."

"You are with me, Mercia."

She smiled, and he loved that turn of her lips as much for its appearance upon her face as the feel of it beneath his mouth. "Then pray, Husband, loosen my braids."

He lifted one from her shoulder, and as he considered its length, let his own eyes stray over a body shaped by the hands of God. Then he began undoing the crossings. At last, the dark shining mantle he had imagined would warm them both caped her shoulders nearly to the floor.

"All of *you* is beautiful, my love," he marveled in her language, then added, "My salvation."

"Maël." Her voice cracked, not from lack of drink but longing.

"Mercia," he answered and swept her into his arms, shouldered aside the bed curtains, and lowered her to the mattress.

There, without hesitation, his wife drew him down to her. And covered herself in his shadow.

"ONCE I THOUGHT you loveliest in sleep," Maël said when he opened his eyes to find Mercia watching him by dawn's light come through the window unshuttered hours past when the room became heated.

Propped on an elbow, head in hand, she raised her eyebrows. "When was that?"

"Whilst there were yet bars between us." He slid the backs of his fingers across her brow and down her cheek. "In sleep, the cares worn upon your face eased. Though there is no sleep about you now, you are even lovelier."

Her mouth bowed.

"And lovelier yet," he rumbled, moving his fingers to the curve between neck and shoulder where earlier he had pressed kisses, the remembrance of which made her shiver.

"I do not think you are cold," he said.

"I know I am not. But, alas, as the women will come to inspect the sheets soon, we must needs be less thorough than on the night past."

He chuckled. "My wife is beautifully brazen. Certes, it is good she was a false abbess."

Reminded of her deception, she tensed.

His smile eased. "Do not be ashamed of what you were made to do to survive, Mercia. Just as I am forgiven, so are you. As my uncle told, though we ought not live in the past, neither should we lock it away out of sight and out of heart. Far better we allow the dark behind to draw sharp contrast against that to which we aspire."

"The light ahead," she whispered, having stood in awe of Godfroi's grace over the loss of his brother whose death, he assured Maël, was not to be borne upon his son's shoulders.

A smile returning to his lips, he said, "As for the ladies interrupting us, it is no concern of theirs that you are no longer a maiden, especially since already we break with the tradition of hanging out the sheets for all to bear witness to consummation."

Mercia had been relieved she would not suffer that display since the fewer who knew of their marriage, the less likely any would draw a connection between Maël d'Argent and the Maël de Chanson he was to become.

Further relieved this morning belonged to husband and wife the same as the night past, she said, "Well then, be thorough, Husband."

"Wife," he groaned.

But no sooner were her lips upon his than a knock sounded, causing a growl to escape Maël, a mewl Mercia.

"I do not believe I could have been clearer my wife requires no tending this morn," he grumbled, then eased her onto her back, turned the coverlet over her, and rose.

Mercia knew it unseemly to stare at him as he sought to recover his cast-off clothing, but though she flushed when he glanced at her, she did not avert.

Another knock.

Maël dropped the tunic and chausses he had snatched from beneath her chemise and instead retrieved his mantle from the chair. Sweeping it around his shoulders, he strode to the door.

It was Lady Robine, and she had not come to look upon the sheets but to deliver viands and drink. If she tried to hide her amusement at seeing her nephew, attired in a mantle above bared calves, falter when she extended the platter, she failed. "For modesty's sake, best I carry it inside, Maël."

He stepped back.

"Good morn, Lady Mercia," the woman said as she glided forward.

"And to you, my lady."

As Robine set the platter on the table between bed and window, the scent of freshly baked bread stirred Mercia's appetite.

"That will sustain you a while," the lady said. "Do you not come down for the nooning meal, I shall bring another platter—and one for supper, if need be."

"We thank you, Aunt," Maël said.

Robine patted his arm in passing.

When he closed the door behind her, Mercia tossed back the

covers. Clothed in her own mantle fashioned of hair, she stepped to the platter and picked from it a thick slice of bread whose crust glistened with butter—and honey, she discovered when she sank her teeth into it.

Looking to her husband, she beckoned with a bob of eyebrows and stepped to the window to gaze out upon the new day.

Maël halted behind her. "But for your hair, you are bare, my lady," he said and opened his mantle and drew her inside its folds. "Lest one of those patrolling the walls looks up when he ought to be looking out."

"Forbid," she said and settled her back against his chest, took another bite, and reached the bread over her shoulder.

They finished it and another slice, then stared out across the castle and land, a view husband and wife would cease to share when Maël left her and returned to England to recover Nicola and Theriot.

Caressing his arm around her waist, exploring the muscles evidencing its strength, she said, "I am not afeared."

He lowered his head alongside hers. "Of what are you not afeared?"

"Of you leaving. I know you will come back to me. When you do, we will make a life together and, I pray, children."

"So we will."

"When do you depart?"

"If not the morrow, the day after. Once I meet with my uncle and cousins, we shall determine the best course. God willing, within a month I shall take you from here."

From here to where? she wondered. Flanders was a possibility, Chanson's brother having offered his nephew the keeping of a portion of his lands. Then there was Paris and the more distant possibility of Ireland where Normans were beginning to settle and one rumor held Queen Alditha had taken her son.

"Have you thought more on where we will go?" Mercia asked as she watched a bird launch itself off the outer wall.

"I have. Though Flanders appeals most since it is near enough Normandy it will be easiest to discreetly remain in contact with my family, Southern Italy may be safer."

Where his people had also begun settling. "That is very far," she said. "Though perhaps safer where William is concerned, what of the unrest there?"

"That is a problem, since I will not be made part of another conquest by Normans."

"Then not Italy." She smiled when she saw another bird spread its wings and follow the first.

Maël sighed, drew her nearer. "What remains of our time together is short. Let us speak of other things."

Certain he meant to resume what Lady Robine had interrupted, she laughed softly.

But he said, "Gytha's missive."

Yet tucked within the psalter alongside the one that began her journey to him.

She peered over her shoulder. "I will not read it, nor ask you to reveal its contents. Even if you are taken from me, still I shall know who I am." She turned back to the window, jutted her chin. "You see that bird flying free of these walls?"

"I do."

"That feels me, Maël." Moments later, the second swooped into sight, and she added, "With you."

"With me," he said with wonder.

She turned, slid her arms around his neck, and against his lips said, "Your love. That is all I need ever be."

EPILOGUE-EXCERPT-PROLOGUE

Wulfen Castle
England, 1352

Cy *love, my heart, the half and whole of me, soon I leave you. Forgive me for being absent from you in all the years I pray to come as you welcome the first of our children's grandchildren into this unlovely world you made beautiful for me. As my light flickers, soon dims, becomes smoke wending heavenward, hold my hand, kiss my brow, and let me go knowing this is not our end but a space between the life we made and when we shall hold each other again. Psalm 31:1.*

In parting, I have a request, beloved Mercia, though you ought honor it only if it speaks well to you. As ever, the missive you wished never to look upon resides in my clothes chest. If even in my absence still you care not for its tale, I would not have you read it. I would have you give it into the keeping of our eldest son with instructions it be passed through our line lest there come a day he or any other wishes to know more of the woman who helped me find the heart lost to me.

Certes, what your grandmother wrote is not you, but be it truth or lie in the black of her ink, it is part of you for having made your light shine brighter. There my argument, and now I return to our bed and pray I awaken beside you come morn. Do I not, open wide our window, look out across the land, and there you will find what feels me flying free of these walls. Waiting for you. ~ Your Maël, in the year of our Lord, 1111

Hector Wulfrith, trainer of the worthiest protectors of the realm, considered the writing that had been no easy thing to read. Not only did it appear penned by an unsteady hand, evidencing the author's many years, but numerous misspellings indicated he was ill-schooled in written English. Either little effort had been given his studies, else the language was not native to him.

The latter, Hector guessed, as much due to the parchment being delivered by foreigners as the intellect required to write something so near poetry it tugged at a warrior mostly immune to tugs.

Lowering the aged scroll to the table, he settled back in his chair and looked to the tallest of those opposite. "This is supposed to mean something to me, boy?" he asked in French the sooner to be understood and rid of his *visitors.*

The one who spoke for both, much strain in his accented voice to sound nearer a man, said with what sounded disappointment, "The names, Maël and Mercia, are unknown to you?"

Though the first had stirred his memory, he was too weary from a dozen hours spent on the training field and too eager to send these two away to delve it. Of greater reason to ignore what might or might not be familiar was the futility of such claims of kinship. Though the third King Edward decreed only those of English birth receive training at Wulfen, this boy was not the first to come across the sea seeking such, several having attempted to enter here by professing kinship to the Wulfriths by way of one or another line of Normans who aided Duke

William of Normandy in conquering England three hundred years past.

Hector shook his head. "Both unknown to me."

The lines of the youth's brow deepening, he nodded at the parchment. "As told, that is only a beginning." Moistening his lips, once more he raised the lid of the cask perched on the table's edge.

Something about the nervous show of tongue disturbed, and more thoroughly Hector searched the young man's face, then that of the boy. Upon returning to the first, he was certain of what poor lighting and impatience to be finished with this business had caused him to overlook. And ground his teeth.

Though more angered with himself than the perpetrators, were they men—and certainly they were not—they would be fortunate to suffer mere bruises for their trespass. As for the temptation to send them away with loud, harsh words, one of numerous lessons taught the stubborn of him slammed to mind.

Allow not wrath to command your actions nor your words, young Hector, Sir Owen had instructed time and again, *else never will you prove worthy of your great commission—indeed, may be denied it altogether.*

Hector *would* honor his name and the great commission nearly lost to him, but he had another incentive for remaining in control—that this ruse caused what had barely interested to beg interest. He would set these two aright, but only after he knew the whole of the promised tale.

He shifted his gaze to Squire Gwayn who stood across the hall with his back to the fire. The young man who should have sought permission to grant these two admittance to Wulfen Castle raised his eyebrows. Lessons were due him, but they could wait.

"My Lord," ventured the one who, said to be the boy's cousin, had given the name Sévère, "here not only further proof

Mace is Wulfrith kin but descended from a great line of English nobility."

Hector looked to the slender hand that once more offered a parchment drawn from the cask, next that one's face framed by a woolen cap, then to the boy of seven or eight years. Though there was no visible silver in that one's dark hair, that did not disqualify him since rarely did more than one child of each generation present thus and more rarely did the silvering appear before the age of ten.

He shifted to Mace's eyes. They were bright, it seemed as much due to their intense green as the polished steel in their depths.

As of one torn from childhood, Hector reflected and began to consider which of his knights would best set the boy on the path to knighthood. In the next instant, he stifled a grunt of disgust. Even absent the deception, there could be no place for him at Wulfen.

"My lord?" Sévère handed the parchment nearer, providing the opportunity to look closer on that one's face.

After further verifying what he knew, Hector reached his scarred hand forward and took the parchment that was either not as well preserved as the first or more greatly aged. Though once it had been a scroll, not only was it creased from being folded flat as parchment ought not be, but it was brittle, deeply discolored, and evidenced shrinkage.

It was good Hector's near vision was sharp. Though the words written on this parchment were well drawn, they were exceedingly small and of great number.

"It is dated forty years ere the one written by Maël to Mercia," Sévère said. "It would be of benefit—" That one's voice cracked, requiring much throat clearing to once more sound near a man. "It would be of benefit do you first look to the name of she who wrote it."

He lowered his gaze to the final lines and read, *Countess*

Gytha, wife of Godwine, mother of King Harold, grandmother of Lady Mercia, great grandmother of England's future king, here sets these words in the year of our Lord, 1070.

A reaction was expected of him, and so greatly was it felt it required extensive control to withhold it from those who watched. Were this parchment genuine, and that was questionable considering how false the one who passed it to him, perhaps training reserved for the English was more the boy's due than the other claimants come before. But as for kinship with the Wulfriths...

He considered Mace again, and those green eyes peered into ones less bright for the grey shot through the same as nearly all those of Wulfrith blood.

"As Maël requested of his wife," Sévère said with more accent and less depth than before, "that has been in the possession of Mace's family for nearly three hundred years—its words as true now as then." A nod. "Pray, attend to it, Lord Wulfrith."

He required no prompting, but he gave a grunt of impatience before angling the parchment toward torchlight and settling eyes upon its words.

Blood of my blood, if this you read, you have done your duty. You, Mercia, are a Saxon strong of mind, body, and spirit. True to the blood, the bone, the marrow. More, you are a Godwine.

I trust you approve of your husband, Canute. More than he is young and of good blood, face, and figure, one day he may succeed his sire to become King of Denmark and, God willing, King of England. If ever you are queen, it will be because your grandmother had a care for her son's daughter. See, Mercia, I make all things right.

Now that you are bound to our kinsman, here I shall keep the promise made by setting down the truth for all, foremost our countrymen, to ensure they rally to King Sweyn's side once it is known his son has taken a Godwine wife.

Though told you were illegitimate, that is not entirely true on one side of it, nor entirely false on the other. Long this mother of a king has borne a tale whose threads were picked and pulled out and rolled into a ball thought never to be woven together again, but for our people and the babes you shall bear, here I weave it.

Over a score and five years gone, one of my sons believed himself in love with a woman beneath his station. Ida was the only daughter of a Mercian thane who, admirably, fathered six sons. However, as her sire was of minor holdings and small reputation, I told my son nay. He defied me but, blessedly, did not bind himself beneath the eyes of the Church but in the Danish custom of handfasting. When I learned of his folly, I ordered the handfasting dissolved. Unfortunately, already you were in Ida's womb. I prayed you a girl lest my son be moved to do again what was undone, and the Lord answered my prayers beyond all hope.

No son did Ida bear, and so greatly she bled that after you were placed in her arms and she named you Mercia, with the last of her breath she begged me to care for you. I wanted to send you away and forget you, but weak in that moment, I gave my word. Though I longed to make a lie of it, your eyes were my son's, the dimple in your chin the cleft in his. Hence, I took you into my household and made a nursemaid of a slave whose babe had died.

Many knew who sired you, but they were commanded never to speak of it and did not, though my son showed interest in his daughter despite being forbidden to draw near. That problem resolved once he was handfasted to a Godwine-worthy lady. Though he had sworn not to love again, even better he loved the one chosen for him, and mostly he forgot about you.

For years, all was well, then the one at whose breast you had suckled revealed to my son's wife it was he who sired you. Trouble there, I sent away the babe growing into a girl and made an example of servants who speak where they ought not. As was due the woman you adored, I sold her across the sea to satisfy the appetites of coarse men.

Thereafter, on occasion I visited you at the abbey where you would have made your profession were it not necessary for my son, Harold, to set aside his wife and wed another to secure the throne King Edward left without an heir. Harold was not happy to part with his Edith, but he did his duty and wed the sister of the earls Edwin and Morcar. As never did I trust that family, I took you from the convent and gave you to be Queen Alditha's companion and keeper of the wardrobe so you could report behavior unbecoming a Godwine wife.

Alditha gave you less to report than the goings-on upon Wulfenshire, but I was right to mistrust her family. Of what use were her brothers to Harold at Hastings? None, though the cowards' absence from the battlefield was of much use to the usurping William who reduced them to earls in name only. Alas, neither has Queen Alditha been of use, refusing my protection and going to ground with my infant grandson. Though one rumor spews she is with me in Denmark, she is not. Another rumor tells she dwells in Ireland, and that is possible. Only the Lord knows what will become of Harold's heir, but as the boy is not yet four, England cannot wait on him.

Though I have gone the long way around naming which of my sons sired you, and surely now you have guessed it was not Tostig, Gyrth, or Leofwine, be it known to all henceforth and evermore, your father was a young and foolish Harold. Twice handfasted, once to a woman beneath him, once to a woman of good standing, the second handfasting was undone for love of England to set the worthiest of kings upon the throne.

For this, daughter of King Harold, you have been chosen to aid the king of Denmark in tearing the crown from the usurper's head. As I know you will not fail me, your husband, nor your people, at last your place in my affections is secure. ~ By God's grace, Countess Gytha, wife of Godwine, mother of King Harold, grandmother of Lady Mercia, great grandmother of England's future king, here sets these words in the year of our Lord, 1070.

Something agreeably sharp and warm, not unlike the thrill of unexpectedly encountering a worthy opponent, sprang through Hector as he reflected on the missive's contents.

Alongside that written by a husband whom death would soon part from a much-loved wife, it seemed a fit for another tale told him long ago, which was the reason the name, Maël, was distantly familiar. And now Mercia.

The Book of Wulfrith, begun by Sir Elias de Morville in the twelfth century, chronicling their family beginning with the sire of the eleventh-century Saxon lady of the House of Wulfrith who wed a Norman knight of the House of D'Argent, included a narrative titled *The Tale of the Lost D'Argent.* Hector's grandmother, tale-giver and keeper of the book, had warned it could be more imagination than truth since it was not written down until a century after its events. Still, she believed its every word—*except for the unicorn,* she had added and winked at the boy who sat at her feet.

So here proof the D'Argent cousin who disappeared from England had done so with the woman who, rather than aid in overthrowing King William, escaped marriage to the King of Denmark's son and instead wed Maël D'Argent? If so, was it also proof the boy standing before him was not only a D'Argent descendant but blood of the last Anglo-Saxon king of England?

Hector set the second parchment alongside the first, returned his regard to Sévère whose lips were pressed so tight one would not know there had been fullness about them earlier. "Intriguing," he said and nodded at the cask. "What else have you?"

Once more the lid was raised. This time it was not parchment taken from the cask but something wrapped in black cloth.

Hector offered his hand and, feeling the brush of soft fingertips as the object was set in his palm, glanced at Sévère and paused over eyes averted above flushed cheeks.

Not a youth, he amended. *So how old? Twenty? Aye, at most one or two steps up from there the same as—*

Wrenching free of remembrance of the one he himself had

laid in the ground, he turned back cloth fine enough to be a remnant of a larger piece used to fashion a lady's gown. Center of it was a silver and gold brooch of fine workmanship—the letter G impaled on a sword whose point was tipped with a triangular ruby.

"You wish me to believe the G signifies Godwine," Hector said. "That it was given to this Mercia as proof of her birth."

"After what you have read and for how valuable the brooch, you must agree there is no other conclusion," Sévére said.

"Nay, I must not agree, *boy.*" He folded the cloth over the brooch. "But if I did, it would change naught."

"But—"

Sévère and Mace startled as the scrape of Hector's chair resounded around the hall.

He straightened. "Whether or not this boy is of the family D'Argent that wed into the family Wulfrith, whether or not royal blood courses his veins, he is not of England."

As Sévère's mouth worked, evidencing a struggle for further argument, Hector swept up the parchments and strode the back of the dais.

"Baron Wulfrith," Sévère appealed as he came around the table, "surely an exception can be made for—"

"Only if you can gain an audience with King Edward and persuade him to believe what you would have me believe. Both highly unlikely."

Nearing, he noted the cask that had been closed following each extraction was left open the last time. Another item lay within, and the one who followed his gaze gasped and dropped the lid, belatedly concealing an opal set in an expanse of silver.

As Hector halted, Sévère fully turned to him and took a step forward as if to shield both cask and boy.

He extended the parchments and brooch.

Doubtless interpreting that as an end to their audience—and nearly it was—anger leapt in Sévère's eyes and convulsed a jaw that would never be hard or broad enough to command the respect of warriors.

Then that one drew a strident breath, scooped up the brooch, and snatched away the parchments. "You know not what you—"

A yelp interrupting words that sought to cure him of ignorance, Hector watched as a tail of fair hair tumbled from beneath the cap he plucked off, then glanced from wide, stricken eyes to those of the boy beyond, next Squire Gwayn. "I *do* know what I do, Sévère," he rumbled, then mockingly frowned. "Or is it Séverine?"

Gripping the items returned to her, the young woman splayed her arms as if to further shield Mace. Fear where there had been anger, she said in a voice now strained not to sound a man but to crawl past a constricted throat, "Forgive me, Baron. It was done to gain your ear since women are not permitted at Wulfen, and I was certain more credence would be accorded my appeal were it not presented by one of the fairer sex."

Before he could respond, the boy said in French, "I told I could present it on my own, Séverine. Now see, you have made a mess of all. Never will I be admitted—"

"Never would you be admitted regardless had *you* presented the tale," Hector growled. He had no reason to side with the woman, no reason to feel anything less than annoyance for the time she had stolen from him, but it was true there was no place for the boy at Wulfen. Too, it was impossible to ignore the chill desperation that had fallen upon Séverine like the blackest of nights when dense clouds and stinging rain blot out moon and stars.

"I am not vengeful, lady," he said, though he knew not if she could lay claim to that title. "Exposing you is enough punishment for your deceit. Now I have duties that need tending." He jutted his chin at the cask. "Take your treasures and go."

Her stance and wariness eased, but she did not trust him enough to look away. Thus, she felt the brooch and parchments into the cask, tucked the box beneath her arm, and closed her mantle over it.

"Again, apologies, Baron. We shall trouble you no more." She glanced over her shoulder. "Come, Mace. The day grows short."

The boy shot Hector a resentful look then followed her from the dais.

Now that Séverine no longer played a young man, she walked like a lady, her gait smooth and bound hair gently swaying center of her back.

"Hold!" Hector called.

Seeing expectancy splash across the faces of those who spun around, he regretted they believed he gave them cause for hope. Merely, he could not have the one who entered as a young man depart as a woman in this place where the latter were not permitted.

There were exceptions, as when circumstances necessitated a baron of Wulfen extend his stay within these walls. So he not leave his wife too long absent her husband at the sister castle of Stern, she would join him here, remaining out of sight of the boys and young men so they not be distracted. Over the centuries, many were the Wulfrith babes conceived in this fortress exclusive to the training of boys into men—and several had been birthed here.

Not so for the current baron, and likely never since no longer did he keep a wife. And dared not take another.

Now as he strode toward Séverine who gave him no reason to be attracted to her, he noted once more her lips were full, having been parted by surprise, hope, and what might be the beginning of a smile of gratitude.

Glad she was on the plain side of pretty that had, for a short time, allowed her to fool him, he halted and held out her cap. "Best not to distract those whose minds must be on matters that will one day determine whether it is life that stands their sides or death."

Hope purged, anger filling that space, Séverine snatched the cap from him, thrust it atop her head, shoved her hair beneath, and pivoted. But before she took a single step forward, she came back around. "How did you know I was not a man?"

Hector allowed a small smile. "You are not the first woman to enter here without permission. As your predecessor succeeded long enough to gain a measure of training, in the two hundred years since that lady humiliated my ancestor, those of Wulfen have been better trained to see beneath disguises that might endanger them and our great commission."

Her eyes narrowed. "A lady, you say?"

"Annyn Bretanne, also an ancestor since later she wed the man she nearly disgraced."

There, a bit of a smile, and though the woman remained relatively plain, it turned her somewhat attractive. "Good day, Baron." Moments later, the doors closed behind her and the boy.

Hector remained unmoving some moments, then called, "To the training field, Squire Gwayn. I have further lessons to impart ere day is done."

But first, Séverine imparted one to him.

Do not expect an angry woman to be compliant, he told himself a short while later when, amid the buzz of astonished boys and young men, he saw the trespassers put heels to their mounts— no cap upon the woman's head.

Dear Reader,

If you're curious about this scene's heading of EPILOGUE-EXCERPT-PROLOGUE, be curious no longer. As much as this is the Epilogue of HEARTLESS, it's the Excerpt of the first book in the 14th century AGE OF HONOR series, releasing the year of our Lord, 2022 (or somewhere thereabouts). Meaning it's also that tale's Prologue, though it could end up being written in Séverine's point of view. Well, providing this brewing new series comes to a boil. Am I excited about what's ahead for the Wulfriths beyond the 8-book AGE OF CONQUEST and AGE OF FAITH series? You know I am!

Thank you for spending precious reading time with Sir Maël and Abbess Mary Sarah—er, Lady Mercia. If you enjoyed the fourth Wulfrith origins tale, I would appreciate a review of HEARTLESS at your online retailer—just a sentence or two, more if you have time.

Up next in the AGE OF CONQUEST series is RECKLESS, the love story of my Anglo-Saxon warrior, Vitalis, and Lady Nicola D'Argent. Watch for its release Autumn 2020.

For new releases and special promotions, subscribe to Tamara Leigh's mailing list: www.tamaraleigh.com

AGE OF CONQUEST PRONUNCIATION GUIDE

Abelard: AA-buh-lahrd
Aelfled/Aelf: AYL-flehd
Aethelflaed: EH-thul-flehd
Aetheling: AA-thuh-leeng
Aiken: AY-kihn
Alditha: AHL-dee-thuh
Alfrith: AAL-frihth
Balliol: BAY-lee-uhl
Bernia: BUHR-nee-uh
Bjorn: BEE-yohrn
Boudica: BOO-dih-kuh
Campagnon: CAHM-paan-yah
Canute: Cuh-NOOT
Chanson: SHAHN-sahn
Cyr: SEE-uhr
D'Argent: DAR-zhahnt
Daryl: DAA-rihl
Dougray: DOO-gray
Ebbe: EH-buh
Eberhard: EH-buh-hahrt
Edelwine: EH-duhl-wihn
Ely: EE-lee
Em: EHM
Emma: EHM-uh
Estienne: EHs-tee-ihn
Fortier: FOHR-tee-ay
Fulbert: FOO-behr
Gerald: JEHR-uhld
Gloucester: GLAH-stuhr
Gloucestershire: GLAH-stuhr-shuhr
Godfroi: GAWD-frwah

Godwine: GAHD-wihn
Gospatric: GAHS-paa-trihk
Grandmesnil: GRAHN-may-neel
Guarin: GAA-rahn
Guy: Gee
Gwain: GWAYN
Gytha: JIY-thuh
Hawisa/Isa: HAH-wee-suh/EE-suh
Hugh: HYOO
Ingvar: EENG-Vah
Jaxon: JAAK-suhn
Lavonne: LUH-vahn
Leicestershire: LEH-stuhr-shuur
Maël: MAY-luh
Maerleswein: MAYRL-swiyn
Mary Sarah: MAA-ree-SAA-ruh
Mercia: MUHR-see-uh
Merle: MUHRL-uh
Michel: MEE-shehl
Nicola: NEE-koh-luh
Ordric: OHR-drihk
Pierre: PEE-ehr
Ravven: RAY-vihn
Raymond: RAY-mohnd
Rixende: RIHKS-ahnd
Robine: rah-BEEN
Roche: ROHSH
Roger: ROH-zheh
Sévère: SAY-vehr
Séverine: SAY-vuh-reen
Sigward: SEEG-wuhrd
Stigand: STIY-guhnd
Sweyn: SVIHN
Theriot: TEH-ree-oh

Torquay: tohr-KEE
Wulf: WUULF
Wulfrith: WUUL-frihth
Vitalis: VEE-tah-lihs
Wynflaed: Wihn-flehd
Zedekiah: ZEH-duh-KIY-uh

PRONUNCIATION KEY

VOWELS
aa: arrow, castle
ay: chain, lady
ah: fought, sod
aw: flaw, paw
eh: bet, leg
ee: king, league
ih: hilt, missive
iy: knight, write
oh: coat, noble
oi: boy, coin
oo: fool, rule
ow: cow, brown
uh: sun, up
uu: book, hood
y: yearn, yield

CONSONANTS
b: bailey, club
ch: charge, trencher
d: dagger, hard
f: first, staff
g: gauntlet, stag
h: heart, hilt
j: jest, siege

k: coffer, pike
l: lance, vassal
m: moat, pommel
n: noble, postern
ng: ring, song
p: pike, lip
r: rain, far
s: spur, pass
sh: chivalry, shield
t: tame, moat
th: thistle, death
t~h: that, feather
v: vassal, missive
w: water, wife
wh: where, whisper
z: zip, haze
zh: treasure, vision

AGE OF CONQUEST GLOSSARY

ANDREDESWALD: forest that covered areas of Sussex and Surrey in England

ANGLO-SAXON: people of the Angles (Denmark) and Saxons (northern Germany) of which the population of 11th century England was mostly comprised

BLIAUT: medieval gown

BRAIES: men's underwear

CASTELLAN: commander of a castle

CHAUSSES: men's close-fitting leg coverings

CHEMISE: loose-fitting undergarment or nightdress

CHEVALIER: a knight of France

COIF: hood-shaped cap made of cloth or chain mail

DEMESNE: home and adjoining lands held by a lord

DONJON: tower at center of a castle serving as a lord's living area

DOTTER: meaning "daughter"; attached to a woman's name to identify her by whose daughter she is

EMBRASURE: opening in a wall often used by archers

FEALTY: tenant or vassal's sworn loyalty to a lord

FORTNIGHT: two weeks

FREE MAN: person not a slave or serf

GARDEROBE: enclosed toilet

GIRDLE: belt worn upon which purses or weaponry might be attached

HILT: grip or handle of a sword or dagger

HOUSECARLE: elite warrior who was a lord's personal bodyguard

KNAVE: dishonest or unprincipled man

LEAGUE: equivalent to approximately three miles

LIEGE: superior or lord

MAIL: garments of armor made of linked metal rings

MISCREANT: badly behaving person

MISSIVE: letter

MOAT: defensive ditch, dry or filled with water

MORROW: tomorrow; the next day

MOTTE: mound of earth

NITHING: derogatory term for someone without honor

NOBLE: one of high birth

NORMAN: people whose origins lay in Normandy on the continent

NORMANDY: principality of northern France founded in the early 10th century by the viking Rollo

PARCHMENT: treated animal skin used for writing

PELL: used for combat training, a vertical post set in the ground against which a sword was struck

PIKE: long wooden shaft with a sharp steel or iron head

POLTROON: utter coward

POMMEL: counterbalance weight at the end of a sword hilt or a knob located at the fore of a saddle

PORTCULLIS: metal or wood gate lowered to block a passage

POSTERN GATE: rear door in a wall, often concealed to allow occupants to arrive and depart inconspicuously

QUINTAIN: post used for lance training to which a dummy and sandbag are attached; the latter swings around and hits the unsuccessful tilter

SALLY PORT: small hidden entrance and exit in a fortification

SAXON: Germanic people, many of whom conquered and settled in England in the 5th and 6th centuries

SENNIGHT: one week

SHIRE: division of land; England was divided into earldoms, next shires, then hundreds

THANE: in Anglo-Saxon England, a member of the nobility or landed aristocracy who owed military and administrative duty to an overlord, above all the king; owned at least five hides of land (a hide being equal to between 60 and 120 acres)

TRENCHER: large piece of stale bread used as a bowl for food

VASSAL: one who holds land from a lord and owes fealty

The Unveiling: Book One

The Yielding: Book Two

The Redeeming: Book Three

The Kindling: Book Four

The Longing: Book Five

The Vexing: Book Six

The Awakening: Book Seven

The Raveling: Book Eight

AGE OF CONQUEST: A Medieval Romance Series

Merciless: Book One

Fearless: Book Two

Nameless: Book Three

Heartless: Book Four

Reckless: Book Five (Autumn 2020)

∽

INSPIRATIONAL CONTEMPORARY ROMANCE

HEAD OVER HEELS: Stand-Alone Romance Collection

Stealing Adda

Perfecting Kate

Splitting Harriet

Faking Grace

SOUTHERN DISCOMFORT: A Contemporary Romance Series

Leaving Carolina: Book One

Nowhere, Carolina: Book Two

Restless in Carolina: Book Three

~

OUT-OF-PRINT GENERAL MARKET REWRITES

Warrior Bride 1994: Bantam Books (Lady At Arms)

*Virgin Bride 1994: Bantam Books (Lady Of Eve)

Pagan Bride 1995: Bantam Books (Lady Of Fire)

Saxon Bride 1995: Bantam Books (Lady Of Conquest)

Misbegotten 1996: HarperCollins (Lady Undaunted)

Unforgotten 1997: HarperCollins (Lady Ever After)

Blackheart 2001: Dorchester Leisure (Lady Betrayed)

For new releases and special promotions, subscribe to Tamara Leigh's mailing list: www.TamaraLeigh.com

ABOUT THE AUTHOR

Tamara Leigh signed a 4-book contract with Bantam Books in 1993, her debut medieval romance was nominated for a RITA award, and successive books with Bantam, HarperCollins, and Dorchester earned awards and appeared on national bestseller lists.

In 2006, the first of Tamara's inspirational contemporary romances was published, followed by six more with Multnomah and RandomHouse. Perfecting Kate was optioned for a movie, Splitting Harriet won an ACFW Book of the Year award, and Faking Grace was nominated for a RITA award.

In 2012, Tamara returned to the historical romance genre with the release of the bestselling Age of Faith and The Feud series. Among her #1 bestsellers are her general market romances rewritten as clean and inspirational reads, including Lady at Arms and Lady of Conquest. In 2018, she released Merciless, the first book in the new AGE OF CONQUEST series, followed by Fearless, Nameless, and Heartless unveiling the origins of the Wulfrith family. Psst!—It all began with a woman. Watch for Reckless in Autumn 2020.

Tamara lives near Nashville with her husband, a German Shepherd who has never met a squeaky toy she can't destroy, and a feisty Morkie who keeps her company during long writing stints. And not to be forgotten—Boog, a delightful mischief-making Pomeranian who visits often.

Connect with Tamara at her website www.tamaraleigh.com, Facebook, Twitter and tamaraleightenn@gmail.com.

For new releases and special promotions, subscribe to Tamara Leigh's mailing list: www.tamaraleigh.com

Made in the USA
Columbia, SC
28 April 2020

93621387R00224